Agony

Of

Faith

The Love Story

All the names, characters, times, places, and incidents in this book are author's imagination. This book is a fiction, a work of imagination. Any resemblance to any actual event, or time, or locales, or person(s) living or dead is entirely coincidental.

ISBN-13: 978-0692319055 (Custom)
ISBN-10: 0692319050

Covered illustration by *designa2z* of *Fiverr.com*

-T o-

Mom and Dad
& My daughter

–T o–

Mom and Dad
& My daughter

DEDICatION

I foremost dedicate this book to my parents (Dad: Eun B. Lee; Mom: Tae S. Lee) who have shown me diligence and patience, all throughout their lives. I want to give a special thanks to my pastor, Abraham Chung, (Chung, Byoung-up) who gave me courage, hope, and anointment. I want to thank Mrs. Chung, the wife of my pastor, for loving me and supporting me for years. I can't forget my aunt who's always praying for me; her name is Eun-ja Lee. I can't thank enough for my daughter—Yoo-Ell: she is the best thing that has ever happened in my life. To my college buddies whom we call ourselves the herd of sheep (Yhang-Tte in Korean because we are born in the year of sheep), they have given me support and friendship I need so dearly. Special thanks to Elizabeth Tuma for helping me with editing. Pastor Hong and his wife (my current Pastor and his wife) for praying for me. My brother (Won) and his wife for supporting me. And to all of my friends God has given through churches, businesses, and diverse paths of my life, they are all very dear to me. I love y'all.

Above all, I thank God for leading me to the desert to make me His friend. Without the grace of His Son's blood, I would not have life.

For Christians who live and die in Christ...

TABLE OF CONTENTS

Introduction

Where does faith come from and make home in your heart?

At first, it molds you into steadfastness and peace.

And as it grows, it takes the wheel of your life, and drives you to adventures where your life is twisted and turned, leaving you destitute.

It spares nothing: it takes everything you got and more. It takes you deeper and deeper into hardship and turmoil, and it even asks for your life.

And many have given theirs gladly.

You can taste the agony of faith in your dried and cracked mouth when it drags you through the valley of death, where faith collides with reality without mercy, leaving you just bare bones intact.

Here is a journey of faith through the roughest winter, the crashing winds, and the towering waves that are about to engulf the very essence of who you are—faith in Christ.

CH 1: CIDY WAKES UP

Cidy (pronounced like CD) suddenly wakes up unusually early in the morning because of a very vivid and real dream. She squints and rubs her eyes with back of her right hand, and opens her right eye with all of her strength, and looks at the time on her cute little red-apple alarm clock, a gift from Jill, one of her Sunday-school kids. It's 4:06 a.m. She is very tired because she slept very late.

She can't help it; she clearly remembers the dream and replays the dream a few times, involuntarily in her head, trying to find its meaning.

She had several prophesying dreams before, but this one is new to her. She tries to think what it means, but the weariness takes over, and shuts her down: Tired from last night's late practice for the company's Christmas show, she returns to sleep instantly; she is exhausted to think much of anything.

She wakes up again as the alarm goes off; it is six, the same waking hour for the working days. She struggles to turn the alarm off, and turns the lamp on quite reluctantly, with the feeling of the heaviness all over her eyes and with the out-of-control fumbling arm. She moans with the dryness in her mouth, but feels the joy of the day to come. The brightness of the lamp hits her eyes causing a sour pain in the back of her eyes. She knows she got to get up and get ready. Stretching and yawning, she feels tired, but she gets up anyway as she tells herself, "Gotta a show to do. Wake-up, Cidy. The show must go on."

She has totally forgotten about the dream: a lot of her dreams are like that—she forgets it until something triggers the memory. She stretches her arms and legs like a contortion artist, and rolls a few times like a dog playing, and voluntarily imagines about Jake—maybe involuntarily. She's not sure. She just loves thinking about Jake: he is quite an addiction for her.

Hugging and squeezing the pillow as if it's Jake, she wishes he is next to her. She turns the radio on; it's always on *89.3*. A wake-up song blasts through her little radio. She awakens slowly but surely. It's funny how she goes through the same routine each day, but she feels renewed every morning, although today she feels less renewed. She kicks out of her single bed, observing the ruined and out-of-place sheets. She puts her bed in order as she hums and sings off-beat and off-note with the radio: She thinks she's in perfect tune and beat. Her body and her head move to the rhythm, like a little girl who is about to get her favorite dessert.

Cidy does her routine to get ready for work: shower, shampoo, etc. She feels exhausted, but she skips through the rooms singing along with the radio. She's not a good singer (That is an understatement.), but she can't help but to sing along with it. She picks up her hair brush with her right hand, and tosses it to her left hand, and mimics a try-out for American Idol. She sings like as if she's an Amy Grant. She knows what she's doing is funny and quite embarrassing if she did it in front of others, but she lives the moment.

She puts on her quick make-up which is not much: a little mascara, some facial lotion, and a few brushes of light-purple-pink lip stick. She smacks her lips, looking into the mirror. She wants to look a little more attractive for Jake today, a lot more.

She usually puts on her work clothes—a professional set with a dash of feminine colors: The gray, blue or black suit with a dress shirt with a bright-yet-soft color—pink, red, yellow, blue, or white. But today, she's putting on a one-piece dress: it's the end of the year with very little work to do, especially today, and she pushes herself for some attention from Jake.

Finished with dressing and make-up, Cidy prepares a usual breakfast for herself: a couple of toast in medium, a large cup of orange juice, three over-easy eggs, and some cereal with cold whole milk. The small apartment kitchen functions quite efficiently—everything is in a single reach. She moves and gets the breakfast done like as if she is in fast-forward motion; she looks like multiple persons moving in synchronized movements. It is usually the same breakfast with slight changes from toast to bagel to muffin; orange to grapefruit to pineapple juice; and different kinds of cereal—usually her favorite is the generic brand of frosted flakes.

Before the first bite, she gives a routine short prayer, with her soft and pleading-but-thankful voice, "Lord, you have given me so much. I'm so happy these days. I wish Jake would ask me out, preferably tonight…. Thank you Lord. I pray in Jesus Christ."

Her voice sounds more pleading than any other days; maybe, it's because it's that time of the year— Christmas. She wants Jake for her Christmas. What a great joy would that be for her! That has been her breakfast prayer for past five years: she can't help but to ask for Jake in her every prayer.

Cidy goes back to restroom after finishing her breakfast, and brushes, flosses her teeth, and rinses her mouth. She thoroughly checks her teeth to see if anything is still stuck between her teeth. She sprays her perfume, and smells it with one long-and-deep sniff; she enjoys the fragrance of rosy spring morning.

She grins as she remembers the last night's practice, and walks out of her bathroom, and walks out of her room as she gives love taps with her right and left hands to all the pictures on her south-side bedroom wall; It's like she's giving high fives to encourage them or celebrate the day with them. There are over twenty children and ten missionaries she supports through various organizations, and there are pictures of her mom and dad, and her friends, and her Sunday-school kids. She prays for them every night as she looks at the pictures.

Cidy grabs her reddish-brown briefcase, and shoulders her light-khaki with a bit of pinkish-blush bag, and puts on her black dress shoes with a slight limp, and hurries out of her apartment. She quickly paces herself through walk ways of the apartment to her car. It's about 6:30 a.m. (give or take a few minutes) as she checks her watch; this has been a routine like a paper boy for past five years.

She sees her white Geo Metro and smiles as if seeing a good-old friend. Her small Geo is old and not attractive, but it's very clean. But most of all, it gives her plenty of space to drive and park comfortably anywhere. All the more, it gives her little worry about getting damaged or stolen. She could care less if it gets scratched or bumped a little—and even getting stolen. It is literally worry-free. She unlocks the doors and opens the door. It is automatic: She gets into the car as she tosses her bag and the briefcase on the passenger side. She heads for the neighborhood H.E.B. (a grocery store in Houston, TX, USA) to do her regular flower shopping.

On December 18th of 2008, about 7 a.m., with just a little more pep on her feet than other days and with a wide-opened gracious smile, Cidy Grant joyfully strolls through an H.E.B. Christmas is everywhere: decorations, songs, smells and all kinds of food. She stops at the floral section, and buys a dozen of roses as she does regularly, some yellow and some red, that are just about to be blossomed.

She considers these rosebuds similar to young, cute teenage girls, who are just about to blossom into beautiful ladies. She loves seeing the rose blossom in front of her as the hours and the days pass by. It feels like magic, because it just seems too wondrous. The roses from the store are placed at work. Seeing, touching, and smelling them really make her days a lot brighter and enjoyable.

Cidy, wearing her long bright-orange dress, steps up to an open counter, greets the clerk with *Merry Christmas*, and pays for the roses. She likes the color orange: it is not too bright but not too shy. This dress is one of her favorites. She usually wears orange for special occasions. It is the dress she wore for her first day at work about five years ago.

She steps out of the store and glides to her car feeling a cool breeze swaying through her hair. It's a great weather in Houston; during the winter, it's quite dreamy here. She gets into her car, and closes the door, and places the roses and her bag on the passenger seat, and turns the engine on. The engine doesn't turn on the first try, but on the second try it makes a roar as she steps on the gas.

Her old Geo Metro is not a Mercedes; heck it's not even a Hyundai, but Cidy is quite thankful for her car. Her friends always bug her to get rid of her junk, and to get a new one. She can afford to buy a new car with her outstanding credit and above-average salary, but she has postponed it several times to support more for the children in the mission fields, her church and other ministries.

She almost bought a white-pearl Hyundai Elantra last year. She really liked it a lot; she went to go see it several times. She wanted it. But she decided it not to because she wanted to support more children.

She smiles, and the radio plays the tune of Chris Tomlin's *Amazing Grace*. Singing along with the tune, she drives to work. After Tomlin's, some Christmas music is playing. She thanks God for lovely and whispering weather as her eyes gorge over the feast of God's greatest show—the scenery and the cool morning air that are created by time and space…and the elements.

Very excited about tonight's company Christmas party, Cidy expects to have some action with Jake—maybe some light conversation and possibly, hopefully, a dance or two. She giggles just thinking about it.

"*Dance would be great. A slow dance…as I lean on to Jake's shoulder….*" she dreams with a shy grin.

Jake has been Cidy's secret crush for past five years. She really hopes he makes a move on her. It would be a great Christmas surprise for her.

Thinking about the Christmas gift for Mom, Cidy suddenly remembers a painful-but-worth-while incident a few months ago at the company—an attempt to change the name of Christmas party by the company's upper management:

CH 2: No more Christmas

"We should change the title of our Christmas party to something of less offensive to non-Christians. I would say less than fifty percent of our employees are Christians. We should respect everyone in our company. I, for one, like to have it changed," Sam Milton, Vice President of Operation, made a proposal at a general operation meeting.

The argument to keep or change the name—Christmas Party—went back and forth—more like back and more back.

Cidy was invited to the meeting because she is in charge of the Christmas party—setting it up and running it. Hearing the discussion, she wanted to cry and witness the Gospel, but she knew it wasn't the place or the time. She kept her cool when she felt horrified to hear such a proposal.

They asked for suggestions for a new name, and the most popular one was "Year End Party" or "Year End Celebration."

Cidy stayed quiet, but waited for Jeff to ask for her opinion, her belief.

Just before the vote, CEO, Jeff Hawkins, asked Cidy, "Cidy, you have an opinion. Please, give us your thought." He knew very well Cidy had more than something to say because he started to "re-attend" church with his family because of her.

Jeff's voice was quite welcoming and calming.

Cidy had more than her opinion; she had her belief, her faith. She wanted to stand up, but decided to stay put. She smiled and looked at each one of them with grace and forgiveness. They got all quiet and waited for her to say something. They didn't really like her much except for Jeff; in fact, they despised her for intruding in their welfare.

The pause was long: Cidy didn't know what to say. No, she had too much say. She needed a little time to think it through or calm herself down. She knew they were just little kids in their hearts with worldly knowledge of debris that had cluttered and tainted their childhood innocence and pure conscience. She made a short prayer in her heart to God for wisdom, and then she cleared her throat a few times and presented her view as her voice filled with her emotion:

> Christmas...ah...it is a religious celebration for Christians. I admit it. But...how many of us...felt...it's a religious celebration? When I think about Christmas, gifts, food, singing, dancing and excitement...joy...oh what JOY...those come to mind. The very first Christmas gift I got, I remember—clearly—was a kitten. I named her, Miko. I got up early that Christmas morning. I woke my mom, grandma, and grandpa up. So excited. I knew they slept late but I got 'em all up...anyway.

They all gave me a gift, but the one I
still remember the most is a little
kitten my mom got it…for me—Miko.

Cidy saw flashes of her times with Miko: she
had to pause a few seconds to let her emotions pass
through. She smiled, and said, "I had so much fun
with Miko."
The officers noticed her joyful smile, too, and
naturally thought about their happy Christmas
moments, those magical and special moments that
just can't be erased from their memories.
Cidy continued:

It was a black kitten with white paws
and a white nose. It was a gift that I
enjoyed for twelve years. Miko
became my friend…sometimes best
friend, only friend….
For me…Christmas is quite a
religious event as well. It is the
celebration of the birth of Christ
Jesus. I believe Him as my savior. I
know…Christ might not had been
born around this time of the year, but
this has been the time for its
celebration for hundreds of years.
Even if we did change the name,
many would still call it Christmas
party because that's what the music
and decoration would say
everywhere. The trees, the music,
the decoration, and the stars…they
all tell the same story—
CHRISTMAS.

We would have to censor so much
to respect everyone in the company.
The Christmas celebration is the
time to share and celebrate. I know
you all have "Miko" in your
memories.
...I think it would be more than fine
to keep its original name—Christmas
Party. I feel there is enough
Christmas spirit in every one of us in
the company.

Cidy made an eloquent argument, and
quietly prayed to herself.
There was silence in the room for a while.
The upper management, although they didn't
have good feelings towards Cidy, was strongly
moved, and agreed with her, and decided to keep its
name.
Cidy was quite happy with the result, but
was sad, and realized it was a sign of the time that
she now lives in—Christianity is becoming more and
more offensive to some, even in the United States,
where the nation is found by the people with
unwavering faith in Jesus Christ.

CH 3: Cidy Arrives at Work

It is 7:30 a.m.

Safely arriving to work an hour earlier, Cidy parks her car, and looks around to see if that Jake's old, beaten-down Ford truck is here. The truck's color is so faded away and rusty, that it looks like an abstract piece of art from afar; it is blue with some faded shades of green and rust here and there.

She once thought the rust looked like blood spattered; she imagined maybe it's Christ's blood on it, making it a holy truck. She thought she went a little too far with her imagination, but a lot things around her made her think of the Bible, God, and Jesus.

Sometimes she thinks rain is like God's way of baptizing those who accepted Christ but never had an opportunity get baptized.

Cidy could spot Jake's truck a mile away. It is one of kind. She really likes it, although it's a raggedy old piece of junk, for its manly qualities—tough, rugged and strong.

Jake's truck has been called many names by girls in the company: a farmer's wheel, a run-down junk, and mostly a piece of shit. Guys don't care for what Jake drove as long as it wasn't significantly better than their car. But Cidy calls it, Jake's ride; sometimes, holy truck. She has a thing for trucks. She doesn't want to drive one but would be more than happy to ride in one, especially in Jake's—with Jake in it, of course. She often dreams of riding in the truck with Jake:

> Sitting tightly glued to Jake, Cidy wears a cute tight t-shirt and blue jeans to show off her figure, and is talking and laughing, inside the Jake's ride while listening to some soft-rock music. Jake's arm is around her, and he is occasionally poking her side, which makes her giggle, but mostly caressing her arms. She feels the love as they are driving to the sunset where there's ocean on the right side and a beautiful mountain range on the left side. And a beautiful love song is playing on the radio, while fresh cool winds are blowing through the window. She feels the love.

Cidy grins almost to the point of drooling. It's the same day dream that she's dreamt for past five years, and she loves it.

Cidy gets her stuff: the bag, the brief case, and the flowers: The bag and the brief case on the right side; the flowers on the left. She gets out of the car, and slams the door shut with a snap of her buttocks. She doesn't worry about locking it. She checks for Jake's truck again, hoping Jake might have made it. Then, maybe, she thinks they can bump into each other, so naturally, so romantically, and share a few magical glares and flirting words.

Her eyes stare at Jake's usual spot; she imagines his truck parked right at the spot. She thinks about parking next to his spot, or parking at his spot, just to tease him. She smirks. With all these parking spaces, Jake parks at the same spot most of the time, and she does the same.

Wearing the same dress she wore for her first day at work about five years ago, Cidy walks towards the main entrance, feeling cool breeze rising up through her dress. She blushes a little because it makes tingles in her lower body. It feels good as she rubs her face against the sweet breeze. The crispy air of the morning is more than inviting, and she is excited about the day to come with the expectation of Jake asking her out.

She enjoys the leisure of being early as usual; she can feel the little things or the greatest things that God gives us for each day as presents—the sky, the winds, the scents, the feels, and the expectations. She feels confidant and joyful more than ever.

"There is something different about today. What is it?" she thinks.

While trying to figure it out, Cidy looks over the building and its parking lot carefully all over again to check if there is something that is changed that she didn't notice right away. Something is definitely different. She's not sure; everything seems to be the exactly the same. But, whatever the reason she feels great, more than usual, since the morning. She's tired but feels like the snowflakes landing on a dog's nose.

"*Maybe it's the season or the party tonight,*" she thinks. She smiles, and enjoys her extraordinary joy and confidence she feels, and continuously walks over to the main entrance: Her steps and strides couldn't hide her feelings either; they are longer and lighter with rhythm.

Wearing the same dress she wore five years ago triggers the memory of Cidy and give her a flashback of her very first day at work:

CH 4: CIDY'S FIRST DAY

Cidy had the interview a month before her graduation around April of 2003. As she prayed for a job, she applied to major companies like any other graduates, but she kept getting an answer to her prayer—Texas.

"Texas? ...hmmm," that was her respond, but she decided to obey because she understood that God wanted her to work in Texas. She always wanted to visit Texas, but never thought about working there. But she obeyed, and applied to several companies in Texas, and even a small one in Houston that she thought it was interesting—the one she now works for. Cidy got two interviews in Dallas and one in Houston.

Meanwhile she already had interviews with a few major companies that she applied to in New York and New Jersey. She received calls that she is hired by two of them, but she turned them down. She knew she was going to find the job in Texas. Her friends at school told her she is crazy to turn down such opportunities and didn't know a thing about the real world.

Cidy majored in art history with master level of Spanish and Chinese, and spoke Italian quite well and Korean a little. She even spoke some Arabic, and she had visited all those countries a few times with Mom. She even enjoyed watching Korean dramas with a great plot and a rich history with exotic customs, and loved eating Korean food especially their spicy ramen. Ramen was a quick treat as well as a meal in a hurry. She had a heart for the world, an inheritance from Mom.

Cidy had much influence from her mom, Karina, in learning foreign languages and their culture, especially their food. She saw Karina talking with people from everywhere in grocery stores or some volunteer events. And Karina always encouraged Cidy to learn as many languages as possible, because it is the only skill you can truly communicate with people from other nations.

And, Cidy just naturally picked-up foreign languages. Her favorite was Korean because it was so easy to learn how to read and write, but she had difficulty in understanding and speaking it. She could teach people how to read and write Korean in an hour or less; she thought it was the most amazing system of reading and writing ever.

With her background, companies were interested in Cidy in sales and marketing.

After interviewing companies in Texas, Cidy got the notice that she was hired by all three companies—two in Dallas, one in Houston—within a month. Two in Dallas were in fortune 100.

Cidy fasted 3 days and decided to come down to Houston where a small-to-medium-sized company with 50 to 100 employees with potential for strong growth (That's what the company's brief introduction said.), because the passage in the Bible she read said to take the narrow road. She felt it meant to take on the challenge of a growing company than settling for an established one.

On the first day to work, Cidy wore the same dress she is wearing today. It was the best first-impression dress she had or she decided. As a girl, she knew how important the first impression is. It took more than two hours to get ready: She tried on over a dozen of different dresses and ensembles, and she tried this and that with make-ups and accessories. Nothing was satisfying. She felt nervous. Dressing-up was one thing she thought she can do without any help from God.

But Cidy calmed herself down and prayed, "Lord, give me peace. I wanna make a good first impression. I'm not satisfied with my look. Maybe, I'm just too worried. I don't know. I'm not really sure what to do. God give me peace and wisdom."

Cidy kept her eyes closed and contemplated upon God's words that she remembered often— *Come to me, all you who are weary and heavy burdened, and I will give you rest. Take my yoke upon you and learn from me, for I am gentle and humble in heart, and you will find rest for your souls. For my yoke is easy and my burden is light.* It was one of her favorite passage in the Bible.

After a while, Cidy became calm, and felt peace, and remembered the wisdom of Esther— being reliant upon wisdom of experienced eunuch who knew the taste of King. She called her college buddy, Jessie, who she felt like had good wisdom when it comes to make-ups, accessory, and putting cloths together. Jessie told her to be simple and elegant with just a necklace and a very light make-up and to wear a single color one-piece dress.

Cidy decided to put on a very special necklace. It was a very special gift from her dad, more like through her dad. It didn't sparkle but had a special design that was one of its kinds. It was a cross, carved very elegantly, made out of a red stone that no one seemed to know what kind of rock it is. She rarely wore the necklace because it was so personal, but today, she felt it was the day.

She put on a light make-up and her favorite one-piece dress, the long and elegant orange one. She felt gorgeous.

Finally Cidy felt good enough to go to work. It was only seven. She had to be at work by 8:30 a.m., and it only took about thirty minutes to get there. She drove to work three times in the morning traffic to make sure she knows the way and the time it takes. Being punctual was something Karina has instilled in her from early on, and she was rarely late to any of her classes, appointments or meetings. Karina always told her, "Be early: Show passion."

So, Cidy decided to drive near the company and have some coffee at Burger King that is only a few blocks away. She didn't want to be late because of traffic, just in case. She had coffee till about 7:50, and drove to work, and arrived thirty minutes early. She parked her car, and walked through the main door on the first floor. It was a beautiful day. She fell in love with Houston's fall weather. She felt nervous but great.

She greeted Peter, the security guard, "Good morning Peter. I'm See-Dee. I don't know if you remember me. About a month ago, I had an interview here."

Peter, a tall but a bit over-weight African-American gentleman in fifties or sixties, smiled and responded with a slow and sweet bass-voice. "I'd remembah a fine lookin' lady like you. ...must be gettin' old. Yo'ah first day work, he-ah?" His slow and that southern twang made her feel special and quite welcomed.

Peter couldn't remember her at all.

"*Did shee say hu'ah name izzah See-Dee?*" Peter thought to himself.

Peter noticed a slim and tall, beautiful, white girl with long brunette hair that shined like if it was a fake wig or a healthy cat's fur. He wished he was young again, because maybe he might have a chance to date such a beautiful girl. But he knew he had more than a handful of trouble when he was young, and he wouldn't want to deal with that again. He knew being young comes with its own troubles and heartaches. He kind of liked where he is now—much less trouble to deal with; life was easy for him now.

Peter took a good impression of Cidy. Not too many of the office workers, especially the ladies, greeted him like they meant it, but he was quite surprised by her genuineness. He took an instant like in Cidy.

"Yes, it's my first day." Cidy sensed that Peter finds her peachy. She saw his eyes smiling. She felt very comfortable with him because he reminded of her of a Mom's friend she met during her volunteer works. She even felt more comfortable, almost to the point of being relaxed, when she heard Peter's sweet base-voice. She thought Peter could be a jockey for a radio station.

"Well…Mizzz….ah…if there's…ah…anythin' I can dooo fo yooo…ah…Mizzz…ahhh…."

"Oh, just call me See Dee, C, I, D, Y …Cidy." Wanting to be a friend with Peter, Cidy slowly pronounced her name, and spelled it out, in a friendly tone, with an unmistakable smile that shows her full-set of teeth that sort of puts a seal of special approval for friendship.

"Well…Mizzz aahh Cidy…." Feeling a bit shy from the kindness shown by her, Peter wished her the best. "I hope yoou ahh work heeah…a looong time." He made a slow gesture and showed the way to the elevator with his right hand making a gliding gesture. He felt much better with that quick acquaintance with Cidy.

"Yes. Hope…I'll be here for a while, too," looking at the building more thoroughly trying catch every little details of it, Cidy responded to him. "See you soon, Peter." She walked to the shown elevators.

"Aaahh right, Cidy. That's whaachooo said—See-Dee. Riiight?" Peter shouted to Cidy because he wanted to make sure he got her name right. He never heard such a name before.

"You got it, right! Thanks. See you soon." Cidy turned her head and answered. She appreciated his kindness. Maybe it was his demeanor, or his kind looks, or his voice, or maybe his name that just made her felt very welcomed and pleasant.

"Best of luck!" Peter gave his final word out loud. He doesn't know what got into him. He just burst out with joy. Even he was surprised of himself.

Cidy walked to the elevator as she heard the echoes of Peter's blessing playing the harmony to her heels' taping on the floor.

She quickly remembered her interview she had here, and the building she had seen. The building was not as unfamiliar as the first time, but it still looked quite vague and unfriendly. She kept on looking around with her eyes naturally to get familiar with the new and unnatural setting.

She stood in front of the elevator with unknown expectation of what's to come for months or years; her mind rolled with fear and excitement of facing a new challenge—work, doing something most adults are doing to make a living. It was her first real job in the real world. She was more than confidant because it was the job God led her to, but she was totally unfamiliar and inexperienced in this area of peoples' lives.

She pushed the button for the elevator, and soon one of the elevators opened its doors. She walked in quickly. She turned around, and pushed number fifteen, and checked herself again against her image on the metal sheet, and breathed in deeply and breathed out slowly to relax, and smiled, soon the doors shut.

The elevator started move up with a little jolt as she felt her heart pound a bit faster and louder. She sensed the nice smell of herself, and heard soft elevator music flowing in the background. She noticed her reflections around the elevator making her to be more self-aware. The time moved very slow as she became jittery in a suspecting surrounding, maybe it was a woman thing. And soon, the elevator came to slow halt on the fifteenth floor; the number sign on the side registered fifteen with little round green dot-lights.

The elevator opened its door slowly. She walked out of the elevator with heightened senses trying not to be alarmed, but she picked up every scent, sound and sight with bit of wariness. That unknown and unfamiliar scent and sight made her tense because of her natural instinct to guard herself, but she calmed herself again and again with the assurance from the scripture that Jesus is always with her. She walked to the company's main door knowing that she can't open the door without the company card.

Luckily, one of the workers was walking out of the main entrance, and held the door for her, and let her in. A male worker took a peak at her and kept the door open. She quietly and shyly said, "Thank you."

She walked to the HR manager's office, following her memory of the place when she first visited for the job interview. Gary Smith, HR manager, was at work early that day, too, and was surprised to see her so early.

Gary liked Cidy's promptness, but thought she's just trying to give a good impression on her first day. He gave her a sign to come in with his smile and a hand gesture.

She smiled back, and pushed the glass door open, and walked in with timidity in her heart.

"Good morning, Cidy," Gary greeted her with wide-opened eyes and with a hi-hand gesture that came almost instinctively. He tried to look commanding and cool, desiring to be respected as a supervisor and to be attractive as an opposite sex. He wanted to make a good and assertive impression on her. He liked her beauty. He thought her long beautiful legs are quite beautiful although they were hidden under her dress, but he could more than imagine them.

"Good morning, Gary." Cidy gave a soft smile back. She was more than nervous. She kept singing a hymn—*it is well*—inside of herself to keep herself calm. It was Mom's favorite hymn and it just stuck with her. It was a habit to keep her calm when meeting people for the first few times where the new setting and the new people made her a bit nervous. Her very first job was exactly like that. Mom gave her much advice how to be calm, but it was not helping as much as singing a hymn inside.

"I didn't…ahh…expect you…so early." Gary tried to find the right words, being busy putting some paper together. "I'm meeting Jeff, in a minute." He stapled the paper gathered. "Please, stay here. I'll be right back." He quickly marched out of the office.

Sitting at the office alone, Cidy saw a few people passing by. They all took a quick peek at her. She tried not to notice them. She kept her soft smiling face, and tried to stay calm. She looked around the office and noticed the somewhat whitish walls, the glass wall towards the office area, the pictures, a large abstract painting, and the open view of a beautiful day. She seen it before, but they all looked very new to her. She felt bored, but sat alone almost an hour humming all the music came to her mind, and prayed a few prayers that she felt she need it.

While opening the door quickly, Gary said, "Sorry, Cidy. Jeff's leaving today for an important meeting in China. I told him we need to hire more people in all areas quickly. It took a while to explain the situation, and Jerry, CFO, was called in to confirm the financial back-up for the hiring. Anyway, I'm so glad to see you. Jeff says hello and sorry that he can't see you today. He really likes you, and expects a lot out of you."

Finishing his words, Gary made it to his seat and placed himself comfortably. He looked at Cidy, trying to find something impressive to say.

There was a long pause, an awkward silence.

Cidy felt obligated to break the silence: Not knowing what to say, she gave a courtesy respond, "Thank you," although it was more than too late.

Then as if something clicked, Gary started to explain some legal stuff and asked Cidy to sign some paper. He gave her a copy of the package that she signed.

He said, "Great. You are NOW officially hired." He reached out with his right hand, and they shook their hands.

She felt his big hand over-wrapping her thin long-fingered hand. Shaking hands with man always felt a bit awkward for her.

He spoke, "Your office will be ready in a few days, a week at the top. Sorry, for the delay. It's been really hectic here past several months. Meanwhile, you can sit in an empty cubicle. I'll show you. And of course, let me introduce you to the people you will be working with."

He walked out of the office leading her, and she followed him showing a small smile, signaling she is with him.

He chaperoned her and introduced her to all the employees—one by one. She gave her best to show the best side of her. All the employees gave her good-impression looks and friendly responds.

She could tell the guys had that smile of appreciation of a beautiful woman, and the ladies had that look of admiration.

But Jake didn't even look at her, maybe a glance, but that was it. He showed little interest in her.

She didn't think much about of it, but from the very first sight of Jake, she had more than a little interest in him. His rugged manly look drew her attention quite instinctively.

Gary finally showed Cidy a cubicle to work at for a few days, and she sat there for about an hour trying her best to pass the time. And Tammy Peterson came over and handed bunches of files over to Cidy, and said with unappreciative tone, "Here you go, Ms. Grant. Knock yourself out." Tammy trumped Cidy, and marched right back to her office. Tammy's back had a big frowning face that Cidy could feel as if it was staring right at her.

One of the Tammy's major tasks, which were to be taken over by Cidy, was coordinating and managing the events with investors, partners and buyers, which took a lot of tedious communication with foreign people, hotels, decorators, restaurants, and the upper management of the company, especially with Jeff, CEO of the company.

Cidy felt Tammy's dislike right away, but she knew this was the job God wanted her to have. She started to go through the files diligently.

CH 5: MORNING RITUALS

Cidy walks through the main door and the lobby, and says hello to Peter, and carries a little chat with him before moving onto the elevator. She enjoys that little moment with Peter every day; it has been like that for the past five years. For her, it's like saying hello to a good friend, an uncle, or maybe a brother. It really starts her day off really well. She notices Peter's age is showing up more and more, but he's voice is still the same, maybe just a little slower than when she first met him, although she couldn't tell exactly. She prays for him every day that he is healthy and be near God.

Walking towards the elevator, Cidy wants to invite Peter for the Christmas party, again. She searches for the invitation, finds one, walks back to Peter, and says, "Hey, Peter…ah…I know you turned my other invitations down for Christmas party before, but I would be more than happy to see you and Rhonda at this year's party."

"Mizzz. Cidy, I appreciate yoooah invi'tation, but…ahh…don't think I'm part of yoooah com'neee. Besiiides, I'm tooo ooold. …neee my sleeep. Ap'preeeciate it, though." Peter, with his sweet southern tone, makes an excuse—the same one he gave every year. He shows his sincere appreciation with his smile. He sometimes wonders about Cidy, if she is for real, because she is just too nice. He often thinks, "*She gotta be an angel.*"

Cidy wonders if Peter practices the line because it's the same line he used it before, and he says it so smoothly, that it's quite convincing. But, she knows Peter is just making excuses. This time, she doesn't want to back off, so she looks into Peter's eyes, and gives him that look of disbelief.

"Peter…? You're like my uncle. In fact, I see you more than any of my uncles. You are my family. I mean it. And I would love to see Rhonda, my aunt, for the first time." Cidy has gotten to know Peter quite well from talking with him for four, five minutes each morning. She feels sometimes she knows more about Peter than lot of her friends.

Peter, too, feels quite comfortable with Cidy. He prays for her quite often that she be protected and guarded by God and angels. This is the fourth time he had been invited to this Christmas-party. She had told him how much fun it was and what she did in the show. He wants to go, but he's not sure.

So he questions: "Can I…ah…really take…my Rhonda…with me?" He is shy, but he really wants to make sure he can take his wife. They don't go out much lately, so he thought this would be a great night out.

"Oh, yes! I would love to meet my aunt, Rhonda." Cidy feels good that Peter is coming and is bringing his wife too. "That is awesome! Please! Your table will be set as special guest. Your names will be on it. Okay? Great! Thank you!" She gives him a quick hug before he can change his mind.

Peter is caught off guard. He had not received a hug from any of the employees in the building before expect from Cidy. Although this isn't the first time she gave him a hug, it makes him uncomfortable. He chuckles and hugs her back. The scent of the roses pleasures him much as well.

"I'll see you tonight, Peter…Uncle Peter…and Aunt Rhonda." Cidy paces back to the elevator.

"Okay…Miizzz. Cidy." Peter never felt so loved by a stranger, now a niece.

Cidy stops at one of the elevator and pushes the button. Hugging on to the roses, shouldering the bag, and carrying the brief case, she feels more than happy, and hums to the Christmas music playing in her head. The elevator door opens, and she walks in. The doors close slowly. She's all alone. She slowly inhales the scent of roses like if she is breathing in life, and brushes them against her cheeks as she delights in every moment of it. She quickly brushes off her enjoyment, and pushes the number 15.

At home, she often holds a rose and brushes its petals against her cheeks and lips: she imagines it's a kiss from her secret love—Jake. It's a habit that reminds her who she is and the desire she has as a woman. And she would drink in the fragrance—the sweet soothing and sometimes intoxicating scent of roses that relaxes and pleases her so much. She often wonders how each flower is designed by God, and does God have any favorite flower like she does.

As the elevator rises to her floor, she slowly but surely breathes in the roses' fragrance and holds it in as if she is getting high on it again and again. The scent is magical. She breathes out slowly. The scent triggers her memory of how Mom would sniff at the roses and how she used to mimic her.

That expression on Mom's face was so happy when she is with the flowers in her garden. She has that Mom's face in her mind very clearly. She can't help it but to smile: The sweet memories of her past are more than alive. She feels the memories that she carries are the real food for her mind because it is so nourishing and delightful for her life.

The rose represents so many delicious memories for her. In her childhood backyard, where Mom still lives, a beautiful rose garden flourished and still flourishes. Although she had a few scratches and punctures from the thorns of the roses, that made her cry, she has a lot of fond memories there: playing with friends, Mom, families, bugs, worms, sand, toys, dolls, dogs, and cats. The best memory about the rose garden is working with Mom. Mom always said, "Horses' dung is great for the rose. It makes 'em beautiful and strong."

Yellow and red roses blossomed so beautifully every year and throughout the year.

She learned to value even animals' dung at early age. She distinctly remembers having regular trips with Mom to Kathy's farm to get some horse dung.

CH 6: Dung from Kathy's Farm

"We're going to get some DUNG today, Cidy," Karina loudly announced it early in the morning of Saturday. It was a beautiful cool day of spring. She knew Cidy loves going to the farm, so she kept as a secret till the morning of the trip to surprise her, and to let her sleep well.

"We're going to Kathy's farm? AWWW'some! Great! Why didn't you tell me?" Little Cidy jumped up and down. She loved the country side: the horses, the ranches, and beautiful wild fields.

Karina enjoyed watching little Cidy being overwhelmed with joy and excitement.

"Where does she get that joy, excitement, energy?" Karina wondered, and she wondered if she was like Cidy when she was little.

Cidy helped Mom with nourishing the rose garden with horses' dung from the ranch of mom's friend about every six months—spring and fall. They drove far out to the country side to get some. She loved the drive. The country side presented itself more lovely than posters with grasses, trees, farm animals, and more. But it was more than just what you can see—the fresh smell, the touch of soft breezes, and the soothing emotion of the beautiful prairie with farm animals loitering; it was God's creation at its best—just awesome and so peaceful.

The worst part of the trip was the stink here and there from something. Mom said it must be skunk's fart.

Overall, the trip was more than worth it for Cidy because she can talk and talk with Mom uninterrupted. Mom made her feel special, secure, happy, and comfortable. But the trip added so much excitement. Cidy couldn't figure out why she loved traveling so much. She felt like her heart would jump out of her chest and dance on its own.

"I want to travel all around the world, Mom. That's what I would do," Cidy screamed her dream out as she often did. She never said I want to be this or that, but she said much about travelling which she did much with Mom.

Karina laughed, and said with a tone of trying to give her other point of view, because she did a lot of traveling, "You have no idea what you are saying. I lived in several countries, but I wished I lived in just one. But I know what you are dreaming about."

After breakfast and a few quick errands, Karina returned home about 10:30 a.m. Karina honked to let Cidy know it's time to go.

Cidy ran out of the house and jumped in the car with joy.

Karina locked the house door.

Karina tried to have as many trips with Cidy as possible, but it was not easy with church events and volunteering. But she made trips to different countries for a week or two each year. A lot of time she had a friend living there, so she didn't have to pay for room and board, only for the plane tickets.

Karina called Kathy last week for permission to stop by and scoop some dung up. It was all set.

She hops in her small-but-efficient white 1983 Honda Prelude, a two-door, small, and sporty looking car that does more than enough for her and Cidy. And off they went.

"How was *Logos*?" As they got on the road, Karina asked about the children gathering on Friday nights at the church.

"It was fun. Mark taught us a new song. We played a game of chasing each other. It's called Pac-Man. When I became Pac-Man, I chased all the boys down and got 'em all out. Chad cried because I caught him first. I said sorry to him many times. Chad is funny but I don't know why he cries so much. He just doesn't like to lose." Cidy went on and on.

Karina loved hearing Cidy's jabbering of her life: they were the entertainment of Karina's life. She showed engaging responds: really, wow, no kidding, and so what happened. Karina's mission—raising Cidy with the love of Christ—wasn't too hard at all: There was more than enough joy.

As they drove out to the country side, Cidy enjoyed having a conversation with Mom, although it was more like soliloquy; Mom was a great listener and always asked the right questions. Occasionally Mom would point out a thing or two, and add a comment or two, but mostly laughed and giggled at Cidy's stories.

They always took some pictures on the way when they saw a beautiful spot. This time it was near an open prairie with beautiful landscapes and horses grazing on the back ground. It was a dream spot. They must have passed this spot least five, six times, but it just isn't the same each time they passed by.

"Cidy, let's take some pictures here." Karina pulled the car over, and took the camera out, and exited the car. Cidy jumped out with the excitement as well.

"Oh, it's soooo beautiful, Mom." Cidy made a comment that Karina usually says.

"Yes, my dear." Karina felt the love of God in that perfect moment—a beautiful daughter and the lovely setting. She felt the beauty of time, the beauty only time can give—the slow, wonderful, musical movement of the nature and the animals. It was so soothing, so perfect, and so lovely. And in the mist of them all, Cidy is there, enjoying and appreciating it all.

Karina often wondered if Cidy is growing up right without having a dad. Cidy looked more than normal to her, and that caused a worry in her as well. She was afraid Cidy is hiding her pain or has pain that she doesn't know yet. Of course there were times when Cidy cried and complained about not having a dad, but it didn't last long. Cidy always looked so happy to her. She couldn't thank God enough.

"Look Mom. There's a pony. She's so cute." Cidy pointed at a dark-brown pony grazing on the grass.

There was a wire fence with wooden posts around the open prairie. Cidy got on one of the post of the fence and hollered at the pony with her sweet, innocent voice, "Hi, Pony. How are you? You look so cute." She waved at it too, as if she met a good friend.

As to Karina's disbelief, the pony slowly galloped towards Cidy. The pony stared at her with friendship. Cidy petted and talked to the pony like it was her long-time friend.

Karina slowly walked next to Cidy, not to scare the pony.

The pony made a nod as to say hello to Karina as well.

Karina petted the pony with Cidy. She hadn't seen anything like this before: a loosed animal coming to greet people that it wasn't familiar with. She petted horses and ponies before, but they don't usually come to you unless they are familiar with you, especially in an open prairie like this. She thought maybe God's involved in this magical moment.

Karina took pictures of Cidy and the pony. The pony seemed to enjoy the moment as well. Maybe twenty or thirty minutes passed by quickly.

Karina looked her watch and said, "Hey Honey, we got to go. Say goodbye to Pony."

"Bye, Pony. I love you." Cidy touched its head, and kissed it, and wave at it as she walked towards the car.

Karina thought it was more than wonderful to see Cidy grow. She thanked God every moment.

They got back into the car and drove to their destiny—Kathy's farm.

Soon they arrived at Kathy's farm. Karina pulled the car close to Kathy's house which is about fifty yards away from the red barn. Karina gave two long honks to let Kathy know they have arrived.

Kathy ran out the house screaming with her arms flapping as if she is trying to fly, "AAAAAh. KARINA! OOOOWWW, it's GREAT to see you! How are you? ...KARINA...."

Kathy was jumping, and Karina jumped and screamed together, till they lost their voices. Kathy's warm welcome was quite hysterical, but it was quite heartwarming.

Cidy stared at Kathy and Mom's over-the-top exciting meeting. She thought it was more than hilarious. She laughed at them. She wanted to scream and jump with them, but she was just fine watching the buffoonery of two adult women.

"I'm so glad to see you too!" Mom's voice hit the highest tone. "You look great! You lost some weight...Girl."

"Really? I'm trying. Well you look great too. You always look great." Kathy was more than glad to see Karina. She owed so much to her.

They met each other at a support group meeting. Karina was invited to speak about her loss of her husband, John. Kathy had lost her son from horse riding. Karina encouraged the group so much. Kathy invited her to her church as a guest speaker, and since then they have been close. Karina visited her twice a year for the dung, and Kathy came by the city, and had lunch with Karina several times a year.

"Let me see. Is this Cidy? Oh my! You are certainly becoming a beautiful lady. How old are you now?" Kathy greeted Cidy with one knee down.

"I'm 7, but I will be 8 in six months. I'm 7 and half. Actually little more than half." Cidy wanted to get older, quick, so she told people she's more than seven, and tried to give precise age to help herself feel old as possible.

As Cidy finished her answer, Kathy hugged Cidy tightly and rattled her a bit a few times. Cidy giggled from the ticklish feeling she got from Kathy's rattles. Finally, Kathy let her go. Kathy stared at her for a while: she was looking at her son for a moment. Kathy's son died when he was 9.

"Wow seven and half. You are growing up so fast. Give me a hug again, Sweetie." Kathy attacked Cidy again. This time, she hugged Cidy even tighter, to the point of squeezing the life out of her. Cidy enjoyed the hugs, although it felt too tight.

Kathy remembered her son when he was about seven. She wanted to cry but held it in well. She grabbed Cidy's left hand. "Let's see what we got here for you Lady Cidy. Come right on in." Kathy led Cidy into her house and to the kitchen, where the breakfast room is.

As soon they entered the house, the aroma of country food slammed them hard. And of course, Kathy's best dish—fried chicken—leads the aroma.

"Fried chicken! Fried chicken! I love fried chicken." Cidy screamed and jumped. She loved Kathy's fried chicken. Kathy and her fried chicken were synonymous and famous.

They sat down, and started to eat after a short prayer.

"Where's Tom?" Karina asked.

"He went hunting with the boys. It was set a month ago. Tom wanted to stay. He says hello." Kathy explained.

It was a joyous time—three girls laughing and talking. Well, Cidy ate most of the time; she never had such a delicious food before. She didn't know why, but Kathy's food just tasted so much better than others, even her mom's.

"I have good news to tell you. I haven't even told Tom. I wanted to tell you—Karina—first." Kathy's voice is a bit jumpy and shaky.

Karina knew something was up; she felt it when she met her at the door, but she didn't want to say anything. She opened her ears and stared at Kathy, and Cidy also became all ears because suddenly there was silence.

With the prolonged silence, Karina's face turned serious: she was afraid it might be a bad news.

"I'm pregnant.... ...Yes! I am!" Kathy watched for Karina's reaction, and when she saw Karina's face light up, she cried and laughed at the same time. Kathy wiped her tear quickly with a napkin. Kathy was a bit scared to share it with Tom, but wanted to tell Karina because she knew Karina would understand how she would feel.

Cidy thought it was funny, "Why would Kathy be crying?" It sounded like great news.

Karina got out of her seat fast, and quickly walked over to Kathy, and folded her arms around Kathy, and petted Kathy's back. They hugged each other for a while. Karina cried with her and laughed with her.

Cidy had no idea what is going on. She was just amazed two grown-up women crying and laughing at the same time, and she was just busy getting her appetite satisfied.

"Tom and I, we...ah...have been trying. I wasn't ready...not really. I prayed to God for another baby, but it didn't happen. I guess I didn't want to.... You know deep in my heart; I was scared...very scared. Tom always said don't worry, in God's time, we'll have another one. I thought it was easy for him to say that. I'm the one who's having the baby, or not, in this case. But one day, I accidently saw him at the barn. He was crying and praying to God that he wished he had another baby. I have never seen him cry before. You know. He's always being so strong and stable. I couldn't believe it. I guess God let me get a peak of his heart. Since then, I've been praying harder, and I tried harder to be healthier. And about a month ago, I felt like I was pregnant. I wanted to make sure. I took the test secretly and I am. But I've been scared to tell Tom. Well…honestly…I'm scared that I'm pregnant. I'm happy too…but….” Kathy spoke with fear and joy.

Karina comforted her with a hug as she petted Kathy's head. Kathy laid her head on Karina's shoulder, and cried like a baby.

Not knowing anything, Cidy cried because Mom and Kathy were crying.

Tears counted the time passing by. And when the tears stopped, their faces brighten up.

“Kathy…what you are feeling is…quite…normal. That's life. We live life with fear…so much fear. Sometime it ruins us, squeezing out every drop of hope in us, leaving us with no room for joy, excitement, and even tears. We become just dry dusty bones just trying desperately to survive, one day a time, one hour, one moment. But we got to trust in the Lord. He will conquer the fear for us. He is our hope. God gave you another child because you are ready to overcome your fear.” Karina consoled Kathy.

“Thank you, Karina. I am ready…ready,” Kathy spoke with joy, happiness, and reconciliation. There was sound of confidence and hope in her voice. She felt comforted and consoled.

CH 7: Jake Wakes Up

Jake hears his phone ring with that signature tone for *T-Mobile*, and he picks it up unwillingly, and looks at the screen (It's 5:05 a.m.), and realizes it's Pastor Kirk, and reluctantly says, "Hey Kirk. Everything okay?" He knows something is up for Kirk to call him such early in the morning. He hopes it is nothing serious.

"Good morning, Jake." Kirk greets, knowing it's too early for Jake to wake up. "Sorry to call you so early. But…I need your help. There are some broken branches in the drive ways and parking. Some are quite large."

Jake understands what Kirk wants, so he gets to the point. "Okay. I'll be right there." He obeys with a dry and groggy and "un-awaken" voice.

"See you soon." Kirk feels sorry to bother Jake too early in the morning, but he knows Jake doesn't mind.

Jake loves Kirk for being so passionate about Christ although he's reaching 60's in a few years, yet Kirk would be dancing with youth and young adults during the worship time, and even Jane, Mrs. Stevens, as well.

Jake figures that last night's strong wind in the area broke some branches, and Kirk has probably checked the church early to make sure it would be safe for the people today.

He stretches a bit and takes a big yawn, and forces himself into the restroom, and peeks at himself in the mirror before taking a shower.

He knows he is getting old, but just can't feel it. He just had his birthday a month ago: he's now 33.

He questions to himself, "*How did I get this old...man?*"

He shakes his head a bit, scrubs his head with his fingers a few times, and gets into shower unwillingly. He quickly takes a shower, and brushes his teeth, and puts his hair in order with a few shake up of his hair with his fingers, and puts his blue jeans on, and slips into a work shirt. He gathers his semi-formal clothes for the office work, and walks out of his apartment.

Walking out, looking at his messy apartment, he tells himself that he needs to clean the mess up soon—the same story for the past 7 years. He just couldn't explain the mess he had.

Walking towards his truck, he loves that cool early morning breeze which helps him to wake up, and can't help but to think about Cidy as usual, and wishes he was married to her.

For five years, his mind has been filled with one major thought—Cidy. Whatever he does and wherever he is, he dreams about her all the time. He thinks he is crazy because that's what drove him—Cidy: She is the reason he had that pep in his life.

(He thinks he is a hopeless case of romanticist, but on the dark side and deep down, he knows he's a coward—just a man without much courage. He has several good solid reasons why he should not act upon his feelings: Number one reason is he doesn't want to ruin his good "relationship" with her. Whatever that means?)

41

"*What a girl can do to you!*" he wonders.

Jake's nightly ceremony of imagining about having a date with her, and finally making love to her drove him nuts. He knows he had to act upon his love, and he swears that he is asking Cidy out at tonight's Christmas party.

CH 8: First Encounter With Cidy

It was about five years ago. It was another beautiful day during the fall. Jake was going to ride bike with Paul, his best friend, after work at the Memorial Park trail. But it was a busy day for accounting department. He was checking out the creditors-and-debtors report, and circling the one's that the company needs to pay by today.

As Jake was telling one of his assistant, Devin, to call one of the oversea creditors to see if the payment is received, HR manager, Gary, introduced Cidy to the accounting department, one employee at a time. Jake was too busy to recognize Cidy's first day as a new employee. As Gary was about to introduce Cidy to Jake, Jake walked away towards his desk, and sat down to make a call to the bank, so Gary and Cidy came over to Jake's desk.

Gary tried to introduce Cidy, "Hey, Jake."

"Yes, Gary. What you need?" Jake had an urgent payment task that needed to be verified. He knew Gary was about to introduce Cidy, but he said what came to his mind. He was thinking about the creditor who just called and complained that they haven't received the payment. He was very sure that he made a wire transfer a few days ago, but some mishap had happened in the wire or something. He had to get this done right away. So, he got on the phone trying to get to the bottom of the problem.

"Jake, this is our new Event Coordinator—Cidy, Cidy Grant." Gary quickly finished Cidy's introduction.

"Oh, Hi." Jake made a quick gesture and gave his right hand for a quick shake, while waiting on the phone.

She shook Jake's hand and said, "Nice to meet you." Although Cidy wanted to say more, Jake got on with his business, so she had to deal with that short introduction.

Jake turned his head around as he finished shaking her hand, and talked on the phone, "This is Jake. What happened to the wire payment to Xin Jian? I wired it three days ago." Jake was just too busy to pay much attention to her, so he just shook her hand out of respect.

He didn't think much about her but saying to himself, "*What a cutie.*" He was a guy too: He couldn't help noticing how cute she is. But the smell of her, it lingered for a while even after she moved on. He wondered if other guys smelled the same thing as long as he did, but he couldn't ask.

He just thought to himself, "*She smelled like some flowers—maybe roses. But I'm not sensitive to scents. What is it?*" He didn't have a dog's nose to say what the scent was for sure, but he was branded with that smell of her, very much. That split second of seeing her got him interested in her, and the smell locked his heart for her.

CH 9: JAKE DRIVES TO CHURCH

Arriving at his truck, Jake taps twice on the hood of his ride, and says, "Gooood morning, Chuck."

He tells kids at the church that Chuck and I did this and that. Kids just love the way he talks about his life with Chuck; kids get a kick out of it, and they all call his truck, Chuck.

He thanks his old Ford truck for being so reliable, "Thanks Chuck. We're going to church to do some work, Buddy." He doesn't remember when he had to fix Chuck the last time. Chuck gives him very little mileage but serves many purposes for him, his friends, and the church, especially when they have to move stuff.

Jake opens the driver side door, and the squeak is returned. He makes a mental note to get WD-40 to kill it. He gets in the truck, and turns the engine on, and the engine roars like a lion. He likes the sound, and shuts the squeaking door, and drives to the church. The radio comes on and plays his favorite tune—*I Could Sing of Your Love Forever*.

Jake rolls the window down, and feels the fresh morning breeze hitting his face. He feels alive and happy although he is yawning and squinting. .He plays this song at the church worship, and just can't get tired of it. He sings alone without missing a word or a beat, and moves his head up-and-down and side-to-side while tapping the steering handle. He is up.

Jake hears his phone ring and turns the radio off. It's Pastor. He answers, "Yes, Kirk."

"Where you at?" Kirk gets to the point with a friendly tone.

"Just around the corner. Be there in a sec. Be sooner than later." Jake makes a rap with his answer. He laughs. He hears Kirk laughing too.

He is just a couple of turns away from the church. He has nothing but respect and love for Kirk. Kirk is like his dad, a close friend, an older brother, and a mentor. There's something very special about Kirk because he always make him feels special. One thing for sure, Jake knows Kirk love him too.

Thinking about Kirk, Jake smiles, and just can't help to think about the fishing trip they had a few months ago:

CH 10: FISHING TRIP

"Jake, it's me, Kirk. Let's go fishing tomorrow. You know the drill." Kirk invited Jake for fishing. It was more like a little revival for the young man in twenties and thirties. It was just another Saturday, but Kirk made it so special.

"I'm on it, Kirk." Jake liked fishing with the boys and Kirk. It was a lot of fun for a short one-day trip. Jake had caught two fish from all those fishing trips, but he learned a lot about Kirk, the boys, and himself.

At 4:00 a.m., the next day, most of the boys showed up, and Kirk was already at the church with the van, already started-up. Jake just drove into the parking lot. They got all the equipment in the van— fishing poles, tackle boxes, and coolers with the drink and food. Some of the boys had gotten quite serious about the fishing and purchased some fine looking poles and baits. By 4:15, they were off to Galveston. The drive to Galveston usually took about an hour and half.

Jake took out his guitar and played the familiar worship songs as usual. They were happily singing for a while, but Kirk suddenly said, "Can't you play any real music like George Strait or Willie Nelson?"

They all laughed, and Jake played some George Straight and other country songs. They had a blast.

Kirk and some of the boys sang off-beat and out of tune, but it was all right. They screamed more than sang, but the love of the fellowship felt deeply among them. It was one great joy ride. Jake and the boys just loved being with Kirk and each other. The fellowship, the friendship, was magical and wondrous. Jake wished the ride would be forever.

Before they knew it, they arrived at the sweet spot that Kirk claims to be holy. They got off the bus quickly, and got their equipment out, and got to their spot in twos and threes. They all had their little clicks or buddies in the church. If anyone is left out, Jake usually took him under, and that's how Paul became his best friend.

Jake and Paul got their stuff and tried to find a spot. Jake let Paul lead. Paul moved around trying to find that miracle spot. Paul had caught three fish last time, much more than Jake had caught in all his trips. Paul had being bragging about it ever since. It always sounded like he caught all the fish in the ocean.

Paul took Jake to his miracle spot. It took almost 10 minutes of walking. It was a nice walk for them to have a talk. Jake felt good that Paul found a little peace and a sense of belonging. Paul really enjoyed Jake's company because Jake gave him confidence and friendship he needed. They liked the bonding that came with walking and talking near the ocean front. From the spot they arrived, they couldn't see the others at all. Paul and Jake started to fish, and had some drink and had a few small talks about work, life and, of course, girls.

Meanwhile, Kirk had one-to-one talk with the boys while they fished. The boys knew fishing was cover-up for consultation or spiritual check-up, but it was more than okay for them. They loved having their spirit check-up with Kirk.

Kirk came around to Paul and Jake. Kirk took Paul aside first. Paul came back after about thirty minutes later smiling. Kirk had his arm around Paul.

"Paul, Romans 8:28!" Kirk said with a very confident and commanding voice. "Jake, it's your turn, Son. Let's have a walk."

They began to walk along the shore as the seagulls made their flying patterns while singing.

Jake had a walk like this with Kirk, now, several times.

It was always quite special for both of them: Kirk felt like he was Jesus taking Peter for the walk to request him to take care of His sheep, and for Jake, he felt like he was walking with Jesus.

Jake broke the silence first. "Kirk, I wrote a new song. I hope the church likes it."

"Hmm...I'm curious. When am I gonna hear it?"

"Well...in a month...just finished it."

"What's the title?"

"*Going Home*. It's about our journey home—Heaven. You know walking the walk as Christ wanted us to...you know...in hardship and failure."

And there was some silence for a few minutes as they walked.

Kirk wanted Jake to say other things in his mind before he started to question him, but Jake kept silent.

Jake always felt a bit naked with Kirk; he felt Kirk knew about his mental and spiritual conditions before he told him.

Finally, Kirk said, "I appreciate all that you do for God...church...and me. You know...YOU, you are...my son."

Kirk said this maybe once or twice a year to Jake: Kirk had a special feeling for Jake because Kirk knew Jake has that rare, sincere heart for Christ. Kirk had a strong feeling that Jake belongs in ministry, so he had been praying for Jake and for Jake's calling for a few years, now.

Jake cherished those words from Kirk. He knew Kirk said the same thing to other boys, but somehow he felt he meant it more for him than the other. And, he somehow did feel Kirk is like his own dad.

Jake appreciated Kirk's comment and nodded, "Kirk, I'm so blessed...through you. I don't know how I can repay you. I love you like my dad."

Jake wanted to say *I love you*, and *you are my dad*. But he just couldn't get his words out like he wanted it. His dad had a very special place in his heart, but they just grew a distant apart as he got older. He couldn't figure his dad out, but he knew he loved Dad and Dad loved him as well.

After a moment, Kirk pushed the hot button without a delay, "You...ah...have a lady you are seeing?" Kirk whacked at the bush. He was one of those guys who didn't beat around the bush especially talking with the boys. Kirk wanted Jake to find a nice girl to get marry and be blessed. He knew Jake is ready for marriage.

Kirk did introduce him a very faithful and beautiful girl, but Jake just dated her only once, out of courtesy. Kirk really thought highly of the girl, and he hoped that they will hit it off because they were both very attractive, and they were both very sincere and humble in their faith. He felt they would be great partners in marriage and ministry, but Jake just wasn't interested in her.

Jake felt embarrassed, but gave an honest answer because he trusted and loved Kirk, "I have a lady...I'm in love with..." His answer got blurry at the end. It was the similar answer he had been giving for the past few years.

"You...ah...asked her out, yet?" Kirk knew the answer but asked it anyway. He had heard this before.

"...No...no. ...I...I...can get over that hill." Jake hated the question. He had been abused by Paul enough with the same question. He could imagine Paul looking over his shoulder to check-up on him and giving that I-told-you-so smirk.

Kirk knew the story of Jake's love. He just wanted to let Jake know he is more than interested in his life, and everything is okay.

"You know it took me three years to ask Jane out. Jane said she's been waiting for me to ask her out for three years. Can you believe that? I was so afraid to ask her out." Kirk gave his honest account with his wife.

Kirk tapped Jake's shoulder, and rubbed Jake's head a bit, and said, "The right time will come. ...Don't be anxious."

Jake got a lot of comfort from that. He was getting anxious and couldn't focus sometimes. He felt like Kirk's words were like from God.

CH 11: Jake Arrives at the Church

As Jake reaches the church, he can see several large branches broken off here and there. He swerves around the parking lot like a race driver, and parks his truck near the biggest one. Kirk was right there waiting.

Kirk greets Jake as he steps out of his truck, "Good morning, Jake." Kirk shakes his hand, and gives him a hug as Jake returns the greeting. Kirk has a big smile on him; he is so proud to see Jake.

Today, Kirk is going to give Jake the calling to do God's work.

"There are some, you can see, here and some at the back as well. I guess the thunder storm hit us good here last night. Luckily, nothing of the church building is damaged. Isn't that amazing! Praise the Lord." Kirk gave his assessment and his feeling.

"I'll get it done in a minute, Kirk. Don't worry." Jake gets to the point and reassures Kirk that the church will be taken care.

"Thanks, Jake."

Kirk's not worried a bit. He knew God planned this for them to meet this morning, so he can give him the calling.

Looking at Jake, he dreams of his younger years.

"How time flies!" Kirk murmurs to himself in a delightful tone, and feels the grace of time that God has given him.

Jake gets a rope from his truck and ties the biggest broken branch to his truck, and drags it to the dumpster. Jake quickly gets rid of all the branches from the drive ways and the parking lot.

Kirk enjoys watching Jake getting the job done. He is surprised how quickly the job is done.

Being messy with debris and sweat, Jake feels exhausted, but he is fully awake, now. He feels awesome: he always felt great after a good laborious work. He could feel the adrenaline pumping through his body. He often thought he belongs in some blue-color work like in construction.

Looking at Jake, Kirk helplessly recalls the first time when he first met Jake at the church parking lot:

CH 12: KIRK MEEtS JaKE

A young man walked out of an old beaten-down truck (the same truck Jake's driving now) wearing a suit and a tie. His suit and tie didn't look quite fitting or matching, and he wasn't familiar to Kirk.

Kirk was just about to leave the church, and go home for lunch. Seeing a stranger in the parking lot made him a bit uncomfortable, so he walked over and greeted Jake, "Hello. Can I help you?"

"I'm ah...wondering if I could ah...give a quick prayer in the church," Jake requested. He found the church sort of accidently, and felt like he was led here to make the prayer he wanted.

Kirk wanted to ask why, but he felt Jake's sincerity.

"I'm...Pastor, here. Let me open the door for you." Kirk never had anyone approaching the church like Jake did before, but he was moved by Jake's request.

"Follow me." Kirk led Jake to the sanctuary, and opened the door, and turned the lights on for Jake. "Take your time."

Jake walked near the cross and kneeled down. Jake bowed his head and prayed. He thanked God for the job and prayed for a place to stay, and a church to attend.

A few minutes later, Jake made an offering to Kirk. Jake had left home with four hundred dollars in his pocket, but made a fifty-dollar offering. He gave to God all he had left with.

Jake said, "Thank you, Pastor. I really appreciate that." Jake made his stride towards the exit.

Kirk had to ask some questions, so he called Jake back, "Hey…ah…young man…wait up…let me…" Kirk couldn't finish his words.

Jake turned around.

Kirk introduced himself, "I'm Kirk Stevenson." He reached out with his right hand for a shake.

Jake gave his hand for Kirk's. "I'm Jake Calhoun."

"Jake…I've been Pastor here, now 9 years, and I had never seen a young man coming to church…like you…give a prayer and make an offering. You know…what I mean…right? Ah…mind I ask you some questions?" Kirk had seen many people who had come for help or money, but not the other way around.

Jake responded hesitantly, "Mmm…ah…okay, Pastor." He reluctantly agreed. He thought that was the kind thing to do.

"Call me, Kirk." Kirk led him to a bench.

It was a hot summer day, but Kirk felt it would be better to have a talk outside than in the office. They sat down. He asked general questions about where and why Jake is here. He found out that Jake's been just hired by a local company and looking for a place to stay. He felt Holy Spirit telling him to provide Jake with room and board. He thought that wouldn't fly well with Jane.

"You got a place to stay?" Kirk asked the question seemed most important to Jake.

"...mmm...God will provide." Jake stuttered a bit and avoided the question or answered it with faith.

Jake had very little money left—a few dollars maybe if he scrapped up all the coins here and there in his truck. He could have stay at a motel for the night with the money he just made an offering with. But now he had no money for food or place to stay. He really didn't know where he is staying or what he is going to eat, but he had peace.

"Don't have a place to stay...huh?" Kirk hit the nail again.

"Well...sir...Pastor...yes...I mean...no...I don't know." Jake's answer was unclear. He felt embarrassed to speak the truth.

"I don't know anyone in town." Jake spoke without a thought. He wanted to leave. He felt cornered. He stood up to leave. He started to walk to his truck without saying a word.

Kirk never brought a stranger home, but he felt Holy Spirit guiding him. Kirk chased Jake down. "Jake, come and stay at my place."

When he heard those words, Jake was shocked. It was like God prepared everything for him. He wanted to say yes, but he wasn't sure. He turned around to see Kirk. He murmured while he was shaking his head a bit of disapproval or out of disbelief.

Kirk insisted, "Jake, I feel this is Holy Spirit's work. I've never done this before. I don't invite strangers home. ...You will be safe at my home." Kirk smiled and chuckled a little.

CH 13: BREAKFAST W/ JAKE AND KIRK

Kirk invites Jake to have breakfast together. "Jake, let's grab a bite…McDonalds."

The magic word—McDonalds—hits homerun with Jake. Being quite hungry from the work, Jake teases Kirk, "You buying?"

"You eating?" Kirk confirms the deal.

They drive to the nearby McDonalds, and order breakfasts.

Kirk pays for it as agreed. They find a table to seat. He wishes he had a son like Jake, so he treats him like his own son. He looks at Jake and feels very proud: Jake has turned out to be a pillar for the church.

Kirk is eager to tell him the dream he had last night, but knows he has to wait for the right time.

Kirk gives a quick prayer for both of them and eats. He looks into Jake's eyes wants to say it, but waits till when they are about to finish. He feels Jake belongs in ministry, and has been praying for it for years.

They talk about work, church, and sport. As they are about done with breakfast, Kirk says it bluntly but quietly, "Jake. …Follow Christ and become a pastor…a missionary." Kirk is looking right at Jake.

Jake stops eating and stares back at Kirk. He feels the destiny calling. He always told himself, if

Kirk calls him to ministry, he will follow because he loves and admires Kirk so much as Pastor, a mentor, and a friend. And he also has been praying for the calling.

Jake holds his breath a little while, and commits without a hesitant in a strong and firm voice, "I will." He is afraid but he has been waiting for this calling for a long time.

Kirk has called several men to ministry and feels very sure about Jake. With the last night vision, he knew his feeling is more than assured.

Kirk says, "I wanted to say this to you for years but waited for the right moment—the time that God had planned for. Last night I dreamed of anointing you."

Jake is curious and asks for the details, "Tell me…about your dream."

"…I was giving a sermon…like any other Sunday. The congregation was there and you. Then a light shined on top of you. I immediately called your name. You walked up the podium. You kneeled down and bowed your head. And I walked towards you, and I kneeled too. And I laid my hand on your head, and anointed you, and blessed you." Kirk gave his account of the dream. "You stood up. And the light was still on top you. I saw the heaven open up. That's it."

Jake grabs on the every word, and suddenly realizes that the calling might mean he has to lose Cidy.

Jake's face turns stoic a bit.

Kirks senses something wrong but keeps it to himself; he figures Jake would have some worries and fears to overcome.

Jake hopes that Cidy accepts him even with the calling. He is excited and concerned. Losing Cidy is just too painful for him.

Kirk sees Jake's fear in Jake's eyes, and reaches out for Jake's hand, and holds them, and closes his eyes, and prays, "Father, give hope and faith to Jake. Use Jake to spread the Gospel to four corners of the Earth. I have seen Jake for years, Lord. He is worthy of your calling. I pray in Your Son's name—Jesus Christ."

Jake agrees to Kirk's prayer with *amen*.

Jake suddenly has flashbacks of the very first time when he committed his life to Christ:

CH 14: JAKE COMMITS

"...He died on the cross, and shed His blood for your sin—every one of them. Yours and mine! He had the crown of thorn on his head that pierced his head. He had blood pouring from his head. He had traces of lashes with blood stain all over his body.... ...The third day...he came back to life..." The young preacher, Nathan, poured out the Gospel with all his heart to the children.

It was at a church retreat for children during the summer vacation. They drove out to a camp about hour and half away, with teachers and kids. It was a lot fun, but Jake loved every word that he was taught. Every word felt like it was meant for him.

On the third day at the evening of *Power Word*, the calling was made after the sermon.

"Anyone who wants to accept Christ into your heart, please come forward and kneel before Christ your Savior! Christ has died on the cross for your sin, and He has shown the power over death by coming back to life on the third day! Give your life to Christ...." Nathan shouted out with all his heart to bring as many children's souls as possible to Christ.

When Jake was ten, the youth-and-children pastor, Nathan, made a strong calling to the kids to accept Christ into their hearts.

Jake knew he had Christ in his heart, but walked up to the podium and kneeled down anyway.

He wanted to give his life for him for sure, and he never wanted anything more than Christ in his heart. He was only ten, but he had love for Christ.

"Jesus, I know you love me. I know you died for me. I will die for you," Jake said those words to himself, when he kneeled down and prayed. He knew exactly what he was saying. He knew what it meant to die for Christ. He felt something touching his body, not like someone's hand, but warmth surrounding his entire body.

He opened his eyes to see if someone is hugging him, but there was no one hugging him or touching him. So he closed his eyes again, and he felt the warmth again. This time he just let it happen. He felt the warmth rising to the point of being hot. He wanted to run away, but he stayed put.

Jake and most of the kids decided to accept Christ that night. Some probably came up because everyone else was doing it.

Nathan prayed for all the kids one by one to accept Christ into their heart by putting his hand on their heads as if he was anointing them. Many kids cried.

Nathan came to Jake.

When Nathan put his hand on Jake's head, Jake felt Nathan's hand to be very hot.

Nathan felt something too; he felt something coming back through him as well. He said something that Jake could not understand. He spoke in a foreign language Jake never heard before. Then Nathan prayed in English. Nathan's prayer went on for a while more than Nathan had planned it. Jake and Nathan had lost the concept of time.

Jake felt his body burning up, and he saw a red cross getting bigger and bigger coming towards him. And the cross just passed through his body. He wanted to scream but held it in.

"Do you accept Christ as your savior?" Nathan asked Jake.

"Yes!" Jake gave his heart to Christ.

Nathan finished his anointing and the calling. The service was over. All the kids went to cafeteria for the evening snack.

But Nathan called Jake over, and mentioned something special he felt, "Jake, I've prayed for many kids, but you're the second one that I've experienced very powerful connection. I couldn't stop praying for you. You felt something, didn't you?"

Jake was shocked that Nathan knew.

"Yes," Jake answered timidly.

"Can you tell me what happened? It will be just between you and me." Nathan was curious.

"It was very…mmm…strange. My body felt warm, not hot. …well it became hot later when you touched me. …and I saw a red cross…getting bigger and bigger, and it passed right through my body," Jake told Nathan of his encounter.

"Okay. Good. Holy Spirit has touched you very strongly. You will have many spiritual battles. Keep yourself close to God, read the Bible diligently, and pray often as possible. You will win against Satan's temptations," Nathan consulted Jake. "God will use you; be prepared."

CH 15: Kirk and Jake

"A lot of things will change. I remember when I decided to become a minister. My Pastor, John Miller. ...What a great guy, great follower of Christ. ...I love him so much. He called me one day to have lunch with him. There he gave me the calling." Kirk pauses; he couldn't help to reminiscence a bit.

"What happened then?" Jake wants to hear more.

"Well, I said no. I told him I'm not a minister type." Kirk pauses again, and looks over to his right as if his past is right next to him.

"Well...." Jake's waiting for the story to continue, and he is quite anxious to hear the rest. He couldn't help it to stare at the same direction as Kirk. He knew there was nothing there, but he looks at the same direction naturally.

Kirk turns his head facing Jake, and looks into his eyes. He smiles and makes a gesture with his hands trying to find a point to start the story again.

"...Oh...he asked me if I love Christ. I said sure. Then he said, 'Kirk, I have seen you since you are five. And you have the gift of love. Every time I see you, I see a little Christ. I know you are called.'" Kirk's eyes are shining, but stops again. He looks outside of the window again, and smiles as if he is enjoying something.

Jake is about to scream, but he waits patiently. He has never become such a big ear before, and his eyes are tightened with focus.

And Kirk continues, "I screamed at him, 'I'm NOT…NOT!' And I got up and left the restaurant. I couldn't handle it. I had other dreams. I had a beautiful girl I was dating. I liked it, the way it was. I didn't go to church for the next six months. My life became a mess. I couldn't work well or do anything right. My girlfriend…she finally left me." Kirk stops again.

Jake could see the pain in Kirk. Jake stays quite.

"I finally went back to see John. John said, 'I've been waiting for you.' I asked him, 'Why didn't you call me?' He said he knew I'll be here sooner or later. I told him my life became a mess since he gave me the calling. I lost my job and my girlfriend. I can't sleep well and eat well." Kirk takes a breath. "And I asked him. How are you so sure of this calling? He said, 'I have been praying for you for twenty years. I know.' I said, 'How come I don't know?' He said, 'You will…soon.'" Kirk wets his mouth with gulp of his orange juice. He sees his past passing right by him.

"How did you know?" Jake questions.

"I haven't told this to anyone because it's too funny…more like silly. I…I flipped a coin. I went into the restroom and said, "God if you want me—head, not—tail. I flipped the coin, and head came up. I did it again; I got head again. I said this is not it. So, when I was by myself I prayed, 'God if you want me, tell me.' I couldn't sleep well. But one night when I was a sleep I heard a voice say, 'You have much work to do.' The voice was so clear I couldn't believe it. I didn't know what to do, but that was good enough for me. And the rest…is history."

Jake nods and smiles. "Coin flip…huh." He thinks that was funny.

Kirk says, "Let's talk more, this Sunday." He knows it's going to take some time for Jake to absorb.

Jake nods.

They leave for their work.

Jake usually loves his morning drive to work: he usually puts his radio on, 89.3, and sings every song with it. The morning drive with his favorite music really sets him in the right mood for the day. But today after the talk with Kirk, he turns the radio off and thinks about his future—a new life as a missionary or a minister: He realizes that a lot of things in his life will change—kind of work, maybe going to seminary, new places to go, new training and learning, and especially "the relationship" with Cidy.

The first and last thing in Jake's mind is— Cidy. He wants to date her at least once. No! He wants to live his life with her forever. But he knows his calling is far more important than his desire for her. Every part of his body desires her so much, but he knows the obedience to God is far more important.

What he knows as the right thing to do and what he desires to do are already clashing with each other: The spirit and the flesh rage on against each other.

Jake prays, "God…I love you. I will go anywhere and do anything that you ask of me. But, you know I love Cidy. I have prayed for her so long and so much. I desire her so much. I love her, God.

You know I love her. Would you at least let me date her once…just once at least? God….” Jake just can't finish his prayer. He wants Cidy so much, but he knows he probably have to give her up. Tears make a shallow pool in his eyes.

Jake looks at the sky and it is so beautiful; White clouds randomly forming and changing their shapes against the background of the blue canvass. They are more than calming. As he changes the direction towards the sun, the sunlight forces him to squint. He looks around, and he knows what he sees with his eyes is nothing but a figment of things that will be gone—even Cidy. He knows only the Kingdom of God will remain forever.

He questions himself, “Can I die for Christ? For real? I sing and pray that I will and I can, but can I really…really die for Christ?”

Jake has known his heart is in the mission field for long time. He would dream about going to foreign lands to witness the Gospel. His dream of going to mission fields started in high school when he made his first mission trip to Honduras for a month.

He smiles while he highlights the month-long mission trip with his church buddies and church adults to Honduras. But one part of the mission trip is always remembered so alive, he can't never forget it:

CH 16: MISSION IN HONDURAS

Two beaten-up, old school buses and a van chugged their way through the mountains and hills in a hot and sticky weather of Honduras. A cool breeze made its way through the open windows of the buses, but it was not enough. It was more than just a tease, but it was better to have it than not. They had no choice; all the rides had no air condition. Jake sweated like everyone else, but he was very excited. Every moment felt very alive with excitement and danger.

Sitting next to a high school buddy, Sam, who played the drum, Jake, talking with Sam, peeked at Julie as much as possible. He loved Julie but couldn't say much to her.

Julie was quite popular amongst boys, but she had her heart set for Jake too. She liked Jake a lot, but she was confused why Jake avoided her. Julie did notice Jake peeking at her, and she liked it. She was quite shy about this love thing, but had much joy of watching Jake singing and playing the guitar. She tried hard to keep her love secret, but did her best to try to meet up with Jake, making it look like it was an accident.

The road was unpaved, but the mountains and forests made the scenery more than welcoming. On the side of the road, there were people selling fruit and fried banana in small cantinas. It wasn't something kids were used to seeing. Jake felt like he was in a totally different world.

On the way to their first destination of that day, they stopped at one of the cantina and bought a batch of baby bananas. They were much smaller than regular bananas. The youth pastor, Michael, said he only paid a dollar for the whole patch. It looked like there were over a hundred little bananas on it. Michael passed the bananas to kids in the buses and the folks in the van.

After three hours of long drive, they finally arrived at their destination—a prison for women only. It didn't look like a prison at all. They stopped at the large metal gate. The native pastor, Lucas, and Michael walked out of the vehicles to talk to the prison guards. Each guard came into the buses and checked the buses for a few minutes, and soon after, they opened the gate.

They went into this facility where there were a lot of small concrete-block huts. It didn't look like prison at all: it looked like a small village. As the two buses and a van made their way through the jail, Jake saw ladies sitting here and there in groups of three or five.

They stopped at the biggest shack in the facility. It was just a simple building with metal roofing that looked like it was about to fall down any minute, and the walls were just concrete blocks stacked. He had never seen a building like it. It was just a plain concrete blocks. There was no door; just a big opening for the main entrance.

Checking the inside of the building with others, Jake estimated that maybe a hundred could sit in. There were no sits, just rows of wooden benches. There were fluorescent lights on the ceiling, but most of the light came from openings on the wall: they were the windows without glass. There was a small stage where the band could set up.

After the band finished setting up, the small building slowly got packed with the lady prisoners. They all wore beaten down blue shirts and pants— the prisoner uniform. Ladies had their hair all tied up or was cut short. Most of the ladies had black hair but a few were blond. Ones that could not find a place in a bench were leaning against the wall standing.

Pastor Lucas made a simple introduction and prayed in Spanish.

And the band started to play and sing, everyone stood up and started to sing along. And as the band played more exciting songs the ladies started to dance as well. It was like a rock concert: people jumped up and down and sang out their lonely and desperate hearts out. About an hour after of singing and worship, Pastor Lucas, the native pastor, gave a heart-pouring sermon in Spanish. Jake didn't understand the sermon but felt every word wrestling his heart.

After the sermon, Pastor Lucas asked everyone to pray with the ladies. Jake reached out and prayed with one of the lady. After few minutes into praying, there was a loud groaning and crying that Jake never heard before. Holy Spirit came down and touched everyone's heart and soul. The place turned into one big crying party; they cried with anguish and repentance. Jake cried like a baby for himself and the ladies; he felt their pain.

The crying and praying went on-and-on, but after a period of time passed, it just suddenly got quieter and quieter, as if someone turned the volume down slowly. Soon people were jerking and wiping their tears off. Jake was sniffling and clearing his eyes with back of his hands, but tears just kept on rolling.

Jake and the group had the hardest time leaving those ladies; everyone couldn't let go of each other. Such a short meeting of people they never met before, but God created a loving bond for them in an instant. Jake's feet were very heavy, but his heart was light. He never knew there could be such a joy in crying.

They were already behind the schedule, so Pastor Lucas urged kids to get on the bus quickly but they couldn't. Jake entered the bus last because he could not stop praying for the ladies.

As the buses were exiting, ladies waved goodbye, and the church members waved back. They all had their heads and shoulders sticking out of the buses' windows. Jake waved back, too, and he never felt so great, so joyful, and so loved.

CH 17: JAKE DRIVES TO WORK

Jake remembers the verse that the yoke of Christ is easier, but he is torn apart because the calling probably means he has to give up Cidy, who has been in his main reason and hope why he got up and prepared himself as neatly as possible and worked so hard. He acknowledges that he loves Cidy more than Christ, but he couldn't help what he felt about her. That is the truth. He sings and confesses he loves Christ more than anything else, but in reality, he is all in for Cidy.

Jake could give up everything except Cidy. He feels funny that he loves her so much; even though, they are not even dating. He knows that his life belongs to Christ and would be more than willing to die for Him, but his body and mind seems to have only one purpose—Cidy.

Jake talks to himself, "*You don't even know if Cidy likes you. And you are concerned about letting her go? Come on Jake! Wake up!*"

This love for Cidy is quite serious for Jake. Rationality can't convince Jake of severing any mental ties with Cidy, so he can truly follow Christ. Jake shakes his head like his trying to throw this pain away—choosing between love and the calling. He bites his own teeth with distorted face, showing obvious pain.

He makes a stop at a red light. He is not focused: He is not himself. He never had to make such a hard choice that slices two great loves of his live—Cidy and Christ. His faith says Christ; His mind and body, Cidy.

For five years Jake's mind and heart have set on Cidy. He never held her hand or kissed her, but the love for Cidy just got deeper and stronger. Just today, already, he had prayed for courage to ask her out tonight a few times.

Jake turns the radio back on to forget about the dilemma. He hears a Christmas song and automatically sings along with it. He sings it much louder than usual hoping to drain his thought out and to kill the pain.

A lot of Christmas songs are playing. But it's not giving him peace nor calming him down. He knows God's in control, but he is quite devastated to let go of his one true love that he finally found. He is more than astonished how Cidy has captured his heart for so long and so strong. He has dreamt about holding Cidy so many times and making love to her.

Jake could see the company's entrance about a few hundred yards away, now.

CH 18: Rose and Cidy

In the elevator, as the soft elevator music flows, Cidy plucks some of the thorns off the roses, and puts them in her pocket. She loves holding on to the roses, but the thorns would get in the way sometimes and cause an unexpected poke of pain.

She often wonders if the roses' branches were used to make the crown of thorn that Jesus was forced to wear on the cross. She imagines the pain that Christ must have suffered as the thorn pierced and cut his head drawing the scared blood of Jesus. It is that blood of Jesus washed her sin away.

She often pictures herself being in the front of the cross when Jesus was crucified, observing the entire process of His crucifixion—Son of God, giving up all His power, authority, and glory, and letting his creation humiliate, torture, and kill Him, so He can die and wash their sin, our sin, my sin away.

Jesus could have stopped the crucifixion whenever he wanted. He could have willed His power to show that He is Son of God with a simple command: He could have called armies of angels to slay all the Roman soldiers and the evil priests of Israel. But He takes the cup of death willingly, which He prayed to God to be removed.

"Couldn't he just die without so much pain and humiliation? Death, itself seems more than overwhelming to comprehend, but the suffering and

the humiliation do not make sense at all." Cidy expresses her pain that she feels about Christ's suffering and death.

It is quite an act of love that Son of God had shown, which Cidy has hard time comprehending the depth and the scope of it, but it is the greatest act of love that she can possibly imagine—Creator suffering and dying for his creation.

"Why are we so precious to Him?" Cidy asks that same question that she had asked so many times. *"What are we to Him? Are we worth it to be saved?"*

She knows she has so much sin in her that she needs Christ. She often wonders how she would have turned about if she didn't believe in Christ.

She decided to be a Christian, a real Christian, at age of 12, and since then, she feels she has done the best for Him.

"Can I die for Christ like his disciples, and like so many of Christian forefathers?" She questions her faith.

Because of her deep thought, she accidently pokes herself to a thorn.

She screams, "Aaahoww."

She could see a tiny drop of blood on her finger. She checks the finger closely, and she can't help but to cringe a bit making an ugly face.

It is nothing serious.

The blood makes her suddenly remember of the cut she got from a rose thorn when she tried to find her cat, Miko:

CH 19: A SCRATCH FROM A THORN

"Miko! Miko!" Cidy cried out in search of her cat, everywhere.

She looked every possible place where Miko could be hiding, but she couldn't find her. Lone Ranger, her mutt dog, happily followed her around like a faithful servant, not knowing she is looking for Miko.

"Mom, I can't find Miko, anywhere," Cidy asked Mom for help.

"Have you looked under the rose bushes?" Mom seemed to know where Miko might be.

Cidy ran out to the back yard as Lone Ranger followed her. She started to search for Miko under the bushes, and finally found her hiding at the center of the back rose bushes against the back fence.

"There you are! I've been searching everywhere for you!" Cidy was more than excited to find Miko. Miko looked okay, but Miko didn't move an inch. She kept calling and enticing her to come out with all the gestures she knew.

Miko still didn't budge; she just stood there like a figurine.

Lone Ranger was jumping around Cidy, but Cidy had all of her attention given to Miko.

"Maybe Miko is hiding from Long Ranger," thought Cidy. So, she tried to chase Long Ranger away to no avail.

Cidy finally decided to craw inside of the bush and get her out. She crawled in slowly, and reached out by stretching out her right hand, and grabbed Miko by a paw, and slowly dragged her out. As she was dragging Miko out, she felt a little sting on the back of her neck. She didn't think much about it.

As soon as she got Miko out, she held Miko tight, and took her inside.

"Mom, I found Miko. She was hiding in the bush like you said." Cidy started to tell what happened with Miko in her arms.

Mom showed her interest. "Tell me. Is Miko okay?"

As Long Ranger making his run around Cidy, Cidy continued her story of how she saved Miko.

Karina, as she was preparing for dinner, listened to every word Cidy said with an amazement and joy.

"I'm gonna go play with Miko, now, Mom," Cidy told Karina her immediate plan.

"Okay," Karina gave an automatic respond.

As Cidy turned around to go to her room, Mom saw a blood stain on Cidy's dress, and said in sort of unbelief, "Is that...blood on you? Come here, Cidy! Let me see that!"

Cidy walked back to Mom, and Mom turned Cidy around, lifted her back hair covering the back part of her neck, and saw a deep cut.

"The bleeding stopped, but I need to clean the cut, Cidy. It a big cut. It's gonna hurt but you saved Miko."

"I don't remember getting cut, Mom. I did feel a sting."

CH 20: WORKING CIDY

Cidy checks to see if there are any more thorns, and hears the bell of the elevator signaling the arrival to the15[th] floor. She gets off the elevator, paces to the company's entrance, and opens the door with the company security card. She's the first at work as usual. She skips towards her office with joy. As she's about to step into her office, she makes a ballerina twirl before stopping at her office door. (It wasn't easy or graceful with the flowers, the bag and the briefcase, but she had to do it as her skips naturally led to the next move—a twirl.) She laughs.

She steps into her office, and glances over to where Jake sits and smiles. She can't see Jake from her desk, but likes to glance at that direction often. She opens the door of her office, and sits herself, and relaxes a few seconds, and opens her purse, and gets a small mirror out, and checks her face and hair, and smiles at herself. She turns her computer on and gets her schedule book out of her briefcase. She places it on the desk and opens the cover expecting to see the picture of Mom, Karina Grant.

Last night, Cidy had a talk with Mom, and Mom brought up that same old story how Cidy hated her name. Cidy brushed it off as always.

CH 21: SHE HATED HER NAME

Michael, a red hair and freckled face boy, an elementary buddy, ran towards Cidy during the recess when Cidy was playing with her friends in the sand dune. She knew what's coming as she caught Michael on the edge of her sight—the daily torture. But she couldn't stop it. The more she tried to stop Michael; the more Michael and the company enjoyed it.

"…a, b, *C, D*," Michael loudly sang the ABC song highlighting the C-D part over and over again, and he changed his ridiculing venue: "I don't *C D*. I do *C D*. Do you *C D*?" Michael continued until he got what he wanted from Cidy—an angry and exploding respond that got everyone's attention especially himself.

Cidy tried to keep calm by not responding like Mom told her not to: Mom said, "Michael will get tired out it, and leave you alone, if you just keep calm, and let him tire himself out. Count sheep up to thousand and breathe slowly. Okay?"

Michael continued his assault on her because he liked her. It was his way of showing his attention. He enjoyed Cidy's respond—getting chased by her. It was the only way he knew how to get her attention, the kind of attention he wanted because he wasn't in for girls' talking or sand playing.

Cidy counted sheep up to nineteen, and that was the farthest she could ever keep her anger down.

Michael could tell he was getting to her because her face showed anger as her face twitched and crumpled up with flaring eyes. He thought she was so cute even when she was angry.

Cidy quickly grabbed some sand in her left hand, and she threw it right at Michael's face as she did so many times before.

Michael dodged the sand easily, and stuck his tongue out, and played the ever-popular teasing song, "Nah,-nah-nah-nah-nah. *You* missed meeeee. *You* missed meeeeee."

Cidy went on the chase mode. She was fast but Michael was faster. He made swift turns around the corners of the swings, seesaws, and other playground equipment. He teased her by letting her get close to him and zipping away. He loved it.

She got angrier and angrier, but she just couldn't catch Michael. A part in her did enjoy the chase, but she hated how other kids made fun of her name too.

She chased Michael until she had no more breath but with fury to punish Michael until he probably died.

The recess had become a very angry time for Cidy.

Kids thought they were just having fun, but for her, it was the time she dreaded the most. She just didn't like herself for being so angry at Michael and the other kids who jumped in the teasing bandwagon with him. It got the worst of her even when her close friends would join in. She felt overwhelmed and distraught when teased by so many kids.

Cidy didn't want to go to school on some days because of the teasing got the worst of her. She hated the Alphabet song. Every time they sang the song, they would stare at her at the beginning of song like a ritual. She could feel their attention—the unwanted attention—and it wasn't pleasant; it disturbed her peace and caused her stomach to turn. Sometimes even the teacher would point at her when they sang that "C-D" part, not knowing Cidy hated it.

"Why can't I have a normal name?" Cidy often questioned about her name that was given to her without any consent from her. "Why can't I choose my own name? It's not fair."

"Mom, I want a new name, please. I like Kathy or Julie. You know something cute and popular. You KNOW one that kids won't tease. I don't like them laughing at me. They don't understand what my name means. Please. PLEASE. PLEASE...," Cidy cried many times begging for a new name.

Whenever Cidy complained about her name, Mom would be understanding and consoled her, and sometimes Cidy would hear the same old story about how her name came about: what her name means, and how her name is so important to Mom.

And that would settle the argument reluctantly on Cidy's side, and she would have to wrestle with her reality. It wasn't fun; it was terrible. Mom would be nice and calm and adhering to Cidy's other causes—most of them, anyway—except changing Cidy's name.

She couldn't understand her stubborn mom; it just didn't make any sense: she felt a name is a name, and no one should be hurt by their own name.

One day, Michael passionately made the same approach to Cidy, trying to destroy her enjoyment and laughter as usual. But for whatever the reason, she kept her cool, this time. She remembered her prayer with Mom a night before: "Lord, let Cidy win against Michael and other kids. Give Cidy patience, not to show any anger. Cidy, you shall win against Michael and other kids with the strength from Holy Spirit. We pray this in the name of Your Son—Jesus Christ." It was the same prayer Mom has given many times, which never worked, but this day the prayer kept her cool.

Cidy felt very calm as Michael made extra effort; he went all out to get his money's worth. He couldn't figure out why she didn't get mad. She just smiled at Michael. Soon Michael's gestures and actions became just too funny for her. She started to laugh and giggle at Michael: She enjoyed the show Michael put on. And the tide turned around: It wasn't about teasing Cidy anymore; it was just having fun. All the kids enjoyed Michael as Cidy kept her cool.

After that, Michael tried three or four more times to get his way with Cidy, but it was Cidy who seemed to enjoy the moment more than him. So, he quit teasing her.

CH 22: Jake's Heart

       Cidy's face keeps appearing in front of
Jake's eyes. He turns the radio off again. He feels
the pain of love. He recognizes that being a Christian
is not easy, but being called to ministry is even
harder as he tries to let go of her. More he tries to let
Cidy go; more Cidy would grapple.

       He remembers the song he wrote about a
year ago. He wrote it by looking back through his life
and holding on to the promise from the Lord.

       He sings it:

> When I trusted in you,
> I thought all things will be all right.
> But I'm in pain.
> And I feel forsaken, Lord.

> Oh, I'm with you my child.
> The faith isn't easy.
> The agony, you must overcome.
> And you will be crowned, My child.
> And you will be awarded, My child.
> And you will know I am with you
> Always.

> When I gave You my life,
> I thought all things will be peaceful
> But I still struggle.
> And I feel You are not here with me.

Oh, I'm with you My child.
The walk isn't easy.
The agony, you must overcome.
And you will be crowned, My child.
And you will be awarded, My child.
And you will know I am with you,
Always.

When I gave You my heart,
I thought You will take care of me.
But I'm still in need.
And I feel I been betrayed.

Oh, I'm with you My child.
The path isn't easy.
The agony, you must overcome.
And you will be crowned, My child.
And you will be awarded, My child.
And you will know I am with you,
Always.

And you will be crowned, My child.
And you will be awarded, My child.
And you will know I am with you,
Always.

    Singing his own song, Jake consoles his heart, and arrives at work, and parks far from his normal spot because he is late. He gets out of his car, and walks towards the main entrance, and habitually looks for Cidy's old, white, and cute little Geo Metro. "Little Whittie," he calls it. Jake enjoys seeing her car because it feels like seeing her. He walks by her car purposefully, taking a longer walk, and gives a couple of tap on it, and says, "Hey Cutie." Jake's alter ego shows up when no one's around.

Jake gets excited from that, and starts humming with a little pep in his steps, and almost hops through the main door, and gives a salute to Peter and marches on to the elevator. He feels silly that he gets this excited just touching Cidy's car, and can't wait for tonight's party either.

He pushes the button, and waits for the elevator doors to open. He practices the Willie Nelson's love song he's going to sing tonight— *Always on My Mind*. It was a song Dad sang often, and he liked it. In his heart he is dedicating it to Cidy. He looks at the mirror image of himself on the elevator's doors. It's a bit blurry, but Jake could see that he has grown up to be quite alike his dad. Sometimes people would say to they are brothers when they are out together.

Jake has a lot of fond memories with his dad. Dad taught him how to sing and to play the guitar, and they sang many songs together.

Thinking about his dad, Jake plays that day when he got his first guitar in his mind:

CH 23: JAKE'S FIRST GUITAR

"…Happy birthday…dear Jake. Happy birthday to you," The crowd sang the Happy Birthday song for Jake. Mom led the song as Dad played the guitar, and all the kids sang along. Jake's little friends from school and church gathered around the picnic table at a park.

Six candles were burning on top of the cake that read, *Happy Birthday Jake*.

As the song ended, Mom looked into Jake's eyes and said, with a few nods of approval, "Go ahead! Blow the candles out."

Jake blew out the candles with a couple of huff, and everyone screamed and clapped. And Dad brought a big box out. Jake had no idea what was in it. It looked like there was a big teddy bear in it, or a washing machine. It was just a big cardboard box. It was standing there for a while; he remembered. He didn't think much about it because it didn't have any fancy ribbon or packaging. He realized it was in a plain disguise for that reason—to be unnoticed by the people, especially by kids. And it worked.

Dad said, "Well…Jake. I hope you like it."

Jake was overwhelmed by the size of the box. He hesitated to open it.

Everyone loudly chanted, "Open it! Open it! Open, open, open…."

Jake opened the top box with ease to his surprise. He jumped to take a pick in it. The very thing that he wanted the most (but was told he was too young for it)—a guitar—was in it. He screamed and jumped up and down. "Thank you! Thank you Dad! Thank you Dad!"

All the kids thought it was a robot or a dog. They questioned, "What is it? Dog? Robot? Bicycle? What is it?"

Jake answered with a loud shout, "Guitar! It's a GUITAR!"

All the excitement fizzled out quickly among the kids.

Jake jumped on Dad. Dad grabbed Jake, and brought Jake up to his shoulder, and hugged him tight.

Jake said, "Thank you, Dad. Thank you. Thank you so much. I love you, Dad."

Dad said, "Mom…Mom got it for you."

Jake released himself from Dad, and ran to Mom. They hugged like they haven't seen each other for years.

Jake said, "Thanks Mom."

Mom said, "Dad got it for you."

CH 24: BACK TO JAKE

As Jake smiles from his fond memory, the elevator's doors open, and the elevator unleashes a few people out. He gets in alone. He checks himself against the shining interior metal sheet again. He is a mess from the work. He smiles at himself and thinks about Cidy.

He prays, "Lord, I know I...probably...need to give Cidy up, but I would love to date her at least once, just once. Please give me courage to ask her out tonight."

The elevator is not moving. He realizes he hadn't pushed the floor button, and pushes 15.

Jake feels like a different man since the calling. He feels the burden of the requirement or the sense of duty on his shoulder. It was something he had dreamed about, but never thought it would be today.

He questioned God's timing on many things, but he knew sovereign God had his perfect timing for all things.

Jake remembers when his little brother called and told him when he decided to be a pastor:

CH 25: GEORGE CALLS JAKE

"Hey, Jake. It's MEEEE, your favorite brother—George." Jake's brother, George, called one night about three years ago.

"What's up, George! Haven't heard from you …what…for six months." Jake was surprised to hear from his little brother.

"Hey. I just wanna to give you up a heads-up. I'm going to seminary, soon," George said something totally unexpected.

"What?" Jake heard what George said, but he was caught off guard.

Jake knew George had a strong love for Jesus Christ, but he had never imagined his own little brother would become a pastor. He knew George lived in church like he did, but he always saw him as just a little brother that he had to watch over and take care of.

Jake always felt George was a nuisance to him, because he always tagged along causing nothing but problems. So, it was more than a shock for Jake to hear George—his little brother— committing his life to the ministry.

"I know, Jake. You think I'm not worthy. I think the same." George read Jake's mind.

"No…. I just didn't expect…you…saying such a thing, today. Well…I'm…I'm…shocked." Jake did his best to cover the truth up, or he had to say some truth why he reacted.

"I've been praying and consulting with Pastor John. He's the one who gave me the calling. I said no, at first. And my life got all messed up. I hit the lowest of low. I haven't gone to church for three months. I wanted to call you. I finally decided to accept God's calling." George just touched upon the highlights of his calling.

Jake thought, "If anyone would be receiving the calling in his family, it would be him. But God has chosen my little brother instead of me." He felt jealous in a way, but also felt proud of his little brother getting the calling.

Jake always remembered his little brother as someone who needs his help, not someone who will be helping or leading others.

"Carol…agreeing to your calling?" Jake felt this question was very important. He knew George has been going out with Carol almost a year.

"No…yes…. I don't know. We're in a little mess, right now. I was in a mess, so it was hard to bring her along. She's upset that I haven't reached out to her. I couldn't get myself together so…. But I decided to accept the calling a week ago. John anointed me privately for now. I called Carol she wouldn't answer. I didn't answer her call for months so…. I love her so much. I'm praying we get back together." George sounded like he had a lot say, but just gave a quick summary.

Jake felt some pain in George's voice.

"My little brother, all grown up. George…my little brother…." Jake kept thinking. He couldn't help to think the growing-up years: How he fought for him, how he taught him to play games, how he helped

him with his homework, and how he took advantages of him. He loved George although he felt George was more trouble than he had bargained for. He remembered how he often wished he didn't have George around, so he can have everything for himself, and don't have to take care of him.

"I don't know what to say. Does Dad know?" Jake asked the second most curious question to him.

"I haven't told him yet. You know you feel like my dad more than Dad. You know...." George said something he always wanted to tell Jake.

Jake heard what George said quite clearly. He got sucker punched. He loved his little brother a lot, but it seemed like George loved him more. He didn't know what to say. He wanted to say a lot, but he couldn't get a word out.

Silence stayed for a while.

George broke the silence first, "Jake! I just want to say I appreciate your love. You took care of me well. You have been a good brother's keeper. I owe you a lot. I love you man."

Jake was crying. He didn't want his brother to know he is crying.

Silence returned.

Jake tried to open his mouth, but he couldn't. He had often wondered if loving "your brother" (in his case his own little brother) would do any good. For years, he felt he was burdened with taking care of a little brother, and on top of that, he would be blamed for many things George had done. He hated George many times, and he really hated Dad for punishing him instead of George. That was just unfair.

"Forgive me, George...." Jake couldn't finish his sentence. His voice shook.

George was shock to hear Jake asking for forgiveness. It was something he didn't expected at all. He didn't know how to respond.

"I love you, Jake. I don't know what you are talking about. It is you who always took care of me. I thank you, Jake." George said.

Silence gathered again.

"I've hated you so many times, and wished you…." Jake, again, couldn't finish his words. He was just too ashamed. He felt like a worm. He never felt this shameful.

"Oh…Jake. I would have hated me worse, if I were you. I was a pest. …I need to ask YOU…for forgiveness. You got blamed for so many things I did. I felt sorry for you so many times. I never understood Dad for punishing you for what I did. Now I do. He was trying to make you a leader or be responsible for me. Forgive me…Jake." George cried.

Jake could hear George crying. It just wasn't a guy thing to do. Jake wanted to quit this quickly, but he knew this special time is given by God.

Jake said, "I forgive you, George."

"I forgive you…Jake."

Silence came back again.

Jake had to have a quiet time by himself, so he told George, "Love you, George. I'll talk to you soon."

"Okay, Jake. I love you. Thank you for everything."

CH 26: CIDY'S BURDEN OF DAD

Cidy, after thinking about Mom, looks at Dad's picture too. She tries not to see his picture if possible because she would get leaky, but today she felt she had to see his face. Dad looks so much younger than Mom because he died when she was just a baby. Her eyes got watery a little as usual: It is the same reaction she has every time she sees his picture—the sadness and the burden of missing him.

For Cidy, the burden turned to nightmares for many countless nights. Like some deep philosophical saying from the East, "*All men must carry their burden—heavy or light.*" Cidy had more than her share of burden on her shoulders before she even knew where her shoulders were.

Dad, John, died a day after her birth. A tragedy, that laid unbearable burden on Cidy's entire life from the second day of her life, was just too much for her on many days, and that burden broke her down like a ran-over, crushed toy laying on the side of a street—all shattered into bits and pieces.

She didn't remember when and how she started to have this haunting thoughts, but she wondered a lot while she was growing up if she caused her father's death like a swap—her life for Dad's. This unwanted whisper of her inner voice would ring in her on a bad day like a police siren that is relentlessly chasing down a run-way criminal.

For whatever the reason, various events would trigger this guilty and haunting thought, mostly at nights when she is alone, and she would fall in to that vertigo of horror, guilt, and despair. She didn't know where she has gotten such an idea; maybe it was from TV, movies, books, or stories that she had heard. She couldn't figure it out. It started in middle school years. She thought it was a passing-by thing like a crush on a boy, but it came and built a tower of Babel with a big flashing sign that said *Cidy Killed Her Dad* in her mind.

When this thought started to rise, Cidy would break down slowly, but she fought back by listening to Christian music, singing hymns, reading the bible, but mostly praying to God. These helped her to calm down and fall asleep tired and exhausted, but it was so haunting in some nights that she could not get any sleep at all. It became long and arduous spiritual war where the winner takes the soul of her.

As a result of such spiritual battles, she read the Bible over ten times by the time she graduated from high school. She enjoyed the boring part the most because it got her to sleep quicker, but the good part made her fall in love with the Word.

The mental pain was so severe and defeating, she often said, "My God, my God why have you forsaken me," like Christ on the cross. When that haunting thought grabbed her, she had the worst of herself: she twisted and turned like she was possessed by a demon, and she would pray and sing quietly to calm her spirit.

The spiritual battle for Cidy was the word of God against her haunting and self-punishing thoughts. It was bad enough not having a dad, but her fight against this evil thought of guilt had taken much toll on her. She would wake up tired with what little sleep she had with her face all puffed up. Mom had no idea, because she never told her about it. She didn't want to worry Mom with her struggle and pain. She somehow thought this was her battle that she alone had to fight and win. So Mom criticized her for sleeping late.

However, because of this arduous trial, Cidy's spirituality and mind grew stronger and wiser than most young Christian girls: her spirituality and understanding of the Word were far beyond her age. She was known as "Walking Bible" by her church friends and especially by the Sunday-school teachers, because Cidy would correct them if they miss-quoted the Bible.

She says, "Hi, Dad," looking at the picture of him. She imagines role playing with her dad often, usually at home where a bigger picture of Dad is hanging.

She continues, "I know, YOU KNOW, I'm into Jake. I hope he asks me out tonight 'cause I'm gonna put on a killer dress that he can't refuse." She grins.

"See you Dad."

She decides to call Mom.

Cidy knows Mom would love her call.

On the second ring, Mom answers with joyful greeting, "Hey Cidy. I miss you."

"Mom, we just talked last night."

Mom laughs and teases. "Yesterday is gone. I miss you today."

Cidy speaks with a bit lower tone, "I miss Dad. I don't know why but I miss him a lot, today." She knows how much Mom misses him too. She didn't talk about Dad as much as she wanted to because she knew how much Mom missed him. But she just couldn't help it on some days: she is overwhelmed by the thought of Dad.

Mom chokes a bit, "Me too." She just can't forget John, after all these years.

Mom continues with the same old story, "John was so excited to have you."

CH 27: John Brings Pickles

"Hey Kay, what you craving for today?" Just like any other days, John called Karina, and asked her if she's craving for anything.

During the pregnancy, Karina craved all kinds of food, some she loved; some horrified by it—potato chips, ice cream, Big Mack, Fries, Coffee, Apple, sushi, etc. She was one mean, eating machine. She loved food more than ever before, even the ones she never thought about eating twice like sushi.

When John called, Karina was struck with the craving for the crunch pickles sold in a convenient store, including the pickle juice. She chuckled and shyly said, "I want two pickles from the Mobil corner store, and ask them for the pickle juice, too."

John was not surprised. He kidded, "I hope I ain't getting a 'Michelin' baby."

Karina laughed. "Get it done, Soldier! The lives of Grants are in your hand."

"Aye, Aye, Captain!"

John came home with an entire jar of pickles.

Karina wobbled to greet John, and kissed him, and swiftly went after the pickle jar. She could smell the pickle and juice pulling her entire body.

She wanted to thank him for the jar, but her thirst gave her away.

Karina carried the jar to the kitchen, and laid it on the kitchen top. She tried to open it several times, but she couldn't open it. She looked over to see if John was around.

John smiled, and quickly moved in, and opened it.

As soon as John opened the lid, she quickly pushed John away with her right arm, and swiftly slipped her right hands into to the jar, and grabbed at a pickle as quick as she can. She went for the kill without any hesitation. She went for the second, and gulfed almost half of the juice.

John just cringed feeling the sympathetic sourness.

It was a great show that Karina put on.

He stood next to Karina watching the whole thing with wonder and amazement. It wasn't his first time seeing Karina acting like this, but it was always quite amazing to see his sweet Karina acting like a hungry Cookie Monster. He just grinned.

After the third pickle, Karina grabbed the jar with both hands and gulfed some more of the pickle juice, and wiped her mouth clean with her hands like a rough and rowdy man.

A few second later, she burped out long and loud, and she looked at John with a helpless grin.

He shook his head with disbelief and smiled.

After she had five or six pickles, she took a break. She was satisfied. She had never been so satisfied by food before.

She slowly wobbled herself to the living room couch. With one hand on her hip, the other hand swing wide, she made her way.

He couldn't help but to enjoy such a funny scene.

She knew he's enjoying the sight and says, "John, wipe that smile off of your face, and get me some napkins."

He got some napkins, came around, and kissed her sour lips, and said, "I love you, Karina."

CH 28: Cidy and Mom

"I know Mom. I hope to find a husband just like Dad," Cidy agrees.

Karina remembers a funny incident that happened during her pregnancy, and decides to tell it:

> You might have heard this. I don't know. I was pregnant. It was at a dinner at church. We were sitting around with other church members. John said, 'Yesterday, I had to go and get a water melon. I tried every store and I couldn't find any. So…I finally bought water-melon-flavored-juice packs for kids.' She drank the entire 12 packs in an instant.

"You know what I said?" Karina prepared for the punch line.

"What?"

"It was eleven and half. I'm sorry. I'm not a pig." Karina throws the punch line. "I didn't finish the last pack. I'm telling you the truth."

Cidy laughs, and Karina laughs.

"I remember the day you were born. It's so clear." Karina couldn't help but to mention it.

CH 29: The Birth of Cidy

Karina knew it would be any day.

John just left for work.

On the way of getting the vacuum cleaner, the pain struck. She screamed instantly and immediately fell to the floor. She instinctively knew the time has arrived. No one was around to help: She wished John had left just a little late. She breathed consciously like she had practiced. The pain resided somewhat, but she knew it will be back soon.

She dragged herself to the phone and called her neighbor, Mandy. The phone rang but Mandy didn't answer. She thought Mandy maybe outside or in the bathroom. Karina held on hoping she would answer, but Mandy didn't answer even after a few-minutes of ringing. She concluded that Mandy is out for something quick.

Karina forced herself to the front door, and opened the door quickly as possible, and looked outside to see if Mandy's car is outside. It wasn't. She knew Mandy isn't too far away, but she couldn't risk herself and the baby. She had to think quickly what to do.

The nearest car Karina could see was three houses down to the right, across the street. The car usually wasn't there at this time of the day. She had no choice but to try to ask them for a ride. She couldn't wait for Mandy. She had only seen them—a young black couple with no kids—usually on weekends. She said hello a few times. She meant to visit them but never had the chance.

It was hard, but Karina wobbled her way to the neighbor's door. She felt like she ran a Boston marathon. Breathing hard and consciously, she knocked on the door with hope that someone would be home. No one answered. She tried to see if there was a bell, but she couldn't find one. She knocked on it again hard, and harder with desperation. No one answered. She knocked even harder and longer. No one answered. Mandy isn't back yet. She didn't know what to do. She prayed, "Lord, I know you are in control. Please help me."

Karina decided to return home and call for the police or the ambulance.

As she walked a half way home, someone screamed from behind, "Excuse me! Did you knock?"

Karina slowly turned around. A young black lady that she had seen before was out with just a bath towel around her. Karina grinned and screamed back, "YES! PLEASE, TAKE ME TO HOSPITAL!"

"OKAY, GIVE ME A MINUTE," the lady answered happily with a loud pitch.

The lady disappeared. Karina walked back to the lady's home. In a few minutes later, the lady reappeared.

"Can you take me home, first? I need to pick up my luggage," Karina explained her immediate needs.

The lady answered, "Sure."

The lady opened the passenger-side door and help Karina get in the car. They got in the car. As the car's engine was about to turn, Karina said with urgency, "It's that house with a green porch and a table outside."

"I know. I've seen you several times with your husband out there. It's hard to miss as you wobble around." The lady turned the engine on, and started to back the car out of the drive way. "I'm Patrice."

"I'm Karina. Sorry! I've meant to introduce myself, but I forgot. I'm so sorry." Karina felt embarrassed but she had nothing but getting to hospital as quickly as possible in her mind.

"Here we are!" Patrice parked the car in the drive way of Karina's home, and got out of the car to help Karina get out. Patrice helped Karina to the door.

Karina opened the door and pointed to the luggage. "Would you get that for me?"

Patrice quickly got the luggage, and put it in the back seats, and helped Karina in, and drove her to the hospital.

"I guess this is your first?" Patrice asked.
"Yes."

"What happened? Didn't you have someone to give you a ride?" Patrice asked the most intriguing question in her mind.

"Mandy, the next door neighbor, was supposed to give me a ride. But she must have gone somewhere quick. I should wait for her, but I'm just too worried." Karina breathing became harder and rougher with occasional screaming. She felt the pain coming and going, but felt comfortable that things will be all right.

Karina asked with much difficulty, "Patrice. What do you do?"

"I worked at a call center. I'm on the phone all day long. I just got the night shift. I hate it. I just got home, and I was taking a shower. I thought I heard something. I got scared a bit."

"Sorry about that. I had no choice. I did the first thing that came to mind." Karina pushed the seat backwards a bit.

"What about you?" Patrice asked.

"I'm a teacher. I teach at the elementary across the town, South Side." Karina answered. "I got a maternity leave.... What does your husband do?"

After a few minutes of chat, they arrived to the hospital. Patrice pulled the car into the emergency, and helped Karina out of the car, and grabbed the luggage out, and helped her to the emergency check-in.

"You can go now." Karina told Patrice.

"Okay. I'll come by with Joshua." Patrice waved her hand good-bye.

The nurse quickly brought a wheelchair, and sat Karina down.

The nurse checked Karina in, and took her to an expecting room.

Karina wanted to call John, but she decided it not to. She felt it would be better if she called after the birth, or later in the afternoon.

Karina felt her contraction getting shorter and shorter. She feared the pain of giving birth because she had heard so many horror stories. She realized the birth is coming much quicker than expected, so she asked to make phone calls. She quickly made call her parents, John's parents, and to her church. She didn't call John. She want to call him after the birth.

About a few hours later, Karina gave a birth to a little baby girl without much of pain. She called John right away, "Hey John we did it. Well…I did the most. We have a baby girl, now."

Karina could hear John screaming and shouting, "I'm a dad now! I got a girl! Girl! Girl! I'm a dad! Dad! Dad! Yes! Yes! Woo-Hoo!"

John screamed, "I'll be there…right away!"

About an hour later, Karina could hear John's voice and rushing footsteps from the hall way. When he got to the room, looking right into her eyes, he quickly moved next to her, and just screamed, "Kay! Honey! I love you." He kissed Karina several times. Karina smiled, but felt the pain of after birth as much as joy from John's excitement. The nurse in the room got a big hug from John as well.

Karina was embarrassed but enjoyed John's joy. She felt good about the birth even more than ever. John always made her feel so special. John kissed her again and again, and she thought he was going to make love to her. She couldn't stop him. She liked it, although it felt awkward. He slowly stopped kissing her. John looked into her eyes with love she always felt so special and wonderful. She told John that both parents will be here by tonight.

The nurse brought the baby and showed a red, flabby, squinting little creature. John showed a shocking face because the baby looked all shivered up and not-as-a-human.

Karina quickly noticed John's face, and said, "John, that's how baby looks like, right after the birth. Don't worry she will look better soon."

John quickly changed his face with a big smile. John announced proudly, "My little girl. I'm

Dad." He reached out for Cidy, and the nurse carefully handed Cidy over.

John held Cidy awkwardly and very carefully like an antique vase that can break with a slightest mishandle. His eyes glazed over Cidy's little face, and looked into Cidy's golden-brown eyes that was barely open and said, "We are gonna have some fun. I'm so grateful for you. I'm John. I'm your Dad. I love you, Cindy." (Cidy's name was Cindy for a few days of her life.)

John hummed a Sunday school song—
Jesus loves me this I know, and kissed Karina, and held Cidy awkwardly as long as he could even when the nurse said, "It's time." John would ask for five more minutes, and the nurse reluctantly gave five more three more times. They all laughed. It was a joyful time.

CH 30: CIDY WITH MOM

"I know the story back and forth. You told me several times." Cidy knows Mom's reminiscing. She could see her.

"Cindy saved our family—you and me." Karina made a sudden point about Aunt Cindy.

Cidy knew about the story how Aunt Cindy saved Mom and her. Although she doesn't remember a thing about how she saved them, she knows the story very well because Mom even made a small journal about it for the family to keep.

Suddenly Karina realizes that Cindy is visiting her. She just got a call from Cindy late last night. She meant to tell Cidy, but she just forgot.

Karina says, "I got good news, Cidy. Guess what? Cindy will be visiting me this Christmas. We're gonna try to visit you as well."

Cidy, surprised, answers back with a happy tone, "That is great. I haven't seen Aunt Cindy for years. I would love to see her. It would be great if I can see both of you here."

CH 31: NAMING OF CIDY

"I wanted to name you Cindy to honor my best friend Cindy. John agreed. I think he wanted to name you after me. But.... So we called you Cindy during the first few days of your life. But after losing John and a few days of trauma, I chose a new name for you—Cidy." Mom explained the how Cidy's name came about to Cidy when she was little.

"It's hard to explain how and where I got enough strength and mind to change your name in such chaos. But, on the day before the funeral for John, I told Grandma and Grandpa to make sure to change your name to *Cidy*. They agreed after listening to the explanation." Mom would continue the explanation.

"The reason I tweaked a bit was because when I couldn't stop crying in despair, Grandpa Matt kept saying, 'See the Lord. Trust in the Lord.' So I decided that whenever I call your name, I'm going to be reminded to trust in the Lord, not to lose faith, and to evoke the memory of my best friend—Cindy—as well. "Ci" is "*see*" and "dy" is "*Thee*" as in Lord Christ. So, your name is supposed to remind me to see the Lord in all matters." Mom made it quite simple and holy about Cidy's name.

CH 32: CIDY AND MOM

Karina adds, "Cindy is hoping to bring her whole family. It's gonna be wonderful."

Cidy, looking at the picture of Mom and Dad, responds with a little delay, "That's even more WONDERFUL! I have never met Uncle Patrick and their kids. It would be exciting. Oh Mom! Tonight is the company Christmas party. I'm so excited."

Karina quickly adds, "They're coming from Turkey. They moved to Turkey a year ago."

"Wow, Turkey. Maybe we can visit them next year."

"Nice, Nice. I would love it."

Cidy suddenly remembers the dream she had early this morning. She had totally forgotten about it. She mentions it quickly before she forgets it again, "Mom, last night I had a weird dream. It's not a bad dream. I think it's good. I saw Aunt Cindy. Wow, how fitting!"

"I dream about Cindy often. I call her every time I see her in my dream. Just to make sure if she's okay. Usually it's nothing, but it makes me feel assured when I verify that she's okay. And, of course, it keeps me close to her as well." Karina adds her experiences with dreams to comfort Cidy.

But Karina becomes quite curious and asks, "What's the dream about?"

"I think God's calling me." Cidy makes a summary of her dream.

"Tell me the details." Karina quickly senses it is the time that she had been waiting for.

Cidy hears the change of the tone of Mom's voice to serious. She figures it's because Mom's just curious.

"Well…. It was strange. I was at the office working. Someone knocked on the door. I said, 'Come in.' It was Aunt Cindy. I was surprised to see her. I got up, and as I walked towards her, I said, 'Hello, Aunt Cindy. It's great to see you.' I greeted her. She appeared wearing all white clothes looking like an angel. She glowed somewhat. She walked towards me, and looked at me with very comfortable eyes, and said, 'Cidy, you are ready now. Go and be blessing for many.' Then, she was gone. That's it. The dream was so vivid. I woke up early. I had forgotten about it. I just remembered." Cidy gives her account of the dream.

Karina soaks in Cidy's every words and doesn't respond. She knows more about the dream than Cidy, and hesitates to say what she wanted to say for a while.

Cidy waits for Mom to say something but didn't hear anything. So she asks the question she had in her mind, "Whaddyiu think about that dream, Mom? You think I'm being called to do some kind of God's work?"

Karina is lost, and didn't hear what Cidy said. Karina responds with a bit of awkwardness, "What, Cidy?"

It was not a respond that Cidy expected but ignores it, "I guess something will happen to me soon…right, Mom?"

"Yes, Cindy said she had her third grandchild. How time flies? When am I gonna get my first...Cidy?" Karina tried to change the subject. Maybe, it is Karina who is not ready. She said something she had in her mind.

"Oh, Mom. I can't just go buy one." Cidy groans and answers Mom's question anyway, but she realizes her dream has stirred something deep inside of Mom.

Karina knows she has to confess. It is the time. She decides to come clean. "Cidy, you know how Aunt Cindy had saved me and you," Karina slowly and deliberately delivers her opening statement.

Karina takes courage, and decided to tell what Cidy's dream is all about.

Cidy's dream has triggered so much in Karina, so she helplessly plays back the death of John, and the birth of Cidy, and how Cindy came to save both Karina and Cidy, and the message she received from Jesus directly:

CH 33: CINDY COMES TO RESCUE

"Kay, be right there. Miss you and Cindy, so much. I can't believe how much I miss Cindy. I just saw her for the first time…just last night. That's it. Yet I can get her out of my eyes." John called Karina to tell her he's coming to see Karina and the baby, soon.

"I know. Cindy is so beautiful. Hurry over. I miss you, too, John. I don't know why but I miss you so much. I guess it's the hospital," Karina answered. "Don't drive fast. We ain't going anywhere. Oh bring some cheese cake. I don't know why but I want some cheese cake."

"Okay. I'll drive carefully. Cheese Cake! Love you, Kay." John was high on life. He never felt so much joy in his heart. He loved Cindy more than he can imagine.

"Love you, John." Karina ended the call.

When John didn't come to the hospital passed the time of expectation, Karina asked Dad to call at John's work.

Matt called John's work, but no one answered.

She asked Dad to make the calls several more times to make sure, but still there was no answer.

Karina had a bad premonition—something bad has happed to John. She didn't like her feelings although they were mostly wrong.

"He should have been here about an hour ago." Karina cried mostly to her dad while other family members and church friends are around. They all felt very awkward; they didn't know what to do. They slowly left, one by one.

"He'll be here soon. Don't worry. I'm sure there's a good reason." Matt, Karina's dad, comforted Karina without any concern. Others followed.

"Dad, it's not like him. It's not like him." Karina spitted her feelings out. She dragged her tired body around the room and the hospital for a while against everyone's advice to stay in bed. Her face became darker and darker. She knew John, too well: He had never surprised her or disappointed her in a bad way. He always called to let her know if he would be late.

Mary, Karina's mom, who had been away for a while, walked in, and asked, "What's wrong?

"John's a little late. Karina's worried something has happened to him." Matt gave a quick review of the current status.

"Honey, I'm sure there's a good reason. Don't worry." Mary gave her quick comfort as well. She had never seen her daughter so anxious.

A few more hours past, and everyone felt very edge. They prayed for John's safe arrival. Karina felt nervous. Finally she fell asleep from uncontrollable fatigue.

A nurse came in while Karina was asleep, and asked for Matt. Matt walked out.

In her dream, Karina met John:

Karina was home doing the dish. John came over from behind and hugged her real tight. She felt much joy and turned around to see him. Their eyes met, and exchanged their love for each other. He hugged her again, and he clung onto her like a baby. She felt loved, but she felt like John was hugging her for the last time.

"I love you, John. Is there something wrong?"

"I love you, Kay. I have something to tell you."

She looked into his eyes. She knew it wasn't good. Her eyes began shaking from the expectation of something tragic.

"I'm gonna be away for a while. You have to be strong. I love you! I love you, Kay." John said the word slowly and with assurance.

She couldn't miss his soft smile. She wanted to ask where he was going but she knew he was going away to Heaven.

She started to cry. She laid her heads on John's shoulder and held him tight, very tight.

Karina opened her eyes with full of tears, and she cried.

Mary, Mother-in-law (Betty), and Father-in-law (Gary) all asked Karina if she is okay.

Matt walked back into the room. Matt said, "I'll be right back." Matt walked out before Karina could say a word. \

About a couple of hours later, Matt came back to the room.

The hours that Karina and the rest of the family waited with dread felt like years.

Everyone's eye and ear were focused on Matt.

Karina saw Dad walking into the room with a heavy face. She knew John was dead from her dream, but she didn't want to believe it. She hoped that he might be alive, and spoke trembling with fear, "Dad, where is John? Is he okay?"

All the family members are dying to hear the news. Matt looked into the eyes of his wife, Mary, John's parents', and then Karina's. He walked close to Karina and held her hand. He had tears rolling, and looked into Karina's eyes, and uttered the words he feared, "John...John is ...dead."

Karina sobbed like a baby. She couldn't stop. Everyone came around her, and comforted her.

As the sobbing got a bit quite, Matt continued, "John died trying to save a family from a car accident. ...He got killed instantly with the car's explosion." Matt tried his best to tell what he heard.

Karina knew John was dead, but couldn't help the shock coming over her body. She shuttered a little and fainted.

John's parents are stunned, especially John's mother, Betty. Betty started to cry out aloud. The shock of losing her son hit her a little late. She was in denial, but she's came to accept the fact as Karina fainted.

The room turned into chaos in an instant.

Matt tried to wake Karina.

Mary is crying while holding to Karina's hand.

114

Matt didn't know what to do. He called for a doctor quickly.

When Cindy learned the death of John and Karina's faint, very late that night, she quickly got on the plane, arrived next to Cindy within 24 hours. It was three days before the John's funeral. She came in just in time when Karina's condition became the worst, and the family was gaining the worst fear that Karina might die too.

When Cindy came to see Karina, Karina couldn't recognize her at first: It took a while for Karina to realize her best friend—Cindy.

They were speechless: Karina cried and Cindy cried holding on to each other; they didn't know how much time had passed. She couldn't let Cindy go, and Cindy understood that.

Karina just couldn't understand her predicament: She never felt such a rage with such helplessness. She only had tears left, and even that was drying up fast. Her face had lost that life; it was showing some ghostly droop.

They had hard time finding words for each other. It should have been time for celebration, but now it was all frightful and sagging sorrow of despair.

On the fourth day of Cidy's birth, Karina asked her parents to take her home. Doctors strongly recommended staying, but she wanted to go home desperately. The hospital just wasn't the place for to recover from sorrow. Parents disagreed, but Karina insisted she will be fine.

Karina also wanted to prepare for John's funeral as well. Things were hectic: the birth and the death made so many people coming and going. She wanted to ask the people not to come, but she knew they were there to pay their respect and love. She just couldn't say no. Luckily, the hospital stopped the visitors after 7 P.M. and before 10 a.m.

It took everything out of Karina. Not a single drop of thought was left in her to sustain herself, mentally or physically. She never felt so vulnerable and weak. She felt like that last leaf barely hanging on a branch of a tree going through the worst winter.

The funeral was held at the veterans' cemetery. It rained hard as if God is sympathizing with Karina. Pastor from her church delivered a short and quick message because of the weather.

Uniformed soldiers blew the trumpet to honor John's service, and a line of veterans fired their rifles over the rainy sky.

She couldn't help to remember when she first saw John in uniform: "*He was tall and so handsome.*"

She received a huge American flag that covered the coffin of John; it was what the country gave for the death of her husband. That was all.

She got through the funeral with help from the family, the church folks, and especially Cindy. Cindy was God sent. It felt like Cindy knew how she felt and what she needed.

Back home, people from John's work, the church, and the school, and the neighbor came to pay their tributes for John. Karina never knew they had so many friends. People paid their condolences, and cried for her. She amazingly got through the reception with grace and poise even she was surprised of her own self. Inside of her, she wanted to chase every one of them away, but she put a smiling mask that fooled everyone. She never knew she could put on a show like that.

After everyone had left, and when home became silent, Karina, holding on to Cindy, fainted. Luckily Cindy was right there to support her. Cindy laid her on the floor. Such a healthy and vibrant Karina dropped like a lifeless mannequin, and fell unconscious for ten minutes or so. When Karina opened her eyes again, she could barely speak a word. Cindy, Betty, and Mary helped Karina change and put her to bed.

Karina's and John's parents worried a lot, and they begged Karina to go back to hospital. But Karina knew there is nothing any doctor in the world could do about her despair. She waved her head side to side with her last strength to say no. And Cindy felt the same way.

Cindy calmed the family with consultations and prayers. They started to have morning devotions and evening devotions. Karina heard them sing and pray each morning and evening. The church pastor, Larry Petel, visited them often for the first couple weeks, but his visits declined slowly since then.

Cindy made sure there are enough flowers (mostly from the rose in the backyard) around to have a sweet and soothing scent to help Karina feel comfortable. She also purchased several CDs of soothing classical music and popular Christian music. She even bought a guitar to play for Karina: she thought it would be great to play some old and familiar music—some Christian, some pop—that they sang together often when they were teenagers.

The new atmosphere of plants and music soothed Karina, but Karina knew that her health wasn't something music and scent can cure.

After a month of taking care of Karina, Cindy was quite exhausted and shocked because of lack of Karina's improvement.

Karina noticed Cindy was wearing down too.

After a month, Cindy ask Gary (John's Dad), Betty (John's Mom), and Matt (Karina's Dad) to return home, leaving just two of them, she and Mary, to take care of Karina and the baby. Cindy and Mary took turns taking care of Karina and the baby, but Mary took care of the baby mostly because she couldn't bear seeing her own child, Karina, refusing to eat.

Karina's feeling of betrayal by God grew penetratingly deeper into her heart, day by day; she became bitter to the core, nurturing that evil and sour root of resentment in her heart.

While in bed, Karina held her breath many times to end her life, but that very last moment she would start panting for air. It was much harder to die than she thought.

Cindy never realized that Karina was trying to kill herself; she just thought it was just Karina's poor health condition that she panted.

A couple times a day, Cindy or Mary helped Karina to porch, and made her hold the baby, and Karina sat there silently and occasionally murmured while holding the baby, and sometimes laughed out loud like a lunatic.

But Cindy and Mary disregarded it. Karina looked like an invalid most of the time. But Cindy and Mary kept the music of hope and the word of faith coming.

As a result, sometimes they saw Karina's eyes brighten up for a few seconds and a twitch on her lips. It felt like a miracle, a sign of hope that should be held on to. But, their hope had a very short life: it would die out by that night: they were tired and exhausted. Dealing with Karina was like a driving a car with four flat tires; you knew it would come to end of the ride soon.

Cidy, with golden brown eyes and blond hair, was a healthy baby, and cried like any other babies for various reasons. Her cry wasn't too helpful because it made Karina cry as well: When Karina heard Cidy crying, Karina just dripped with tears of her own as well. Maybe it was out sympathy, or maybe it was out of despair. Maybe…Cidy's cry helped Karina to hold on.

With every little consciousness left, Karina kept blaming herself for John's tragedy and Cidy's misfortune. She told John to go back to work because there isn't much he could do: She said to John with a grin, "There's nothing to worry now. All the hard work is done…by me. Mother and the baby are healthy. Just come back and see us after the work tomorrow." John returned home with both parents with joy on the night of Cidy's birth.

She thought what if she had asked John to stay, and be next to her like he wanted to. The company would have let him stay with her for a couple of days, and Karina would have like that too. But she felt it wasn't necessary. She felt good. The birth was much easier than she expected: it only took a few hours of labor. *"Why didn't I let him stay?"* That simple question just kept pounding her head like a thrashing hammer, and nothing could stop it. This same thought just kept playing over and over again in her mind, whenever Karina found herself awake and conscious.

She was convinced that it was a punishment from God for her wrong doings. "*What else can it be?*" She repeatedly thought. "*What did I do wrong to deserve this?*" She argued against God. She hated God that she loved all her life. She lost all her wisdom and common senses; she had become dysfunctional.

Lying or sitting, she thought about giving up her life constantly; a contemplation of death was a regular exercise of her waking hours: it was the only way she knew how to fight again God—suicide. But whatever the reason she slept well a few hours at night, a few hours in the morning, and a few hours in the afternoon. But her death wish was quite real, and she deliberately took on that path to death.

The first thing Karina tried was not eating: she couldn't eat well anyway, so she tried even harder not to eat. It wasn't too hard—not eating. She felt it was luxury to eat, anyway. "*How could I eat?*" She thought thinking about John and their love.

Cindy coaxed and pleaded to eat. "Come on Karina. You have a baby to raise." Every meal was a battle: Karina trying to die versus Cindy trying to keep her alive. Mary couldn't handle the pressure, so she avoided even watching Cindy trying to feed Karina.

To help heal Karina's heart, Cindy bought a nice used guitar from a local musical instrument store after a month. Cindy and Karina used to enjoy singing together. Cindy played many of Karina's favorites: CCM, country, soft rocks, hymns, and even Sunday-school songs. The songs were great medicine for both of them. It reminded them of their fond memories of youth, and soothed them with the familiarities of their teenage years. Karina's heart softened with the songs, but not for long.

And Cindy gave Karina spiritual medicine everyday by crying together, holding her hands, reading the Bible, singing gospel songs, and turning on hopeful Christian music, but mostly praying. Cindy took this endeavor day by day, hour by hour, with prayer and faith.

After two months, Karina overheard Mom telling Cindy to return home. She didn't say anything. She didn't care whether Cindy left or not: She cared for nothing.

Karina lost so much weight, and her remaining showed very little of herself. She slowly but surely achieved her goal—death. Even she couldn't recognize herself whenever she saw her reflection. She asked herself, "Who are you?" She embraced death as it lingered around her.

It was about the end of the third month, Karina could tell Cindy has lost a lot of weight too and is sick too: Cindy coughed a lot and had very little smile left. Karina did feel sorry for Cindy, but only prevailing thought that was in her mind was her own sweet death. And she knew her death wish danced around her because she entertained with delightful rhythmic music knowing it will end all of her misery.

But, she made that last plea to God, "God, I don't know what to do. I'm all torn and twisted. I do not want to live, not like this. I need my John back. I love him so much. I can't live without him. God! Give me my John back. Please…please…please…."

It was Saturday, very early in the morning or late in the night. While deep in sleep, Karina heard a voice calling her name. She ignored the first call thinking she imagined it. When she heard her name for the second time, she said, "Dad?" She knew it was neither John's voice nor Dad's voice, but Dad was only man who she could think of calling her with man's voice. The voice sounded very calming and sweet. When she heard the call for the third time, Karina peeked through her bulged eye-lids with all her strength. She saw a very sturdy looking man with a glowing white gown. Karina realized it is Jesus.

Jesus reached out, and grabbed her hand, and said, "Karina, my daughter." He looked into Karina's eyes.

Karina felt warm and loved. She never felt so loved before. She blinked her eyes with a little smile. That was all her strength would allow her to do. She thought see is finally going to die, and Jesus came to take her home personally. She was happy and ashamed to see him, but more than comforted by His presence.

She tried to get her upper body up, out of respect. She knew she couldn't do it, but she want to show an effort, But to her surprise, she got her upper body up with much ease.

Jesus said, "Follow me, my daughter, Karina." He let go of her hand and turned around. He slowly walked out of the room.

Karina got out of the bed with ease, and followed Him to the back door, and to the backyard. She couldn't believe she could walk by herself. She followed Him. She stood in front of Jesus.

Jesus hugged her for a while; Karina hugged Jesus back. She never felt so loved. She said, "Lord, please take me. I'm weary and hopeless. I cannot go on. I beg of You. Please, Jesus…please.

It felt eternity has passed. Jesus let Karina go.

"Kneeled down, my child."

Karina slowly and awkwardly kneeled down. Jesus put his right hand on Karina's head.

Karina felt warm first on her head, and the warmth spread to her body. She felt hot all over her body very soon. Then, she felt a bit of electricity flowing through her body as she felt her arms shaking a bit. It felt as if the time had just stopped. The electricity flow got stronger and stronger, and her whole body shook a bit. She clinched and made a tight fist because of the painful, electric, and pulsating sensation throughout her body. She felt her body shaking especially her arms and fists. Her body clasped to ground, and she grasped the grass. And she fell even more close to the ground, and she grasped deeper into the grass as her fingers delved under the ground. She felt like her body becoming one with the ground. She didn't know how much time has passed. Then the electricity flow drained slowly and slowly, and everything became calm and quiet. She raised her body off the ground a little, and stood up.

Then He slowly and softly spoke looking into Karina's eyes, "Karina, my daughter, I know your pain. I love you. I have a plan for Cidy. She will be my voice for many. You have to raise my Cidy, well."

As Karina lowered her head feeling the burden of the assignment, and raised her head to see His face again. He was gone.

Karina looked around to find Him. He was gone.

The morning sky was so calm and so beautiful. The fresh air and the sweet morning dew were just so wonderful. She felt the beauty of God's creation. She felt hungry and thirsty. She wanted to eat Mom's fried chicken, strawberry yogurt, peaches, and more. She had so much appetite for food she couldn't believe it, but first of all, she needed some cool water. She felt very thirsty.

Karina walked back inside the house all by herself.

When Karina walked back into the house, Cindy was praying in the living room as she was waiting for her.

With eyes opened brightly, Karina slowly said in a very soft voice but happily, "Cindy, get me...a...a cup of...water." Karina could see the shock and the joy in Cindy's face and her whole body.

With unexplainable joy, Cindy jumped and couldn't make a sound for a few seconds.

Karina sheepishly gave a big smile in return.

Cindy couldn't believe her ears and eyes, and finally screamed for Mary. She forgot about the drink and the baby sleeping because she was so shocked that Karina just spoke very clearly while standing up all by herself.

"Karina has spoken. Karina talked! Mary! Mary! MARY! Come out! Karina talked! MARY! MARY! MARY!" screamed Cindy again.

Mary ran out from her room with erratic thumping of the floor, but the joy on Mary's face shined throughout the house.

"Karina!" Mary cried with tears, and hugged her daughter very tight for a while. Karina tried to hug Mom back but she couldn't. She felt much better but she realized she still needs to recover quite a bit.

Cindy joined in. They were hugging and crying for a while.

"Mom…," Karina said in a small voice with a smile. "Water, please."

Now remembering Karina's request for water, Cindy quickly ran and got some water.

Karina drank the cool water slowly. She felt refreshed. And put on a smile that made Cindy and Mary cry again with tears of joy.

CH 34: MOM'S CONFESSION

"Of course! You told me several times." Cidy speaks the words that came to her mind, naturally.

Karina feels it's time to tell Cindy everything. "But I did not tell you I received a direct message from Jesus."

Cidy waits for Karina to say something more. She sensed the importance of what Mom is about to say, but she doesn't hear anything.

Karina had asked her mom and Cindy not to tell anyone about the message she received about Cidy to anyone until the time comes. Karina knew it was very important for Cidy to grow up as normal as possible until Cidy is ready to hear the message.

But today, Karina feels obligated to tell Cidy the message.

Karina has kept this in her heart for too long.

Cidy asks, "WHAT message, Mom?"

But she hears nothing.

"Mom! MOM! What MESSAGE?" Cidy ups her volume.

Karina says very steadily, "Jesus told me, personally...He had a plan for your life. You are to be His voice for many. ...From the day that I received that message I have been healed and lived strong. I tried to do my best to raise you well. It's been so long.... I forgot about the message. I knew I had to tell this to you, sooner or later, but didn't know when."

Cidy is astounded. She has never heard this before. She feels the importance of the message, and questions Mom, "Why didn't you ever tell me this, BEFORE?"

"I didn't want to hinder you…from growing up, NORMALLY. I knew there will be…time to tell you…all this. After hearing your dream, today…I realized it's THE time." Karina explains herself.

Cidy now understands everything is planned by God for her or God Himself. She feels something very heavy lifting off from her shoulder—the burden and the blame of not having a dad around.

CH 35: Cidy's Pain

"You don't have DADDY. You don't have DADDY." A couple of girls in playground chanted with eagerness.

Cidy had fought with them, but it was a fight she couldn't win. So, she ran away from them, but the words kept ringing in her head. Tears rolled while Cidy found a hidden place to be alone.

Cidy had that love-and-hate relationship with school. She loved her friends and learning, but the teasing about her being fatherless and other things were just too painful. Being teased about her name was hurtful enough. But about being fatherless was just something she could not face up to.

Cidy imagined playing with Dad often:

"Daddy, what would you like to eat?"
"Okay I'll make you some
pancake...."
"And you want bacons, too. Okay."
"You have to eat all of eat. Okay?"
"What would you like to drink,
Daddy?"
"Okay, here is orange juice."

There were times when Mom would ask who she is talking with, and she would answer, *Daddy.* And Mom played along happily.

In her dreams, Dad would play games with her, talk to her, and hug and kiss her like she would imagine. Cidy wrote about her "dad dreams" in details in her diary because she remembered them in such details: smell, color, sound, and feel.

And she would go back to her journals, time-and-time again to read them and to relive them, and she would smile sometimes and cry the others. Her dreams often made her feel like she grew up with Dad.

One day, Mom said, "I know you miss Dad a lot. I miss him too. You have to let him go, so he can work for God. God took him to heaven to work with Him. You will meet him soon. I promise you. Okay?"

Cidy nodded and questioned, "Dad works for God?"

Karina responded, "Yes, Dad works for God, now. He is very busy."

CH 36: CIDY'S FREEDOM

"Mom, this pain, we feel…, it is meant to be." Cidy makes a profound statement.

"Yes. The pleasure and the pain." Karina agrees "I remember it…like it was yesterday…when I first fell in love with John."

"I just love your love letters. I can recite a few of the poems Dad wrote. It is so cute." Cidy adds her coin of thought to the love of her parents.

"I know. I have several favorites of my own." Karina reads the poems once in a while when her love for John comes alive for whatever triggers it— smell, sound, or just out the blue.

"Which one?" Cidy wants to know.

Karina feels embarrassed and loses her words.

Cidy always elaborates Mom and Dad's love in her mind through what she heard and what she read from their love letters.

For a short love story, they sure had a lot of letters to prove it. There were not just a few letters but three boxes of letters that were sent to each other. Cidy couldn't believe the huge pile of love letters, but she read through every one of them several times like if it was her own.

That was one of her favorite past time when she was growing up. She would giggle and laugh at the things that Mom and Dad wrote to each other. Sometimes she would read them with Mom. They all sounded corny like a love songs on the radio, but she loved every one of it. Dad loved writing poems to Mom, and there were over a hundred of them.

Cidy recites one of her favorite poem in her mind:

> Last night I kissed your lips,
> Like I did that night.
>
> I woke up with such a joy.
> Still feeling your warmth in my arms.
>
> Your lips, your body…
> I dream the same dream.
>
> I don't want to wake up.
> Karina, Kay…I love you.

It just never seems to get old for Cidy. She loves their love story, and knows every line like her favorite movie.

"Well I have a favorite one," Cidy covers up Mom's shyness quickly. Cidy tells Mom one of her favorite poem that Dad wrote:

> Ding Dong, Ding Dong…
> I hear the bell ring.
> But it's your name—Karina.
>
> Swish Swoosh…
> I feel the wind blow.
> But it's your soft lips—Karina.
>
> Cookies and Ice cream…
> I smell the sweets.

But it's your fragrance—Karina.

Every bite I take,
Every sight I see,
Every sense I feel.
I dream of you...Karina.

Karina laughs and says, "I love that one, too."

Cidy laughs with Mom, and says, "I wish Jake writes me a poem like that. I would die."

Cidy always wished someone would write her a corny poem like that. She even thought about paying someone to write her a love poem in middle school. She thought that would be silly but she wished for one dearly.

"He will. You deserve it." Karina answers.

"Mom, Karen is coming to see me too," Cidy bursts out. "She called me last week. I forgot to tell you. I have been so busy with so many things."

"Great! How's she doing?"

"She's doing great Mom. She got her law degree a few months ago. She just got engaged. Michael...Michael is his name. He got his law degree with her. They met at the law school. Karen is bringing him too. I guess she wants to show him off."

"That's great. And her dad?"

"Her dad is doing fine too. He's getting married to his longtime girlfriend." Cidy answers Mom.

CH 37: Cidy's Best Friend, Karen

"Hi, Karen." Cidy sat next to Karen on the way back home in the school bus. She heard something tragic has happened to Karen, and it showed on her face: She wasn't the same: she wasn't playful with boys like she usually is.

Although they lived in the same neighborhood, same street, Karen and Cidy were just an acquaintance. Cidy met Karen during her middle school years, when Karen moved to a house nearby.

Karen usually played around with boys a lot. She was pretty and very outgoing. Boys liked her. Cidy usually played with girls, and felt jealous because all the boys liked her so much.

But Karen wasn't the same lately. The rumor was her mom passed away from a car accident.

"Hi," Karen reluctantly replied in a low and dragging tone.

Cidy slowly moved her left hand to grab Karen's right hand. When Cidy grabbed Karen's hand, she quietly prayed for Karen's peace.

Karen felt comforted, and realized Cidy was praying.

"Can I come over?" Cidy asked Karen for a visit.

"I don't know…. It's a mess." Karen wanted someone to be with her but she wasn't too sure.

"Well…we can clean up together then." Cidy smiled at Karen.

"It's a major FUCKING mess. …I didn't know how much Mom…." Karen showed part of her anger, sadness and frustration, and she couldn't finish her sentence. She wanted to cry, but didn't wanted to look weak. She breathed with roughness.

"I will help. I love cleaning." Cidy felt awkward a little.

Karen opened up a little. She knew she need a girlfriend, someone to talk to. They started a conversation.

The bus came to their stop. Karen and Cidy walked to Karen's home while carrying on their conversation. Karen never felt good to have a girlfriend.

They arrived at Karen's home in no time. Karen opened the door, and they walked in. The house looked like a war zone.

Cidy went to work cleaning up the mess, and Karen helped out. They talked and worked, and talked some more. Karen showed a few smiles. Karen felt like she had a real friend for the first time in her life.

Since the first visit, Cidy visited Karen almost every day for a year after school, just being next to Karen most of the time, and helping her with school work and other chores.

Karen's family was in a shamble after their mom passed away. But, with help of Cidy, Karen took on the mom's role little by little: Cidy helped her to clean, laundry, and cook as well.

James, Karen's dad, got inspired by Karen' actions and Cidy's help, so he shaped up, got tougher, and took on more roles as well. It was hard for James at first, but he did his best without breaking down in front of his children.

Karina helped Karen and James too, but with her work it wasn't easy. But James had more than appreciated Karina's and Cidy's support.

Karen came around a bit, about a month after the loss of her mother, and recovered quite well by the first year. Cidy being next to her did wonders. Cidy cried with Karen many days and nights. Cidy didn't force anything on Karen, but she would pray with her often. Karen felt the presence of God whenever Cidy prayed for her. Cidy didn't say much in her prayer; she simply said, "Lord please help ease Karen' pain." That simple prayer was all that Karen needed.

After a month after the tragedy, Cidy invited Karen to church on Sundays which Karen accepted happily, and James was happy to bring his whole family to church as well.

During the senior year of high school for Karen and Cidy, James had to move because of his job. It was not an easy departure for Cidy and Karen, but they always stayed in touch and talked about everything.

CH 38: Back to Work

"Karen is so pretty and very smart. She will become a good lawyer," Karina responds.

Cidy looks at the time. She needs to make a few calls quickly to make sure the party is being prepared properly. "Mom, I love you. I'll call you tonight. I gotta go."

Since Cidy took the charge of Christmas Party, She has made it very exciting and fun: it became a half talent show and a half Christmas celebration.

The talent show got hotter and hotter each year because of the increased purse of winning and just pure fun and excitement: any group winning the talent show wins a thousand dollars this year. Last year a group of employees singing Air Supply songs won. They were simply awesome.

This year, it will be held at a Hilton hotel much bigger and nicer than the last year one. Usually comedy won second or third place. Cidy made sure comedy makes a place in top three where there is a prize. The second place wins $500, and the third $200 this year. Cidy loves comedy, and she always enters the show in the comedy section. This year she hopes to win the first place. She and her click, *009 Girls*, are entering the show again.

CH 39: JAKE WORKS

Jake goes straight to the restroom to change.

Mark was there. (Mark was searching for Jake in the morning to brag about his date with Sandy.) He is so glad to see Jake. He gives the biggest smile Jake had ever seen with bright smiling eyes.

Jake knows it's the date that Mark had with Sandy last night.

Shooting his double finger-guns at Jake, signaling I-told-you-so, Mark makes a bold claim, "Jake, I'm gonna marry Sandy."

Feeling quite jealous and dumbfounded, Jake teases, "What! You had ONE date with her! You're not really serious about Sandy? Come on, Mark." He knows Mark has been a player all his life.

"I'm...dead serious, man! She IS THE one." Mark shows his commitment enthusiastically.

Jake, changing into his more formal working clothes, teases even more. "Sandy...she's more than just a look, man. I'm surprised she went out with you. She KNOWS you're a player."

"Come on, Jake. I AM not a player! Not anymore! You know I haven't dated a girl for a long time...what...ah...almost a year. I've never been so sure!" Mark displays his seriousness about Sandy once again. "I'm gonna marry her, Jake! I love her! I DO!"

"Sandy…she got class. I wouldn't have guessed it. But, she's a lady. I don't think it will work out with you, man. Besides, you'll change your mind about her in a week or two. You know it, Mark!" Jake reveals Mark's past and tests Mark's seriousness again. He feels some jealousy as well. He wants to tell Mark how he feels about Cidy as well, but he just couldn't. He is afraid the word might get out.

"Jake! I haven't date a SINGLE girl for a year! Whole year! 365 days! I'm ALL in with Sandy." Mark confesses his love for Sandy again. "Last night, it was so special. I had tingles all over my body all throughout the night. Still tingling. Look man! I can't keep myself calm. I've never been like this with ANY girl. She's the one…one and only. I…I feel it.…" Mark rambles on with no fear: he doesn't care if anyone hears him or not.

Jake finishes changing, and double checks his looks. He again wishes he could say something like that about Cidy because that's how he feels every time he takes a peek at her. He throws more punches at Mark. "Mark …I'm sorry. I'm not trying to put you down. But I know you too well. You just want another trophy on the rack…that's all."

"Jake…I'm through with my past. I can't explain this. There's something special about Sandy. She just drives me…CRAZY. I WANT her more than anything else in the world. You KNOW I have been on hot trail for Sandy for a year. I'm not KIDDING. I LOVE HER. I LOVE HER." Mark shows his full-out emotion.

Jake comes right back. "Mark…do you know what commitment means? It sure ain't having a new lady every few months. When Sandy falls for you, you'll get tired of her…just like every other girl you dated." He is losing his fire power. He is almost convinced that Mark is telling him the truth. Jake feels sorry for himself because he feels so much jealousy: He envies Mark's state of being in love...in so much love.

"That's WAS me. I AIN'T denying my PAST. But I'm NEW. I'm DIFFERENT, NOW." Mark knew Jake would say things like this. He didn't mind it. He has the same fear about himself—what if his mind changes like Jake's prophecy. But he feels he can face all the fear with the love for Sandy.

Jake stares at Mark's eyes for a few seconds. He feels Mark is serious, but doubts.

"Sandy, she is not answering my call, Jake. I need your help. I need your prayer." Mark was looking for Jake's help from the beginning.

"What if Sandy says no...she's not even answering your calls. I think she is finished reading you. The whole company knows you. Sandy knows you. I know you." Jake felt bad for being the Devil's advocate. He wishes Mark the best. But, he feels Mark is not ready for marriage, not ever.

"I don't care what you say Jake. I'm gonna have Sandy as my wife. This is for real. I couldn't sleep one minute. Look how I'm pumped up, man. I need her. I will die without her. Help ME, Jake! What do I do?" Mark felt lost and desperate, something he never felt before.

The power of love has grasped both Mark and Jake.

Mark explodes with his feeling for Sandy; Jake tries to control his feeling for Cidy.

Jake has never heard Mark asking for help on anything, and besides love is the farthest from his expertise. Mark cries for help, but Jake has no idea how to help.

Jake doesn't want to say he has nothing, so he fakes it. He nods and says, "Give me some time to think about it."

Jake walks out of the restroom and goes to his seat. He is jealous. He has been dreaming about Cidy for five years with nothing to show for, but Mark had a date in a year and is screaming that he's going to marry Sandy.

"*How things seem to roll for ungodly man,*" thinks Jake.

CH 40: Karina Calls Mom

After the call with Cidy, Karina is determined to call Cindy and Mom. She wants to call her best friend, Cindy, first, to break the news, but it is about dinner time in Turkey. So, Karina calls Mom, Mary, first.

Karina speed dials Mom; it's number two: They are best friends.

Mary is very excited to receive a call from Karina. She, with a very upbeat voice, greets Karina, "Karina! How are you my Little Pumpkin?"

Mary is getting older and has fewer and fewer friends to talk to, so Mary dearly waits for Karina's call every day. It's the excitement of the day for her. Although Karina calls her mom almost every day, Mom anticipates Karina's calls all day.

"Mom, I have news about Cidy." Karina urgently makes an intro for her call.

"Cidy's got a date with that...Jake guy?" Mary is slower with her speech now days, but still knows how to throw the punch line first.

"No, Mom. It's more serious than that." Karina wants to tell all the details.

"Serious? Tell me.... Hmm, what is it?" Mary is all ears. She senses it's important but not bad news like a car accident or an unexpected medical problem. She is excited. She is hoping for something exciting to get her heart pounding, because as she gets older, she doesn't get to hear much of any

141

exciting news that pumps her blood flow like when she was younger.

"Well…I was getting ready for work. Cidy called. After the usual, when I told her that Cindy is coming to visit me, she told me she had a dream about Cindy." Karina pauses to let Mary gather her thoughts.

"And…." Mary gives a go-ahead sign. Mary has forgotten about the prophecy Karina heard. She has kept it as secret too long, not that she has forgotten permanently.

"In her dream, she was at the office working. Someone knocked on the door. " Karina paces the story for Mom to catch all the details. "So she said, 'come in.' It was Cindy…walking in looking like an angel. Then…Cindy looked at Cidy with loving eyes and said, 'Cidy, you are ready now. Go and be blessing for many.' Then, Cidy said she was gone." Karina tells all the details that she heard.

Mary remembers well—the incident that happened about 26 years ago when Karina almost killed herself with hunger and depression, It pains Mary that she had given up on own daughter Karina when God hadn't.

CH 41: MARY'S AGONY

It was another beautiful morning. Mary waited for the birth of her first grandchild for eight months now with greatest expectation since she received the news from Karina that she is pregnant. Mary and Matt were sipping their morning tea when the phone rang.

Mary said, "It's from Karina. I'll get it."

She guessed it right.

As soon as she picks up the phone and before she can say a word, she hears, "MOM, I'm at the hospital. It's little…ahhh…earlier than expected. Ahhhh…. See you soon. Ahhh…. I gotta go!"

"We'll be there right away."

Karina hung up the phone.

Mary hung up the phone. She ran to Matt and screamed, "Matt, I can't stop this jitter in me."

"What's wrong?" Matt felt alarmed, but he noticed a smile on her face that gave Matt major relief.

Mary sat next to Matt. She stared at Matt and held Matt's hand tight. She felt like she could almost jump out of the house. "Karina is at the hospital. We got to leave now. I'm so nervous and happy. It feels like I'm the one who's having the baby."

"I'm gonna be Grandpa. Wow! Life is wonderful." Matt can't help his excitement either.

"You know I've already seen the baby in my dream. I saw a beautiful young lady saying hi to me." Mary had a vision of her granddaughter just about the time when Karina realized she was conceived. Mary's dream was right on the dot when Karina confirmed her pregnancy a few days later.

Matt heard this several times. "It's amazing Mary. I don't know how you have these dreams." He wondered about the amazement of Mary's dreams. Most of her dreams were prophecies that came true.

Mary told Matt she received this gift when she accepted Christ into her heart when she was just eight-years old.

"I'm special. God gave me this gift. Don't like it when it's...bad."

When Mary had a bad dream, she didn't want to share it. She had a bad dream a few days ago that she didn't share it with nobody: *John was holding a baby. He said to Mary, 'Mary, she will be a very special baby.' But John was crying.*

It was a very short dream, but Mary understood that John will die soon...very soon. But she didn't want to say anything. She just knows that she needs to keep her composure when this tragedy hits.

Mary was compelled to tell Matt, but she knew this is something that everyone had to take it as the tragedy hits. She already had her tears in the morning. She cried and prayed for understanding. She heard a soft voice saying, "I have allowed this." She didn't understand it, but she had to accept it. She acted as if nothing is wrong.

Mary and Matt quickly packed up and went to go see their daughter. It took several hours of driving, but it was an exciting trip. She kept her acting up well. Matt didn't suspect anything wrong with her.

That afternoon, Mary and Matt walked into the hospital with their heart filled with joy. Mary never felt so much expectation before. She heard her friends talking about the joy of having grand kids, but she never thought it was this exciting. She totally forgot about her bad dream.

As Mary and Matt walked into to Karina's room, John was holding the baby, and Karina had a big smile on her face. Karina's eyes greeted them first with welcoming brightness, and Karina said, "Mom, Dad...you guys are here so early. Dad...how fast did you drive?" Karina gave a playful side stare at Matt. Karina's greeting wasn't what Mary expected but it was more than welcoming.

John looked up as he was watching the baby. John greeted, too, "Mary, Matt...good to see you."

Matt replied, "My heart was here hours ago. Congratulations John!"

Matt and Mary made their ways to their baby girl—Karina. They stared at her for a while and share some words. Mary felt so proud to see her baby girl becoming a mother. Mary thanked God for His over-watching of her daughter.

Matt held the baby for a while.

Matt had a face that Mary just couldn't remember seeing: He was glowing. Mary wondered if she was glowing too. Mary wanted to hold Cidy as well, but she waited patiently. Matt couldn't let go, or he didn't know he was holding Cidy all by himself too long. Finally, Mary had to ask Matt if she can hold the baby.

Matt handed the baby over. Mary held the baby, and she felt the magic, the miracle, and the wonder of life. She was totally amazed about her daughter having a baby, now her grand-daughter. It was just too overwhelming, too wonderful, too incredible, too amazing. But, Mary kept remembering the bad dream, so Mary felt she should hand over the baby to John.

Mary said, "John, this is your daughter. Enjoy her." She already knew John only had a few days or a few months with his baby.

John took Cidy again and he danced.

Mary wanted to say be careful but didn't. She went next to Karina, and had a mom-and-daughter talk.

Meanwhile, Matt, tired from the long trip, fell asleep in the corner quickly.

Mary could hear John singing a Sunday-school songs to the baby. It was such a heavenly time, but she just couldn't get over her dream. She had a swift face change that Karina noticed.

Karina asked, "Something wrong, Mom."

Mary had to say something quickly, "I was worried if I left the range on or not." Mary quickly got out of that one. She told Karina she's going to restroom. She got out and went to restroom.

In the restroom, Mary asked God, "What do you want me to do? I know something bad will happen, but what? Is John really gonna die? What am I supposed to do? I can bare this, God. What is it? God, give me wisdom."

Mary lost her composure. This was the worst moment in her life that she can think of. She can't imagine her daughter losing her husband when the baby is just born. She wondered if she can stop this

146

tragedy from happening. She instinctively felt John's going to die. How and why she didn't know. It was already set in motion.

Mary often wondered about the future if it was already set or it was what we make of it. From her experiences, she felt they were fixed, and we were just playing the part that was already set in motion...like a rock rolling down the mountain. It was destined or predestined. Then, Mary realized everything that she ever did was done with her choice. She did what she decided to do. She was confused.

All Mary can do was try to give much time as possible for John to be with his daughter and his wife without intruding. And she hoped that her premonition was wrong.

Mary went back to the room. John was still holding the baby. A nurse came in ask for the baby back. John begged to hold the baby little more. Mary almost cried. She told the nurse, "Please let him hold the baby as much as he can." There was something of plea in Mary's voice.

The nurse reluctantly agreed with a smile.

John smiled at Mary. She smiled back.

As the night slowly rolled in, Karina begged everyone to go home and come back tomorrow. She was too tired.

Mary wanted to tell John to stay with Karina, but she couldn't.

John repeatedly asked Karina if he can stay next to her, but Karina refused. She was exhausted; she want to be alone.

Mary wanted tell her daughter to let him, but she could tell Karina is very tired from giving birth and greeting visitors. She could tell Karina wanted to be alone to have a good-night rest.

The nurse came back and asked for the baby for the fourth time. Finally Cidy and John was separated.

Mary wanted to stop this tragedy from happening, but she couldn't. She felt like a crazy woman. She observed every moment knowing how precious they are for John. John looked so happy that she thought he looked more like a clown. She had never seen anyone so happy.

Mary loved her son-in-law. He turned about to be a perfect son-in-law. He had prepared a lovely home for them to start out a family a few years before the marriage. Mary was so proud of John: he was a faithful Christian, hardworking, and very handsome. Mary did feel sorry for separating them when they were much younger.

They got out of Karina's room and headed for home, but Mary said, "Let's go see Cindy again."

John quickly agreed, "Good idea…I miss her so much…already."

Mary wanted to cry, but she didn't want to look like a crazy woman. They went to the babies' room. They looked through the glass where the baby was sleeping. John was glued to the glass.

John said, "My dream came true. I always wanted to have a little girl. I got one. I'm a dad. I prayed for this for so long. God is great."

Mary thought, *"Silly. Nobody dreams about becoming a dad."* She knew how simple and godly John is. She hugged John. John hugged her back, not knowing why.

And Mary said, "John…you are a dad. God has answered your prayer."

Matt tapped on John's back as if he is telling John that he had done a good job.

Mary was scared, but trusted God.

Mary and Matt went to John's place. Night quickly got darkest—as if to foretell what is to come.

"Matt, I want to thank God for Cindy, our first grandchild, and great health for Karina. I'm gonna go pray for a while," Mary said before going to bed. She lied why she wanted to pray. She went to pray to change the destiny that is set: she asked God to let John live.

Mary prayed that night for a long time. She prayed and argued that Karina needed her husband to raise the baby and be provided for. Mary prayed desperately seeking to change the destiny. After couple of hours of prayer she felt calm and accepted the destiny set by God—whatever that maybe—even the death of John.

A beautiful morning faithfully arrived with the orange sun with cool breeze blowing from East. Mary heard birds singing and enjoyed the falling leaves making their acrobatic landing on the grass. It was a perfect day.

John was already up preparing breakfast— coffee brewing and bacon sizzling. The smell conducted much joy into the heart of Matt that he started to hum. Matt's heart was more than content: Never thought he could get so excited in his late fifties.

Mary could tell both of man were walking on rainbow and playing the tune of highest joy. They weren't saying much, but their steps and their faces told more than enough to feel their warmth of happiness.

They soon had breakfast John prepared. Matt smelled the food. It was extraordinary. And he chewed the food with more vigor than usual. Matt acted like when they first started dating. It was something Mary hadn't seen for a long time. Mary loved it, but she knew tragedy was just around the corner. They quickly got through the breakfast.

Mary said, "John…let's go see Cindy before you go to work."

"I would love to… but the company called last night saying they need me early. But they'll let me leave early. Sorry. I wanna go see Cindy, so badly. It's killing me. The keys are here. You know the drill." John cleared the plates from the breakfast table.

Mary wanted to say this could be your last day to see Cindy, but couldn't. She did her best to do what she felt it was right thing to do. As John was about to leave, She stopped John. "John let me pray for you real quickly."

John hesitated, but smiled and said, "Great!"

Mary asked Matt to join in, too, and prayed, "Father in heaven, I know you have a greater plan that we don't understand. Give us wisdom and love for you to understand and accept it. I thank you for Cindy. Please help John…. Please give him understanding…give him courage to do the right thing…give him love…your love…give him strength to carry your cross…. I love you Lord. In Your Son's name—Jesus Christ…we pray. Amen."

John felt something touching him, very strong, he couldn't explain. He had an expression on his face that he wanted to say something.

Mary felt something very strong in her.

Matt felt Mary's hand so hot. He almost wanted to let go.

Mary could tell John had some words stuck in his mouth. She had the same problem.

John had to go to work. He quickly said, "Thanks Mary. I…I…will. I…mean…thank you…for your prayer. I'll see you soon."

Mary wanted to say be careful, but she couldn't. She said, "See you soon."

Mary followed John to the front porch and waved goodbye as John pulled away from the house and drove off. She knew this could be the last moment she would see him.

Mary was overwhelmed by the dream and the reality. She quickly forced herself to the restroom. After locking the door, she quickly kneeled and prayed for a while.

Later, Matt knocked on the door, and said, "Honey, are you okay?"

Mary had tears dripping down her face, but she managed to pull out a soft and comforting tone of voice. "Sorry Matt. I'll be out in a minute." She washed her face.

She felt her premonition dreams were not gift; she felt it more like a curse—knowing the future. But she knew God gave it to her for a good reason.

This time, the gift gave her a little more time with John, and Mary had a time to pray with him and to appreciate him one more time. She knew she would be the only one who would be calm enough to take the families through such a tragedy. She needed to be strong and calm.

Soon, Mary and Matt drove to hospital. Matt was quite excited to see the baby again.

"That little bugger. I'm SO attached to her. Already! I can't believe it." Matt said as he was driving. He continued about his experiences as Grandpa. He couldn't stop.

Mary felt unbelievable joy as well, but her heart burdened knowing something bad will happen to John soon. Mary made a quick prayer again, and asked God to keep John alive.

At the hospital, Mary and Matt went to see the baby first. And soon, they had a great time with the baby and Karina. It was a picture perfect family.

About noon, John's parents came to the hospital. John's parents were much older than Mary's. They decided to stay in an inn nearby the hospital.

It was a great family gathering—lots of laughter and joyful words. People continuously visited.

Karina breast fed the baby for the first time.

But there were several instances where Mary was out of it because of the burden of worrying for John and what would that mean to the baby and her daughter. Because of the joy and the commotion, no one paid much attention to Mary.

It was about the time that John should have arrived.

Karina started to anticipate for John as she asked for the time.

Karina casually said, "John should have been here by now."

Matt said, "He'll be here soon."

Mary felt something bad has happened already, but couldn't do or say anything. She said comfortingly, "John's in God's hand. He's all right. He'll be here soon."

When Karina show more concern about John's well-being, Mary commanded Karina, "Be calm. Be in peace. We are in God's hand, especially you and John. Trust in the Lord. Karina!"

Matt had already called John's company twice—no one answered. Matt paged John as well. Matt said, "Don't worry Baby. He'll be here soon."

John's parents were not worried. They felt there was a good reason why John's being late.

A Little later, nurse came in and asked for Matt. He walked out, and he returned to the room with a stoic face. He said in a very cold voice, "I'll be back in an hour."

Karina knew something bad has happened now.

Karina fell asleep unwillingly just from being so tired: She had another long day of greeting people from school, church and other acquaintances.

In her sleep, Karina murmured, and she woke up crying, and said, "Where's John? Mom! Mom!"

Mary smiled unwilling and said, "What's wrong? Oh…you've must had a bad dream."

"Mom, John's not here…is he?"

"He'll be here soon. Don't worry. We are all in God's hand." Mary did her best to comfort Karina.

Karina felt alarmed. Karina got up started to pace herself around, and she drank some water. She started to fidget.

Mary walked over and held Mary and said, "Baby…don't worry. John is more than fine. You know he is in God's hand. Don't let this get to you."

Everyone was so cheerful that they couldn't understand why Karina's acting so nervous.

"Mom I just saw John in my dream. He hugged me and kissed me. Then…he said he loves me, and he disappeared." Karina described her dream. "I still can feel his warmth on my cheek."

Mary comforted Karina, knowing and now realizing that John was probably dead. She just confirmed her premonition by Karina's dream. She put Karina back in her bed again.

Mary sat next to Karina, and held Karina's hand, and comforted her. Mary kept repeating that we have to trust God in all matters. Karina cried and worried with her exhausted body. Karina tried to stay awake but fell asleep again.

When Matt returned a few hours later, it was about 11 p.m. His face told the story of tragedy, and he said looking into Karina's eyes and holding her hand, "John…is…dead."

Gary, John's dad, felt his life draining out of him, but he walked over to his wife, Betty, and hugged her and cried with her.

Matt walked over to Karina. Mary was with her. Soon everyone got around Karina and consoled her. Karina cried and cried, and she fainted.

Betty fainted.

Mary told Matt to get a doctor for Karina and John's mother.

A doctor came in quickly ran in and checked for Karina and John's mother. He said, "They're fine. It's the trauma. Just be near them and comfort them." Then, he left the room.

Later, when Karina woke up again, Matt looked into his daughters beautiful eyes, and opened his tightly shut mouth, "John died trying to save a family from a car accident."

Karina screamed and cried, "No! No! That's not possible. NO! NO! NO! ...No! He's not dead! It can't be. No! Where's my John. Where is he?" Karina continued her rant until she got exhausted and fell asleep, again.

Mary kept her composure. She kept praying for Karina mostly. She quickly realized she had to prepare for funeral and try to keep Karina and the rest of the families calm. She felt lost, but she was the only one here who had right mind to do the right thing.

But both families that were so cheerful and loving had quickly become a house of tears and sorrow.

Karina woke up crying, and looked into Mary's eyes and cried.

Matt was nearby. He approached Karina quickly, and said, "Trust in the Lord. Keep your eye on the Lord. See the cross. See the cross."

Karina reached out for Matt. Karina hugged him. Karina cried, "Dad. What am I gonna do? Dad, I don't know what do?"

Matt cried with her. "We have to trust in the Lord."

Betty cried again aloud.

The room became full of sorrow.

Mary asked, "Karina, Baby, we need to prepare for John's funeral. Let me have the phone numbers of the people I need to contact."

"It's in my purse. Please call Cindy to come quickly. She said she'll try to visit me when I told her that I'm having a baby. It would be great if she can be with me. You can call her now. She should be awake in Germany." Karina made the most urgent request of what she need it—her best friend.

Mary made the call quickly to Cindy. She made a collect call from the hospital pay phone.

"Hello." Cindy living in the other side of world answered.

Mary could hear kids crying and screaming on the background. It was very hard for her to say what has happened. She heard another *hello*. Mary finally opened her mouth. "Hello, Cindy. This is Karina's mother, Mary."

"Hi, Mary." Cindy answered, but she didn't hear any answer right away. So, she spoke what's on her mind, "Good news? The baby is born? Karina told me she's going to name the baby after me. I'm so...so...honored. Blake! NO! NO! Sorry, Mary. My hands are full with two boys."

Mary didn't want to tell her the bad news anyway, so she waited as long as possible.

"Mary...are you there?" Cindy got the situation under control and returned to the call.

"Yes, I'm listening." Mary's voice was down. It was unintentional, but she couldn't help it.

"Something is wrong...right?" Cindy felt something is wrong from the voice of Mary. "What's wrong? Is there complication with the baby? Is Karina all right?"

There was silence that said more than the words. Finally Mary broke the news. "Baby is fine. It's John. ...John passed away. He tried to help some people from a car accident, but the car exploded. He died."

"No. No! ...Oh...NO! ...How is Karina?" Cindy's voice was breaking apart.

Mary could hear Cindy crying. "She's not doing well. She's asking for you. Can you come…immediately?" Mary made the request Karina asked for.

"Yes. I'll be there right away. Please tell Karina that I'll be there right away." Cindy's voice told the pain she felt for her friend.

Mary returned to the room. "I just spoke with Cindy. She said she'll be here right away."

"You think she can make it today." Karina showed how she really need her best friend.

"I don't know if that would be possible. She got kids…don't you think she'll be here at least a week later." Mary gave her honest opinion.

Mary stayed awake with Karina, while Matt and John's parents went to John's home to get some rest.

"Mom, I don't think I can live anymore. How can I go on?" Karina spoke lifelessly.

"As your dad said, see the Lord…see the cross. John did not die for nothing. He saved two boys, I heard. You must overcome this. God will give you the strength." Mary gave her encouragement. She noticed Karina isn't listening.

"Mom…I can live like this. I feel I'm cursed. How can God do this to me…to my baby…to my John? John is such a great person. He's been nothing but good in his whole life. He knows I can't live without John." Karina started to cry again.

Karina fell asleep around 2 or 3 am. Mary's presence helped Karina to be calmer but it wasn't much help at all.

Mary prepared herself well for this tragedy: through her prayers she got her heart ready for this ordeal.

Now, she saw her daughter's face being without life. She got so scared that she might lose her daughter as well.

Mary prayed and prayed. She prayed out of fear and for love of her daughter. She fell asleep next to Karina as she prayed.

It was about 8 a.m. A nurse walked in. Mary realized it was morning. She got up and went to restroom. She looked herself in the mirror and realized that she's not well either, but she needed to get the job done—getting ready for the funeral and taking care of Karina.

Mary went back by the baby's room. She saw little Cindy sleeping so peacefully. Mary cried for the baby. She was not sure how Cindy will grow without a father. She wiped her tears gently and went back to Karina.

Karina was still asleep.

Mary felt tired, but she felt okay. The reality just crept in her mind and dragged her down, but her faith kept her up.

Around 10 a.m., Matt and John's parents showed up. Karina got up and went to restroom to prepare for people visiting. Karina returned and greeted the family, and started to cry again. Matt comforted her and kept repeating the words—*See the Lord, See the Cross.*

Mary never imagined such a tragedy would happen to her or her family. She knew things like this happened every day, but somehow she felt her family was immune because of her faith and her obedience to Christ.

Soon people started to pour in; people from the church came in first than from the school. It was crowded. They all wanted to stay longer, but had to

go because there were just too many people. Nurses
told them they can't stay too long. They were given
ten minutes at the most.

    Time quickly passed.

    People visiting slowed down.

    The night came.

    Mary returned from her rest. Matt and John's
parents left to get some rest as well.

    Mary and Karina found themselves together
alone again.

    Karina had tears but no more words. She
looked deadly tired but worse—she looked hopeless.

    Then, came a knock, and a face Karina
could never forget walked in. Mary hadn't seen Cindy
for so long she could recognize her.

    Cindy ran to Karina and hugged her. "Rina.
It's me Dee." Cindy was happy to see Karina, but
she felt the weight of the calamity.

    "Dee! Dee!" Karina loved Cindy's voice.

    "Yes, Rina. It's me. Your best pal." Cindy did
her best not to cry.

    Karina erupted with tears. She hugged her
Cindy, and cried and cried.

    Mary cried softly feeling the suffering that
Karina might be going through.

    "How you get here so quick?" Mary had to
ask.

    "I turned everything over to Pat, and got on
the next flight. They do favors for the army. They
even gave me a first class seat for economy. I got
here very comfortably." Cindy answered Mary's
question.

    "Mom, I need to get out of here. I can't stand
it. And I need to get ready for the funeral too." Karina

suddenly collected her mind and said something Mary couldn't believe.

"I don't think you should go anywhere. I don't think doctors will let you out." Mary was worried about Karina's health.

"MOM, I'm fine. I need to get out of HERE. I can't stand it. I WANNA go home." Karina repeated her request with a pleading voice.

"I agree with her, Mary." Cindy supported Karina.

"Okay. We'll see." Mary agreed.

Karina and Cindy talked all night as Mary slept in the corner.

Mary woke up several times from Karina's crying. She felt sorry for her daughter. She never felt so helpless. The most critical time in her daughter's life, she couldn't do a thing to comfort her. She felt the pain that life can throw you into; it can be more than unbearable.

The morning came. Mary saw Karina still sleeping and Cindy wide awake. Cindy gave a smile. Mary returned with a smile, and got up, and walked to restroom. She sat on the toilet and did her nature call. She wiped herself and went to wash her face. She looked herself in the mirror. She looked ten years older than when she arrived.

She thanked God for everything. She forced herself to thank God. She didn't like her prayer. She felt some anger in her. She knew it was toward God. She didn't know what to say. She never felt angry toward God before. She quickly washed her face and put some make-up, and she walked out of the restroom.

"Oh, Mary, it's me Larry, the pastor." Pastor Larry Petel from the church greeted her on the hall way.

"Got the funeral all taken care. Actually, Mr. James Hayden did it. He's the deacon in charge of funerals. It will be Friday 11 a.m. at the veteran's funeral ground. We will take care of all the rides for you." Pastor quickly gave the funeral summary. "Your families just have to be at the funeral. The army and the church have everything set."

"Pastor Petel…"

"Larry."

"Larry, thank you very much. We really appreciate that."

"We're all in shock. We are doing our best to help Karina. We love John so much. I still can't believe what happened."

They slowly walked back to the room.

Matt and John's parents came. They all held the baby. More people came to visit. Karina made a request to go home, and the doctor reluctantly agreed.

The family returned home. At home, more people showed up to console Karina.

Mary thought Karina looked well…too well.

Evening slowly approached.

"The funeral is tomorrow," Karina said with a blank face. "I want everyone to be ready."

Karina walked into her room.

The morning of the funeral came.

Karina was all dressed up and ready to go. Mary prepared the breakfast, but Karina didn't eat or drink anything. Cindy and the rest of the family members tried not to get Karina upset or aroused. They tip-toed around Karina's emotion.

A knock came and Matt opened the door. A church member said he brought a van to take them to the funeral.

Everyone got on the van quietly. It was very silent. Karina stayed very quiet.

"This is not a sad day. It's a day to celebrate my husband's life." Karina suddenly burst out with her feeling. Let's sing a hymn together. They sang *It is well with my soul*. As they sang together, Karina started to cry, and Cindy and Mary followed. John's parent's cried a loud too. John's dad, Gary, cried the loudest. He just couldn't bear sending his son before him. John's mom holding on to her husband cried quietly. Even the driver started to cry quietly.

They have arrived at the funeral. It was colder than usual. It rained hard. There were over three hundred people. Pastor gave a quick sermon. The church folks sang a memorial song for John. And the veterans fired several shots for the honor of John's service, and they methodically folded the U.S. flag that was on top of John's cast and presented to Karina as a symbol of John's honor and sacrifice for his country.

Karina accepted the flag and gave it to Mary. She held her tears and kept her composure quite well.

John's parents kept on crying throughout the funeral. After the funeral, people made their tribute to Karina, Karina's parents and John's parents.

After the funeral, Karina and the families returned home to have the funeral reception. The church members prepared all the food. Karina looked like she was enjoying the crowd. She was conversing and laughing with the people so well; Mary couldn't believe it. As the afternoon approached, people started to leave one by one. Karina gave everyone a graceful goodbye to each one of them.

As the night approached, the church folks cleared everything and left. The house became quite. Karina went into her bedroom. You could hear her sobbing, so Cindy walked in. Cindy came around and cried together. After a while, Karina just collapsed on Cindy; she fainted. Cindy laid her on the floor.

Mary and Betty walked in because Cindy asked them to come in.

"Don't worry Mary. She will wake up soon." Cindy comforted Mary.

Cindy had seen this before, so she wasn't too worried. But she didn't feel good about it.

All these had taken toll on everybody even Mary.

After about 10 minutes, Karina opened her eyes and looked around. "Mom, Cindy…thank you for everything. I couldn't have done this without you."

"Baby, you haven't eaten anything for whole day. You need to take care of yourself for Cidy." Mary displayed her concern.

"Cidy…yes…my baby…how is she?" Karina responded very slowly.

"Let's get her up and put her in bed first." Cindy addressed the immediate need.

"Okay." Mary agreed.

They slowly pulled up Karina's body.

"Let's get her into something more comfortable." Mary suggested.

"Good idea." Cindy agreed.

Mary, Betty, and Cindy got Karina changed to a night gown. And they took Karina to her bed.

Karina wasn't dead, but she wasn't exactly alive. She fell asleep right away.

Mary, Matt, Cindy, Gary, and Betty got together in the living room and didn't know what to say. There was a silence, a silence from sadness, shock, and fatigue. Mary pleaded for help inside, and looked at Cindy. Mary felt Cindy was sent by God to help the family.

Cindy said, "We'll have morning and evening devotions. We will pray to God for help, and worship Him, and read the Bible. We will fight through this and win. It's not gonna be easy. In fact, it will get worse before it gets any better. It will be least a month before we'll see any improvement. I have seen wives who lost their husbands in battles. Most of them take at least a few weeks before they are able to gather their composure to function properly. I can't believe how Karina got through today. It's a miracle. I didn't think she could handle it, but she did it with such a grace. I still can't believe it. I know Karina: She's gonna make it through."

Gary beat the table hard as he screamed and shouted, "This is NOT right. No! Damn it! Ahh. Ahhh...." He ran out the house slamming the door behind him. Matt followed him.

Three ladies looked at each other. They held their hands together and prayed. They cried. Mary and Betty let their pain out. They wailed and screamed. The pain was just too much for them. They comforted one another. They lost the grasp of time.

Mary looked up and saw angels around the house.

"Look at the angels!" Mary pointed at them.

Cindy couldn't see anything, but Betty said, "I see them. I see them."

They cried and held each other even more. Mary started sing the hymn—*It is well with my soul*. Cindy and Betty followed along.

They started to clean up and got ready for sleep.

And Matt and John's dad walked in.

It's was a nice four bedroom home that John had fixed up. He bought it a few years before the marriage, so he can have a place to start his marriage and to bring his family up. Mary and Matt had a room. Gary and Betty had a room. Cindy slept with Karina and Cidy.

Morning arrived after the long and tiring funeral. Mary and Betty had the breakfast going. Matt and Gary sat in the living room watching the morning news. Cindy brought Cidy out from the room. Cindy handed over the baby to Matt, and walked back into Karina's room.

They got around the breakfast table and had a delicious breakfast. After breakfast, they got the Bibles and the hymns out, and had a devotion. They read the New Testament's Gospel of John as Cindy suggested. They decided to read one chapter per devotion and share their thoughts.

Everyone felt joy and quite hopeful even with the loss of John. They enjoyed taking care of Cidy as they took turns. But it was Karina that was hard to take care of: She just refused to eat.

Mary tried to feed her several times and gave up. Only Cindy could handle Karina.

Mary enjoyed watching and taking care of Cidy, but watching her own daughter getting closer to death wasn't something she expected.

Every morning and night, Cindy would give an encouraging word to them that all things are in God's hand and everything will be all right.

Mary felt Cindy sounded like her, always being positive about the outlook.

A month went by quickly. They expected in a month Karina would recover, but she had gotten worse. Doctors came by and said there's nothing they could do. A slow process of seeing her own daughter getting worse and worse killed Mary and Matt.

Matt screamed at Karina several times, and he gave up because Karina didn't respond at all. Both families tried pretty much everything to get Karina self-sufficient because she needed to recover for the baby.

The house became unsettling because Karina's unwillingness to get well, so Cindy asked only Mary to stay with her to take care of the baby and Karina.

Matt left and John's Parents left.

It was just Cindy, Mary, and the baby with Karina.

Mary would over hear Cindy talking to her kids and her husband over the phone unintentionally. They were nice cordial calls in the beginning, but the conversation became more and more pleading from Cindy asking her husband for understanding.

It was around second month, Mary lost much faith in Karina's recovery. She didn't like the fact that her first daughter, Karina, would die, but it looked like it was inevitable. Cindy would say otherwise, but Mary accepted the reality. She couldn't believe herself either, but she gave up on Karina, her favorite daughter.

Mary prayed and prayed for Karina but she didn't get any answer, but she enjoyed and loved watching and taking care of the baby. She fell deeply in love with the baby, Cidy. She knew she could raise the baby if she had to. She slowly and coldly made a mental gap with Karina. She decided that Karina is just another woman that she's helping out. But it wasn't easy; every day was a test of her true self. She drove often all alone to a nearby park, and prayed and cried in the car.

The church folks came by and gave them a relief for a day sometimes, but the chore of taking care of Karina became too hard for Cindy. Mary noticed Cindy's physical health is in the verge of danger as well.

One day Mary answered the phone, it was Cindy's husband, Patrick. He usually requested for Cindy right away, but today, he spoke directly Mary. Patrick pleaded with Mary to return his wife because his family is breaking apart. Mary didn't know what to say but *I'm sorry* repeatedly, and she told Patrick she will return Cindy right away.

Cindy heard the conversation and realized it must have been her husband. She asked for the phone. Mary could hear the loud pleading voice of Patrick. Cindy asked for one more month, and she said she would return home even if there's no improvement.

Mary now had another big problem in her hand—Cindy's family. She now knew Cindy's family is going through turmoil because of Karina. Patrick's plea for her wife back sounded more than reasonable.

"Cindy, you can go back home. Don't worry about Karina. She's in God's hand. She'll be fine,"

Mary lied thinking that's the best way, and she was afraid that Cindy's family will be ruined.

"Karina needs me. She needs me. I can't leave her like this." Cindy was torn apart between her family and a friend. "I can mend my family when I go back, but I can't fix Karina if I leave her now." Cindy put her family on the line for her friend.

Mary was touched, but she didn't want to be responsible or be blamed for destroying a family. Mary could hear the pleading of Patrick in her ears— *Please, Mary. I need…we need Cindy here. I'm losing it here. It's chaos here. I think Cindy has done more than enough. Please let her go now.*

Mary begged, "Cindy, you done more than enough. Karina will be the same with you here or not. You are a great help, but I can take care of her. Don't worry. You have your family to take care, Cindy. You may leave." Mary's words were convincing but her tone of voice was weak.

"I can't go now. I will regret this rest of my life if I lose Karina. I can't bear that. I need to give her all I got. It won't be too late then. I can't go, Mary. I love Karina too much." Cindy displayed her commitment strongly.

Mary turned around and walked away. She felt small as a mother. Cindy was the one who sounded like mother. Mary never realized that she had no faith at all. After all these years of telling people to have faith, it was her who needed faith.

Mary had lost her faith after a month of long struggle with Karina's refusal and her ever worsening condition. She couldn't look at her own daughter's drooping, and now-ugly-lifeless face. It felt like she was staring at a ghost or even worse—death.

Karina didn't speak a word. She didn't ask for anything. She didn't even ask for her own baby not even once.

Every day, Mary helped Cindy taking Karina out on the porch or near the window. And they put Cidy on her lap, but Karina never showed any sign of life. Karina drove away anyone and everyone by being cold and lifeless. Cidy would be on her lap crying, and still Karina showed no sign of any interest.

Mary knew Cindy did everything she could: Cindy even bought a guitar and played songs Karina. But Mary saw how Cindy was getting worse too. She realized Cindy had lost quite a weight, her voice had weakened, her faced drew less smile, and her attitude showed much irritation.

Mary didn't know what to do with Cindy. She appreciated her undying loyalty and love for Karina, but the fear of Cindy getting sick and breaking her family apart got to Mary. She prayed hours, but she didn't get any comfort at all.

Mary resented God for killing both her son-in-law and daughter, but she resented more for killing her daughter in such a grinding and painful death. She felt it would be better off if her daughter died instantly like her son-in-law. She revolted and prayed to God to take her daughter right away without pain. She didn't know if it was a plea, or protest. She had lost much faith in God.

Mary was just going through the motions of prayer and worshipping. She felt empty, very empty. All her experiences of God added up to nothing that she could rely or trust. This wasn't the kind of God she knew or she had experienced. She read about Job, but she thought Job had it much easier—losing his kids instantly. Seeing Karina so close to death for so long was more than a torture for her.

Cindy got cranky, and she would scream at Mary, Karina, and even herself. She dashed out of the house many times, and be back in an hour or two. Cindy's word in the morning devotion and the evening devotion had less and less hope and authority. Cindy didn't look into Mary's eyes much anymore.

Luckily, Mary had Cidy, her grandchild. She would forget about all her problems and worries when she was taking care of Cidy. It was the only thing that kept Mary in sane. She ate and took care of herself because of Cidy. She fell in love with Cidy. She felt more than confidant enough that she can raise Cidy when Karina died.

It was almost three months since the ordeal started. It was about time Cindy would be returning home, leaving Mary all alone to take care of Karina and Cidy. Mary overheard that Cindy promising to return home in a week if there was no sign of any improvement of Karina. Mary was relieved but still worried that Cindy would never be the same in health or in her relationship with her family. Mary knew Cindy started to cough about two month ago and had gotten worse—a lot worse.

Cindy looked better in shape with much lost weight, but her face told another story. Cindy started to look more like Karina.

It was Saturday morning, very early morning; she just got up to go to restroom and return to bed. She noticed that the baby was asleep. Mary loved smelling and seeing the baby. She smiled and went to bed again right next to the baby. Then, Mary heard a loud call for her from downstairs, "MARY!

MARY! KARINA IS TALKING. GET DOWN HERE. MARY! MARY!"

Mary quickly ran downstairs and saw her daughter standing in the living room with a slight glow on her face. Karina looked at her and smiled. Mary hadn't seen that smile for so long that she cried and ran to Karina. Mary hugged her daughter and cried, "Karina, my baby....my baby...."

Cindy came around and hugged together. They cried for a long time. It was all mumble jumbles of the same words of each other's name and that they loved each other.

After all the crying, Karina asked for water.

Cindy quickly got a glass of water.

Karina gulped the water in one shot like a whiskey, and smiled. There was life in her eyes.

And Karina told what happened: Jesus came to her, and led her to the backyard, and anointed her, and told her to raise Cidy well and that He has plan for her.

CH 42: Karina and Mary

"Cidy is now ready for whatever God has planned for her. Isn't it amazing, Mom? ...I shouldn't have made you go through those three months of horror. Mom. I'm so sorry. I want to thank you again for everything, Mom." Karina thanks Mom for the suffering that she made her go through.

"I'd put it aside a long time ago." Mary doesn't want to remember those three months of horror. "I thought I was gonna lose you, Baby. I lost my hope and faith in God in those three months. I don't want to remember it. It was a test, I failed."

Karina realizes Mom's pain of losing faith in God. "Mom, you didn't fail anything. You made it through. We made it through. I gave up on God long before you did, but He didn't give up on me or you. He is faithful even when we are not." Karina comforts Mom.

"I couldn't bare the fact of losing you. But I accepted, when God didn't.... I resented God and you. I gave up. I love you so much, so I hated God for taking you away. It wasn't fair. I was very angry inside. I didn't like the way he was taking you. I'm sorry Karina. Please forgive me." Mary lets her deepest thought shown. It is the burden that she wanted to share with her daughter for a long time.

"Mom, there's nothing to forgive. I should be the one asking you for forgiveness. I should've been stronger, but I got weak and rebelled against God.

172

I'm the one who needs forgiveness, Mom. I cracked right away. I thought I trusted in God, but when he took my John, I lost faith in Him in that very instant. I gave you so much pain, Mom. I'm so sorry. I love you." Karina shares her deepest regret as well. She had no idea Mom had such a burden for such a long time.

"I love you, Karina." Mary cries. She feels something very heavy being lifted off of her shoulder. "I love you so much, Karina. You have been a good daughter and a good friend. I thank God everyday…for you."

"I love you too, Mom." Karina cries with Mary.

Suddenly Karina remembers that she might be visiting Cidy this Christmas when Cindy visits her, so she invites Mom to join them, "Cindy is coming to see me. We might be going to Texas to see Cidy. Won't you and Dad come with us? It would be great."

"That would be nice. It would be great to go see Cidy. Matt would love it. Maybe we can rent a van and travel together. No, it's winter. We shouldn't drive." Mary is very excited about the trip, but has the fear for the weather.

"Don't worry Mom. We can drive in Texas, especially in Houston. The weather down there is quite nice during the winter. Mom, that's a good idea. We'll take the plane to Houston, and rent a van, and travel together. Just like the old time." Karina encourages Mary.

"Sweet. I'll talk with Matt. He's getting some fertilizer. Call you tonight." Mary loves it.

"Okay, Mom. Talk to you, tonight." Karina feels the joy of Mom's excitement.

CH 43: Back to Cidy

Cidy's mind is busy reviewing her memories and sketching the unknown future.

"Will God take me to a remote corner of the Earth, or will He ask me to minister kids in some special out-reach somewhere," she contemplates about God's plan for her.

She is just as excited as well as sad to leave the places where she called home, work, and church. The uncertainty of her future and the comfort of her routine collide leaving her in a deserted island where she is very lonely and uncomfortable.

She knows her life is making a turn to a new and uncharted place where she will be doing God's work full-time. She had a feeling one day she might be called to do ministerial work. But, she is still shocked that it was planned from the day of her birth.

"How can that be possible?" She is baffled.

She thinks about Jake, again. It is her greatest pleasure. Thought of Jake is constantly there with her like a hot chocolate drink that she just can't refuse. Jake has been the joy of her being.

Her greatest pain of leaving and doing God's work is letting her love, Jake, go. All her wishes and fantasies being with Jake are about to become just fantasies. She is heartbroken, but knows God has a bigger plan for her life.

"Maybe Jake was planted by God to keep me from chasing a wrong guy and getting my life all

messed up." She reasons her current situation.
"*What is ahead? Where is God taking me to?*"

(Cidy came to Houston, Texas, knowing
nobody, but trusting in God that He will watch over
her. And that's exactly what happened: God took
care of her well, very well.)

She has tasted the success of the world
without giving up or compromising her faith a bit. In
fact, it is she who influenced the world by bring in
people to Christ and showing them the love and the
wisdom of God. She has been a faithful servant.

She quickly checks if all the props and the
food are ready.

It looks like everything will be fine.

She is ready for the night.

Now, she has to make sure her part of the
show is prepared perfectly. And only way she can
make sure of that is to practice her part as much as
possible. She feels confidant she is ready for the
stage, but she wants to make sure. She takes out
the script for the show tonight, and practices her
part. She is hoping to win the first place with the
girls. It will be nice if she won the first prize as a
going-way token to remember.

She loves to let herself lose in the talent
show. She feels the need to scratch the itch that she
builds up over a year to go crazy especially in front
of the people. She isn't usually outrageous or
comical, but she has her comical side that just pops
out of nowhere. She just loves comedy.

She knows she has a serious funny bone in
her. She's not sure where she gets it from. But Mom
keeps saying—*It must be from your dad.*

CH 44: Cidy's First Comedy act

"Okay, okay class, today, actually I mean this hour, we are going to learn 50 states and their capitals of the United States of America." Miss Rodriguez, 4th grade teacher, spoke loudly, slowly, and very animatedly to the class.

Kids just loved Miss Rodriguez and were animated by the opening sentence by Miss Rodriguez.

"Who can name a state besides New Jersey?" Miss Rodriguez asked as she turns and dances around with her index finger pointing everywhere.

Cidy raised her hand very high quickly with so much vigor and with the noise of *wooh-wooh*, that Miss Rodriguez had no choice but to pick Cidy—again, but she waited and raised the tension in the class.

Miss Rodriguez loved Cidy because she was so off beat and silly. Cidy was her favorite student. Cidy represented innocence and joy of being a child to Miss Rodriguez.

Before Miss Rodriguez pointed her finger to Cidy and called Cidy to give an answer, Cidy volunteered herself by jumping right up. Cidy saw Miss Rodriguez's eyes are on her.

Cidy, standing straight-up like a soldier, screamed with strong commitment, "I have a confession to make, Miss Rodriguez!"

It was not what Miss Rodriguez or the kids expected, but then again it was Cidy. So, Miss Rodriguez sort of played along expecting the unexpected from Cidy. "What, Cidy?"

Cidy pointed her index finger to the ceiling with her eyes following the direction of her index finger, and stuck her buttocks like a duck, and gave a magical twitch of her buttocks like a duck. And there was a silence for a few seconds, creating anticipation for something to come.

And Cidy farted out loud and long. Even she was surprised of her own fart being so loud and long.

Everybody just blasted off the floor and rolled over for a while. The class became totally out of control. After a few minutes, the class was still in roar, and it even made a few shed tears because they laughed so hard and so long. Once they started laughing they couldn't stop. Others imitated her quickly. The loud "artificial" sound of farting quickly filled the classroom continuously.

Then the class became so silly and out of control that whatever anyone said was just too funny. The class became one loudly-blasting-and-popping bag of laughter. The entire class time was spent on laughing.

Miss Rodriguez laughed and enjoyed kids' silliness. She just was afraid they might be bothering other classes. Besides that, she didn't mind. She remembered her younger years weren't too much different, although she would get punished for such an act.

Miss Rodriguez was the most popular teacher with the kids, but not so much with the parents and the school. Kids just swarmed around her like bunch of little bees. Kids went home and talked about what happened in her class, but the parents felt the kids weren't learning anything. Only thing they like about Miss Rodriguez was that their kids liked to go to school, but that was it.

Miss Rodriguez felt kids today were slaved to learning this and that, and had little time to be kids. She remembered how her childhood was filled with joy and laughter, so she tried to give them that freedom to be kids because they will soon be adults before they knew it. And once kids grew up, they can't go back to their innocent childhood when you can laugh about anything.

Other teachers came around to see what's going on, and they saw what they heard—a class of kids just laughing and jumping and running around. It was a zoo. They thought they were there to prevent exactly what was happening. They had no idea what happened. It looked like a chaos.

Miss Rodriguez had a ball; she could not stop laughing either. A moment she will not forget. She never laughed so much in her life. Maybe she did when she was a child. She first thought it wasn't funny at all and kept her composure, but as kids started to roar and got out of control with laughter, she started to laugh too.

Other kids soon followed this and made it a trend for a while making the school little more tolerable for kids and intolerable for a few teachers. There were always a few teachers who had to have complete control over their kids, and they weren't going to have this shenanigan. But most teachers thought it was very funny and liked it because it helped them make the day go by a little quicker and easier.

The school became more bearable for the kids and most of the teachers, but a few teachers had built a strong resentment for Cidy and Miss Rodriguez for making the school a joke. The trend lasted for a month and got those few teachers very upset. Cidy felt the heat from them.

So one day Cidy again suddenly stood up and said loudly, "I'm so sorry for causing so much trouble." The whole class laughed again. They didn't know why they were laughing but it was just funny for them. Even the teacher was flabbergasted; Ms. Rodriguez wanted to say something but decided to just laugh it out and let it go. But this caught on too like a fire: Kids started to stand up in the middle of the class and say the same thing.

Eventually Cidy was called to the principal office for causing a stir again. Karina was called in to the office as well, and they discussed about the incidents. Karina wanted to laugh, but she didn't want to disrespect Principal.

Cidy got three days of detention for it.

Karina reluctantly agreed and apologized for the commotion that Cidy had caused. At home, Karina just laughed with Cidy and advised her not to make any sudden announcements like that anymore. Cidy loved Mom for being so cool.

CH 45: Back to Cidy

Cidy looks at her face in the window to make sure she got that right facial expression for her act. She tries different ugly faces, cute faces, and fun-ugly faces. She laughs at herself.

Other employees as they walk by could see her through the glass, but Cidy forgets that sometimes. People are pointing at her and laughing, but she has no idea. She is too focused.

CEO, Jeff, passes by and becomes curious to what's going on. He sees the whole thing, and he couldn't help but give out a loud laughter. He is just amazed about Cidy. He thanks her a lot for the company success. It has been nothing but unexplainable success with Cidy's arrival. He knows it's not a coincidence. He taps on the glass. Cidy turns around. He waits until she sees his eyes, and he gives a little wave and a wink. She returns a wave and a large-but-shy smile. He walks away.

Cidy is just as surprised and as well as embarrassed to see Jeff and others staring at her like if see an ape in a zoo.

After just seeing silly gestures of Cidy, Jeff walks back to his office with a big smile. He tilts his head realizing that Cidy is different—in a good way.

CH 46: Jeff's Secret Weapon

Jeff gave Cidy a direct line to get approval for the events' set-ups and details. He knew that the upper management team wouldn't like a non-management employee having a direct line with him, and the upper management team showed their displeasure by frequently displaying their disapproval for whatever Cidy tried to do.

But he wanted all the events or meetings with the investors or buyers done with care and respect without any delays or flaws, and he secretly wanted to talk someone about the employees' well-being or morale because he knew employees' spirit affects the bottom line of the company's performance very directly in the long run. It was something he couldn't measure with numbers, questionnaire or survey. He needed someone who relates to employees well without getting involved with their work, and Cidy seemed to fit that profile perfectly.

He hadn't told anyone, not even Cidy, but he wanted her to accomplish much more than her job description as Event Coordinator.

He never asked Cidy about how employees felt about the company or gave her any assignment about such, nor did he ask her to increase the employees' moral or spirit. He just wanted her to give him ideas, or he wanted her to help him to read employees' mind a little better by just talking with her freely.

Of course, Jeff foremost wanted to make sure the company's events for the buyers or investors done properly without any slip-ups or disasters.

One of the reason Jeff knew his company had better success than other companies was because he brought people together in natural and friendly setting through different types of events to do business. It was his way of bring the people together to get the deals done more effectively and creatively. He realized when people saw each other face to face in a friendly and joyful environment they talked more freely resulting in business deals quicker and better. He intuitively knew it was those events that really made quite a difference in the company's performances in short and long run.

Jeff, after the disaster and having heard the management's complaints about Tammy, admitted and committed to replace Tammy from event coordination at least. But, he wanted more than someone to replace what Tammy was doing; he wanted someone who can be an inside connection with the employees without her knowing it. He wanted someone's honest opinion besides the management team, so he can make the right decision.

He knew the management had their own survival rule. They sometimes had to make things bigger than they are or keep some information to themselves for their survival, and he understood that. He wasn't trying to sabotage the management team or try to control them. He just wanted to make the right decision for himself, the management, and the employees—the company. He felt he had to be somewhat shrewd to be successful.

And Cidy was going to be Jeff's secret weapon that no one expected, and he certainly had his doubt about his hidden plan for Cidy. So he gave Cidy direct excess to him, and he enjoyed having conversation about the company and many other things with her.

He wished many times he was married to someone like Cidy or Cidy. He felt she had so much wisdom and intuition about the people at such a young age and she was so funny. He often wondered if she received such wisdom from God, because she often talked about God as her friend. He often consulted with her about his problems with his wife and children as well. He didn't know why he would be opening up his deepest burden to her, but he felt consoled and comforted. Cidy always said to him don't lose your first love with your wife. He asked what that meant, and she said, "You already know the answer in your heart."

After a couple of months at work, Cidy solved the problem that Jeff and the company couldn't resolve—Tammy. He had so much appreciation for Tammy because she was the one who helped him the most get the company going from the very early stage. Without her, he knew the company would have gone bankrupt a long time ago. She stayed up many nights with him to prepare for investment proposals and sales presentations. She was the Swiss knife for him in all company matters. As the company grew, her place and work just moved further and further away from him.

Jeff was going to fire Tammy because of all the pressure from the employees, especially from the management. From Tammy's lack of adjustment to the company's growth, he realized how important it is for the employees to work together and appreciate one another: It was that intangible camaraderie that made all the difference in the tangible outcomes.

He knew firing Tammy will have a conscience back-fire foremost for himself, and disapproval from the early employees who feel they have been pushed aside. He knew he would feel like a back stabber for the rest of his life if he fired her. So, he often called her up for a cup of coffee, or stopped at her post for a small talk. He always had Tammy in his mind. He knew she would still be here with him even if the company had failed and everyone had left. She gave him so much courage and support in the early years; he always had a little memo with him to remind him of her early indispensable help: it said—*Tammy gave her life for the company*.

After a few months, Cidy came up to his office. It was after a big round trip from Asia. He was very tired, but he was always glad to see her. She walked in and said a few words and gave him a proposal package with the front page that read—*FEAD*. The small subtitle read *Friday Employee Appreciation Day*.

Jeff went through the proposal with the budget request of $80,000 per year. It was asking the company to pay for employees' Friday lunch and special thoughtful gift for different celebration or memorial. Usually such a package had to be approved by the management team first, but Jeff gave her a different route for her approvals.

He approved the FEAD with much disapproval from the management.

Employees loved it. They called it "feed-me" day, but they did really feel the company appreciated them. Jeff enjoyed the event. He tried to attend it as many as possible, and signed on all the cards that were given to the recipients. He tried best to be a friend to his employees. It was great for him to talk to his employees at least a couple of times a month, and he felt connected with them knowing their special events—birthday, graduation, special achievement, and sickness.

Jeff remembered seeing Sandy at FEAD. He had never seen such a beautiful girl before. He enjoyed talking with Sandy. He tried to get her as his private sectary, but Cidy advised him not to. He remembered how he decided to see more of his employees just to see Sandy.

When Jeff wanted to sign on the FEAD proposal, Jeff called CFO, Jerry Jackson, to his office, and Jerry came to his office right away.

"Jeff, we can't do this. Next five years going to be rough. You know it. I can't sign this off." Jerry made it clear.

"Jerry, sit down. I know how you feel. How can I explain this? I feel something very special about this girl, Cidy. I think she is like a golden girl. She helped me breathe again. She solved Tammy. I can't believe it. This FEAD thing…I think…it will work out." Jeff tried to convince Jerry.

"Our reserve will make us through three years max." Jerry backed off a little.

"How's Max and Susan?" Jeff changed the subject purposely. He knew Jerry long enough he will back him up.

"They're growing up fast…too fast. They don't talk to me anymore." Jerry knew Jeff's got him.

He was just trying to cover every base, and coming years didn't look good with the worsening economy across the border. He felt the company isn't immune to it.

"We should get together soon. I'm gonna call Vicky to call Samantha to have dinner together. Vicky loves your kids. They are so well behaved and smart. My two little ones are just a major pain in the ass. They are just spoiled rotten. I don't know what to do." Jeff made a best effort to appreciate Jerry.

Jerry had been a great finance overseer. He made sure every penny was counted for.

Later that year, with FEAD every Friday, Cidy proposed a scholarship program for college students or professional-training students costing another $100,000 a year supporting $10,000 maximum per kid per year.

"We need to give hope to some of these single moms that their kids can go to college or professional-training school. They can't afford it. What we are paying them is not bad for double-income families, but for single moms it just gets them through." Cidy made an excellent pitch for the scholarship program.

Jeff signed on the scholarship program too. And again, Jerry disagreed.

"Can they get a student loan to help out?" Jerry questioned Jeff.

"Yes, they can. But it really becomes burden for them after school. It took a long time to pay my student loan. It's not fun. That's what Cidy said." Jeff said.

Jeff knew that the company can go through hard time, and what he agreed to do with Cidy can bring the company down much sooner. He knew if the company had no money, there is no company. But, Cidy talked about God's blessing. He wanted to test God. He wanted to know if God existed like Cidy said, and he was willing to risk the company's future.

He often felt like he was in love with Cidy. She gave him something he never had or something he was always seeking—that joy for life. She seemed to have that.

"Cidy, you are going to break my company." Jeff often joked with Cidy.

"God will bless you for taking care of the needy." Cidy mentioned about God's blessing again.

"You think God will bless me." Jeff wanted to know.

"He says that if you help the poor He will help you." Cidy stated God's blessing without any hesitation.

Jeff remembered signing off FEAD and the scholarship project.

Jerry complained several times in private and in the management meetings that the company is not on the solid rock to give out such money like Halloween candies.

In private, Jeff said to Jerry what Cidy said, "God will help the company if the company helped the poor."

Jerry reacted, "You don't even go to church. You don't even believe in God, Jeff. Do you?"

"I talked with Vicky about attending church recently. She said she's been thinking about it too. I remember going to church when I was a kid, but I stop going in high school. It just got boring, or I fell in love with girls that were not church goers." Jeff responded in matter-of-fact tone.

"Hmmm.... I got nothing against church. I went to church a little too. I liked it. I don't know. I never thought about going to church since college. I think it's just bunch of bologna." Jerry gave his honest opinion.

FEAD and scholarship fund program made a lot of employees feeling good about the company. Before, they thought the company was just another company, but when they saw the company, CEO, the management really cared about them, they felt very much gratitude and royal. They had sense of belonging and felt very proud working for their company.

He never thought such events and programs could bring the employees together so successfully and increase their performances.

After Cidy's arrival, all the employees always checked the company schedule to see what's happening each Friday, some Saturdays, and the biggest event of the year—the Christmas party with the talent show with diverse employee awards.

Above all, Cidy brought much laughter and joy to the company. Jeff called it—love. He felt love from his employees, and he felt he loved his employees as well. He even secretly visited employees that were in hospital with his wife. But the words got out. It was Cidy who advised him to take his wife to visit the sick in hospital. Vicky was loved by his employees since then, and that made him feel very good about his wife as well.

Vicky became a good friend with Cidy. She thanked Cidy for helping his husband and the company. She realized Jeff changed a lot since Cidy came aboard. She called Cidy out for lunch several times to talk about their family problems and to get help. She always praised Cidy to Jeff.

Jeff thought the Christmas party that company had was fine until Cidy brought the Christmas Party proposal. The proposal made the Christmas Party into a fun and exciting program. There was dancing competition, talent competition, and funny awards. Of course it cost much more money. But, everything worked out great; the company's sales always increased even the worst of economy. It was a great cause to celebrate.

The awards at Christmas party were just too funny. It was more like recognition or make-fun-of-things, e.g. the biggest foot, the guy who looked the strongest, the one who wore the ugliest shoes, the sexiest pants on the floor, etc. Each year it was different. Most of the employees got a twenty-dollar gift certificate.

The company helped out the poor neighborhoods and schools as quietly as possible. Cidy made sure there would be no news coverage or bragging by the company. Even employees didn't know that their company helped out with the local charity works.

Cidy said, "This is how God said to help the neighbors—secretly."

The company couldn't explain the phenomenon that was happening in the company—employees started to really worked together very well. There were more laughter and commotion in the company, but the company made more money.

The upper management couldn't explain the deal either, but they knew Cidy was at the center of this. They never mentioned in the meeting because they didn't wanted to make it official. They didn't want her to be in the upper management team, but Jeff didn't mention about the Cidy's amazing role in the company either. He knew the magic Cidy brought to the company because even he enjoyed working. He could never prove Cidy's affect in company's performance, but he knew it.

Jeff knew Cidy had bought some enemies with her success. It was a very unusual thing. The upper management team felt defeated after five years of negative projection had been missed by mile. They couldn't believe how their own company performed better each year when their competitions did poorly.

Whenever Cidy came into Jeff's office for approval or request, he purposely had a long talk with her. Cidy made him feel comfortable and happy. He liked knowing about little things about his company. He liked her a lot as a girl, as an employee, and as a friend. He sort of felt enchanted with her, but he made sure he doesn't cross the line, although he was tempted many times.

He imagined having Cidy as his lover or mistress.

Cidy never seemed to show any sign of coming on to him.

He felt she was just too innocent.

But above all, he didn't want his relationship with Cidy to be awkward at all. He didn't want to lose her as an employee, bust mostly as a friend. She was his treasure—a great employee and a friend—the secret weapon.

Jeff always thanked her and gave her appreciation for the success that Cidy has brought to the company, and she thanked Jeff for his appreciation.

She always said to Jeff—*I just did what is right. I'm just trying to make the company more like a family and friends. Family and friends—that's who we are.*

After the first year of Cidy, the employee turnover ratio dropped virtually zero, very few left the company. HR manager was praised for his work, but the upper management had no simple explanation for the company's success in low employee turn-over ratio. They said it was the bonus they paid each year which became bigger each year and quite large. The company paid the employees for the profit as much as they can, because Jeff wanted to share the fruit of their work as much as possible.

And of course, the bonus helped the employees' moral, but Jeff knew it was because the employees started to work together better that their bonus got bigger. They started to show more care and dedication for the company and for each other. He knew it was Cidy who closed the gap between the employees, and between him and the employees.

He started love his employees. He felt they were just workers passing through, but Cidy made him to think that they are brothers, sisters and friends. He wanted to make the company like a family—a one big happy family. He tried to talk the employees as much as he can. He made time for them. He prayed for them as well.

With the economy facing the worst and with the company's projection of negative performance for past five years, against all odds, the company profited in a record-setting number. He and the management team were surprised by their performances, and gave major bonuses out to all the employees for past five years, while their competitions were cutting employees and down-sizing, and having record losses.

Jeff thanked God for bring in his family back together, success in the company operation, giving him faith back, but mostly for Cidy.

CH 47: Cidy's New Life

Cidy can't help thinking about what Mom just told her—*God has a plan for her life*. The dream she had and the message that Mom received years ago coincide perfectly.

Cidy looks through the window, and notices her reflection, and sees the clear blue sky with a few clouds flowing, and thinks about her future life. She meditates again, *What is God's plan for me.*

A lot of things will change, Cidy concludes.

As Cidy slowly turns around, all the *009 Girls* rushed in to her room. With the excitement of tonight's party, the girls giggle and ramble like teenage girls. They are jumping out of control like their third-grader kids. She thinks that girls will be girls. She gets up and shares the joy and excitement. They become louder and louder.

"Okay girls…CLAM it DOWN! Got work to do." Tammy steps in and pours the cold water over the excitement, and tries to get down to business. She is more serious than others, most of time as well, but she means well.

Cidy looks at the girls and stops at Tammy, and can't help but to thank Tammy for all the great time that she had here. She knows she's going to miss Tammy the most.

Tammy says, "Cidy! …what? What's wrong?"

Cidy quickly covers up and smiles. "You look so beautiful today!"

Tammy smirks, and senses something is not right, but she has an urgent matter to discuss—the talent show.

"Okay. Jayla, Amanda, Sandy, ready? Paula, Kathy, ready? Jin, Julie, Cidy, Nadeera, ready? I'm set. You guys better be ready. The show time is only several hours away." Tammy slams the girls down for the preparation.

Each girl answers Tammy with an empathic *yes.*

Cidy kept staring at Tammy and Sandy, mostly. She couldn't help it. She loved all the *009 Girls*, but Tammy and Sandy were the ones she couldn't forget. She remembers, when she first started working for the company, many called Tammy—Mrs. T, T Rex, Terrible Tammy, and other awful and cursing names. But now they just call her Tammy or Sweet Tammy.

Tammy noticed Cidy's stare again, and says, "Cidy…say what's on your mind. What is it?"

"I'm hungry. When we gonna go eat?" Cidy has to say something quickly.

"Hold your hungry horse, Dear. We go eat when we check off our list, first. First thing, first." Tammy shows her tough side when she has to. She has that voice of authority that can't be easily denied.

Tammy is going over all the details again.

Cidy acts like she is paying attention….

CH 48: TAMING OF TAMMY

It was the final interview—the interview with CEO, Jeff Hawkins. They said it was more of a formality of saying "Hi" to CEO. But whatever the reason the conversation between CEO and Cidy had gotten quite long. She could feel he was trying to let her feel comfortable about him or just trying to lower her guards—whatever the case she enjoyed it. They said it would only take a few minutes with Jeff, but it took about an hour or more.

"You are quite interesting. Love your stories." Jeff made a compliment towards the end of the final interview.

"Thank you, Mr. Hawkins." Cidy returned with a big smile.

"Jeff."

"Okay, Jeff."

Jeff made his final words before saying *Welcome aboard.* "I'm gonna be honest with you, Cidy. We are hiring you to take over some of the roles, especially events and functions coordination, that Tammy Robertson is in charge with…. You either have to work with her or fire her…. We will give you three months to decide…. Nice meeting you, Cidy. Welcome aboard." CEO gave an honest job-at-task to Cidy, and reached out for a shake.

"Me too." Cidy shook Jeff's hand involuntarily. She really had no idea what her tasks is although she has a concept of it.

After leaving the CEO's office, Cidy stopped at the HR Manager's room as she was instructed before having the final meeting with CEO.

The company hired Cidy to replace Tammy, but the company said they are "up-grading" her. HR Manager, Gary Smith, laughed when he said it.

Gary briefly explained about Tammy: "She started working for the company from the day one or close to the day one. She got the company settled down, and made sure everything got in order. She sacrificed a lot for the company's current success, but gained a bad reputation for her overzealous attitude for perfection in recent few years."

He concluded, "That is a nice way of putting it."

After a brief pause, he smiled, and he observed for Cidy's respond.

Cidy wanted her own assessment of Tammy, so she stayed calm.

Then Gary continued, "She is in everyone's business and has little control of what she says. She is like a "mini" CEO that no one can stand up too. Tammy makes everyone quite miserable, but no one can say much to her because she is the hero of the company. A few have tried reasoning with her, including me, but she didn't take it too well. That's an understatement. We even had a long talk with CEO. He's pretty much a great guy and a good leader, except when it comes to Tammy. Tammy was one of his first employees, and he feels he owes great debt to them especially her. He couldn't fire her. Her title is now General Manager which stands for everything and nothing. She has no one under her. She is no longer part of any management team, but she just kept her role of the company as the company grew. All the upper management advised Jeff to fire her several times, but he refused. Finally, he decided to try something different. He decided to hire someone new—you, Cidy—to take over some of what Tammy does and see if Tammy can still work in the company as "general helper" keeping the same damn title— General Manager. You got this, Cidy."

"Is there anything I need to know about Tammy?" Cidy had to ask because Gary had a look that he want to say something more.

"Well…you are gonna hear this anyway. Mind as well." Gary was itching to say it. "We had a major disaster in one of our major events with our business partners. We lost a major client from a silly and minor incident. We almost lost one even before that, but we manage to salvage the client with much effort from Jeff."

Gary stopped briefly, knowing that Cidy will ask what had happened.

"What happened?" Cidy asked as expected.

"It was a minor incident. Tammy… (He was going to cuss, but held the word in) got into the client's face over a minor incident. He touched the wall arts making them look unbalanced, and she made a simple degrading remark to instruct the client to keep his hand off. The client got offended but kept quiet throughout the event and cancelled all his business ties with the company. The company lost 10% of our revenue through a single offending incident. More painful for Jeff was such an incident was foretelling and warned by other employees. As a result, Jeff had a hard decision to make of letting

Tammy go or keeping her. At least, he knew we had to hire a new employee for the event coordinating for investment, buyers and sales. The company decided to hire a culturally diverse and detailed oriented yet people-friendly woman to make sure company promotional events and parties are done properly and successfully without offending any buyers and investors."

"I see." Cidy gave a cordial respond as Gary made another brief stop.

Gary seemed to gather his thoughts, and he spilled his last words. "After interviewing over fifty ladies, Cidy, you are our first choice. CEO personally hand-picked you. He had never done this before at least since I got on board. He usually went with the consensus, but this time he hand selected you. I said you are too young to have any savvy to handle the task or deal with Tammy. ...I'm hoping...you prove me wrong."

Cidy felt good, but also felt unwanted pressure.

Gary observed Cidy again as if he was trying to catch any sign of disturbance.

Cidy thought, *I guess he's having this conversation to see my responds or check my mental status. Is he recording this?*

"I'm gonna come clean with you, Cidy. Here's what I think. Maybe...you already know this. Jeff wants to keep his hand clean. I think he wants to fire Tammy, but he can't himself for friendship or loyalty or whatever. So he hires a hired gun for the job. So, he...all of us at the management can keep our hands clean. I think it's a slick political move by Jeff to keep his image clean. I wish you the best of luck with Tammy." As he said his finally sentence, he rose from his seat and offered his hand for a shake. "Just check with me on your first day. You need to sign a few more paper. Okay?"

"Yes. Thank you." Cidy shook his hand and nodded.

When Cidy came to work for the first day, everyone except Tammy showed a welcoming smile. Cidy remembered the company's warning about her. Her first assignment was to keep Tammy by somehow working with her, or fire her. She had a very daunting task besides getting to know her job; her first task in the real world wasn't an easy assignment; in fact, quite demoralizing—firing someone was the last in her mind.

Cidy started to work with Tammy while trying to tame her or while deciding to fire her; her first option was to work with her, naturally, and keep her in the company. So, she, first, tried to find as much about Tammy as possible.

Tammy was in her early forties divorced with two kids in high school—one boy, one girl. She graduated from a top-notch college with double majors in business and chemistry. She was smart and tough. She was an over-achiever, a perfectionist, and a bully. She got the job done with the expense of others' feeling and time. She received most of the credit in early company's success, but created a lot of animosity in the company since then. Only person who appreciated her work was Jeff, and that was all it mattered to her.

Cidy asked Tammy for additional files in the know-how of the company's event preparations. Tammy didn't cooperate with Cidy at all; she gave Cidy hard time as much as possible.

Each day, Cidy tried to communicate with Tammy to learn the ropes and the plays that company had when it came to the event preparation and coordination. She had done preparation for parties and events in college, but not for any company. She had to learn something very new for the first time, and she was not getting any help. Tammy just gave a lot of empty promises and excuses. It was very frustrating for Cidy.

Others in the company felt sorry for Cidy, but they couldn't come out and say anything. They didn't want to cross Tammy, not openly. A few employees did call Cidy anonymously and encouraged her. But for Cidy, encouragement did little to help her solve Tammy.

Tammy got harder and harder to deal with, each day, and Cidy was on a verge of firing her. She was tempted. She felt firing her will solve the problem quickly. She thought about threatening Tammy that she had the power to fire her, but somehow she didn't think that will work. She wanted to make it work by not threatening and not firing. She fasted three days to tame or be in peace with Tammy. She didn't get any answer from her prayer, but gave her enough confidence to handle Tammy.

Working with Tammy and learning about her position during the first month at work, Cidy learned very little.

Cidy visited Jeff, and complained about Tammy. Jeff didn't say much. She knew he was in a bear trap too, but had to let her frustration out hoping to return her burden of Tammy back to Jeff. She was on the verge of quitting.

"I'll have a talk to her." Jeff reluctantly responded with heavy face. He never had so much weight on his consciousness before. He had never turned his back on his friends before. It wasn't his way of life. Tammy was one of his dearest friends; he felt he had debt to Tammy that can never be paid back. Tammy was his arms and legs and that force that never gave up when he couldn't pay the employees for three, four months.

Jeff probably had a talk with Tammy, but she didn't change.

In fact, Tammy became even tougher than ever. She felt Cidy was just a fresh, innocent girl in a jungle where she had the upper-hand with shrewdness and experiences. She toyed with Cidy. But, Tammy did feel something different about Cidy, because Cidy didn't get angry or showed any sign of anger as much as Tammy would like to see. Tammy pulled every trick in the book, even tried tripping her a few times when she passed by her on the hall way. Luckily, Cidy didn't fall: She sort of skipped, hopped, twisted, and turned, and walked right along as if she enjoyed it. It was lame, but Tammy wanted Cidy out of the company like an F-16 lifting off from a carrier.

After two months, Cidy had to stand up and take charge, or she had to quit or fire Tammy. Her first job was killing her: It was a fight of her life, more like a beating. She doubted about her answer from fasting and reading the bible that she should take this poor-paying job, instead of all those glorious ones. She was lost: She prayed about the job. She didn't want to fail. The fear of failure was making her miserable. But each day her daily devotion before work gave more than enough spirit to deal with Tammy and her own self-doubt just for that day. It was like that verse—Today's trouble is enough for today.

Cidy played reserved and calm, but it looked to Tammy as if Cidy is a coward and a pushover.

Tammy was the experienced boxer taking on a novice challenger stepping into the ring of the real world. She was going to stick and slide, having the fun of her life by making Cidy miserable.

Cidy prayed and sought for wisdom. She tried to find out Tammy's weak spot or what makes Tammy tick. She realized Tammy was just a perfectionist doing her job the best way she knows how—perfect. Tammy felt much of the success of the company is her accomplishment: Tammy's ego in the company exuded in her every word. What Tammy needed was a mother figure giving her assurance that everything is okay, but that was not easy: Tammy was older, and had dominating characteristics.

Tammy was having fun with Cidy: Cidy was her favorite dessert--a nice big slice of cheese cake with real-dairy whip-cream with a big juice cherry on top. She never knew Cidy could fire her; she was totally out of the loop.

Tammy never gave Cidy an inch. She felt threaten that Cidy is going to eventually take her job away, so she tried to keep her lunch tray instinctively. But Cidy's cool demeanor and smile made Tammy soften up after two months, but not by much to be noticed by Cidy.

After two months, Cidy fasted again for three days for wisdom about Tammy. On the third day, Cidy had a feeling that she should tell her, *I love you*. She prayed about the answer. She had no idea how to love someone like Tammy. She prayed more, crying for help. Then she realized that it was not her who loves her, but it is Jesus that loves Tammy through her. Cidy repented, felt good, and made a plan to invite Tammy for breakfast, and to give her a present, and to say *I love you*.

At work, Cidy, before leaving home, asked Tammy for a breakfast date at Denny's next day. Tammy had no idea what's planned for her. Tammy thought she won the fight. Tammy loved Denny's, so she agreed; besides, she thought, *I'm getting a free breakfast as well, so…might as well.*

Next day, they met at Denny's, and had a breakfast. Tammy ordered everything she liked and more. She was going to enjoy a nice breakfast, and stiff Cidy as well. Eating her favorite food and giving a big fat check to Cidy made Tammy feel over exhilarating. While eating, Tammy lowered her guard as if she won the fight, and talked about a lot of things.

Tammy and Cidy talked about three hours: Tammy opened her heart and talked about her tough childhood and life. She didn't know why she was talking to Cidy about all these things of her past. She wasn't herself. She felt a wall crumbling down around her—a wall that she has built to protect and guard herself from the world. This wasn't in her plan. She opened up so much that she felt vulnerable. She didn't like it that Cidy knew her too well, now. She thought, *Am I losing the fight against Cidy. No! I need to stop. She might pull the rug under me.* She stopped talking feeling she fell into a trap.

After three hours of mostly listening, Cidy said, "I got a gift for you Tammy. Wait here."

Tammy was surprised to hear the word—gift. It was not her birthday.

Cidy brought a dozen of roses in red and yellow, and a beautiful bird figurine, and said,

"Tammy, I love you. ...I know you have much fear about me. ...I really need your help. ...And I do really love you." Cidy looked into Tammy eyes.

Tammy was waiting for a punch line, but Cidy kept staring into her eyes. Her eyes got all watery. She tried to stop feeling vulnerable. It's not something that she wanted to show to anyone, especially Cidy. She hadn't heard those words—*I love you*—for a long time. She just wanted to be loved and be appreciated for her work, but received very little of it. She couldn't hold it anymore; she poured. She wailed.

Cidy got around the table and hugged Tammy.

Cidy didn't say anything, just hugged her.

Finally Tammy hugged Cidy back, and said, "I'm sorry Cidy. I'm so sorry for giving you such a hard time. I...I..."

"It's okay. I know.... I love you...Tammy." Cidy shared the tears with her. She didn't know why she was crying either.

"Thank you. I really need that. I love you, Cidy. I'm sorry...so...." Tammy panted. She tried hard to recover her composure, but all the sorrow that was locked up for decades just burst out. She never felt so relieved.

Cidy obeyed to God, and God opened Tammy's heart for her. She learned if she obeyed to God, He will do his part—the greatest miracle of all— opening people's heart.

"I don't know what to say, Cidy. ...." Tammy went on for a while.

When Tammy stopped crying, talking, and got her composure back, Cidy asked her for help, again, "I really need your help Tammy. Can you help me?"

Tammy laughed and smirked, "I'm your man, Cidy. I'm your man."

Since then, Tammy became Cidy's right-hand woman, and helped Cidy in every possible way. Tammy reported anything and everything to Cidy, and Cidy kept her ego in check. Tammy's perfectionism and Cidy's understanding of the people worked in perfect harmony.

The company was very surprised that they worked together so well.

Jeff felt relieved because he didn't have to fire Tammy: he was able to save his conscious by keeping Tammy.

CH 49: CHECKING THE LIST

Today, Tammy keeps the girls in order. She has made a list of all the details that needs to be done precisely. She points out each member. The girls think the last night's practice was it, but Tammy has a long list that she's going over.

A girl whispers loudly enough for everyone to hear, "Can't handle this. I'm just glad it's only once a year."

"I can hear you, Jayla." Tammy meets her nose to nose, and frowns.

All the girls giggle and laugh.

Tammy puts her hand up signaling to quiet. The girls stop giggling.

Cidy enjoys every moment. She glares at Sandy and wants to talk to her about her date she had last night, but she knows it has to wait.

"Sandy, you missed last night's practice— our final practice. I'm on to you. We're on to you." Tammy knows something is up with Sandy too. All the girls know something is up with Sandy, but she isn't talking. They tried to get some scoop out of Cidy last night, but she didn't budge either.

Sandy wants to shout to the world what happened, but she knows better. "I was a bit dizzy and sick. You know I stayed home." Sandy lied.

"Yah, I went to Buckingham Palace last night to have date with Prince Williams." Tammy makes

her point. "You know we'll find out sooner or later."
She gave that all-knowing stare at Sandy.

Sandy gives a blank face.

Cidy winks at Sandy.

Tammy double checks again. The girls
answer with "Yes, ma'am." Tammy is a perfectionist.
The girls don't mind Tammy because she's more
than sweet most of the time. To them, Tammy is
Sweet Tammy, now. Only a few remember Tammy
as Mrs. T.

Knowing there are only a few more months
left with them, Cidy can't help it to observe Tammy,
Sandy, and all the girls much closer than usual.

Tammy feels Cidy is different today, but lets
it go for now.

"The show must be perfect," Tammy thinks
out loud because that's her prerogative.

"Pay attention, girls. We are going to win the
first place, this year. Right!" Tammy isn't tall, but her
words and tone of voice just sucks in the attention of
everyone.

"Yes, ma'am!" Girls respond in chorus.

"I CAN'T HEAR YOU!" As each word got
louder and higher, Tammy goes into her tough
sergeant mode.

"YES, MA'AM!" Girls shout even louder.

"Cidy, I can't hear you!" As she points her
finger right at Cidy, Tammy warns her to pay
attention.

Cidy smiles and straightens her posture.
"Yes, ma'am!"

Tammy's bully attitude takes Cidy to a time
travel to her childhood when she first experienced a
bully:

CH 50: Kevin, the Goliath

That Sunday, Cidy had been taught about King David. She clearly remembered the Sunday-school teacher's word, "You stand up and fight against evil. God will fight for you. You will win." She had taken the lesson into her heart. Although she felt too weak to face Kevin, the lesson gave her more than enough confidence to stand up against the school bully—Kevin.

Kevin never bothered girls much, but Cidy didn't like Kevin bullying other boys. He was a sore in her eye.

"Move over Tommy before I kick your ass!" Kevin's words ringed around the playground, striking fear in everyone, even Cidy. It was at the playground during a recess, like a déjà vu, when Kevin bullied another boy.

Tommy quickly moved away knowing the consequence if he didn't.

It was a lovely and peaceful day, but on this playground, there was fear, like any other days, among the kids as Kevin made his way through pushing boys around for fun.

Cidy remembered Kevin being a nice kid, but she had no idea when and what happened to him. He just became a mean bully, one day.

It was time to act for Cidy. With the word she learned from Sunday school, she decided to become a "King David" like she was taught. She walked over to Kevin.

Kevin saw her coming over, but didn't think much about it.

But soon, she quickly got in to his face, and loudly said, "STOP it, Kevin!"

That wasn't what Kevin expected from her. He was shocked but realized that he needed to get in control, quick.

Suddenly, all the kids turned their faces to where Cidy voice came from, and realized it was Cidy facing up to Kevin. They quickly gathered around her and Kevin, like a bunch little ants around a chip of cookie.

Cidy could see the tiny brown freckles on Kevin's face, and stated firmly and sharply with her cute girl's voice with her left index finger pointing at Kevin's face, "Kevin, you ought to be ashamed of yourself picking on someone smaller and weaker than you! Kevin, behave and be a good boy!"

Kevin had a mean streak in him, and kids knew it, especially the boys. None of the boys were willing to challenge him anymore; a few already had and learned their lesson painfully. He was the boy to beat. He was athletic, strong, and even cute, but whatever the reason he just enjoyed picking on the other boys.

Kevin was surprised but tickled that Cidy confronted him. He gave a little nose laugh first, and slowly tilting his head stared at Cidy, and walked up a step closer to her while lifting his chin up slightly to right, trying to put some fear in her. Kevin learned this from a movie, and he practiced at home many times, and it worked like a charm. Most fights never even got to the first base: Kevin's stare and a few mean words would finish it. He stared down at Cidy like he had done so many times to other boys.

Cidy was a tall girl but not as tall as Kevin. Kevin knew most of the kids would back off, by now, when he gave them the "death stare" right up to their faces, and he expected her to back up. But whatever the reason, it didn't work on her, and Kevin felt a little unwanted pressure. He didn't want to back down, especially by a girl. And he didn't want to beat her either. It caused a little dilemma in him that made him shake his head slowly.

All the kids were afraid that Kevin would beat Cidy up or push her down hard, but they, on the other hand, wanted to see Cidy get whipped as well. They knew what was brewing; they had seen this before. A few strong and big boys tried to take on Kevin and lost the fight quickly and painfully.

Kevin had that natural instinct in fighting. He realized it after his first fight that he had a mean punch and was a pretty good fighter. That was when he beat *Numero Uno*—Big Kyle, a fifth grader. That shocked all the boys in school. All the boys feared Kevin.

Kevin wanted to end this quickly because it just didn't look good for him. As he squinted his eyes even more tightly and angrily trying to display his furor more seriously as possible, he tightened his fists. He never expected a girl to stand up against him, but he didn't cared, now. He was going to make her kiss the ground hard. He slowly lifted his fist targeting for Cidy's face but suddenly words from his Grandma rang in his ears—*Don't you ever hit a girl, Kevin! That would be greatest shame in our family. You hear!*

Cidy saw his fist and got scared, but remembered her Sunday-school teacher saying, "Goliath will not fall if you don't fight him." She didn't know how to fight against Kevin or boys. They always pushed, shoved, and wrestled. This was not something she was used to. She remembered getting fights with the boys before, but they never had gotten to the point of hitting each other. They pushed her, and she managed to push them just as hard settling the dispute to a standoff. But she had seen Kevin fight, it was different: They threw punches hard at each other. She feared she would get beaten up by Kevin, but she trusted in the Lord and continued without backing off.

When Kevin hesitated hitting her, Cidy took a step even closer to Kevin meeting his squint for squint, staring up at his blue eyes. She thought, *Kevin is cute but he has to learn a lesson about bullying other kids.*

If they weren't fighting, kids probably thought they were going to kiss each other. They stared at each other like two cobras going at it each other—a show down in the playground. All the kids' eyes were locked in, and they were very quiet trying to catch every word spoken and not miss any action.

Cidy opened her mouth first, and spat those solid words like a respectable teacher, "I'm disappointed in you, Kevin. I don't think you're a bad person. I don't know what's got into you, but Kevin, I know, you are not a bully. Now go and play with your friends nicely, and leave Tommy alone. He hasn't done anything to you."

Kevin felt ashamed, but fuming, he got even closer to Cidy. Now their foreheads were touching each other. Kevin knew Cidy was not his match but he didn't care. As Kevin lifted his fist even higher, Cidy didn't back up, she got even angrier and stomped her foot.

It looked like he was going to throw his punch, but Kevin instead of throwing the punch said sharply, "Mind your own business, you little...!" He shoved her away. Kevin shoved her hard as he can, and Cidy fell hard on the ground. Kevin smirked expecting Cidy to cry and back off, but she came right back at his face. Kevin felt a little intimated by Cidy, now.

Staring right up into Kevin's eyes, Cidy quickly lashed back, "Tommy is MY friend and YOUR friend too. We grew up together. We are ALL friends, here. Friends don't pick on each other."

The words Cidy spoke made perfect sense to Kevin but still felt very angry for Cidy stepping in and ruining his pride and reputation. He felt disgraced by her. She was going to ruin his reputation as the "baddest" boy in school. He had no choice but to put her down, but his thought process got all messed up with his Grandma's voice repeating in his ears. A few seconds slowly flowed feeling like an eternity for everybody.

Cidy threw the final words, "KEVIN, you are going to be a good man. This is WHERE it's going to START!"

Suddenly, Kevin's heart changed. He wanted to grow up to be a good man like his Grandma always said. He remembered his spoiling grandma always saying to him, *Kevin, you will be a good man. You will put your trust in God.*

When his Grandma passed away a few years ago, Kevin had anger that he couldn't control; he was angry at a lot things since then. Those exact words from Cidy made him remember his grandma. Remembering Grandma's words, he lowered his fist and his head, and turned around, and backed off, and walked away.

Kids couldn't believe what had just happened.

Kevin wanted to cry remembering Grandma, but he got out of there quickly. He was ashamed.

Cidy walked away too, and everybody went to their normal screaming-and-laughing mode in matter of seconds. Kids talked about the incident for a few days, but it wasn't a big deal for them.

And Kevin started played with other kids fine and even with Cidy. He lost a lot of his mean streaks after the incident. In fact, he now became a protector for kids getting bullied. He quickly became popular among the kids. Kids loved him now. He became new "Sheriff" of the playground.

CH 51: CIDY AND JAKE

Cidy nods that she ready for the tonight's show. The *009 Girls* make a circle following Tammy's order. They put their right hands in the middle and shout, "Break a Leg!"

As the girls return to their spots, Sandy turns around and gives a look to Cidy saying I need to talk to you right now.

Cidy gives a quick nod because she knows she needs to talk with her. She returns to her seat, and sitting, she sees Jake passing across the office. She enjoys the sight of Jake. She is amazed how one guy can take so much control over her thoughts.

She evaluates Jake: Jake, Jake Calhoun, isn't handsome but caught her eye. He is tall and lean, not muscular, and has dark brown hair and hazel eyes. He is a quiet and strong type, not much of a party dude or an attention getter. He is a riddle to other girls as to her.

Girls in the office like him but hate him as well, because he just won't respond or reach out to them like the others. Cidy likes that about Jake. Girls kid that he might be gay, but they know Jake likes girls because Jake would stare at girls sometimes and veer off when he gets caught. He is a gentleman, kind and courteous, but his lack of interest in girls drove girls wild, even Cidy. Jake has no idea that girls and even Cidy have so much interest in him.

Cidy is afraid Jake is just a Sunday Christian. She feels the burden of letting Jake go because she senses she will be leaving the company soon for Christ. She starts to doubt about her prayer answer that Jake is to be the love of her life.

Jake paces through the offices looking busy, and today, he is busy but finds time to check Cidy out from a far. He knows he is going to miss seeing Cidy. His heart is breaking.

Jake too evaluates Cidy: Cidy is cute and petite. She isn't glamorous but has enough to make guys seek her attention. Most of the single guys and several married ones in the office have tried to get her interest. A few have made daring moves and failed. Guys like that Cidy don't give them a cold shoulder when they try to bait her but gets a "kind-but-no-thank-you" respond. Cidy is *Cool Cidy* to many guys in the office.

For Jake, he is in love with her for five years, and knows very little about her. He is glad she's a Christian, but worries she is not serious enough about her faith as he is, especially when he has received his calling this morning. He hurts deeply that he might have to let her go because of his calling.

Cidy remembers when Jake asked her out,
Jake came to her office and bluntly and coyly said, 'Can you…o…I mean…ah…would you…ah…have a dinner with me?'

Cidy can't help it to smile thinking about that whole week when five guys asked her out for dinner:

Jake was the fourth guy, that week, who asked her out, and totaled to five by Friday noon of that week. She detected something is up: one guy asking out was more than flattering but five, in a week,—something was definitely up.

Later Cidy learned that a week before the "asking-out" week, five bachelors in the company made a bet to see who can succeed in getting her for a date. Five bachelors made every move as possible to get a date with her. She enjoyed the attention. But, she decided to turn the table against them and secretly told each one of them she would give a text answer by Saturday morning.

Cidy wrote to each one the same message—I really like you. I was surprised when you ask me out. I was waiting. But I don't want any else to know about us dating. I want this kept as secret …. You know. So please come to Ciao on I-10 and Gessner, 7 pm tonight. Please don't tell anyone. I hope to get to know you. I will see you there. Love Cidy.

They all thought they had the date.

Later Cidy heard that all five guys got there, and they were surprised to see each other. They realized they been had by Cidy but they were very happy.

Cidy wanted to date Jake but not like that.

Jake makes sure he's not too close but not too far to see Cidy. He feels silly but this is just as far as his courage would allow. He saw the *009 Girls* walking out of Cidy's office a few minutes ago. He knows they are up to something for tonight's show. Last year they won the second prize for acting silly. He and the company employees just had a ball with their acts. All the employees still have fun talking about their last-year act.

Jake's is singing again: this time a Willie Nelson song—*Always on My Mind*. He has Cidy in his mind—always. He remembers time when he wrote love songs for Jane in college. He still remembers a couple of songs he wrote for her; it is very hard to forget. But now he writes love songs thinking about Cidy. He plays them home, often. He's got over twenty songs he wrote for her.

CH 52: JAKE'S LOVE SONG

December's cool breeze was just nice enough to leave the windows open for Jake. It does get cold after late evening, but it was nice till then. With the windows opened, it really helps the air get refreshed in the apartment. He just came back from Church's prayer meeting. He took his jacket off, and crashed on the sofa. It was an old one, covered with a thin spread sheet, which just kept coming off. He should have washed it years ago, but he never got around it. That was how he liked to think of it: Not lazy but just hadn't time.

He always felt very lonely about this time of the night. He always wished for Cidy to be next to him. Although his heart belonged to Cidy, he had a young girl in a church in mind tonight, but he just can't make a sense of being with her. She was just too young. Kerrie was there tonight. She made a strong approach on him. She stared him and gave him that unmistakable look that says *I'm into to you*.

He regrets maybe it was him that gave Kerrie too much sign that he's interested in her. He didn't mean it. It all started out as innocent gestures of playful tease since she was little. He saw her as just a little girl, although Kerrie is a very attractive girl now. Most of the boys were more than attracted to her. It was up to Kerrie to choose who she wanted to be with. Jake never called her except once or twice for some church picnics or events, but he never said anything to make her think otherwise.

Kerrie made a move that shook Jake's heart.

He started to pray. He knew his heart is for Cidy, but Kerrie was more than attractive alternative. He couldn't help it to ponder about Kerrie versus Cidy. He felt he's betraying Cidy and God.

He had known Kerrie about seven years. He had seen cute little Kerrie grow up to be a find lady. She was in middle school going in to high when he first saw her. Kerrie had long beautiful black hair and big lovely, greenish eyes that were just so beautiful, and she was just so adorable. He had mentioned to her how cute she was during her high school years at the church, and he had seen her grow up. Kerrie just turned twenty. She was so beautiful, but Jake can't get his mind to think of Kerrie as a girl to him.

He decided he's just going to ignore her, and hoped the best for her. He felt sick how easily he's love for Cidy could be rattled, but he guessed maybe it was a test on his love for Cidy. He felt bad that he didn't really pass the test in a flying color.

He quickly reached out for his guitar. He practiced the songs he wrote for Cidy. He strolled in C major and sang these words:

> You are so beautiful.
> Like the calm sunset lake.
> Giving me so much hope for life.
> Can't promise you the heaven.
> For I will fail you in many ways.
> But I promise I'll love you forever.
>
> You'll always be my world.

For I breathe you for my every
thought.
I'm praying for you every night.
Can't promise you the stars.
For I will fail you in many ways.
But I promise I'll love you forever.

I'm so glad you are mine.
I'm so glad you are mine
I'll be lost and lonely like a
wondering wind,
If I don't have your love.

Can't promise you the moon.
For I will fail you in many ways.
But I promise I'll love you forever
Can't promise you the moon.
For I will fail you in many ways.
But I promise I'll love you forever

CH 53: Jake's Pain

      Jake is busy today and this week especially. His department has to make sure most of the end of the quarter and the end of the year paper work are done. All the other departments are loosened except the accounting department. But his mind ping-pongs back and forth between Cidy and the calling.

      Jake returns to his desk, feeling good that he had seen Cidy and bad that he won't be seeing her anymore. He wants to see Cidy as much as possible before quitting the job. The mixed emotion churns the inside of him.

      He feels maybe he was never meant to be with Cidy. But he had prayed for her love so many times and so much. His steps are heavy as he feels his heart trapped.

      He wonders if God kept him from Cidy, so God can use him in his ministry.

      He thinks, "It was just last night that I was singing a love song for her."

CH 54: CIDY

Cidy checks for any e-mail, just in case if she needs to be ready for anything unexpected for tonight. The company e-mail messages are mostly all routine ones—all the little announcements that people don't really care for. There is one for tonight's Christmas party.

She has been praying for Jake to be her husband for five years now, and she really wants to start a relationship about now, and to date him a year or two, and get married, and have a normal, happy life, although that's all been changed this morning.

She, being a woman, knows her destiny of beauty would be the same like all other women of the past: She too will get old and lose that attractiveness she feels it would be there forever. That has been the history for woman: young and popular; old and revered.

That's how God made women, she thinks.

Cidy wishes she had waved at Jake, but knows better. But after this morning's conversation with Mom, she knows drastic changes are coming to her life very soon because God has a plan for her life: She will be involved in some sort of ministry, somehow.

She hasn't much to do today, but worries what she is going to wear to the party.

Suddenly, Sandy walks in says, "I want to thank you for everything. It's so hard to keep it inside."

Cidy has forgotten about Sandy because of her own priorities. She knows about the date that Mark and Sandy had last night. She is dying to know.

Cidy says, "Sorry, I was about to go and have a chat with you. Let's hear it. Give me every little, hot, sizzling details, Girl!"

Sandy is hyper and starts talking too fast.

Cidy clams her down.

Sandy takes a breath and says, "Oh my God!" Sandy has a big smile, and slows down to say, "I played cool and reserved as much as possible. I tried not to giggle and laugh too much like you told me. It was hard. Mark got nervous that I didn't respond to a lot of his quickies to get us going.... I had a wonderful time." Sandy went on for a while.

Cidy enjoyed every word. She nods and digs in for more details. She lets Sandy let all the air out of her.

Finally, Sandy stops with a relief.

"Did Mark ask you out for the second date?" impatiently questions Cidy.

"Yes. And I said, 'No,' like you told me to," Sandy quickly answers proudly.

"Good." Cidy gave Sandy a confidence nod and a smirk as if she has gotten the whole plan down.

"I told Mark if I get involved with him it would be for marriage, not for fun. I said, 'If you ain't thinking of marriage don't even think about calling. I know you're a player and all. I ain't answering if I'm not thinking about you for marriage either.' ...Just like you told me too." Sandy quotes her own words such an animation.

Cidy feels such an adrenaline flow being a major part of Sandy's love life: She feels like Sandy being her avatar of sort. She just hopes best for her.

"Good. Did Mark call you back?" Cidy probes.

"Yes. He called me last night a few times about an hour after he dropped me off. I didn't answer it like you told me. And he tried to kiss me when he dropped me off. I turn my head quickly and walked away from him. He called me several times today already." Sandy's eyes are wide opened, and she proudly answers Cidy and gives all the up-to-date details.

"Nice. Mark has to play the game of love. Not hit and run." Cidy tries to make some sense to Sandy. She knows Sandy is in love with Mark and Mark is on a hot pursuit for her.

While talking with Sandy, Cidy misses Sandy because she knows she has to leave her and all the friends in the company behind. It feels like Cidy just met Sandy yesterday.

CH 55: SEtting Up HOt SanDy

Cidy knew right away when she first saw Sandy a little more than a year ago that Sandy would have problems in the company or cause problems. It wasn't Sandy exactly: It was the boys, or both. She knew boys would not leave her alone. So from the very first day of Sandy coming to work, Cidy asked Sandy to come in to her office and had three, long hours of talk. Mostly they talked about nothing, or everything.

During the final thirty minutes of talk, Cidy told Sandy to stay close to girls avoid man as much as possible. Sandy understood that had been her problem with other work places. Cidy then promised her that Sandy will find the right man if she followed her advice. That was the "gospel" Sandy needed. Sandy needed an adviser that gave her cold advice. She has turned 27 just a month ago; she really wanted to find a right man to settle down.

For the first month, Cidy had kept Sandy close to her and the girls so Sandy won't fall for any guys especially Mark. She didn't want give Sandy any room for guys to approach her, but even then, guys still approached her. Mark, known not to date company girls, made several smooth moves on her. Sandy couldn't help but to bash her eyes and show interest to Mark. But Sandy took the advice of Cidy: she didn't date him. More like, Sandy didn't even given him a chance. Cidy knew Mark had an irresistible charm; even she had hard time saying no to him four years ago.

After a month at work, Sandy found herself liking a couple of guys in the company: Jake and Mark. Sandy had set her heart for Mark and a distant second choice, Jake.

Cidy knew Sandy would choose Mark: All the girls chose Mark. It was a no brainer, but she also knew Mark would choose Sandy also because that was a no brainer too. She just had to have a plan to get them together properly.

Cidy knew Mark is a player, and Sandy a golden girl. Sandy just needed some guts to play tough to make this thing work.

Cidy told Sandy not to give any guy an eye, a flirt, or some space that they can slide in and make a move.

Sandy didn't like the idea but decided to follow. She felt she had nothing to lose. But, as soon as guys started to hit on her, especially Mark, Sandy felt the heat and wanted to give in, especially for Mark. Sandy would run into Cidy's office sometimes or call her at night asking for advice.

Cidy gave Sandy cold advice that she needed to make herself known to Mark and all the guys that she's not a player or teaser. She calmly counseled Sandy, "Be patience just for a year and then go out with Mark. Mark's not gonna give up on you. I'll promise you. He will pursue you even harder and harder. He's gonna find out you're the real thing."

Sandy had no idea what Cidy was talking about, but she didn't want to lose Mark. However, she decided to trust Cidy all the way, because, so

far, her easy acceptance of guys' date gotten her
nowhere.

As Cidy predicted, Mark's pursue for Sandy
did become more aggressive and more romantic:
Mark sent flowers and called her frequently, which
Sandy never accepted and answered. Mark would
call Sandy on different numbers and get hung up
when Sandy recognized Mark's voice. Sandy played
her role well as taught, and was amazed how Cidy
knew exactly what Mark would be doing.

About a year passed, Cidy told Sandy she
can date Mark if she wants to but warned her, "Don't
play easy."

Cidy said, "Don't be easy on the first date.
Don't laugh at all his jokes and let him get too close
to you. Let him treat you like a lady. If he doesn't
open the doors for you, walk away. If he tries to kiss
you, you got to refuse."

"Wow…I can't believe it. I can't have fun on
the first date?" Sandy questioned.

"Yes and no. Just keep the distance. You
can let him think you've been playing him. Don't take
things too fast. Once he feels that he got you, he's
gonna lose interest in you. Mark's been a player all
his life. No girl gave him a challenge. He's gonna
have to stake his life for you…just follow my advice."
Cidy kept her serious face and spoke in even tone to
make sure Sandy got the message.

"You think so?" Sandy wasn't too sure, but
she knew she could trust Cidy because everything
happened as exactly as Cidy said it would.

"Now this is very important after the first
date. You tell Mark this just before he lets you out of
his car. Don't call if he's not interested in marriage,
because you're not into dating for fun. And make

emphasis that you are not going to accept his calls if you are not thinking about marrying him either. You need to tell him THIS. If he keeps giving you excuses or sweet talking to make a move on you, just leave. Just leave wherever you are. Got it! You've got to stick to the plan, Okay?" Cidy coached Sandy.

Sandy listened very well.

"How do we know if we meant for each other if we don't continuously date?" Sandy asked an obvious question.

"I know it doesn't make any sense, but love doesn't make sense either. And certainly, Mark never made any sense either, all his life. We'll go plan B if this plan doesn't work. Trust me Sandy. He is not going to let you off of his hook." Cidy was pretty sure how Mark operated.

CH 56: Love for Sandy

"What do I do now?" Sandy is dying to know.

"Just keep calm. We'll play hard to get. Mark's gonna go crazy. I know it. He's hooked." Cidy continues her explanation, and builds up confidence in Sandy.

Sandy is nodding but she's not showing any sign of confidence. She doesn't understand this "hard-to-get" game she has to play for her love. She just wants to run after Mark and kiss him till they both die.

Cidy sees Sandy's desire for Mark, and Sandy's confused.

"Don't worry. Mark ain't going nowhere. He probably will come to your desk. When he comes, you must ask him to leave. If he doesn't, you just walk away and come to my office. Okay?" Cidy tries to make sure of all the details covered.

Sandy is confused: she doesn't know why she can't be honest with her feelings. She shows confusion on her face.

"Sandy, you trusted me so far. I didn't think you can pull it off, but you have waited faithfully for a year. We're…no…you are almost at the finish line. Trust me. Make Mark think that you are not serious about him. He will not give up on you," Cidy speaks with conviction.

"Okay. I'm sorry. I get carried away with my own feelings. Never felt so strong for a guy before.

Never been in love this deep before. I'm just so afraid to lose him. That's all." Sandy's face shows more comfort, and she smiles to convey Cidy that she has gotten it.

"All right, Sandy." Cidy walks up to Sandy.

Sandy stands up.

They hug for a while.

And Sandy leaves the room.

Cidy hopes that Sandy can wait for just a little longer.

"Love is such a hard game to play," she murmurs to herself.

CH 57: SANDY

Sandy, in her seat, is more than excited about the last night. She wants to confess to Mark that she loves him so much. She wants to run after him. She kept looking around to see if Mark is coming over to her. Her heart is pounding like a base drum. She is afraid others can hear it too.

She never had a guy that pursued her with so much passion and persistence for so long. And she is in love with him, maybe, from the very first sight.

He has sent flowers, letters, texts, and calls, and not to mention his frequent approaches. Every time she received a letter or some flowers, she felt exhilarated; she wanted to chase Mark down and give herself up. But, Cidy said no, wait for a year.

A year felt like an immovable mountain when Cidy first said it. But, Sandy somehow knew she had to have faith in Cidy, and managed to wait a year. It seemed like an eternity, but she had a lot of fun hanging out with the girls. She felt like the *009 Girls* are her best friends she ever had, especially Cidy.

Although Cidy is a few years younger than her, Sandy feels much respect for her because of her wit, leadership, wisdom, and friendship. She went to church with Cidy a few times. It was kind of awkward, but she's now going to a church, near her home, after receiving Holy Spirit. She's learning about Christ and faith, but she prays a lot because Holy Spirit leads her, although it's not something she is used to, yet. But she likes praying for the love of her life—Mark—and many other things she has no idea what she is praying for.

Sandy can almost grasp Mark. She feels he's everywhere and watching her. She feels a bit nervous. She knows she's got to wait like Cidy advised.

Sandy met boys on her own ways, and they all turned out to be very hurtful. She felt used. But she couldn't stop falling in love with them.

Now, she wants to settle down, and to have a family of her own. And it would be more than wonderful for her to have that family with her one true love—Mark.

She can't believe how she was able to resist Mark for so long. Mark just seems to have perfect timing and touch; he would make a memorable yet not-to-pushy contact with her in every possible way in most surprising moment.

Mark is not stalking her but Sandy could feel his presence everywhere: He is in her mind.

Sandy is shocked how exactly Cidy's prophesy that Mark will continuously purse her came true.

CH 58: MARK ASKS SANDY

A few days ago, Mark approached Sandy again.

Sandy intentionally waited for Mark, and passed by him.

Cidy said it was okay to give a chance to Mark and to date him now. She told her when Mark approaches her give him some goodies and lure him in to ask for a date, but don't get too excited, just play cool.

Mark never would have guessed that Sandy just made a move on him. She gave him a warm smile.

Sandy was afraid that Mark finally lost interest in her because Mark's hello wasn't as inviting or alluring as before.

Mark was desperate and lost much of his cherished confidence for Sandy. When she gave him a warm smile, he doubted himself. He didn't want to make a fool out of himself, again. But he mustered a little courage to say a few word: He stuttered like a broken record and couldn't find any cute words that were so easy for him, "Hi, uh…Sandy…. It…ah…ah…mighty fine…of…to see you." Mark had no idea what he just said. He felt like a blank gun.

Seeing Mark squirm like a bashful boy, Sandy smirked. It had been her all these times trying to hide her true feelings by basically keeping silent, but now Mark is squirming. He had no idea how his presence was just overwhelming for her, but today she feels like she had the upper hand.

"Hi, Mark." Sandy smiled bashfully and showed her irresistible shyness but inquisitive glare. She saw Mark's eye beaming suddenly.

Mark had been faked by that smile and the look so often, but he couldn't resist it, again. He bolstered all the courage he ever had to ask out for a date. He never had this problem before with any girl. He felt silly, but he was in love with her. He was in pain. His new idea about love was that it is painful than he ever imagined. He started to understand the pain the he had caused to the girls of his past.

He shyly spoke with uneven pitch, "Hey, hmm…Sandy. I…eh…eh…I…know you are not interested in me. But won't you…ah…just give me a chance." Mark's body turned back and forth while his mind was going on and off…flickering. He couldn't believe himself either.

He never asked a girl for a chance. It was not something he said to ask a girl out for a date. He coached many guys asking girls out, but this wasn't one of them. But he couldn't stop his body and mind from acting on its own. He just wanted a single chance from Sandy to prove himself that he is a worthy man.

Sandy brightened her eyes to show interest. Mark caught on and continued on with a little more confidence, "How about…ah…dinner tonight?" It sounded bad to him. He wanted to rephrase it. He wanted to say something more fancy but that was it. He sounded corny and unattractive, and he knew it. He was regretting what he said and how he said it. He felt low.

Sandy took a time just enjoying the show. Seeing Mark sweat was quite an entertainment for her. Sandy could see Mark getting weaker and weaker. Mark was just about to walk away, and Sandy agreed with joyful voice, "Sure, but not tonight. I have a practice with the girls." She had practices all this week. She didn't know what to do.

Mark was shocked. Mark lost his words a little. "Oh…really. …Great. I'll pick you up after work." He heard the words, sure, but he didn't quite catch the details, so he quickly jumped to his gun. "What? Did you say yes? You said yes, right?"

"Yes. I said *yes*. I will call you for the details. Mark, I got to go." Sandy stated it quite commandingly. She turned around and left as if she is busy, but she needed quick advice from Cidy. She made a quick getaway. She quickly left the spot giving a quick gesture and words of *I'll see you soon.*

Mark had no choice. He was just stunned. He tried to collect himself from the shock.

Sandy went to Cidy and told her what happened. They hugged and jumped like little girls.

Cidy advised her to date Mark, Wednesday, the night of the final practice. She told Sandy to come up with a good excuse for missing the practice.

CH 59: Mark's Desperation

After last night's date, Mark can't stop thinking about Sandy. He is going crazy because Sandy won't accept his calls. He is in love, but is afraid that Sandy might not think of him as a serious candidate for husband.

Mark is in sales, and is the hottest bachelor in the company. He is sharp and rugged looking at the same time, and he has that Elvis Presley smirk with a bit of southern twang that girls just died for. On top of that he is funny and very engaging. He is the total package that the girls could not resist—the future, the charm, and the looks.

He is the prince of the company not just with the looks and the charm but with his sales performance and his commanding role among the sales crew. He's like the "quarterback" of the company.

All the ladies in the company know who Mark is, and most of the bachelorettes dream about Mark, knowing that they had no chance at all. Making thing worse for the ladies, Mark is known for not dating company girls. The explanation is that he doesn't like the extra complication after the break-ups with a company girl.

Mark doesn't understand the complication that came with the break-up. He feels like he treated them nicely and courted them with his money, and if he wants to end the relationship, it shouldn't be any problem. But girls hate him for luring them in and throwing them off aboard.

He would date girls, have a short relationship, and drop them when he lost interest in them; more likely, he found a new girl to pursue. He never connected with all those lovely ladies he dated, and he didn't understand it either. He feels bored with them quickly. He just has too many girls lined up. Girls are easy-come and easy-go for Mark.

He doesn't sleep around with girls like people think; nor he is sex crazed like many imagine. He isn't a one-night stand guy either. Whenever he felt like he and the girl are about to have a serious relationship which usually happened after having sex, he just feels the pressure of commitment and moves on to a new challenge.

But Sandy is a whole different BBQ for Mark. Mark likes to think of girls as BBQ, something he couldn't refuse. He refers Sandy as his kind of BBQ—sweet to your mouth, tingling to your nose, and damn sexy to your eyes.

He knows his game too well when it comes to girls: He eyes the girl in pursuit a bit, and throws some cute catchy lines with his cowboy charm, and he reels them in slowly but surely like a pro. He feels like it's a sport of some sort; he just feels he's good at it.

But whatever the reason, Sandy just does not work with all his charm and tricks in the world.

But his pure effort and sweat over a year finally came through: He had a date with Sandy last night.

The date was so mesmerizing.

Mark is constantly reliving it—every second of it.

It was a powerful experience. He never had such an experience in dating. Every second with Sandy gripped his mind and body.

Mark makes several trips to Sandy's desk hoping to see just a glimpse of her. It is not like him, but he has to see her. He waits for her there, but she doesn't come around. He searches the entire office, but finds her in Cidy's office. He wants to walk right in and make a fool out of himself. He wants to beg her for her love.

Mark's feeling is quite silly but desperate.

What is this desperation, Mark thinks. *Is this love that people talk about?*

Mark makes another trip to Sandy's desk. She is not there. He goes to see if Sandy is still at Cidy's. He sees Sandy walking out with Cidy.

Mark wants to chase her down, but spies Sandy to see the back of her just a little. She disappears.

Seeing her beautiful blond hair crossing through the office space, and watching her walk with a slight sway, and feeling her body curves with his eyes drop his heart.

"What has got into me? Sandy, Sandy, Sandy…. I love you." Mark talks to himself.

Mark's walks to where Sandy just got on the elevator, and tries to breathe in the air where Sandy was just standing. He feels her presence. He is hopeless in love with her.

His mind explores the dinner date he had with Sandy:

CH 60: MARK DATES SANDY

Sandy called Mark.

She stated her business like she was told: "I only have a Wednesday night to see you. Pick me up at my apartment at 6:30 pm. Are you ready?"

"What?" Mark sounded like a little boy who didn't know what was going on.

"Are you ready for my home address?"

"Oh…yah. Yes." Mark barely got the words out.

Sandy gave her address, and told him to wait for her at the front office, and quickly hung up the phone.

That just drove him crazy. After a year of chasing Sandy, he finally got a date, and he had no idea what to do. He was so good with the girls. It was the girls who followed his order, not the other way around.

Mark cancelled everything with his friends and buddies for that night.

He waited for Sandy at the apartment's front office like Sandy told him at 6:30 p.m. sharp. Sandy didn't show up until 6:45. He jumped out as soon he as he saw her coming around the corner. She was wearing a yellow top, a soft greenish yellow skirt, and matching sexy yellow high-heels. She was stunning: She was one in a million. Her neck line and shoulder line were amazingly sensual for him. He couldn't take his eyes off of her.

He had dated many girls but Sandy was the best he had ever seen. He blushed and felt her beauty hit him in the face like a sucker punch. His mouth opened and dried up quickly as he stared at her beautiful face: blue eyes, long blond hair, soft half-egg cheeks, and lovely chin line with red lips. He lost a track of time as Sandy walked over to him.

He waved at her with a joy of little boy seeing his long-waited friend: It was an involuntary action of his gladness of finally dating Sandy.

She waved back. She could see the joy and the excitement in his face. She loved his glaring stare. She felt her heart pounding faster and faster.

He smiled. He could almost hear a beautiful, romantic music getting louder and louder as Sandy came closer and closer like the movie scene: He was the leading actor falling in love with a beautiful woman.

"Sorry. I'm late." Sandy looked into Mark's dark brown eyes. She liked what she saw. He looked like a movie star and had the charm as well. She couldn't believe she was dating Mark—the Mark that every single girl dreamt about in the company.

"Hey. Waiting for you is like a sweet chocolate bar." He gave his honest feeling. He didn't feel like he glossed anything. He really felt good about waiting for her.

"That's a nice compliment, Mark. Thank you." Sandy made a step toward the car door.

Mark opened the door.

Sandy stepped in as she observes Mark looking at her legs. She felt bit naked, but felt very sexy. She wanted him to touch her legs because she just shaved them for him. She smiled short and courteously. She watched him as he came around to get into his seat. It felt as if time is passing in a very slow pace. She had been out on a lot of date, but she never felt this excited before. She felt like a high school girl going out on her first date.

He didn't know what to say or do, so he just started the engine and drove away.

She reminded herself to be calm so he won't get the wrong idea that she is going to easy. But, she was already too much in love. She repeated Cidy's advice to her heart.

He never felt this jittery before. He was trying to find words to please her, but he couldn't say much. This date with Sandy was totally different from all others he had.

"I picked out a small Italian restaurant. I hope you like it." That was the only thing he could think to say. Sandy's beauty blinded him. *Be calm, be cool*, he talked to himself.

"Great. I love Italian." Sandy played along. She was too excited too. She couldn't help fidgeting a bit. She was afraid Mark would catch her being nervous.

Mark searched for words; meanwhile, he couldn't help but peeking at Sandy's body—legs, face, bosom, and hands. Mark just couldn't focus. He was afraid she might think of him as pervert. He tried to be calm, his mind kept repeating, *She is hot!*

Sandy noticed his eyes wondering around her body, but she enjoyed it. She liked that he likes her body. She was in love. She wanted to make love with him right here and now, but she didn't want him to notice her inner feelings.

Silence was awkward, but they enjoyed each other's company.

He turned on his favorite CD with soft and jazzy love songs. He wanted to make the trip special. The car became a nice cozy place for two. She enjoyed it. She felt very special being with her love of life—Mark.

She realized he was nervous. The "Mark" being nervous—it was funny and cute. She tried to relax him a bit by carrying a small talk about weather, movies, and music.

Soon they arrived at the restaurant. He got out quickly and opened the door for her. She gave her right hand to him for help. He smiled big. He couldn't help it. He almost drooled seeing Sandy's beautiful legs and a peak at her bosom.

The touch of Mark's hand gave a self-aware electric shock which was very special to Sandy. She felt the tingle all the way back to her tail bone. She never felt so special by a single touch of man's hand. She got out, and he led her to the front door of the restaurant. It didn't look expensive or cheap either. She felt comfortable.

He opened the restaurant's door, and they walked in the restaurant.

A waiter questioned if it was for two.

Mark made a gesture with his fingers verifying the question and spoke softly, "Two."

They followed the waiter, and sat in a nice, corner table for four. There was a small candle light in the middle. He deliberately sat next to Sandy, not across from her. She looked into his eyes and he looked into her eyes. Time stopped. She knew she was in love. He knew he was in love. Sandy could feel the heat on her cheek, so she covered with her palms softly trying her best not to seek any attention to her face. She decided to look at the menu and cover her face for a while.

Mark's eyes couldn't leave from Sandy's eyes. He had never seen such beautiful and enchanting eyes before: They were unmistakable jewelry that Creator has made just for her.

They order their dishes and red wine.

She didn't drink much but liked to take a few sips of it.

They talked and ate.

She tried her best not to laugh too much or giggle. She played her part of being a calm and lovely lady as best as she can.

He tried his best to get her going. He pulled out most of his favorite jokes and stories. He felt lost when she gave a calm and collective respond to his funny stories. She loved his jokes and stories. He felt silly. One thing for sure, he knew her eyes were glued to his.

He couldn't help it to notice every little details of Sandy—ear rings, her intoxicating perfume, and lovely necklace that kept sparking at the right time to catch his eyes, and her lips kept inviting him to kiss her, her nose that stood so lovely in the middle of her face, and her eyes that was so hypnotizing. He knew he was eating but all his senses were being overloaded. He wanted to reach out and just kiss her so many times, and to spill his gut out and say *I love you*.

She felt his glaze over her face, shoulder, arms, hands, and bosom. She loved his attention. She felt so loved. She felt so conscious of every word she said, and felt she could see every word that he spoke. She had never had a dinner like this with any man. The feeling of love was more than intoxicating for her. She felt high. Her eyes were bigger, heart pounded faster, and lips reached both sides of her ears.

Four hours passed quickly. The waiter came around said they had been closed for thirty minutes, now.

Mark and Sandy returned home.

She wanted to lean on his shoulder, but kept herself stable.

He wanted to take her home and make love to her.

As the car came near her apartment, she said, "Mark, it was a wonderful evening. I enjoyed it. But, I want to make one thing clear. ...I'm passed the age of dating for fun. I need to see a man who is serious. I heard a lot about you. I need someone who wants one woman, and wants to be married. If you are not thinking about marriage don't bother to call me. ...And I'm not answering your call if I'm not thinking about marriage with you either. I'm getting too old for this. I need a man not a boy. Again, it was wonderful." Sandy mustered all of her inner strength to pull out the line she had been practicing all day.

Mark was silent. He didn't know what hit him. He never had a woman telling him anything like this before. He was thinking of kissing and making out. He thought he was going to get some sweets from Sandy, but out of the blue, he got a cold statement of something he never heard before. He was still trying to figure out what she just said. He lost his mind.

He parked his car as she instructed, near the entrance of her apartment.

She tried to open the door by herself.

"Wait. Let me get it for you." He quickly got out and opened the door for her.

She gave her hand again. She felt that tingle, but it went all through her body like a small orgasm. She blushed and bowed her head to cover her face. She collected her thoughts and raised her head. He was still holding her hand. She pulled her hand away. He didn't want it to let go.

He pulled her closer and closer, slowly to kiss her.

She coming to her senses pushed him back. She practiced it in her mind many times as Cidy told her.

He felt embarrassed and said, "Sorry. I didn't...mean.... I'm sorry."

She turned around and walked away without saying goodbye. She was getting weaker inside. She didn't think she could have refused him if he pulled her in one more time.

He didn't know what happened. He couldn't figure it out. He thought he had a great date. He felt drunk with love. He knew this was love he never felt before. He wanted to run after her, but he thought she might scream or slap him for it. He watched her as she slowly disappeared to her apartment.

Sandy wanted to turn around, and see him for one last time before she went inside her apartment. She knew if she did he would run after her, and then, nothing could have stopped her from giving all of herself to him. She knew she had given him the cold shoulder like Cidy told her to do. It wasn't easy. She hoped Cidy's advice was the right thing to do. Mark was the first guy she ever wanted to give herself after the first date.

CH 61: First Encounter

About a year ago....

Cidy told Sandy to coldly refuse Mark's offers or one-liners that will want to make her say *yes* for a year, and prophesized that the true love game between them will begin.

Cidy advised, "We are not gonna play Mark's game of love-'em-and-leave-'em. That is not love. We're gonna play the true game of love. There's got to be respect. If Mark's not gonna respect you than there's no love. So you will refuse his proposals for dates with cold and courageous heart for a year." Sandy had little idea what that meant, but decided to follow her advice and say *no* for a year.

Mark had heard of a blond bomb named Sandy from the boys. He heard the boys talk about girls like that a lot, so he didn't pay much attention to it. But he was curious. The boys told him she usually eats lunch with Cidy and her girls.

Mark decided to check her out because he was curious but not really interested. He set a rule for himself—not to date company girls. He stood in line with the boys, and boys gave him a cue where Sandy was.

A beautiful blond girl was in front of them about five feet away.

Mark noticed her even before the boys gave a cue. Sandy was a kind of girl guys just can't take their eyes off. She was a natural beauty—a woman that could cause a war between nations. He saw her from a far once, but he didn't take any serious attention to her beside he couldn't see her face clearly. He waited calmly for her to sit somewhere.

He led the boys to sit not to close to her but close enough for him to see her face and eyes clearly. He chose an excellent spot to view her face.

He liked what he saw. He licked his chop like a predator for his prey. He knew he will get her in a few days or sooner. He just had to make up his mind. He really didn't want to break his rule.

Mark gave Sandy that look, and Sandy couldn't resist his stare. She was interested in him instantly. She couldn't help noticing him just like any other girls. Her eyes would meet his often.

He walked over to her and poured out his charm.

"Hey, Blondie. Guess you're new. Welcome aboard. I'm Mark. How you like it so far?" He gave his trade mark smile reaching out for a hand shake.

Involuntarily, she gave her hand. She felt the heat as Mark held on to her hand. She liked his bold and smooth approach. She saw Cidy's face of disapproval. "I'm Sandy. Nice to meet you, Mark. I'm sorry but I'm eating with my friends. If you don't mind...." She did her part as coached.

"Sorry ladies. Enjoy." He took the sign. He decided to continue his hunting after lunch.

He waited for her at the hall way.

"Hey, Sandy. Nice timing. I was thinking about you." He casually approaches her, again.

"...Really?" She was hooked.

They had a little rapport again. She thought she could handle him, but she already felt like he owned her. She quickly realized how charming he was. Cidy's warning was ringing in her ears. She made up her mind not to be persuaded by him.

He said looking right into Sandy's eyes, "Sandy I love to have a dance with you. Know a nice club we can two-step. Can I have your hand?" He slowly but surely reached out half way to meet her hand.

Suspecting it was that pick-up line, she gave him a cold stare, and said, "Sorry Mark. No thank you." She walked away with her heart pounding. She wanted to turn around and give him a smile, but didn't, like Cidy had told her not to.

He smirked and felt like he met a decent challenge, but it was nothing he couldn't handle. He thought, *Playing hard to get. I'll get you…soon.*

After a few days, in the coffee room, he caught her as he planned, and he gave her a wink and a look, again. There were others around, but he gave a clear signal to her that he's into her. He made sure everyone knew it. She couldn't help it to bash her eyes. She didn't like her reflex. She kept herself calm, acting like she didn't notice anything.

He recognized the flash in her eyes. It was a go sign for him. He stepped outside, and waited for her exit on the hall way, like a lion waiting for his prey with patience. His move never failed him.

When she walked out with her friends, he walked up to her, and greeted her and her friends kindly. He made extra effort not to forget the other girls: he presented himself to the ladies, "I'm sorry ladies but I've a catching-up-to-do with Miss Sandy here. Mind if I borrow her for a few second?" Girls knew what was going on; they said, "See you later."

They parted with that I-know-what's-going-on glance and smile to Sandy.

Mark noticed Sandy was in a bit of panic mode. He quickly calmed her down with a few gentle remarks, "Sandy, you look mighty fine today. Love your soft blue dress. I bet you like to dance. What you doing this weekend?"

She showed sign of interest and automatically responded, "Nothing much." She was surprised of her own uncontrollable responds to him.

He made more small talks, timing when to throw the hook. He finally threw his hook. "Sandy, I love to have dinner with you. I know a nice French restaurant we can enjoy. Whaddiyu say?" Mark slowly but surely reached for her shoulder with his right hand expecting to touch her.

But she quickly moved back and answered, "Sorry Mark. No thank you." She moved her shoulder away just in time, and turned around, and walked way.

He waited for her to give a "peeking-back" glance, but it never happened. He lost his balance a bit wondering what happened.

He gave Sandy his best one-two punch which never failed him, but against his expectation he got turned down. He laughed inside thinking, *I see it in your eyes…I know you want me*.

CH 62: CIDY TALKS TO SANDY

Cidy doesn't feel comfortable thinking about Sandy's last impression. She knows Sandy wants to express her feeling, but she also knows Mark wants the challenge of winning Sandy's love. How does Cidy understand about human nature is also mystery to herself.

She feels that she better make sure Sandy feels assured. She gets out of her chair, and walks out of her office.

Cidy walks to Sandy.

Sandy is quite glad to see Cidy, and quickly pulls up a chair with a greeting smile.

Cidy sits down and comforts her by saying, "Sandy. God loves you, and He will make this happen for you. I promise you. You will not lose Mark."

Cidy understands that Mark is more than hooked on Sandy, but Sandy doesn't want to lose him.

Cidy takes Sandy out of the building. They find a bench nearby. And they continue their talk.

Cidy advises Sandy some more, "You are like the treasure Mark wants, but you have to test his heart. Then he will take you seriously and realize that you are not a player but a treasure."

Sandy is listening. She knows she heard this before. She never felt like a treasure. She always felt pressured to please the man.

Cidy pauses and tries to see if she can read Sandy. She sees Sandy is comforted.

Sandy is comforted, not by words, but by Cidy's presence. She wonders how Cidy's so strong and assured. She respects Cidy.

Cidy reaches out and softly grabs Sandy's right hand. "You have to win Mark's heart the right way, or you'll be just another chalk mark for him."

Cidy knew Sandy had soft spot man: Sandy would be just too nice to every man.

Cidy had explained to Sandy about controlling her feelings toward the boys: She told her she had to keep the distance from the boys. "Sandy, you are very attractive to man. It could be a curse."

Sandy just couldn't understand what the jealousy was all about. Her boyfriends all got just very upset with her being friendly with other boys. She didn't cheat, but they just felt insecure about her being so nice to other man. That's how Sandy thought.

Cidy explained, "Man and woman we feel insecure about our love, or jealous. It is a sign of love. As we get older, we have to learn to behave differently, and respect our lover's feeling. Especially you, Sandy. You will give other girls much insecurity as well. Just keep girls close to you as friends, and keep one man, Mark, close to you as husband, lover, boyfriend, and best friend."

Sandy knows that Cidy had explained this to her some time ago that men are very possessive just as women are, and we have to learn to keep distance with each other.

Sandy really likes the word husband, and says, "I love Mark. I don't wanna lose him. Don't you think I played enough hard-to-get?"

Cidy smiled and replied, "No."

Sandy opened her eyes wide said the same word with disbelief, "No....?"

"Sandy, do you think Mark would be still chasing after you, this seriously, if you gave in?"

"Well...."

"Mark is a player. You have to get him out of that player mode. He will not play you. He has to earn you."

"Earn me?"

"You can't fold now. You have to play tougher. Mark probably thinks he won, especially with the date. You are gonna play cool for a month. Let Mark sweat it out. He will bring you a ring and ask you for marriage. Then we'll talk."

"A MONTH! A RING!"

"Don't worry. It will go quick. Just play cool, tonight. You can smile and talk with him but don't flirt and give in. Mark will lose interest in you if you play into his game. You've gone out with him. He knows what the prize is worth. He's gonna have to ante up, now." Cidy gives her cold advice.

Sandy acknowledges and realizes that everything went exactly as Cidy had predicted, so she is going to trust Cidy all the way through.

Sandy had tried pleasing guys and went out with a couple of guys when working for another company. It didn't work out well. Girls and guys they all talked trash about her because of those dates. Nothing happened but the guys just bragged about it as if they scored or others just exaggerated, so she knew she had to change her game. She knew she was a quite genuine woman.

Sandy had never let anyone play this hard get, but Cidy's plan worked marvelously for her.

Sandy wants to have her man, Mark, and she feels this is the best catch she ever had or dreamed of. She is more than assured by Cidy; she is calm, and trusts Cidy.

Cidy feels Sandy can pull this off.

Sandy's phone rings with the music. She looks at her phone and says, "Mark. It's his fifth call today."

"He's relentless." Cidy opens her eyes wide.

Sandy says, "Thanks Cidy. I trusted you so far. I'm not gonna give up now."

Cidy gives Sandy a warm hug.

CH 63: Mark's Present

"Man. ...she's not at her desk, again. She's not answering," Mark talks to himself. He's chasing himself back and forth. Sale reps have never seen him so anxious before. They can tell he's saying something to himself.

He sweats because Sandy isn't answering his calls, nor she is at her desk. He feels like she is avoiding him purposely. It's killing him.

He couldn't sleep through the night because he felt so wonderful from the date, but he got anxious when she didn't answer his calls. He called her an hour, two hours, and three hours, after he dropped her off. He thought he was going crazy. Giving so much attention to just one girl wasn't his thing, but it felt very good—painfully good, now.

He is finally feeling love for the first time in his life. He wants to give Sandy everything he has. He wants to propose to her for marriage but he thinks, *I dated her, only once. I don't do this kind of thing.*

He had never been turned down by a girl before, especially after a great date. He always had his ways with girls. It was the girls who tried to invite him to their home, but Sandy said don't even call if I'm not thinking about marriage. He couldn't believe his playing this marriage game.

He is in love for the first time. He sits at his desk and plays the last-night date with Sandy in his mind over and over again. He feels heavenly and thinks, *Sandy is hot but she's a more than a lady. How about that? It took me a year to get a date with her. And now, she wouldn't even answer my call.*

He is anxious, and decides to visit Jake to spills his guts out. He quickly runs out of his office to meet Jake.

He sees Jake at his desk with a heavy face, but he feels his problem is bigger and more urgent. He calls out Jake. Jake meets him. They walk to a quite spot.

Mark says, "I don't know what to do. She won't even answer my call. I called her five time already in last few hours. I don't want to lose her. How do I show her that I'm serious? I'm not playing with her."

Jake smiles and says, "You are one lucky dude. Sandy is one that everybody is eyeing on, and you got a date with her. That's awesome." Jake focuses on the positive.

Mark is chewing himself up.

Jake has never seen Mark like this before. "Cool Mark. Wow! Mr. Dude. The Dude. The Man. Even Mark can be like an average Joe." Jake teases Mark.

Jake gives the advice his best friend Paul gave, "Man up, Dude. Be a man! Shout to the world that you love her. Show her that you are serious."

"How?" Mark is desperate.

"Give her a ring!" Jake answers without even thinking about it.

"Ring! You think that would do it?" Mark gets the idea.

Jake has no idea. He blurs, "I'm just saying…you know."

Mark couldn't hear Jake's words: He is too focused on buying a ring now. He takes off and walks out of the building.

Jake doubts, "He is not going out to buy a ring. …Is he?"

Mark gets into his car and goes to mall to buy a ring. As he drives, all he can think about is Sandy:

> I love Sandy's smile, her voice, and her sexy body. How did I get into this mess? I don't marry a girl. Not now. I'm too young. Wow, I must be in love. I'm just dying inside. I got to see her soon. I got to hold her. I need to make love to her. …I met her a year ago. I had a sacred rule not to go out with a company girl. …But when I saw Sandy, I felt the challenge never before. I just couldn't resist Sandy. I love her damn too much now. It's weird. I was afraid to commit. Now I want to commit. I want to marry her. I want to take care of her…forever. Is this love that people are talking about? …Whatever…. I'm in love. I love Sandy.

Mark drives to the nearest mall, and parks his car, and runs into the mall. He goes directly to a jewelry shop, and shops for a ring. He instantly spends about five thousand dollars on a beautiful blue sapphire ring with his credit card. They are trying to wrap the ring for him, but he tells them not to, and takes the ring in his hand, and put it in his pocket, and leaves the store almost hopping. He feels like a little kid going to Disney Land for the first time.

CH 64: CIDY THINKS OF JAKE

Cidy leaves Sandy with a big smile and gives a short cute girly wave. Sandy waves back with the same cute wave.

Cidy is more than happy for Sandy. She just wishes she had her love going too. She is just baffled about how to get Jake moving. *Maybe it was never meant to be,* she doubts.

Walking back to her office, Cidy has Jake in her mind, and feels something...like a destiny with him. But she is again bothered by her calling. She doubts her love Jake again, *I barely know him except for seeing him almost every day for past five years at work. How did Jake got into my mind, and stayed there for this long?*

She's back to her office, and takes the seat.

She shakes her head a bit and contemplates again about Jake, *Jake would be the last person that I would be interested in. Sure he's tall and lean with a little above-average look, but with no sense of humor or character.* She is trying to find a good reason to stop this non-sense—virtual love with Jake.

Whatever it is between Cidy and Jake just couldn't be explained: it is that love thing. In her mind she plays the same tape again about her thoughts about Jake and her, and all the little encounters with him.

"Did curiosity cause all these confusion, misconception, in my head," Cidy tries to reason her infatuation about Jake as she has done so many times. She dreams about holding his hands, kissing him, and talking with him a lot, especially when she goes to bed. She knows from her prayer he is her destiny, but as the years passed by she doubts the answer to her prayer.

Then again, she would make that extra turns and purposely try to take a peek at him without getting caught. She felt all giddy about this teenage-like crush on Jake for five years. She enjoyed every day at work because of her love for Jake.

CH 65: Cidy Wants to Pinch It

Cidy, because she was late than usual, had to park her car little further away. As she drove by, she saw Jake getting off his truck. She wanted to hunk the horn and say hi, but just gave a turn of her head and let the sight of Jake just flow in her eyes. She wanted to stop the car, and jump out, and give him a big hug and a smooch.

That would make his day.

She parked her car, and walked towards Jake, hoping he still be there. And he was. He was arranging some sporting equipment and balls in the bed of his truck. She thought it would be a good idea to strike up a conversation.

"Hi, Jake."

He turned around. He looked a bit surprised. He replied hesitantly but with a smile, "Oh…hi… Cidy."

There was a short pause. So, she questioned, "Hey, what's with all the sporting goods?"

He responded naturally but with his head turned away with a bit of stuttering, "Ahhh…. It's for the church retreat…for games. You…you know."

She thought he would strike up a conversation, so she can get closer to him. But he never seemed to show any interest her. She knew their eyes would meet often, but she wasn't sure.

She stood there staring at the back of Jake and peeked at Jake's buttocks. She smirked a bit. She was always fascinated how man's buttocks were quite attractive her, and she liked the way Jake's buttocks are—tight and cute. She wanted to grab it, maybe give a pinch, but felt silly thinking about it. She hoped Jake would say something.

She didn't hear any words from Jake, so she decided to mention that she loves going to retreats. "I love going to retreats." It came with little higher pitch than her usual voice. She felt bit nervous too. Maybe she wanted him to hear her cuter voice. She was shocked that her pitch was so much higher than usual. Excitement of talking with him got the better of her or in this case worse.

But for her, when he didn't respond, that few seconds passing felt like a torture, she felt quite disregarded. She never had a guy being so rude to her before. She knew Jake was in his own little world, but this was just too much for her. She turned away slowly, and just walked away feeling disdained by him.

CH 66: JAKE 1

Jake is busy working, but couldn't help but to think about Cidy. He has been like this for past five years, and he loves his days at work because of her. He especially loves it when she comes over to talk to him about anything, although he turns into a stoic rock.

He just can't explain his reactions to her. She had that magic that makes him a robot—a broken one.

He is very serious that he will ask her out tonight, although he is more than afraid now they won't be compatible for his chosen work. He knows she probably will reject his next career move, but he just wants to have that one alone time with her to remember and share his love with her. He knows it might not be a good idea. But he couldn't just throw away the five years of love for her.

He prays, "God just let me have one date with Cidy. Give me courage to ask her out tonight. Lord I beg of you. Don't let me chicken out. That's just been the story of life. Give me courage Lord. In Jesus' name, I pray."

He is trying his best to pump up his courage.

CH 67: JAKE FUMBLES CIDY

It was Friday during the summer about three years ago.

He had all the sporting goods and other equipment for the church weekend retreat. Coming to work, he heard the goods and the equipment get loosed in the bed of his truck. So after parking the truck, he got on the bed of his truck and started to rearrange them. While rearranging the goods, he thought heard Cidy say, *Hi.* The voice of Cidy was enchanting, but was also a great surprise. He froze. He wanted to say something cute and catchy, but he couldn't find any word.

His dream girl giving a hello where there's no one around was the moment he had been waiting for, but he got into the shock mode; he couldn't respond coolly and properly.

He replied hesitantly but with a smile, "Oh...hi..., Cidy."

That took some courage from him. Meeting with the girl of his dream, and saying those simple words when no one was around was more than daunting for him. He started to sweat and just couldn't figure out why he sweated in front of her all the time.

Cidy questioned, "Hey, what's with all the sporting goods?"

He tried to man up, like his best friend, Paul, always advised, and ask her out. He thought this was a great opportunity. But, trying to think of two things at the same time never worked too well with him: The motives—trying to answer the question and trying to ask her out—clashed.

He responded unnaturally but with his head turned away and said with a bit of stutter, "Uuhhh.... It's a...uh...uh...for the church retreat...for games. You...know."

Jake was building up his courage but acting like his busy with the arranging the sporting equipment that spattered all around. When he finally got enough courage to say something and ask Cidy out, she was gone.

He felt very foolish. A chance lost. His love all had gone wrong.

He regretted that about himself—always being indecisive and lacking courage.

He always prayed to God for that moment of solitude with her, and he had it. Now it was gone.

He didn't feel good about himself for a few days, but he kept his composure. His desire for her reached even higher after that short conversation: He would busily move around the company, just to see a glimpse of her. His pretense of running around made no sense to his fellow workers in the department. He made up excuses that he needed to exercise.

CH 68: Note of Jake

Jake is in his early thirties, 33 to be exact. He feels shame to be so shy and has no courage when it comes to girls. He doesn't feel old but the number doesn't lie. He wonders how time had just swept under his feet so quickly.

He wonders about the life God has planned for him. He wants to go the end of the earth to witness Christ like Christ has commanded. He knows, when the Gospel is preached to all nations, all languages, and all the tribes, Christ will return, as He had prophesized.

He is fascinated by life, his own life: How God has raised him through his family, churches, friends, and acquaintances.

The past seven years have been most exciting and blessing for him as he led the church's praise and worship team, and helped out with the Sunday school, and fellowshipped with fellow Christians, and helped the company to grow, and most of all fell in love with Cidy.

CH 69: Jake and Houston

Jake was 26 when he started working for the company, and that is how his life in Houston started:

He tried his best to find a job near his hometown, but the economy wasn't good or his credential wasn't good enough. He searched the Internet for months, and finally got a small company in Houston, TX to take a risk on him.

The company was only three-years old and very small with less than 20 employees, but had potential for growth. That's what the company description said. The company had the same problem of finding employees because of their size and the low pay. Graduating from a small community college, Jake was not too attractive for companies either. The company and Jake were perfect matches for each other.

He drove down from New Jersey with the same truck that he still drives—the truck Dad bought for him for college.

It was summer of 2001. Houston was much hotter than he expected. Jake didn't have A/C in his truck, and the hot humid air coming through the window just gave him the worst welcome to any city he had ever been.

He came for an interview and was hired that same day as he expected. The company told him they were desperate, and he played the same song. The interview was more like a plea from the company. The company's most important question was—*When can you start?* The same as Jake's—*When can I start?*

After he was hired, he first decided to go to church and thank God, and went on a search for a church. As he was driving around asking people for a church nearby the company, he got lost. He didn't know where he was. Then, he saw a small church, and drove in, not knowing that would be the church he would be attending for next several years.

When he drove in and parked his car, Pastor Kirk greeted him. Kirk usually left for home for lunch and a light break by during that time.

They said hello.

Jake explained that he wanted to pray to God and thank Him.

Kirk showed him to the main sanctuary.

Jake gave a quick "Thank-you" prayer and had a small chat with Kirk that became a long one.

Jake told him he needed to find a place to stay because of his new job here in town, but to his surprise, Kirk invited him to his home for the next few days before Jake finds a place to stay.

Jake couldn't believe it: God had already prepared his place to stay. He didn't have much money and was quite worried that he might have to sleep in his truck for a while.

But Jake stayed at Kirk's for two months, soundly and comfortably.

Jake gave his entire first month salary as his "first-fruit" offering.

Kirk realized Jake gave all of his first-month salary as the "first-fruit" offering, so Kirk and Jane took care of Jake like their son even more.

Kirk told Jake to save the next month's salary to rent an apartment.

Jake worked to improve the company's accounting system as the company grew quickly, but as the company grew much bigger than they expected, they had to hire more experienced corporate accountant to keep up with growing counting work and finance tasks.

He didn't mind, because he knew the company now needed a better accounting expert to implement more sophisticated system, and to have better organized accounting department. He knew he was blessed to be learning so much more.

CH 70: JAKE 2

Jake gets back to work. He's doing his paper work—checking the receipts and vouchers date and making sure all the date are properly inputted with their unique file number. He senses that he might be working for the company maybe a year at the most, no a month at the top.

Jake is all messed up—having mixed emotion with the calling and his love for Cidy. He is not sure if his going to ask Cidy out anymore. He's afraid it would be just too much even for a Christian woman to marry a minister or missionary, or worse, she might just say no to him when he asks her out. He likes to think there is too much complication as he weighs the love matter on his hand and trying to make sure he does the right thing.

Jake sort of feels small if this is his cop-out excuse for him for not asking Cidy out tonight, again. Five years of secretly loving her shows up empty because he is afraid of rejection. He feels very stupid that he just couldn't ask her out for a date, all these times. Only way he had a date was through an introduction from other people. That was how he had few of his dates.

The last date he had was over a year ago. He had to take the date. An older church member, who Jake had a good relationship with, introduced Jake his niece. She was very pretty, and her name was Jill.

He liked her beautiful face and lovely body, and she had strong faith in Christ that they both of them felt very attracted. But he couldn't erase Cidy's face while talking to her. He kept thinking about Cidy: how it would be so nice to have Cidy across the table instead of Jill.

Jake told the girl he's not ready for a relationship and complimented her how beautiful and elegant she looked.

CH 71: Return to Cidy

Cidy looks around the company and misses the people already. She starts to cry, so she calmly walks herself to restroom. She sits herself on a toilet and quietly let her emotion out. She prays that she will do whatever God asks of her, but she can't help but to count her friends and peers in her life in Houston.

She wants to call Mom again but holds it in. She can't help it to think about Mom:

Mom had been the solid foundation in her life.

Cidy now knows how difficult it had been for Mom to raise her all alone.

Mom had a few chances to remarry but had to refuse because of her. She knows how much Mom misses Dad after all these years.

After a while, she walks out of the toilet slot, and after checking her face, she heads back to her office. Her each step now rings creating a time stamp everywhere she walks. The wall is watching her. The lights are focused on her. People are paying attention to her every move. She feels overwhelmed, and her senses are overload. She quickly returns to restroom. No one's there.

She stares through the mirror and sees her past with Mom: *Mom always had a hot breakfast and bagged a nice sandwich, a fruit, a bag of chip and milk for lunch. She always enjoyed her lunch, and*

Mom always put a Bible verse in her lunch as a word of encouragement.

She didn't do well in math and science generally. Mom never complained and always prayed with her for wisdom from God for understanding. Mom's comfort and prayer gave her strength so much throughout her life.

In high school, Cidy brought a boy home to help him with his school work—David Stone. David was a hopeless case, but he reached out to Cidy for help. She sensed David liked her, but she thought she can handle it. She decided to help David anyway.

Mom usually came home about 30 minutes after Cidy came home. But that day Mom came home just a few minutes later. Mom sensed trouble right away.

Mom called David and Cidy to the kitchen table and asked them to sit down.

Mom bluntly said, "David, YOU will go to jail. I promise you. Cidy is not that kind of girl. I KNOW you have done this before, but THIS time you are going to Jail."

Cidy and David were shocked to hear such a heart-piercing threat, but he was more scared that Karina somehow knew of his past. David quickly ran away in a panic.

David looked like a fine kid just needing some help, but was a serious predator.

Karina later told Cidy that God had warned her to beware of a boy named David, and Mom added that she sensed danger instantly when she heard Cidy was bring a boy named David.

Karina said, "I knew it was the boy you are bring over to help. I knew I had to tell him in his face to get him off of you."

Cidy heard David was sent to jail for raping a woman a few years later.

She has so many thoughts about so many different things. She wonders why she remembered that incident about how Mom saved her from David.

Mom is a great protector in her life.

Cidy calms herself down, and decides to take on the destiny head on. There is nothing to fear. She knows God saved her from many dangers that she knew and did not know about. Now it is up to her to do the job that God's commanding.

She returns to her office again. While walking back to her office, she steers her head where Jake is sitting hoping to catch a glimpse of him, but she can't see him, naturally. She knows it is a long shot.

As she turns her head around back to her office direction, he is walking towards her.

She feels very happy to see Jake's face: She really wanted see him since the moment she woke up.

As Jake comes close, she becomes quite aware of herself with heart racing quicker and quicker. She wants to stop him and tell him that she loves him. Oh how she wishes to make such a bold move. She smiles and says, "Hi, Jake."

And as usual, he is a beat behind in his respond as if he is reluctant and forces a smile back with a *hi.*

He passes by her taking a peek into her eyes.

She returns to her office feeling good that she just saw him. She wonders and worries if he has any inkling of her interest in him. She wishes she was a man so she can make the move. She hopes with a prayer that he would be asking her out tonight. She wants to have at least one date with him.

She looks out to the window toward the work area and tries to capture every little detail of the floor and the peers. She checks each one's name and makes a mental note of them.

CH 72: Jake 3

Jake just saw Cidy's beautiful eyes.

Seeing her is the greatest pleasure for Jake. It stings him and halts all of his nerve system for that split second.

He was barely able to pull out that simple word of greeting—*hi*.

It is always her who greets him first and gives him that undeniable smile that makes him unconscious for that split moment. It is a love shot. He knows it. Her presence reaches the core of his heart, mind, and soul.

And that scent that she carries; it takes Jake to another world. Her scent lingers in his mind long after she is gone, conjuring up fantasies with her. He wishes that he could just hold her in his arms, forever, inhaling her scent.

He returns to his seat and wishes that he had stopped and carried a conversation with her.

He regrets again for that missed opportunity because he had practiced so many times how he was going to start and carry a conversation with her.

At home he practices many lines of greeting Cidy and having a wonderful chat:

Hey, Cidy. You look great today.
Love the way you smell....
Hi. I have seen you here for years
now.... I really like the way you look

and relate with the people. Would
you like to see a movie with me?
Hey, Cidy. I was wondering if you
like to go see a concert....?
I love to have a date with you. Would
you give me the honor to court you?
Hey which church do you go to?

He feels sorry for himself and seeks courage
from God like he had done so many times, although
he doubts himself. He feels he is a loser. He's has
been a dud all his life. He has no love life.
He never had any meaningful relationships
with girls.

CH 73: JAKE'S LOVE LIFE

Jake had many puppy loves when he was just a little kid. He liked girls a lot, but he was more interested in playing games with boys. It wasn't until high school he started to have heavy crush on girls that felt like torture and heaven.

His first real love—more like a crush—was with a girl named Judy Chang, a Chinese-American girl, in high school. She attended the same church as well. She was smart, cute, slim, and very sexy. She had long straight black hair and big black eyes that he dreamed about diving into.

To him, she was a perfect girl, and he knew she liked him too, because she would come around and start a chat, which he enjoyed very much. He knew she was dropping hints, but he was a dud in that department—making that major move to ask a girl out for a date. Finally she went out with another guy in the church. He felt sorry for himself; He just didn't know why he couldn't take that next step.

With Michelle, he had a similar result in his senior year of high school.

And one girl friend he had in college left him for his best friend in college.

CH 74: Inside of Jake's Head

Jake feels there's something wrong with him when it comes to girls; he feels he has a major problem having intimacy with them.

He knows he can't live without a girl because he enjoyed their company so much and had so much sexual desire for them.

He worries that he might have the same result with Cidy. He is down, realizing maybe he is just a dreamer that never has any piece of the action. He feels all those prayers and devotions just went right down the drain. He is drawing her in his mind—her beautiful face, bosom, legs--dreaming how he could have dated and married her for years by now.

He never understood how he fell in love with Cidy. He never had a talk with her lasting more than 3 minutes, and if they did, they mostly talked about business matters.

Cidy never showed me any interest, he thinks.

He likes how she looks: petite and tall, long brunet hair, and her beautiful golden brown eyes.

He is afraid, if she got to know him well, she might not like him, either, and furthermore, he is afraid he might not like her if he got to know her well too. He just worries too much when it comes to his feelings and other people's feelings.

He shared his feeling for Cidy with his best friend, Paul, from the church. Paul always advised him: "Man…, love only comes a few times or only once in your life time. You GOT to take the risk, so you won't regret it…the rest of your life. Gotta man-up…to love a woman!"

Jake feels silly but Cidy is the reason why he gets up in the morning and goes to bed fantasizing about her. His love for her gives him life. The love consumes him perpetually: he day-dreams and night-dreams about her. She is the drug of his choice.

His fellow workers caught him many times just staring towards empty space where Cidy would be if you were to follow the line of his stare. Of course, you couldn't see her from there, but that's the direction Jake always stared at—where she would be.

When they asked Jake *what's he staring at*, he would say *my dream*.

Jake would see Cidy coming around the corner and walking away a few times a week: Those were he's favorite moments in his life.

About a month after Cidy joined the company, he remembers her passing by as their eyes met—he got mesmerized by her beautiful golden brown eyes shining on her beautiful face.

He had seen many girls' eyes before, but her eyes were like a piece of jewel he had never seen it before. Her transparent and shiny golden-brown eyes were the most sensual and beautiful eyes he had ever seen. He thought he liked blue or hazel eyes, but once he saw her eyes, his favorite became her golden-brown eyes.

Cidy is taller than most girls with the height of 5' 8" or 9" depending on the shoes she wore, but shorter than him. And the way she swayed her long skirt that just covered over her knees and her shiny brunette hair dancing beautifully and sensually with her skirt always played that romantic dance music.

Seeing her everyday makes him fall in love with her deeper and deeper: that little peek here and there is the day-maker for him. He would take a walk purposely around the office hoping to meet or bump into her, and they do because of his and her efforts to see each other here or there collided randomly with the deliberate precision of love. She usually says hi and moves on because she is as shy as he is.

CH 75: CIDY'S VALENTINE

Because of the Valentine Day came in two weeks, Cidy prayed for her husband-to-be. But the simple prayer became a serious 7-day fasting by just drinking water, orange juice, and some wine.

She usually fasted twice a year, full seven days each one. She prayed for various things in her life: Mom, Grandparents, friends, peers, church, missionaries, children at church, the unreached nations, and for other personal matters.

But this time she decided to fast for her husband-to-be. She really wanted to know if Jake is to be her love of life, because she somehow fell in love with a man she barely knew.

She felt calmer than ever before (maybe it was because the lack of energy from not eating), although she was starving and in pain from fasting.

The *009 Girls* were accusing of her of having secret dates, because she didn't have lunch or dinner with them for that whole week. She managed to fast by drinking a lot of different kind of juices to keep her energy up so she can do her work at least. She did fall asleep earlier and quicker than usual.

On the seventh day, she just finished praying for Mom, her Sunday-school children, and the foreign children and pastors in mission fields she supported. She was ready to leave for work. It was her last day of fasting that she promised to God, although she was thinking of extending it until she heard the voice from God telling her about her fate with Jake.

As she looked around the room and saw the picture of Dad, she smiled and said, "Hi, Dad. I'm praying for Jake. I mean I'm praying to find out if Jake is the love I need to wait for."

She exited her apartment, and she walked to her car. And as she was about to open the door, that funny feeling as if someone is whispering in her ears, she heard the name—Jake.

She turned around to see if there's anyone around. She didn't see anyone. She definitely heard the name, Jake.

God didn't come out and say, "Marry Jake," but that small voice she heard was more than enough. She first thought it must been hunger that caused her to imagine. But she kept the answer in her heart. Since then, that voice kept her eye on one man—Jake.

CH 76: Karina's Present

Karina senses that Cidy would be going through a whirlwind by now. She gets urges to call her but holds it because it's already a broken pot, and she knows Cidy has to know the truth and needs to obey it and deal with it.

Karina, instead, calls her younger sister, Mandy. Mandy lives not too far from her, now. (Mandy moved nearby a few years ago.) She talks to Mandy quite often, and meets her often too. Mandy is like her best friend now that she is all grown up.

"Mandy, you won't believe the story I'm about to tell you."

That got Mandy's attention quickly.

Karina talks to Mandy about the event in the morning, and the message she received from God over twenty years ago.

Mandy remembers the suffering Karina went through because she visited her many times to help Mom and Cindy, but because of her own family, she couldn't help as much as she wanted to.

Mandy remembers fasting and praying she did for Karina. She knows that God had miraculously cured Karina, but she has not heard of the message Karina heard from Jesus directly. It is the first time that Mandy is hearing about it.

While talking with Mandy, Karina reaches into the memory of her childhood.

CH 77: KARINA, MANDY, AND PAUL

Karina is two years older than Paul, and three years older than Mandy.

They loved each other but they had their own shares of sibling rival.

Karina always felt she had more responsibilities and less attention. She felt Mandy got all the attention and got away with more misdeeds.

In her high school years, Karina had a huge fight with Mandy, because her favorite shirt went missing. It was found in Mandy's closet, like Karina suspected.

Karina never asked any questions to Mandy. She just lashed out at her little sister, because she had done this a few times before and she had much grudge against her for a lot things.

But Mandy insisted in her innocence this time.

Karina felt this was the opportunity to revenge all of her anger she had gathered and piled up against Mandy. She had the proof, and the parents weren't around. It was time for sweet revenge.

Karina didn't give Mandy an inch. She went for the kill to show Mandy not to mess around with her.

Mandy pleaded her innocence. She cried and cried saying she was sorry for all the things she had done wrong to Karina. But, Mandy stuck with her innocence in this case. That made Karina even more mad and resentful.

Paul seemed to be going back and forth enjoying the fight between his sisters. He was grinning all around his jolly face: He was enjoying the show.

Karina shouted to Paul, "Get away! It's none of your business."

That night, Paul teasingly confessed that it was him, who played tricks on them. He took Karina's shirt and placed it in Mandy's closet. He further disclosed that he thought it would be fun to watch them fight.

Karina cried for thrashing her anger around and having such a grudge against her little sister. She tasted her own sinfulness; she was so ashamed. She ran away for a couple of hours. She didn't know how to ask Mandy for forgiveness. She prayed and cried—for God's forgiveness.

When Karina returned home, Mandy was the first to greet her.

Mandy said, "Where were you? I was worried. It's okay, Karina. All is well." She felt relieved to see Karina, her friend and a sister— sometimes a mother.

When Karina heard Mandy's words, she was able to say, "I don't know what came over me, Mandy. I'm sorry. I'm…truly sorry."

"It was me. I set you up for this, or I set Paul up for his devious act. I'm sorry for taking your clothes. I won't do it again." Mandy apologized for her misdeeds. She always wanted to look like Karina. Karina was Mandy's role model in every aspect of her life.

Karina hugged her little sister, and cried together for a while.

That night Paul got a whopping from Dad that he won't forget.

From that incident, Karina learned a valuable lesson—not to judge any event or any one unless you know all the details, and don't jump into conclusion. She felt so guilty of herself for hating her sister for so many things. She repented many times. She never knew how mean she could become over a shirt.

Karina learned a lot about herself, and decided to let go of things that weren't important. Since then, she gave a lot of her favorites, especially clothes, to her sister, her friends, and the needy. She literally became a saint.

The family was back to normal quickly. Karina sincerely apologized to Mandy several times, and tried to amend with her by baking cookies for her and playing with her more.

Paul, in front of the entire family, apologized for his "evil" act, and had to clean up the house for a year.

In fact, the family became never closer.

The sisters shared much of everything. Paul's mischievous act transformed the sisters into angels. Parents couldn't believe how the two sisters got along so well.

Being the oldest made Karina responsible for Mandy and Paul. She didn't like the role, but took it with fate. She babysat her sister and brother often when the parents had a night out. Those nights were hard on her because Paul would test her patience and authority. For Karina, taking care of Paul was the hardest.

Paul loved pushing Karina to the limit although he loved her. He felt he should be the one in charge, but it was her always telling him what to do. That agitated him to push her buttons by teasing her and disobeying her. He tortured two birds with one stone: paying back the child-like treatment from Karina and having fun. He constantly drew up a new scheme to get her screaming.

One time when Mom and Dad were out for some military event, Paul put some paper and aluminum in the microwave and made fire. He was out of the picture when the fire got started. He thought the fire and the smoke will surely bring her down; He found himself just giggling and imagining about her screaming out of control.

While doing her homework, she smelled some smoke from the kitchen, and ran into the kitchen quickly, and found smoke coming out and fire piercing through the microwave. She was about to go into panic mode. She screamed fire a few times and skipped around trying to figure out what to do.

Then, she told herself to calm down and think.

She calmly sized the fire to be easily controllable and not too dangerous.

She put out what's left of the fire calmly with a cup of water, and spotted Paul around the Kitchen entrance, peeking the whole incident. The smoke spread quickly and fast throughout the house and it didn't smell good. She quickly opened all the windows and the doors to remove all the smoke. After the smoke cleared out, she started spraying the scent spray all over.

She could tell Paul wasn't happy as he thought he would be.

She punished Paul severely that night. Her anger was intentional and demanding: she told him to clean up the mess and get into push-up position afterwards, and do not move. She learned a thing or two from Dad. He followed her order. She watched over him with anger. She knew he meant it for fun, but it was dangerous and went too far. She had to punish him for possibly starting a fire and getting the house in awful stink.

Paul being a strong and healthy boy felt it was an easy punishment, but after thirty minutes, he arms started to hurt. And soon, he started to sweat. He didn't want to ask for forgiveness. He wanted to take the punishment and defy her.

She started to talk to him trying to put some sense into him. She always seemed to have a way with words.

He loved her, but he just wanted more respect from the family especially from Karina.

Karina softly spoke her words, "Paul you know I love you. You're my friend as well. We played together a lot. Yes, we fight and argue, but you know I love you."

He got weak soon as he heard those words and wanted say I'm sorry. But his pride got in the way: Paul and his man's pride were inseparable.

She knew him too well: she knew he wasn't going to apologize.

She continued, "What you did today is not acceptable. It could have started a bad fire, and have hurt us, and quite possibly even have killed us. I hope the smell of the smoke is out before Mom and Dad get home. You will not like what Mom and Dad have to say about this, especially Dad."

He knew she is more than right. If Dad found out of this, he knew it will be the worst punishment he would ever had, and that meant probably paddling, grounding, and cleaning for weeks, maybe years. He suddenly realized it will be a bad night if he didn't settle quickly with her.

He reluctantly apologize to her, "I'm sorry for what I have done. I went too far Karina." He just said what he had to say besides he couldn't keep up the push-up position any longer either.

She allowed him to get up and help circulate the air as much as possible, and she put Mandy as the look-out post if Mom and Dad are here.

When Mom and Dad arrived, Karina, Paul, and Mandy had done enough air circulation and covered up the entire house with a few scent sprays to pass the smell test. They acted little too proper and too cheerful.

Mom and Dad knew something was up; everything looked too perfect and even smelled great. But they were tired, very tired, and went to bed quickly.

CH 78: A CALL FROM LINDA

An office lady pages Cidy, "You got a call from, Linda. She says she knows you from high school."

Cidy doesn't recall anyone named Linda right away first, but decides to accept the call.

"Yes, this is Cidy."

"Hey, Cidy. It's me, Linda. Fort Lee High." Linda quickly and brightly introduces herself.

"Linda…." Cidy phases her voice out with doubt of knowing her, and checks her memory.

"Hey, Cidy. I just wanted to thank you," Linda states joyfully and doesn't mind that Cidy doesn't remember her.

"Well…. You welcome, Linda." Cidy reluctantly accepts.

"You…don't remember me? Really?"

"No…. I'm sorry…."

"Cidy, you saved me from that predator, science teacher, Jeremy…Lexton."

Linda left the school after the incident. Cidy only had a short acquaintance with Linda through the incident, so she had forgotten about it.

"Yes…Linda. …I remember you, now."

CH 79: CIDY SAVED LINDA

Jeremy was a well-liked teacher. He was good with the kids, but Cidy felt something not right about him. She didn't think much about it, but one day she realized Jeremy might be a predator because she usually caught Jeremy with pretty girls, especially blonds. It never dawned on her, but with repetitious sightings of Jeremy with pretty girls, she unconsciously felt uncomfortable as well as attracted to him.

In her junior year of high school, a pretty blond girl, named Linda, that caught all the boys' attention and even male teachers', was asked to stay after the class by Jeremy Lexton.

Cidy was in the same class. Her sixth sense kicked in; something just didn't feel right. She pretended to leave the class with others, and waited a few minutes outside the hall, and made quick entrance back to the classroom making an excuse that she left her book.

When she quickly walked in, Jeremy's hand was on Linda's shoulder. He got surprised, and jerked, and took his hands off from Linda very quickly.

Cidy acted as if she didn't see anything and hollered, "Hey Linda. You done? Let's go."

So Linda followed her out, and they talked on the way to next class.

Cidy first talked friendly building up some rapport, and made some probing questions, one leading the other. Finally Linda told her something felt wrong in there, but it was slow and very hard to resist.

Cidy needed more evidence to get anywhere with her haunch that Jeremy Lexton may have gone too far with other girls. She guessed Jeremy likes pretty blond girls. She asked other pretty blond girls if they had any strange encounter with Jeremy. None of them wanted to talk to her.

She felt something was definitely wrong. Her investigation made a discovery that a pretty blond girl moved away and had a suspicious rumor about her sudden move. She got her number somehow, but she didn't want to talk either.

She told this to her mother, Karina, and Karina filed a full complaint requesting a full investigation to her police friend.

After a few months of secret investigation by the police, the science teacher, Jeremy Lexton, got convicted of sexual molestation of under-aged girls.

CH 80: LINDA THANKS CIDY

"Cidy, I wanna thank you for what you did. I liked Jeremy a lot. Honestly, I had a crush on him. I know it was wrong, but he was very likeable person. I think I could have been his prey. But you saved me." Linda is very thankful.

"What made you call after all these years, Linda?" Cidy is grateful to hear from a friend.

"I'm a mother now. I have two little girls. I worry about them a lot. You know. And I remembered you suddenly. I called the school, and English teacher, Mrs. Pirrer, answered. She's still at the school. Can you believe that? She gave me your mom's number. She says they go to the same church. And your mom gave me your number." Linda gives a quick wrap-up.

"How are you doing? Where are you now?" Cidy wants to know.

"Good…. You know…. It's not easy being mother and wife. But there's joy. I'm in Dallas. My husband relocated here, a year ago."

"Hey we should get together. I'm in Houston." Cidy feels good that a friend calls after years later and thanks her.

"I'm gonna try. I'm all tied up with two kids. But you are welcomed any time. I'm forever indebted to you, Cidy." Linda's voice shakes a little.

"Thanks." Cidy genuinely feels Linda's thankfulness.

"When I have to go to Dallas or nearby, I'll call. What's your number?"

They exchange their numbers and hang up.

Cidy smiles and feels proud of her good deed. She wonders if other girls that Jeremy ruined are living okay. She realizes how fragile a life of woman can be yet still be quite resilient.

CH 81: JAKE 4

Jake remembers seeing Cidy earlier from a distance when the *009 Girls* rushed out of her office, looking like a bunch of little giddy girls up to something no good.

They are together quite often. The word is that they will be doing a musical comedy tonight. Last year they dropped every to the floor. It was unforgettable performance. Jake had never seen anything that hilarious than what he saw: 9 grown-up girls singing, dancing, and acting with funny and cute outfits was just over-the-top outrageous.

Cidy wore an animal costume—a pink bear. It was a parody of *Sound of Music*—the lonely goat song. But they sang it as lonely bear. When the two bears tried to hug, they both bounced off of each other. It was very funny.

He has learned that she is unique and quite loving girl that knows how to reach out to other girls, especially the ones that are left out. By reaching out to left-out girls, she unintentionally formed a click that guys called, ***009 Girls or Bond Girls***. It was a joke until Sandy joined.

There are actually 10 girls including Cidy now, but the coinage stuck with them. They are a mash of outsiders or misfits from the view of most of the guys. They just didn't look like people who would be hanging around with each other.

CH 82: Bond Girls

Cidy's click—*Double O' Nine Girls* or *Bond Girls*—means odd ones of nine. It started out as Three Odd Girls, but when they reached seven somebody started calling them *007 Girls* (hence, the Bond Girls) which meant *Odd Ones of Seven*.

Usually girls had their own little clicks for whatever the reason, and it was not easy for a new girl to find their own little click in time. Many of the girls in the company were usually paper or communication supporters, and the upper management treated them with less attention or respect.

Cidy was young, just out of college, but she had confidence and self-assurance that you can feel and recognize. She quickly became popular among the girls and the guys. But she tried her best to be with the girls that are alone. It was something she learned in her early years. She didn't mind hanging around with unpopular ones and giving them attention as a friend and a colleague.

She, with title of General Coordinator, coordinated most of company's inside and outside functions and events and a lot other things that just couldn't be categorized. She just took over them without additional compensation or direct orders from the top. (The company didn't mind what Cidy did for the company employees voluntarily, especially without any compensation and complaints.)

She did not pretended to be nice to other girls, who seemed to be left out, but she actually made effort and stuck with them to make sure they felt like they belong in the company. If any of those girls couldn't find their own little click in time, she took them under her wings. That wasn't in the Cidy's job role, but she made sure the company or she made everyone feel welcomed or has someone to lean on.

As she took on the left-out girls one by one under her wings over the years, the number of Cidy's girls just grew. And they were diverse with a bit of eccentricities (mildly stated). (Frankly, most of the guys didn't find them attractive.) They were international and odd, but interesting. And the latest one was a Muslim girl, Nadeera, who couldn't fit well with others girls because of the way she dressed and talked with the distinctive Arabic accent, but Cidy took her in too. She had created her own little gang, whether she wanted it or not, and they hung around with each other a lot.

Guys talked about them a lot mostly to make fun of them, but they had some jealousy of their friendship. *Bond Girls* always looked like they were having so much more fun than the others. Even ladies started to have some jealousy over them.

Finally, someone who did looked like a Bond girl joined the *009 Girls*—Sandy. All the guys went wild when Sandy joined the company. For the first few months, what every guy talked was about their encounters with Sandy. Of course, their encounters were usually seeing her from a distance, but they still enjoyed talking about it. And they would elaborate about their encounters mixed with their little fantasies with her.

Above all, *Bond Girls* were known for their act in the Christmas Party. They always brought out a variety of entertainment—singing, dancing, and comedy. They had their own little celebrity status in the company, now, which no one really gave a dime for, but for them, it was the friendship they shared more than anything else. Fame was the lasting in their mind, although they enjoyed been appreciated a little.

Each day, they really enjoyed coming to work because they cared for each other. And with the latest addition, Sandy, the *009 Girls'* status had risen to a whole new level of recognition and popularity. Now, guys bothered them to get an introduction or a hook-up with Sandy. Sandy really put them on the map.

CH 83: A NOTE OF HOT SANDY

Who wouldn't want a woman like Sandy! All the male employees thought the same thing in chorus.

Sandy is known to guys as *Hot Sandy* or *Sexy Sandy*. She is the girl every man would fall in love within the first sight, but over a year, she has gained a solid ground on her respectability.

Now guys started to call her by another name: *Lady Sandy*, *Ms. Sandy*, or just *Sandy*. But *Hot Sandy* was the preferred name from the beginning.

A lot of the girls said, "If I that body, I'll go pick up a millionaire in a sec."

When guys said *Hot Sandy*, they said it with passion and emotion; you could feel their simmering breath spreading around the room.

Hot Sandy was an awesome blond hottie. She had the entire package: the looks, the sound, and the most of all—the behavior. She had that girlish motion that would make any man cry, and when she talked with that girly pitch, guys just drooled losing the concept of their own existence.

Guys were mesmerized by Sandy. And Sandy knew it, but this had been her life—guys just coming around and dropping like dead flies around her. A lot of boys asked her out knowing they would fail, but they had a story to brag—asking Sandy out for the rest of their life. It really wasn't about getting a date with her from the beginning. They knew they never had a chance. But they always sent their love through various methods: gifts, flowers, and telegrams. And they were the stalkers—a few cute ones but mostly creepy. It was not easy being a beauty queen.

Most of the guys on the same floor made their routine to say hi to Sandy, paying their tribute to her. And some even came from different floors to just see a glimpse of her. Even CEO liked her a lot, too.

The word in the company was that CEO tried to get her to be his personal secretary, but Sandy refused. No one could verify it, but the rumor made sense, because CEO had no business of talking with Sandy, but he would make a round trip around the office and say hello to all the office ladies and men just to say *hi* to Sandy. Before Sandy started working, there was no such a trip by CEO. They all knew what was going on. He would usually stay extra longer with Sandy, and she would give him the honor and the respect with that deadly smile and seductive voice.

She knew the boys are just being boys, just wanting to be recognized by her, and she gave them their treats—a smile and a *hi*. She never realized how many guys she made happy each day, but the girls weren't too happy about her "make-boys-happy" smile. They were very jealous.

She hung around with the girls most of the time: Cidy demanded her to do so. She would talk to all the girls as possible, and she would purposely be with them and avoid men as much as possible.

And of course, there were daring men that came and tried to strike up a conversation or ask her out for date even when Sandy was with other girls.

For them, she replied softly, "Thank you, but this is not an appropriate time. You can talk to me later." Guys were confused if they were turned down or not. But when they went to see her alone, Sandy turned them down gently.

As a result, she had gained good reputation among the ladies and the guys. Ladies really appreciated her for hanging around with them; they felt honored that she would spare her time for them.

This wasn't easy for her because, for her, guys were more fun to be with, but she wised up and became girls' girl. She had been hurt for being popular with boys, and she didn't want that to happen again.

CH 84: Mark Has a Ring

Mark comes back to the company with the ring, and visits Jake again, and talks about Sandy this and that, and shows him the ring that he just bought, and keeps talking about Sandy this and Sandy that.

Jake is more than busy with his work, but he couldn't help it to listen to Mark with awe, because he is shocked to see the playboy Mark with a ring, they just talked about. He envies Mark's boldness and decisiveness, and feels the pressure to do the same thing. But he knows he's not that kind of a guy.

Jake wants to tell Mark to go away because of his envy, but he can't because Mark is his good friend. Mark confides with him a lot of things, but he just felt too envious of Mark's current bold move because Mark is going to do something he wants to do—propose for a marriage.

Mark stares at the ring and talks about how he should surprise her. "What should I do, Man? Should I give it to her now? Got any idea, Jake?"

Jake reluctantly responds with a stutter, "To…tonight? …ah…at the party…would be ah…a…great…moment."

Mark jumps and tightly hugs Jake.

Mark screams, "Jake, I love you, Man! I'm gonna kiss you." Mark kisses Jake. Jake turns his head just in time to get the smack on the cheek.

CH 85: MaRK anD JaKE

Mark and Jake started to work together about the same time.

Mark always felt comfortable with Jake. So, he shared a lot of his feelings about a lot of different things with Jake, because he felt Jake as a solid stone that he can count on. He just felt good about Jake although he knew Jake wasn't much of fun at all. He just couldn't explain his comfort with Jake.

Mark called Jake sometimes late at night to talk about life and girls. He even told Jake that he is interested in Cidy but she isn't really his type. He confessed he tried to lure Cidy for a date but she just wouldn't budge, not a bit.

Jake was shocked when Mark said he's interested in Cidy. He wanted to say she is his girl, but he couldn't. He felt bad about himself, keeping his feeling to himself. He wished he could call Cidy like Mark did.

Jake had invited Mark to church several times and witnessed Christ to him several times as well. To Jake's surprise, Mark did come to church with him a few times. Mark was not sure of this faith-in-Christ thing: he felt his life had been just fine. He didn't know what the fuss is all about. But Mark respected Jake's faith, and he knew there's something in Christ that gave Jake that solidity or stableness that Mark could definitely feel and is drawn to.

Mark quite didn't feel like he was a sinner. He felt the world was a great place to play, a sort of playground. He cheated in school to get the grade, but he felt that was something everybody did. He hurt a few girls by dating and dropping them, but he didn't feel like he took any advantage of them. He never forced anything on them; He never promised them anything.

But Mark felt alone many times even when he was with a beautiful girl. There was something Jake provided for Mark. Mark thought it was a guy thing, a friendship. But other guys he hung around never seemed to give him that solid ground or rebuke that he needed it.

Jake always told Mark, "Don't mess with girl's heart! It can come back to bite you, or even haunt you. They aren't made to be broken."

Mark didn't take Jake's advice serious until he heard one of his ex-girlfriends made a suicidal attempt after he broke their relationship up. He heard she moved out of state. He did realize what he was doing to the girls wasn't good for them. He tried to stop but it was hard.

Jake always envied Mark's charismatic aura and his popularity. He didn't know why Mark would befriend him, but he didn't mind. He tried to be the best friend he can be although it wasn't easy because he felt like Mark was having all the fun and the attention.

Jake prayed for Mark, that he would find Christ as his savior and the Lord. For Jake, Mark was like a devil himself keep teasing and taunting him, but Jake knew Mark is his friend.

Mark felt Jake was a tight wad who needs a life. He always teased Jake to get a life—go to parties, see some girls, have some drink. Jake's life at church—praising and worship, and teaching the kids—looked dull and uninteresting for Mark.

When Mark was talking about sexy girls, Jake never seemed to respond like the other guys. Jake kind of nodded as if it was nothing. Jake did respond to sport, but that was about all the common Mark felt with Jake. But, Mark felt unusually comfortable with Jake; he never understood it, why.

Mark had many drinks with Jake, and Jake always listened well. He felt like Jake was his psychiatrists. He always felt good talking with Jake, and felt great after talking with Jake. He wondered if he feels comfortable with Jake because Jake listened to him and gave him advice he need it, although he hated when Jake witnesses Christ.

Mark always remembered that one time Jake said after the home team—Texans—won the game:

> It was a Monday night, because on Sunday's games Jake couldn't make it: Jake is too busy with church on Sundays.
>
> Jake questioned Mark, "Did you know that there's a bigger game going on for your soul?"
>
> "What?!" Mark understood the question, but he didn't understand what Jake was trying to say.
>
> "There's a fight, a war, a game raging on for your soul."
>
> "You talking about…Christ again…right?" Mark became

attentive, but he felt it was another religious talk, right away.

"Yes. You saw the sacrifice and the fight the Texans players went through to win the game.

"...Christ died on the cross and shed his blood for your soul. He sacrificed His life to win your soul." Jake just had to witness Christ to Mark, again.

"My soul...is the prize?" Something connected with Mark. He, like others, had heard about Devil trying to steal or deal for one's soul

"Yes. It is the greatest prize! Bigger than Super Bowl." Jake's voice got stronger.

"Super Bowl! ...my soul...bigger.... How's that possible?" Mark sort of got the idea about the sacrifice of Christ to win his soul.

"I don't know all the details, but there's something of great value...of your soul. It has been paid for...by the highest price...the death and the blood of God's only Son—Jesus Christ." Jake spoke the Gospel as simply as possible.

"You believe there's hell, Jake?" Mark didn't know how to respond, so he spoke whatever came up to his mind.

Jake felt Mark want to veer off from the subject.

Jake didn't let go. "Mark, I don't
know a lot of things, but one thing I
know and I need to tell you…is GOD
loves you, and He let His only Son
die on the cross for you, your sin,
your soul." Jake pours his faith out
with conviction.

"…Man…that's enough. Go
home Jake. You're ruining the whole
thing. Just go! I don't wanna hear it!"
Mark wanted to hear more, but he let
his pride get in his way.

Mark was confused. He liked his life the way
it is. He had everything he wanted and maybe
more—success, girls, family, health, cars, money,
looks. Only thing missing was some gap, a hole, in
his heart that just can't be explained. He always felt
there is something missing in him. And he feared
dying: he dreaded one day he will get all wrinkled up
and die. He tried not to think about it, but it was
staring right at him in the least expected time.

After Jake's witnessing after the Texans'
game, Mark always felt something behind his head
when he watched any kind of game. So, he wanted
to know if there's really a soul or a spirit that
separates from his body. He read the Bible secretly,
searched the Internet, and bought some books.
None really satisfied his questions.

He finally decided to try prayer to test, if God
exists. He didn't know how to test if God existed in
any other way.

One day as he was driving he asked God to
show Himself if He really exists. He kept looking
around for God's manifestation. It was a beautiful

day. A day moon that was bigger than usual hung on the sky on fluffy clouds, loitering as cars are busy on the earth. He searched in the clouds as if there would be God's face or something. He decided that was sort of goofy.

But one night, he dreamed something he can't forget:

> A man he hadn't seen before was walking with him. He didn't know where he was. It felt like a park trail in a beautiful morning.
>
> Mark said, out of courtesy, "Hi, how you doing, man?"
>
> The man replied, very knowingly, "Hi, Mark."
>
> Mark was surprised. "...Have we met?" He tried to figure out who is this man who knew him by his name.
>
> The man answered with a soft smile looking into Mark's eyes, "Mark, I knew you before you were born. And I have shed my blood for you. OF COURSE I know you."
>
> Mark, very stunned, questioned the man, "How you...? ...you, God? How...? ...This is just a dream. Isn't it?"
>
> The man answered, "Seek me with all your heart, and you will find me."

Mark woke up vividly remembering the dream, but he never told this to no one because he didn't wanted to sound like a religious freak like Jake. He didn't dream about things like this. But he had been reading and watching a lot of religious material, so he figured it was his imagination making it up. He wanted to talk with Jake about it, but he didn't want Jake to know about his desire to know Christ, either.

But the challenge the man gave in his dream kept him up with the Bible reading and researching about Christ.

He secretly went to several different churches and asked pastors and ministers "How do I know God exist?"

None of them gave any good answer that Mark wanted. They all said pretty much the same: read the Bible, pray, look at the nature, or they gave their personal experiences about meeting God.

Mark was dying with these questions: Does God exist? Why did He have to die on the cross instead of just commanding the sin to be washed away? Is there Heaven and Hell?

But the main question—the existence of God—just couldn't be answered.

He finally decided to ask Jake. He invited Jake over, and questioned Jake as soon as Jake made his way into his home, "Jake, how do I or you know God exists?" Mark was very seriously.

Jake never heard Mark's serious tone like that before, and it was the same question that he had trouble answering to anybody. His faith had waivered before. He knew God exists, but how is he going to answer it him. He walked over and sat on the sofa.

Mark sat across waiting for an answer.

Jake's long pause gave much doubt to Mark.

Mark hits the heart of Jake. "You don't know either. Do you?" He sounds quiet sarcastic because he is disappointed in Jake.

"I know. I KNOW he exists right here, right now." Jake proclaimed his faith because he had experienced God's miracle several times.

As Jake proclaimed his faith, Mark and Jake felt something move or touch them. They looked around involuntary and quickly. Mark was stunned. He felt something but he couldn't explain what it is. Jake felt it too and knew it was Holy Spirit. They stared at each other for a few seconds agreeing with each other of what just happened.

Mark couldn't deny the existence of something in his house. It scared him. "Okay that's enough." He felt something come in and through him. He felt warm and got hot.

Jake never felt the presence of God so strong before: He felt something go through his body or touch his body. It was similar to that same experience he had when he was a kid at the retreat. His body felt quite warm.

Jake said, "You felt it too. Didn't you? You felt it. I see it in your eyes. Let's pray, Mark." Jake made his way to Mark. Jake sat next to him.

Mark distanced himself from Jake, quickly. He wasn't going to give up this easy. He had too much pride in him to let go of all his ways of thinking and living that easily.

"I need more proof…more proof." Mark thought out loud.

Since then, Mark prayed to God and read the Bible on his own much more. He didn't want to tell anyone that he was a Christian or becoming a

Christian. He felt silly, but he couldn't deny his own experiences in the spiritual world.

Jake knew Mark changed. Mark would ask more Bible-related questions as if he just wanted to know, but Jake knew Mark is into it. Jake tried his best to show patience; he knew he could not force Jesus into no one.

Jake prayed for Mark to come into the world of faith—having a personal relationship with Son of God—Jesus Christ.

CH 86: Return to Mark

Mark is about to explode. He knows Jake is not paying attention to his words, but he has no other choice but to share his feelings about Sandy with Jake. Jake has been his "go-to" guy about all of his problems, but he has never imagined that he'll be seeking help and confessing about his love for Sandy like this to Jake. It is always other guys seeking advice or wanting some coaching from him.

Jake works and pretends to listen at the same time. He heard this before, but today the intensity has reached to new level. He could tell from the tone of Mark's voice. There is that pitch in his voice that you can feel the urgency, pain, and most of all—love.

Mark sings his pain out loud: He explodes, "Yes! I'm gonna tell the whole world like you said."

"I'm just saying!" Jake tries to back out of his idea. "Calm down, Mark. Be cool." He is scared what if the whole thing backfires.

"*How would Mark be able to work in the company? How would Sandy be?*" Jake worries.

"It's gonna be great!" Mark assures himself again.

"What if she says no?" Jake is afraid for Mark and Sandy.

"I don't care. I have to tell her how I feel. I want the world to know." Mark thumps his chest.

"You only had ONE date." Jake starts to reason with Mark.

"That's ONE too many. We should've gotten married, yesterday."

"Are you sure about this?"

"Solid! Rock solid!"

But for the first time in his life, Mark asks Jake to pray with him, "Hey Jake pray with me."

Jake is stunned. "About your proposal?"

Jake wished that he could pray the acceptance prayer with Mark, but not a prayer for a successful proposal. But he did wish he could pray with Mark. How your prayer comes true!

Jake's thought process makes Mark more impatience.

Mark quickly grabs Jake's hand, and closes his eyes, and makes a deal with God. "God. Jesus. I love Sandy. I want to marry her. Please let her accept my proposal, tonight. I will give you my life if you give me Sandy."

There is a pause as if Mark wanted to say something more but he couldn't, or Mark wants Jake to say something.

"I pray this in your Son's name—Jesus Christ." Jake closes the prayer. "Mark, you know you just made a deal with God. You know that?"

"I know. If Sandy becomes mine, I will give my life to God. I will. I mean it." Mark proclaims his side of the deal.

Jake is flabbergasted. He wishes to make a deal like that with God. He has never been this bold with his prayers. He envies Mark's courage. He couldn't propose to a girl in front of all those people—not in a million years.

Mark's now singing a country love song—
Could I Have this Dance—and dancing to his own
singing. He is out of tune but keeps the beat, not
bad. He sings it with joy. He grabs Jake and forces
him to dance with him. Jake follows the two-step
dance as Mark leads and sings. All the guys in the
accounting department are laughing to the sight.
They overheard most of it.

CH 87: A Note of Cidy

The company is first in Cidy's life; the church second. But in her heart it is the other way around. Her passion for church is second to none. She is a Sunday-school teacher who is quite involved in kids' lives. Oh, how she loves the kids at the church! She feels like she is friend, sister, teacher and mom to them. She loves giving them hugs and prayer. She loves the little one dangling around her like little ornaments on a Christmas tree. She would usually talk with them once or twice a week over the phone before she met them at the church on Sundays.

The church's Sunday school had almost tripled with the arrival of Cidy. She rounded many kids up near the church every way she knew. She would carry candies and church brochures to the neighbors often. She did this voluntarily mostly by herself. She was known as Candy Lady, or Senorita Dulce in the apartments near the church.

Some of the church members loved her for her amazing effort of bringing new kids to church. But some were against it because the kids were rowdy, poor, and most of their parents weren't at the church with them.

When there was a special function like retreat or lock-in, she would be with them for Friday night, Saturday day and night, and Sunday. She spent a lot of her own money to provide gifts and food for them. It was a great joy for her. She loved seeing them grow, and hoped her loving and teaching would have faithful and positive affects in their lives.

She always told them, "Live like Christians should, and pray like one, and you will hear God's voice." Her experiences with her prayers and God gave her personal testimonies that she can share with kids. Sometimes her message with kids didn't go well with their parents, but she gave the message according to the Bible.

One of the lessons that didn't go well with some of the parents was how Cidy taught about the story of David and Goliath. She just had to add her words, which was the same words she learned from her Sunday-school teacher, "Goliath will not fall without a fight. You take the challenge from a Goliath in your life and step-up to the plate with faith in God. God will give you courage and strength to fight, and the victory." And she gave her encounter with a bully when she was little.

Within a month after the message, two boys and a girl got into fights in school. And a mother of one of the boy's parents was very upset with Cidy. Pastor had to step in for her trying to stop any ugly incidents in the church. She learned later about the complaint from other ladies in the church.

The mother still confronted Cidy even after all the explanation and peace-making by Pastor. She was a pacifist, and got very upset that her boy got hurt as well as hurting the other boy.

Cidy was advised just listen and apology if she was ever confronted by the mother. She did as she was advised.

She was very much hurt to hear such harsh words from a mother she thought she knew very well, but she felt good that the boy, Randy, stood up against a bully. She knew Randy's life will take a more faithful course because of his faith.

Her life was busy: work, church, Sunday school, friends, and family. They kept her running busy joyfully. She had a list of people to love and care. She loved them all dearly.

Only thing that she was missing in her life was her love, and she hoped and prayed her love— Jake.

CH 88: LUNCH FOR THE *009* GIRLS

It is lunch time, but Cidy's dreaming.

Her personal phone rings with that musical tone from her favorite sci-fi series—*Doctor Who*. (Everyone enjoys her ringtone, especially Cidy herself.) She checks who it is: it's Tammy. She answers the phone, "Hey Tammy. Something is up?"

Tammy shouts, "Yo, Cidy. LUNCH! Get your pretty little ass down here, NOW. All waiting for YOU. Move your skinny hinny, Girl! NOW!"

"Be there in a sec." Cidy smiles, promptly answers, and gets out of her chair. She has totally lost the pace of time; hence, she forgot about the lunch date with the girls.

Walking towards the elevator, she reminisces about a lot of things. All the years that she has worked here feels like a dream, a quick ride of roller coaster that just ended a little too early—that feeling of unwanted detachment.

She quickly hastens her steps, and looks around if Jake is near. It is quite involuntary act of searching for Jake. He is not around. She feels very sad that she probably won't be seeing Jake either.

It is 12:15.

She arrives at lobby. She knows this will be her final Christmas party with the girls, and thanks God for everything.

CH 89: CIDY AND THE COMPANY

Cidy didn't like fasting: she loved food too much. She ate much more than people thought, but she kept her weight down quite well. She never knew how, but she suspected her fasting did some wonders for her weight. She dreaded it, but she managed it by drinking lots of orange juice and water, sometimes even some wine. She tried other juices but orange worked the best.

She fasted now for the third day for the right company to work for. And God gave her the word of taking the narrow road after her devotions and fasting, and she kept seeing the word—Texas. So, instead of taking a safer and more impressive job, she took a small company in Houston with the potential for growth.

That was how she got to the company she is working for now. All of friends told her not to take. It was a hard decision that only Mom supported.

The company grew a lot with Cidy on board. As a result, she received much higher pay than other companies after two years of work, and she had much solid position in the company. She was not in a management position, but she was treated like one by the employees, although that didn't go well with the upper management people. She was well loved and respected mostly by her fellow peers.

But the upper management managers had some fear of insecurity from Cidy because of the unexplained success that she has brought to the company. They felt like she did something that they were supposed be doing—helping the company grow. They just couldn't explain the phenomenon in the company's performance, because they all predicted negative growth boldly for past five years.

The upper management was quite awed by Cidy's performances: the details of taking care of the companies functions, both big and small with great success. The functions or parties, that she was in charge, did wonders for the company's expansion, closing deals, and acquiring new investments. She always made quite an impression on the people that the company invited. Her knowledge and experiences with many nations and their cultures impressed the investors and clients from foreign nations as well in-States business partners.

The employee turn-over ratio dropped nearly to zero with her aboard. They said it's because of expansion and growth, but no one in the management knew any company like their own. Employees reviewed their company with the highest satisfaction in the industry. The company had been exposed in the national and local TVs and magazines as *Happiest Place to Work*, *Best Place to Work for*, and *Fun Place to Work*. It was publicity that no one could have pulled off. As a result, the company had an amazing pool of people with great talents wanting to work with them.

With the success, Cidy unknowingly made enemies in the management: The management didn't like employees talking about her as part of the management or discussing with her about the problems they had with the company. She stepped on the management's face quite involuntarily. She thought the things she did and asked the company to do was best for the company, and they were.

The upper-management tried to scheme or collude to get rid of Cidy a few times, but things didn't work out. They desperately hoped that she would get in trouble or cause one. But each time, she came out like a golden goose, laying another gold egg.

Cidy had come to realize her political situation in the company. It wasn't something she bargained for. She never wanted any power, but she somehow had gained it. Her voice started to matter, especially to Jeff, CEO, and to the employees, especially the female. And that made her position difficult sometimes. Jeff always told her not to worry because he is backing her all the way.

CH 90: Lunch With the Girls

Cidy meets the girls at the lobby and heads for Whataburger with them.

During the lunch, Cidy looks into each girl's eyes showing love and attention as usual; but today, much more than usual, because she senses her time with them will be over soon.

Paula senses something is up; she says, "Cidy, are you okay? Since the morning, there is something. I know. What is it?"

"I'm fine. I'm just so glad to be with you. I love and appreciate y'all so much." Cidy covers it up quickly.

"No, we are," Paula quickly disagrees checking the approval of the girls. "You know what I'm most thankful about you Cidy? It's that PMS rest you made it happen."

(Why Paula brought that up, nobody knows. Maybe it was Paula who benefitted the most from it.)

Other girls they all jump in and pitch in their praise for Cidy.

"God made it happen, and Sandy was the boys' heart changer. And you girls gave all your heart and effort to make it happen. You are wonderful. I love you." Cidy wants to cry. When she said I love you, Cidy's voice breaks down a bit.

All the girls sense something is up, but no one wants to say anything.

Cidy barely escapes from crying. She coughs and covers it up. She feels like every second so precious and magical. There is sense of dreaming that overwhelms her like she is heaven. There is so much joy and laughter. She hates to leave them, but the destiny calls her. And she knows she will be walking into the greatest journey of all—The Great Commission.

CH 91: PMS REst PEtition

(It happened about ten months ago.)

More than 65% of the company employees were females, but they were mostly paper and communication supporters. The company gave the same treatment as other companies in regards to their female employees' benefits or care—nothing more, nothing less.

But some girls in the company had a very strong PMS headache, and they need a room for them to take a rest for a while or more desirably, a day off. They really needed that time off for their "woman" problem.

Several ladies came to Cidy to make complaints or seek favors for their "female" condition, and she did try to do something with Jeff. Although Jeff supported Cidy's idea of giving a day off and having a special "rest" room, the upper management team disagreed strongly.

The management team said it will cause a lot of disruption and unwanted disapproval from non-benefiting employees. They threw in a lot of speculative problems that could cause, not to mention, cost.

As a result, the company looked like it was resisting giving any favors to ladies over men. But Cidy being a woman knew that PMS headache can be quite troublesome for some ladies, and understood many just couldn't voice their complaints because they felt embarrassed. So she decided to have a petition drive to provide this relief for the girls in the company.

She had to have a petition drive because the company management was against it, although Jeff supported it. The management team said they did not wanted to change the company's policy because it was not a normal practice anywhere, and they said they didn't want to set any precedent for giving special provisions for employees that are not set by the law.

But, because Cidy brought a lot of small changes in the company that made big impacts, which made the management look obsolete and against the employees, the upper-management thought this will be great opportunity to get rid Cidy. They instinctively knew their roles, and the management never felt as united as one before. They wanted to see how the tides of the employees' opinion would be after a week or two of petition drive. And they knew the petition drive was not going to be easy. There were rumors that men were totally against giving any special treatment to ladies only. All they had to do was to wedge in the employees opinion apart as much as possible acting like their hands are clean.

Jeff knew Cidy had walked in to a death trap. He couldn't help her on this one at all. It was a cause more for women only, and it was unprecedented. He felt his hands are tied. He didn't want to go against the management team and the male employees. He did voice out that the company should let the employees decided, which meant the company employees need to show their overwhelming support. That was all Jeff could do to help Cidy and the ladies.

The rumor got out that company is a turmoil with an unnecessary and favoring issue, and the company was quickly divided into two—the man against the woman. There was even a rumor that the company make a black list of any employee who supports the cause.

The stage was set for Cidy's demise.

If she succeeds, which looked very unlikely, the management could agree to the cause reluctantly, and save their faces. But if she fails, which was the likely destiny, they had the leverage against her, and they can put scorching heat on her to quit or pressure Jeff to fire her. They felt like it was a "god-sent" opportunity to get rid of their pride-robbing thorn—Cidy.

Jeff told Cidy that only way to turn the tide in the management is to have a solid support from over 80 % of employees, and he warned failing could have devastating effects in the company's short-and-long run. And finally he mentioned that she would have very hard time staying in the company.

She knew there was very little to gain if she succeeded in the cause, but a lot to lose when failed: The company had to deal with the ruined employees' morale, and she would probably have to resign. She prayed to God what was the right thing to do. God was silent. She knew the answer before praying, but she wanted to hear it from God whether she should take on the cause. Her fasting for the cause gave a positive stand with God. Whether she succeeds or not, she decided to pursue the matter anyway; she had no idea what she went up against.

Jeff wished her good luck. He couldn't separate himself from the management because this was a major issue that no company had tried before, but he really wished Cidy the best. He decided to stay neutral as much as possible: he couldn't lose the male employees as well as the female.

The upper management personally voiced out their opinions that Cidy was pushing the envelope too far, and the issue can divide the well-running company to the point of great fall. They said this to position themselves to get rid of Cidy. They felt safe because they gave a unanimous voice. Many employees understood that Cidy could sabotage the company, and they feared for the worst—a severe political division—men against women. This could cause the company to dysfunction terribly.

However, most employees loved their jobs and did not want to move to another company. The fear separated even the ladies apart; they said one thing to supporters and another to non-supporters.

Cidy and the *009 Girls* designed various flyers with kisses and perfumes on it and passed them out saying support your sisters, wives and friends. It encouraged the men to take care of the weaker vessel of their fellow workers as the Bible say.

The fliers cause much commotion in the company: Men generally said, *This is not fair. How are we going to know if she has it today? What about for men, what if we have a headache?*

The cause really divided the company—men vs. women; supporters vs. non-supporters. And many really didn't care as long as they can keep working at the company.

Men had no idea what women really wanted, because they literally had no idea about PMS. They felt they came to work with all kinds of trouble and headaches, and they felt women should do the same.

It didn't look good for Cidy. She felt like she stepped into a major dinosaur dung, and she wasn't going to look pretty at the end. Worse, she thought she could bring the company down.

Employees' relations with each other started to feel edgy. They didn't know what to say. They felt like a pawn that was pushed around by people with "loud" voice.

For Cidy, this was the hardest time she ever had. She could be the cause of the down-fall of a very successful company. She struggled. She was blinded by the good cause. She prayed and prayed crying to God. God was silent.

The *009 Girls* never saw Cidy so distraught.

Cidy lost her confidence and joy. They were falling apart too. Two girls said they can't participate anymore.

Cidy said she understood because even she wanted to quit.

Soon two more said they can't do the passing out the flyers anymore.

Cidy asked Sandy and the remaining of the *009 Girls* to pray with her by fasting three days. Sandy and the remaining girls didn't really have faith but agreed to fast and pray with her. They got together early in the morning, 5:00 a.m., when no one was at the company, and they prayed for wisdom, and the change of hearts in men, and courage in ladies to stand-up for their sisters.

Sandy had the hardest time fasting, but she kept her bargain. On the third day, she received Holy Spirit; she started to speak in tongue. It was a language no one could understand. Even she said she didn't know what she was saying.

Sandy said, "My tongue…it's moving by itself. When I try to pray…it does its own thing. It's crazy. I think I'm crazy."

Other girls were amazed. They thought Sandy had gone nuts. But they would hear Sandy talking fine, but when she prayed she spoke in a different language that no one seemed to recognize.

Cidy said, "Sandy, you have been blessed. God gave you a spiritual gift—speaking in tongue. God has baptized you in Holy Spirit. I'm so glad for you. I have sought for a Holy Spirit gift for many years and haven't received anything like yours."

After fasting for three days, all the *009 Girls* bonded together with the witnessing of Sandy receiving of Holy Spirit. They got together, and decided to give it one more try. They continued their morning-prayer meeting. They knew it was a sign from God that He is with them. The remaining girls turned their heart to God for sure, and they recommitted themselves to the cause.

The *009 Girls* decided to silently make their statement by passing around coffee and snacks, during morning break and after lunch, to all the employees—both men and women—for a week. Many ladies joined the *009 Girls* for the cause by helping to serve, and over twenty girls came to join their morning-prayer meeting after hearing that Sandy received Holy Spirit. And a few others received the gift of tongue and two ladies got their pain healed during the morning prayer as well.

Mark heard that Sandy was fasting for the PMS-rest cause, so he led the cause in the sales department. Sales department became strong supporters. And Jake too made his voice heard in the accounting department to support the sisters in the company, and they became strong supporters as well.

After three days of fasting and serving the employees for a week, the *009 Girls* and other lady supporters went around the company for the petition to be signed. When talking with guys, Sandy was always there with her smile. She couldn't say much because she had very little energy left because after receiving Holy Spirit she continued to fast as Holy Spirit led her. Almost everyone signed even the ones who voiced out strongly that it is unfair favoring the ladies in the company. (Sandy's fasting moved many guys' hearts: she never looked more beautiful. Her face glowed like an angel.)

They all jumped on the band wagon for providing extra care for the ladies, and the ladies promised to take care of each other's work load to prevent any work clogging. It worked out perfect. Ladies who could not voice out their private issues were very happy, and felt very loyal to the company. Most of all, ladies felt indebted to Cidy and *009 Girls* for making something impossible happen.

The company's output and the overall working environment became much better after that. And many ladies work on weekends to meet their deadlines on time: they knew their body well. None of them abused their privileges for the sake of others.

CH 92: Back to the *009 Girls*

Girls yap in groups of two or three: they rehearse and talk about all kinds of things. They are rowdy, but just don't care for much. They feel like they own the world with the show coming up.

Tammy senses that Cidy is more of listener today than ever. She knows something is definitely up, but the show forces Tammy to put everything aside even her feelings for Cidy. When their eyes meet, Cidy smiles with her whole face telling Tammy that she is fine, but Tammy knew something is hidden behind her smile. Tammy needs to make sure the show is prepared perfect in every detail, so she naturally loses focus on Cidy's matter.

Tammy urges the girls to fill their stomach up quick and move on to the practice quickly; she sounds off, "Come on, Girls. Ain't got much time to waste. Let's chow up, and head-up for our final practice, Girls. Move it!"

They quickly finish their lunch as ordered.

They move to Tammy's church, and run their final practice to satisfy Tammy's picky desires. They are all giddy about the tonight show. They know they are going to make fools out of themselves, but they won't trade their lives for the coming moment.

They return to work around 3:30 p.m. after a quick practice at Tammy's church. They don't have much to do, but they are supposed to be at the office till four.

When four hits the clock, everyone in the company rushes out to get home to get ready for the party.

It is the biggest and the most exciting event of the company each year, and this is it is going to be the biggest ever.

And Cidy and Jake are no exception.

CH 93: KARINA CALLS CINDY

To Karina, Cindy is more than a friend; she is like a savior. Karina owes so much to her, and she has shown her appreciation for her friendship by keeping her close and always sending her gifts. Of course, Cindy dears their friendship as well, and sends gifts to Karina too.

Karina wanted to make the call to Cindy much earlier, but her work didn't give her any time.

Now with a break, Karina calls Cindy to tell her that the prophesy is being fulfilled.

Cindy answers with a voice of love, "Hey Rina. What's up?"

Karina laughs. She always enjoys Cindy's up-tempo and high spirit, but she knows Cindy has her own wounds to lick.

"Hey, Dee. I miss you so much." Karina truly misses her every day. She longs to see her so much: It has been almost seven years they haven't seen each other.

"Me too." Cindy doesn't hesitate to give her feeling as well.

"Got…something very important to say, Dee." Karina gets to the point quick.

"What? Are you getting married?" Cindy senses something important, not of tragic, but of significance.

"NO! It's about Cidy."

"Is Cidy getting married? It's about time."

"No. She's not getting married."

"Okay. What? What's the news?"

"I was getting ready to go to work this morning. Cidy called. We exchanged greetings, and she said she saw you in her dream. I felt it was something important right away, but I acted cool. She said you told her that she is ready and needs to go. And it hit me like a hammer. Everything came back to me. I knew it was the time to tell her everything. Time to come clean. And I told her about our encounter and the prophecy told." Karina replays what happened this morning.

Karina's words bring the memory of agony and triumph for Cindy: The four months of taking care of Karina broke her down to crumbs and rebuilt her completely new. It was the time when she lost the most precious thing in her life and got it back— the faith in Christ.

CH 94: Cindy's Agony of Faith

After two months of taking care of Karina, Cindy looked herself in a mirror and found an unrecognizable and terrifying face: Sadly it was her own self. It was ghastly looking face that she feared. It was one of those faces in horror movies. It was herself because it would do the exact same thing that she does, but it was not herself. She couldn't believe what she had turned out be—a face with no hope, a face of horror.

Birds singing and the cool breeze did little for her. She used to love all those little things in life that make each moment so special.

She was tired physically and tired of living as well, just like Karina. She thought she was doing the right thing to help Karina recover, but her life had turned totally upside down—her health is destroyed and her family is about to or already broken apart.

I have ruined my life, my family. …God has ruined me completely. What am I doing? Cindy couldn't believe where she had end-up. This wasn't in her script. She never imagined falling into such a dark and endless trap for helping a friend—a best friend.

She had many chances to return home, where everything is joy and happiness with some daily grinding work of taking care of kids and her husband. But there was something in her just won't give up, maybe pride.

Even after two months of taking care of Karina and neglecting her own family, Cindy still begged Patrick, her husband, many times just for another month to take care of Karina.

Cindy never heard Patrick so furious and threatening before: He attacked her with a threat of divorce and called her irresponsible mother with words she can't imagine coming out of her loving husband's mouth. He ranted on-and-on and even cussed at her. She felt like a trash that's been rotting for years, stinking up the entire neighborhood. She wanted to die; she wanted to just disappear. She wanted to cry but couldn't: She had even lost hope to the point where she didn't care for anyone or anything. But where she got that last straw of will to trudge on, she cannot say.

Karina's mom and dad advised her to stop the insensible act and to go back home to take care of her own family. They begged her often to leave, especially Mary.

It felt like a back stabbing every time when Cindy heard such words like she had done enough and she should go home.

She didn't even know if there is a home to return.

Her own parents called her many times to return home and take care of her own kids and family. She felt pushed around, cornered and manipulated to return home, although it seemed like the wisest thing to do. She couldn't handle the pressure. She didn't know what was the right thing to do.

She now began to question herself constantly of her motive, *Is it right putting everything I love in jeopardy for a friend? No, best friend?*

She realized she just might die right next to Karina, and lose herself and her own family as well. It was the cost of loving her best friend: It was just unbearably and too expensive.

Karina was looking worse than ever with no sign of hope: She looked like a zombie—eyes almost looked like a bulging balls of horror with full of blood vessel making its way to the corneas, and you could not tell if she was asleep or awake because you could always see her eye lids slightly open. She looked scarily and haunting with a face with little life and hair all diffused and with just bones barely attached keeping up her body frame. It was a miracle that she was alive.

A doctor came once a week to check on Karina. It felt he was coming to see if Karina was still alive.

Cindy felt like she needed IV too. Her view of Karina's recovery changed drastically, and she couldn't help it. Everything felt dark and hopeless. Not a prayer or a hymn could give any hope or strength to her. No, not anymore. She gave up hope, but whatever the reason she begged Patrick for one more month to take care of Karina.

It was Cindy's will; her own stubborn will to see it through to the end—to the death of Karina. She knew Karina can't live too long like this. So she decided to that she is going to be next to her best friend till death separates them. She didn't know if it was love or her just un-breaking will, but she felt it was the right thing to do even with the risk of losing her own family, not faith—just her own stubborn will.

At the least or the best I can do…for Karina's death, Cindy thought.

And Cindy, even after two months of no prevail, still summoned Mary each morning and night to have a devotion to God. She knew Mary was just being cordial and following along, and she started to feel the same way about the word of God and their prayers—dry and ritualistic. The Word was not alive for them, and their prayer was not faithful. But, Cindy coerced Mary to continue doing the devotion because she thought it was needed it to save Karina. The devotion became a ritualistic ceremony like witches chanting their spells.

Cindy thought about killing herself too many times. She felt the death would bring so much peace to herself because she didn't have to deal with the failure, the pain, and the loss.

What good is it to live, God? God, God, talk to me. She doubted much of her faith which became sour and twisted just like Karina's.

With furious anger, Cindy demanded answers from God, "What are YOU doing? Are YOU gonna kill us, both? You are CRAZY! We have loved you so much. You KNOW that. Why aren't you answering ME, God?"

Then, Cindy tried to do her best to remember any sin that she had committed or any wrong that she might have done to any one and try to amend with them—God, friends, relatives, and acquaintances—by asking for forgiveness. Many were surprised to receive calls from her and felt very disturbed because she kept apologizing for things they couldn't quite remember. She was going crazy: She popped into laughter often. She slowly lost touch with reality.

Her love for Karina died out. Her love God died out, too. She didn't know why she was holding on to her friendship that is killing her and taking the very thing that she loves the most—her family.

Why lose everything for a friend? She's gonna die anyway. That was Cindy's conclusion: Her fiery hope in God turned to ashes of darkness and cynicism.

She knew for sure that God had sent her to take care of Karina. She didn't hear any voice, or see a vision, but she knew it was God's calling her to take care of Karina right away when she heard the tragic news. She knew she needed to be here to take care of Karina. She knew it by heart. But she wasn't sure any more.

The third month was the worst. She never felt so disconnect with God before. She doubted all her experiences with God. They all felt like something she just imagined; something she just made it up as if God was somehow involved. Her faith died.

Patrick reluctantly agreed for another month, more like two weeks after furious arguments and fights for two, long weeks. Cindy's love for Patrick died with the devastating-word fights. She never felt so resentful of her husband. She cursed him in her heart. She murdered him many times in her mind.

Her burden became heavier and heavier. She was about to lose everything that she valued in her life—the best friend, loving husband, and very possibly her two adorable boys for neglecting them. She could constantly hear her boys crying and begging her to come home. She kept talking to her boys as if they were next to her, *I love you, and I will be home soon…very soon.*

She tried her best to keep her smiles, but she couldn't. She never cried so much before. Her cry sometimes turned in to hollow laughter of disbelief and darkness. She couldn't sleep well. She started to hate everything, even herself. She got mad at Mary and Karina and started to scream at them often.

She hated that Mary didn't give much support. She felt Mary was Satan himself always playing that devil's advocate: Mary kept piercing her faith with sympathetic words—*We all will die. Karina's death can be blessing. You should go home*.

Worse, Cindy started to feel like Mary was more than right. She felt she should have just left everything behind and went home to take care of her own family. She knew she had to salvage what's left of her family, soon. She missed them so much: her two little boys—Moses and Joshua—and Patrick, her loving husband, who now had turned bitter and angry. She missed making love with Patrick. She dreamed about making love with him often.

Worst of all, her body was breaking down as well. She coughed and her eyes were red most of time because of lack of proper rest. Her legs weakened, and especially her right leg felt quite numb. Her face and Karina's face were becoming more and more alike, each day. She thought she might even die with Karina, here.

Her mind parked in one thought—should have left after the funeral. Her spirit was but a smoke of a dead fire—worthless.

But that mask of hope, a fume, made Cindy clang on to God or herself. She didn't know what she was holding on to. Maybe, it was out of habit or out of desperation. She never cried out to God like this before: Her cries were loud and screeching. She beat the floors and the walls. But she didn't feel like God was listening to her prayer.

But one day, she didn't know if she was asleep or awake. But she heard a voice asking her a question, "Are you willing to die for Karina?"

She looked around to see if there was someone around. There was no one but Karina sleeping. She knew she wasn't well, but she knew she heard a voice asking a very simple question.

She couldn't answer the question, or her answer waivered back and forth. It was a struggle and a fight to answer the question.

She kept asking herself, *Can I die for Karina?*

She kept saying no..., and said yes later. Then, she would say no, soon after.

She had a family to take care and a loving husband. She couldn't give up her life for Karina—No; she couldn't not give her life up for Karina—No way.

This question put her on her knees, and she cried to God for several nights. Finally as death being so near her, she said, "God you know I love Karina. I don't know if I can give up my life for her. ...But I will try. You know I will try. I love Karina, God. If my life can replace for hers, I'm willing to give you mine. God please let Karina live. Take my life." She couldn't believe what she said to God, but she knew she said it sincerely.

She felt defeated, but she came to conclusion that she is willing to die for her friend. She was willing to let everything she dearly loves go. She cried, but she felt free. She trusted God will take care everything—her two little boys and Patrick. She wasn't afraid to die.

She called Patrick and didn't try to convince him or tried to make excuses anymore, but kept repeating that she loves him and thanks him for everything. Patrick didn't know how to respond. His anger didn't seem to rattle her anymore. His tone of voice and attitude changed: he kept asking if she is okay. She told her kids how much she loves them and how much she appreciates them. She called her parents and told them the same thing. She called her friends and acquaintances telling them the same thing.

She felt light and relaxed as she waited for her death, for her best friend—Karina. She hoped and prayed to God that He takes her life and saves Karina's. She never felt so close to God before. She was able to put on a smile, and praise and worship Him again. She didn't like the way He did things, but she felt comfortable with it.

A morning came and the night came, one day at a time, and somehow the third month was slowly but surely passed by. She let everything go even her own life, but she had peace she never felt before. She didn't have hope of what she wanted, but she felt free to give up her life in Christ's way.

She looked at Karina with love she never felt before. Although Karina's eyes were a bit horrifying to see, she glazed at Karina as if it was the last moment to see her, and Karina stared back at her with an eye of discontent and disapproval. Karina's emotionless face with hollowing eyes gazing at her like a zombie was frightening. But the fear became smaller and smaller with her serenity of accepting God's will and her willingness to give her life up for her friend.

She woke up many times, and she didn't know where she was. She didn't even know her own name either a few times. The pain and the suffering had gotten toll on her so much that she felt severe pain and aches in her body and head, and her menstrual cycle stopped. She couldn't eat well, and if she ate anything she threw it right back up.

Mary called a doctor over to check on Cindy. The doctor said Cindy and Karina need to be hospitalized. But Cindy kept arguing with the doctor what good is it gonna do to be hospitalized.

Cindy was correct: There was nothing that the hospital can do, but watch them die.

One night, only with will and a mere breath left, she woke up next to Karina's bed and found Karina not there. She panicked that Karina finally took her life as she dearly pursued it.

She dragged her body around the house and the outside of the house to find Karina to no avail. Finally, she opened the back door and was greeted by the coldness of the winter morning smothering her face. Then with a squint, she was able to spot Karina kneeling in the middle of the backyard. Karina was glowing.

Cindy thought it was just too strange seeing Karina glowing and being out there in the cold morning all alone.

She doesn't look dead. thought Cindy.

She, more than exhausted, called Karina aloud with all her strength. Karina didn't move. Cindy repeated again. Karina showed no respond.

Maybe she IS dead. Cindy worried.

Trying to approach Karina, she heard a voice saying, *Let her be.* She looked around if the voice came from anywhere, but she couldn't see anyone except Karina. She was very tired, but she knew what she heard. So, she immediately obeyed and came back inside. She waited at the living room, but she soon fell asleep.

When she woke up with the voice of Karina calling her, she felt refreshed and revitalized. She knew she was touched by God. She had her strength back.

After taking care of Karina and hearing what happened to her, Cindy called Patrick right away.

"Hey Patrick, Cindy has recovered. I'm coming home soon."

"I'm sorry, Cindy. I have wronged you, so much. I'm SO sorry…." Patrick tried to amend their relationship. He knew he had said too many ungodly words to his loving wife, the love of his life.

As soon as Cindy heard Patrick's voice, Cindy cried because God already amended their relationship.

There was silence.

Cindy didn't know what to say but said, "I'm so sorry too, Patrick. I love you. I wanna come home. I'll be home soon."

"I'm sorry Honey. I love you too. We are okay here. I'm used to the kids now. Or…the kids are used to me. …We're fine. You can come home whenever you want to. I'm so sorry for being so childish. I just missed you so much, and the kids were just impossible. I'm sorry, Honey. Forgive me."

"I'm sorry too, my Love. I'll try to be home quick. Are the kids up?" Cindy wanted to hear the boys' voice.

"No they're still in bed. I'll call you when they are up." Patrick answered with tears jerking.

"Okay…my Love. I love you. I'll make it up to you…."

She wanted to make love to Patrick so much. She missed his touch and warmth. She had been afraid that she was going to lose him and her children, but now, she was free from all that fear and burden.

Karina quickly recovered. Cindy too quickly recovered. Within a month, both of the families, Cindy's and John's, reunited. There was joy and celebration like no other. They thanked Cindy over and over again.

On the day Cindy left for home, Mary drove them to the airport. Sitting at the back seats together, Karina kept on crying while holding Cindy's hand, and they spoke of many things of their past and future. They laughed, cried, and hugged many times. It was a drama only dearest friends that have gone through the driest and stormiest desert together can share.

At the airport, as Cindy was about to enter the separation line, Karina started to cry again like a little girl that just lost her mom and can't find her, and she cried with such emotional burst that people thought something tragic has happened.

Cindy couldn't help but crying with Karina.

Cops came and asked if everything is okay.

Mary had to tell them everything is fine.

The cops and the crowd just stood there in awe to see two adult women crying like as if they just lost their loved ones in a tragic accident.

Finally Mary cried too: She tried to calm them down first, but she lost herself as well.

Cindy can't remember how long they cried, but their cries became quieter. Maybe they got exhausted. Crying was good: it made them feel much better afterwards. Maybe Holy Ghost had touched them.

Mary broke Cindy and Karina apart because of the time of plane departure became closer.

Cindy made her way through the inspection line. Cindy saw Karina slowly disappear from her as she got closer and closer to security check line. Their eyes never separated from each other, and they continuously waived at each other, on and off. At some point, Cindy couldn't see Karina anymore, but she felt her presence.

On the plane, Cindy wrote her experiences down.

She returned home as a different woman. She became more humble, and understanding. She didn't try to beat the Word into people anymore, she tried hard to show the love of Christ even when it was the hardest.

There was something in her now that knew God will be with her no matter what, especially in a situation even when she felt like God's not there at all. She felt the death wasn't something to be feared, any more. She became more than a warrior: She passed the test, the agony of faith that purified her like the pure gold with the glory of the triumph

CH 95: Back to Karina and Cindy

"I knew the time would come. I forgot about it...totally. How old is Cidy now?" Cindy senses the destiny playing out.

"27"

"Cute little Cidy...27. Just can't imagine. It's been 27 years." Cindy is amazed how time has passed by so quickly. She doesn't feel any older than 20, but she knows she isn't the same woman physically. The years have taken toll on her body especially her face, but she is very glad that God has allowed her to age gracefully.

"Yes. My little princess is now 27. And she's has received the calling from God. I'm ready to accept her destiny." Karina looks around the class room. "I'm afraid what she has to face is not easy but that's what God wants. Isn't It?"

"God will work with her and through her. Cidy will be his servant. ...Hey. Our whole family is going to U.S. We are very excited. I know it would be your first time seeing Patrick. He's very excited to meet you, too." Cindy tells the decision Patrick and she has made a few nights ago. She has told Karina her family might be coming, but now it is a permanent decision.

"Awesome. I missed you so much. We can visit Cidy together. We'll have wonderful time together."

CH 96: Going to Christmas Party

Worrying about what to wear, Cidy drives home.

She has plenty to choose from, but what. Being a girl means knowing what to wear, and she feels like she does an excellent job of putting together an outfit for any occasion. But today, she wants make a good impression on Jake. She wishes to have just one date with him, and to tell him that she will be doing some sort of God's work. She is hoping, but realizing it would be probably very unlikely he might be willing to come along.

Girls in the company call Cidy odd but tasty. They like her conservative yet catchy fashion. They thought Cidy didn't dress cheap nor expensive and her fashion seemed mild but had sprinkles of hot pepper that just can't be explained. Maybe, they felt comfortable with Cidy that she didn't tried to grab everyone's attention.

She enters her apartment quickly. Covering her hair first, she takes a quick shower. She needs to get dressed up as quickly as possible because she is the coordinator of this party, so she has to be there early. She knows everything is probably set and ready to go, but she feels the responsibility and is somewhat worried.

But today she really wants to look special for Jake, and that attention-seeking takes an extra time. She remembers when Jake stared at her from a distance when she wore one-piece pinkish dress for a company party. She quickly wears it and likes it.

She never wears all out pink because she feels it is just a little too childish now that she's all grownup, but a dress with a bit of pink flavor mixed with light purple feels more than "royal-ish" yet cute enough for a teenager.

The lower-end of skirt reaches just below her knees. It not too revealing for many girls, but she feels it's quite appropriate and sexy. Displaying her beautiful shins, ankles, and calves is more than revealing enough. She likes it. And she sprays her home-made perfume she made; she learned it from Nadeera. She has a smell that no one else has. It really smells pretty nice—dreamy and romantic.

She puts her make-ups: eyeliner, mascara, a touch of face lotion, a touch of blush, and a pinkish purple lipstick to match her dress. She smacks her lips and winks at herself with a cheesy smile. She likes what she sees. She selects the ear rings and her necklace to match. She checks and double checks herself on the mirror. She feels confidant and sexy. She gives a little fist pump and shouts, "GO GET HIM, GIRL!" It is a spirit acknowledging that she is going to knock Jake down tonight.

She closes are eyes for a few seconds and thanks God for everything.

As she is about to walk out the room, she looks at the pictures of girls and boys from India, Africa, and South America that she sponsors through various Christian organizations.

She never shared about this part of her life to anyone except Mom, but this support gave her a lot of joy in her life and that extra perk and steadfastness that people are drawn to her. Reading about how kids, missionaries, and churches being supported each month makes her feel great and awesome, and gives her that fountain of joy sprouting in her heart, and creates that aura about her—very comforting and magnetic.

She supports them quietly and secretly, but that good work shows through her face, heart, attitude, and walk. She has tears and love for the children of the world, especially for the weak and the poor.

This charity is something Karina did too. Actually, Cidy learned it from Mom. They have this secret sharing of their fruit in the supporting of mission fields.

And every other year, they purposely visit various parts of the world where they support.

It became a great vacation as well as strong bonding for them, but most of all it became a strong spiritual-growth experience.

Cidy looks into the kids' and missionaries' eyes and prays for them and kisses them with her hands like she always does. She is quenched with the rush of all the joys that are brought by these kids in the far corners of the earth, and has flashes of joys that are received from them.

CH 97: TO INDIA WITH MOM

During the winter of 2006, they journeyed to upper north-eastern region of India. They have seen poverties in Africa and other parts of Middle East, but India was one of the worst they had ever seen. The extreme poverty shocked both of them. It was basically a Stone Age living with constant hunger. But the wells and churches they help built gave the kids, the families and the missionaries they supported in the area—hope and faith.

The place in their schedule to visit and stay for two weeks was a *Bridge of Hope* center in a remote village in northwest India near the Pakistan border.

They were exhausted from over 20 hours of the plane ride, but the van ride to the remote village from the Mumbai international airport was even worse.

They did stop at a small village to sleep before continuing the travel to their final destination. They got out of the van feeling every bone and muscle screaming, but the foul smell smacked them on their faces first. But they got used to the smell in a few minutes.

They stretched and walked around to feel better, and saw stars and stars abundantly stretched out on the sweet night mellow sky with the beautiful half-moon shining so warmly. It was dark but the night was so beautiful. It wasn't a sight you can see in a city in the U.S.

They were shown to a room or a hut: no bed just blankets and pillows on the floor, maybe some hay under the blankets. It wasn't too visible at night with a flash light. They were given some water in a large bowl to clean and shown where the outhouse was. They had done this before but it wasn't easy. They took care of the business as quickly as possible and got to bed.

They had one of the sweetest sleeps ever. They both slept like dead fish. They had no idea where they were at and what they slept under, and they forgot about the foul smell.

They got up earlier than they thought. They thought they slept over a day, but they only had eight hours of sleep. They felt refreshed. The morning sky was clean and crisp with fluffy white clouds moving to a slow music of the wind.

They quickly wash their faces, and ate some Indian food they were given. The driver, the missionary, and the hostess family all ate with their hands. It was uncomfortable for Cidy and Mom but they ate with their hands (They were given forks and spoons.), licking their fingers and hands for every grain of the rice and every drop of sauce. They had a lot of laugh with the hostess family, the missionary, and the driver while eating.

They shared a few stories together about the U.S., and they heard a few stories of where they were at before their travel started again.

They forgot how painful it was to ride on the van.

The morning came, and they had delicious and laughing breakfast. They thanked the hostess.

They got right on the van, and headed for their destination. The continuous rattling of the van caused by the unpaved road was quite nauseating. In fact, both of them vomited a few times. It took them two days of travel from the airport in a beaten down van that sounded like it was going to break down in any moment to arrive at their destination—a Bridge-of-Hope center where the missionary Cidy supported ministered.

When they got to the center, it was about 5 p.m. There was a large hut in an open field with a wooden-stick fence around it. The van honked loudly and long twice to let them know they had arrived. Cidy and Karina felt sick, but relieved that they stopped.

When they got out of the van, they stretched and saw the beautiful sky that spread above them as if God was greeting them. It felt like the open arms of God. They forgot how sick they were from the rough ride.

Missionaries and the teachers first came to greet them. Cidy knew Mom wasn't feeling well because she wasn't either, but she was shocked how Mom was able to put on such a big smile to meet the greeters.

"Hellrow, welcum to the Bridge of H'Up Centerr." One of the ladies greeted them with a heavy Indian accent.

"Hellrow, I'm so glad to see you. I'm Sankaran." The tall, skinny missionary with big dark eyes made a greeting. He hugged Mary and Karina. He was the one Cidy supported.

"Hi. It's great to be here." Karina and Cidy hugged the rest of the missionaries and teachers.

As they were greeting, they could see kids leaning and peeking behind the fence.

A missionary told them that it is a place where kids could come after school and get help with their homework and learn the Sunday-school music and the Word from the Bible.

One of the ladies led them to the field inside the fence. There were over fifty kids anxiously waiting. Kids were told to stay inside the fence and be proper. But the Kids quickly surrounded Karina and Cidy. The kids were so cute and beautiful although many looked unhealthy.

They were bombarded by questions and greetings from all the kids: "Welcome!", "Hi!", "Hello!", "Thank you for your support!", "Are you from U.S.?", "What's your name?", and "How old are you?"

Karina quickly picked up a little girl, who looked unhealthy and weak, but Karina decided she is the one to receive the most of her attention.

Cidy followed Mom and picked up a small boy that looked very weak as well. Kids swarmed around them constantly asking questions, but they seemed to be living in heaven because they had such big smiles and authentic joy.

The teachers told Karina and Cidy that the kids have a gift for them. The teachers started to call the kids to line up. Soon the kids started to sing a Sunday-school song—*Jesus Loves Me This I Know*, other Sunday school songs in English and Hindi. Cidy and Karina sang with and danced with them. It was Heaven. Cidy and Karina quickly forgot about their pain, or the pain just disappeared. Cidy felt like she was floating on the clouds. Kids with big black eyes were angels from the Heaven.

Most of the kids were outcasts in their neighborhoods and in their nation. They were called *untouchables*. It meant that if anyone above their social cast touched them, he or she became unclean or contaminated. So people hated even talking to them. Worst yet, these kids were abused by other kids in school. (It was illegal to treat people based on their cast, but it was a common practice.) It was like a curse from the birth. It was depressing for Karina and Cidy to see such boys and girls with the lives that are already carved as failure and cursed.

But these native Christian missionaries gave them hope by teaching them that they are loved by God and Jesus Christ—the Son of God—who has died for their sin and rose again from the death on the third day. And they are not cursed but blessed, and they are not poor but rich.

The missionaries told them of many miracles that these children have done with the faith they had been taught. They called out a boy whose name is Anshi. He ran over to them. And they told the story what Anshi did:

Anshi's mom had been sick for over five years. She had done everything she could and had gotten very poor along the way. She reached out to every possible cure and witch doctors, but she had gotten worse and worse in both health and finance.

Meanwhile, her son, Anshi, had been left alone and was reached out by one of the missionaries. And Anshi had been visiting the center for fun, food, and friends. But mostly the teaching of the Word had been planted in the Anshi's heart, and his faith grew day by day. One day Anshi, learning the story of how Jesus' disciples had healed the sick, went home, and laid his hand on his mom, and prayed to God for the healing.

And miraculously, she was healed. Mom couldn't believe she got healed from the sickness. She went around the village telling what had happened. The boy and his mom became a great witness for the Christ in the village. And several families in the village came to Christ, and the missionaries were able to build a small church there.

It was really hot there.

But they were able to meet the child and the missionary they supported. They supported them through the organization called GFA (Gospel for Asia). Karina supported five children and three missionaries and Cidy supported seven children and five missionaries.

Cidy and Karina met so many children that they fell in love with. They cried as if they met their long lost children, and they blessed all of them. And they knew these were the family they will be together in the heaven and live forever. It was one joyous moment after moment.

As they stayed in the area for the next four days, they saw how the kids, and their families, and missionaries lived in harsh and unimaginable conditions. These native missionaries lived in the same harsh environment as their neighbors: usually an entire family slept in a tiny mud house more like a hut. But they were happy; they were so happy and excited to work for Christ.

The children gave Karina and Cidy gifts: letters they wrote, and small presents made from clay, wood, or rock. Some just gave them rocks. It was a token of their heart.

Karina and Cidy couldn't help themselves from crying and laughing. Children's big dark eyes with that big smiles melted Cidy and Karina's hearts like chocolate on a hot summer day.

Cidy repented that she should have supported more of them.

CH 98: Cidy Hopes for Jack

Cidy imagines teasing Jake a little bit and finally being asked out by Jake, and she would say *no*, just to make sure he meant it. Jake makes her happy. She wonders about God's plan for her and her desire for Jake would coincide or collide. Her bet is on collide but hopes for coincide.

She quickly closes her eyes and prays for Jake to be her love, but she finishes with the words: "Not my desire but your will be done." She feels the heart ache of letting Jake go for Christ as if someone is carving her heart out, very slowly and deliberately. It is not easy for her, but she knows her priority— Christ, first. She doubts herself, that if Jake pursued her, she might not get her priority straight. She is little dazed, and decides to focus on now.

She knows Jake is always at the party usually just talking to a couple of his buddies. She wants to hit on him hard tonight so he has no choice but to ask her out. She feels she had to make a move, tonight, because she knows she has very little time left for her. How? She has no idea. She really likes him, so she drops another quick prayer for his courage to ask her out. She wants to see if he is her true fate.

She quickly leaves her apartment and dashes for her car. Her heels makes nice drum beat against the concrete sidewalk. It's a beautiful afternoon with such a beautiful sky: The soften-up baby-blue sky lying on the background, the cute white fluffy clouds posing in the air, and the sun slowly dipping on the other side creating light-purplish shade make the late afternoon more than spectacular. It feels like the perfect day to fall in love with Jake.

Cidy gets into her little, white, shabby Geo Metro, and drives to the hotel. She checks her phone to see what time it is. She's a bit late. Although she is quite confident that everything is ready, she wants to be at the hotel early to make sure everything is set and ready. It is going to take about twenty minutes to get there, so she calls Mom.

"My daughter, Cidy. I've been waiting for your call." Karina is so glad to hear her daughter's voice. "How'd you handle the day?"

"It was sad and special. Every little object in the office seems to be so alive. Every person seems so special. I kept wishing I should have treated them better and said one more greeting. I lost it a few times. I had to go to restroom to let it all out. I kept staring at my close friends. They all seem to say *I love you* and *I'll miss you*. Everything feels like a dream." Cidy drives through the roads carefully.

"And Jake...?" Karina lowers her tone and tries to see if Cidy is handling the calling all right because Karina feels Jake is the biggest obstacle for Cidy.

Cidy feels something special in her heart when she hears the name—Jake. She wants to say so much. "...Mom.... I love Jake. If he asks me to marry him today, I know I be very shaky, but I know what to do Mom. I need to make sure he's willing to accept my calling. I don't know if it would be that easy, Mom. I love him so much. I just want to date

him…least…once…least once. You know…. I'm
trying to impress him tonight. I would like to have that
just one date. Is that wrong…Mom?" Cidy watches
the cars ahead and turns on the street to the hotel.

"I think you can handle it Cidy. You know
your priority: God is first. Love you, Cidy. I'll talk to
you soon." Karina knows Cidy is driving, and she
heard it enough to know Cidy is going to do the right
thing.

"Love you, Mom." Cidy hangs up the call.

Cidy wants to have a love like Mom—the
kind of love that people dream about.

CH 99: CIDY'S "LOVES"

In elementary, there was Job.

Cidy had crush on Job because he was funny and cute. He was always making funny noise in the class room that got him in trouble, but she loved him for his humor. He teased her a lot, but he teased a lot of other girls too. His goofy acts and energetic play in the playground got her attention.

One time, Job kissed her while playing together once. It was a blind attack that she had no control over, but she liked it, although she fussed about it. Maybe Job was returning the attention she had given him: she shared the sandwich Mom made with Job often. She was sure Job was the love of her life.

In middle school, Kurt made all the right moves to get her heart pounding. He always would say things that would get the class roaring which teachers didn't mind much. She had three classes with Him. He was the class clown with the heart of gold: He always helped other kids who need help with their school works and other things. He once threw a roll during lunch time and started a food fight. He got into a serious trouble, but kids loved him. And she loved him.

She enjoyed Kurt's foolish acts and adored his kind acts. He came up with a special greeting for Cidy: He said, "Cheerio, Cidy, be jolly." A few days later Cidy came up with a touché, "Aye, aye Captain

Kurt." Kids thought they were boyfriend and girlfriend. She wished, but he never got serious about any girls. He never sent any Valentines cards to her. She was disappointed but loved him anyway.

In high school, Kurt grew up to be a fine boy, but he hung around with boys more. She occasionally had a chat with Kurt, but that was it.

In high school, she thought she's going to find her true love like her mom at church or school but nothing serious happened. Robert was her favorite. He was tall and dark that a lot of girls liked. He was a quiet and strong type. She had crush on Robert, but he never asked her out for date. Other boys asked her out for date, but she just didn't have any feelings for any of them. So for the prom, she went with one of the boys that she felt better than the other.

In college, Jerald, Michael, Steve, Sam, and few others that she dated once or twice never worked out. She just didn't hook with them. There was attraction but no connection.

It was funny how love seemed to elude her, or she kept dodging the Cupid's arrow.

CH 100: Cidy and Reconciliation

While driving to the hotel, Cidy picks up her phone on the side to check the time again, but the phone somehow slips through her finger and lands on the floor. As she searches for her phone with her right hand, she drives carefully but bit awkwardly. She's feeling for her phone with left foot and with her left hand now, but she couldn't find it.

She knows she will be on time, but looks down quickly, and sees if she can spot the phone. She can't see it. She makes sure the road ahead is clear, and dips her head down a little longer to see where the phone has landed. It was close to the accelerator paddle. She looks up the road to make sure it is still safe again. She pushes the phone near her reach with her right foot, and she bows down, and picks up the phone.

When she lifts her head up again, she felt very strange: the scenery around changed completely. It was unfamiliar: She could not recognize the streets that she was on.

She turns her heads left, right, and back, but she could not recognize where she is. She is scared. It looks like a part of town where she had never been.

What happened? Where am I?

One green neon sign catches her eye—a very brightly-lit sign that reads *Paradise 7*. It looks like a major, five-star hotel, at least, and feels very luxurious and welcoming. She does what comes natural: She drives into the hotel parking lot, and gets out of the car, and looks around. She forgets she's lost being observed by the spectacular beauty.

There are people talking, walking, and getting in and out the car. The surrounding is very clean and presentable. It is very well decorated with flowers, shrubs, trees, ornaments, and there are statues of lions and eagles. She steps toward the entrance that you can't miss. She figures you might as well check out the hotel and ask for the direction back to the hotel.

It's much better than the ones you see in the movies, she thinks. "Wow, this must be a top-notch, five-star hotel. I didn't think there was such a hotel in Houston."

The fragrance of flowers is everywhere. She loves the exotic scent of the flowers which reminds of her backyard growing up. The sky in the background is amazing too: there are stars and stars. She can see the galaxy. She had never seen so many stars before. But she feels the urgency to find out where she is, but the scenery and the scent keep her calm and comforted.

She walks through the main entrance where two gentlemen standing across each other dressed in dark-blue suits with long double tails, gold-plated buttons, and *Paradise 7* emblems on their chest collars.

They say in chorus and harmony, "Welcome to Paradise."

She smiles and walks through the main entrance. She forgets to ask where she is at because of the majesty and the grandiose. She feels like she was just sucked in.

A beautiful piano music is playing. It is very comforting and entertaining. And the lovely oriental carpet under her feet feels heavenly. It has most fine and beautiful detailed work of art. Most of the walls have lovely paintings with elaborate gold frame, and beautiful antique furniture is here and there. The sweet aroma of peach is more than heavenly. She feels elated. All the details are so perfect.

It must be one of those luxury hotels I only hear about. She reasons.

But she quickly comes to her senses that she needs to know where she is. She tries to reach the counter as quickly as possible, but her senses are overwhelmed by the beauty and the scent. Her head is constantly turning to observe the exquisite beauty. She can't help it but to make steady steps towards the counter.

As she reached the counter, the clerk greets her, "Welcome to Paradise." He sounds as if he was expecting her.

She quickly blabbers with urgency, "Where am I? Where is this hotel? I have never seen it before. I'm lost."

"Yes...Miss Cidy. We have been waiting for you. Your room is 717," the clerk responds calmly with a comforting smile, and put the key on the counter, and slowly pushes it toward her.

"What? ...what...ARE you talking about? How? ...you know my name!" She stutters with disbelief.

"What's happening? How does he know my name? This can't be real." She talks to herself.

She echoes the same thought over and over again.

The clerk gives her a moment to calm down. "Ms. Cidy. Your room is ready. It's all been paid for by Mr. John Grant." The clerk gives a comforting smile in his eyes.

"JOHN GRANT...! That's MY dad. Is HE here? Is HE really here?" She screams with shock.

She forgets about everything. Hypnotized, she grabs the key and heads for the elevator as if she knows exactly where she was going. Just as she got to an elevator, one of the elevator's doors open, showing the sign going up. She gets in, and pushes number 7.

She couldn't think anything else but her dad. The doors slide and meet in the middle, and the elevator moves up displaying the each floor number on the top of the doors. Her heart beats louder and faster. The whole body resounds with her heart beats. She has only one thought in her mind—Dad.

For how long had she longed to see her dad? For how many times had she cried for that moments only a dad could comfort? All those times—school events, church events, her birthdays, and just normal everyday things—she felt left out because she didn't have a dad next to her. Finally she gets to see her dad that she has desperately longed for her entire life.

She feels tears coming out of her eyes and making their ways down her cheeks, and she lets them drip on the floor. She jerks a bit. She softly wipes her tears softly with her fore palms, and breaths in deep to calm herself down. And she checks her face on the wall, making sure she looked ok. She cleans her face quickly. As she breathes in deep, she smells that lovely scent of flowers again. This time, roses. It calms her down a lot. The elevator reaches to 7th floor with a sweet ring.

As the elevator door slides open, she runs to the room 717 in a split second as if she is pulled by a force. She seems to know exactly where she is going. She halts at the door 717. She takes in a long breath; a thousand thoughts pass by her. She slides the key in and opens the door almost unconsciously.

As she opens the door wide, a gentleman wearing a dark blue suit with his back turned takes the center stage of her view. He stands at a window and the light from the window spots him like a star of a show almost making him look celestial.

The room looks so meticulous and exotic; it was unbelievable. It must have been an executive suite, or one of those fancy rooms for the rich and famous. Every painting, vase, table, furniture, rugs, carpets, ceiling decoration, details, and that smell of roses that she remembers so well make the place so inviting and fabulous. She is afraid and awed; she stands still at the door. She feels like eternity is passing by.

The gentleman slowly turns. He sees her. He has tears in his eyes. He says in a sweet baritone voice, "Come in, Cidy. I have been waiting for you."

She can't believe what she heard. She is slow to respond observing the moment and replaying the voice she just heard over and over again.

"Dad?" She speaks not so confidently with a shaking and weakening voice. She can't believe what is happening. It is the moment she dreamed about for all her life. Her body is shaking with sheer joy as well as with the fear of doubt. She makes an intentional and difficult forward movement as she is drawn to her dad with a force that completely surrounds her body.

"Yes! Cidy! It's…me…Me…. You're DAD." As he slowly walks towards Her, John loudly and welcomingly answers with open arms.

She always had a picture of him. She cried on that picture so many times. She had that young handsome man Mom fell in love with. He looks just like how she would imagine but with little more facial lines and gray hair.

She can't hold herself anymore; she runs to him, and hugs him. She cries as her tears flood her face. "DAD!"

He runs toward her. He grabs her and hugs her.

They cry and cry for eternity.

She feels so happy.

He feels her joy and pain in her tears.

She cries till she is exhausted. She pants irregularly.

While holding her closely, John wipes her tears away with his thumbs as he holds her face. Oh, how long had he desired to hold her? He feels overwhelmed and exhilarated.

They stare at each other with tears just pouring down like a sweet rain. She thinks she is dreaming. She knows she is dreaming, but it just feels too real to her.

After all the crumpled-up emotions about her dad who was never been there for her are drained out, she gets her sense of reality back, and she quickly pulls away from him.

She calms herself a bit and spits the truth out, "How can this be? You are dead! This is not real! What is this? Who are you?" Her eyes stare right at John's trying to pick up any lies or pretentions.

He puts on a soft and understanding smile. He knows it's not something she can believe or comprehend. "I am...your Dad." He tries his best to tell her the truth. He is a bit shaken too. He's trying to find words to explain.

"I know I'm dreaming but this is so real." As she shakes her head, she gazes at his eyes again to see if it is him.

"I don't know how to explain this but this...IS...real. It's a special arrangement by God...for you and me. It's a gift." John slowly and calmly explains.

"What? God's arrangement? ...gift?" She doesn't understand what he is saying.

He explains steadily and calmly again, "Well...you are in Paradise. I asked God for this special arrangement for a long time. I wanna to meet you, see you, and hold you for a while. He said *yes*. And...I didn't know it would be now."

He pauses a little and gives a kind smile and continued, "You look so wonderful, so...so beautiful. I watched you grow up every day, and I see every moment of your life. I know you miss me a lot, but I never miss you or Karina...not a single day. There are so many times I wish I could be with you or be seen by you. But.... Well...I've prayed for you and Karina every day."

"Mom said you died helping a family from a car accident." She mentions the event that gave so much pain to herself and Mom. She actually wants to know what happened; she wants to hear it from Dad.

"Yes. I…I don't regret what I did. I…would do…the same…knowing I won't be part of you…and Karina's lives," John speaks with heavy heart. He has hard time accounting the tragic life of Cidy, but wants to show her what happened.

There is some silence. She is touched by Dad's love for her and Mom as well as fellow human beings.

He says, "Cidy, I wanna show you something, something…very special. Come…."

He leads her to a beautiful crystal door to the left. Cidy follows him. John holds her hand. It is a double door like the one that leads to a porch or veranda. As he opens the doors, he leads her to a green spring country-side prairie. The soft spring-sun warms up the day as the cool spring breeze teases them with welcoming kisses.

A farm with a barn, a huge close-fenced ranch, and a small, run-down country house make the scene with beautiful blue sky with spots of white clouds here and there. The wind sweetly hums through the grass and tree branches serving that fresh country smell. And Kids play around like a scene from a story book.

"You see those kids playing. The little blond boy tagging along the older ones…well…that's me. They are my brothers and sisters." John reminiscences with joy.

He continues, "I'm the youngest of five. My brothers and sisters always took care of me, but couldn't play with them because I was too young for them. After we grew up, we just couldn't see each other as much as we wanted. They were busy with their lives. I was busy with mine. I miss them a lot."

He points out each one describing who and how they were like when they were growing up.

John's childhood passes by like a movie.

He accepts Christ when he is seven when his Pastor prays with him.

His trouble making doesn't stop, but he talks to Christ and God like his friends. He must have been the most trouble-causing little boy that town had ever known, but he grows up to be a fine teenager:

He is much like any other boys growing up in a church with a family that is trying to do their best with what they got. He works hard helping out with the farm work.

He gets lots of love from his brothers and sisters, his parents, his neighbors. He is very adventurous and daring. He doesn't know his poor. He loves hunting with Grandpa and his brothers.

He doesn't hurt anyone, but his desire to explore and discover causes much trouble for many. He takes his friends for a trip without telling his parents and their parents. They disappear into the wilderness for a few days. Finally they are discovered by the town search organization. He gets into to a heap of trouble and is punished very severely for scaring the whole town.

He disappears often at nights with his friends for a night adventures to spy on unusual neighbors and for other weird stuff he is curious about with his friends. He is always breaking things apart to see how they work. He is a major menace to family and to the town, but he makes everyone around him feel very special. He seems have that genuine love and care for people and animals.

He has his core friends that are always getting in trouble with him for doing silly things in school, but always doing a lot of the dirty work for the school and the church as well. People just couldn't figure him out: They hate him much as love him.

He is talking to a couple of boys in high school.

He explains to Cidy, "I have my share of wrong doings. I know I caused enough trouble for five boys. But, this one hurts me the most."

CH 101: John's Addiction to Porn

In high school, a few boys call John over after a gym class, and show him a pornographic magazine. He is instantly hooked. He couldn't keep his eyes away from it. His heart races like he never experienced before. (He never felt such a rush of an excitement and thrill before.) His mind and body are sucked in by the pictures in the magazines. He has never seen girls exposed in such manners before.

His mind struggles. He knows it is evil. But every time the boys call him over, his body follows the voice on its own will: his body desperately sought out for the fix for its eyes. He laughs and jokes with them saying things about women he had never even thought about. He gets high on the pictures. His body and mind never felt so intertwined as one; the surge of energy in his body and the focusing of his mind feel intoxicating. Those images of women burn inside his heart and mind, and build a living quarter there. He lusts for every one of those girls on the magazine—constantly.

Since then his desire to have a woman as a sexual partner grows immensely. He stares at girls and imagines them like the girls in the magazine. He becomes more and more fixated by girls' existence around him, and he notices himself becoming more and more attached to them not as friend but as sexual objects.

373

He liked girls before sexually, but now it is purely sexual. They are sexual object to play with rather than friends.

Before he did fantasize about holding hands and kissing them often, and having sex with them, but now more vivid wild sexual encounters dominates his thoughts all day long.

He imagines having sex with pretty girls in the school and how they looked naked like the porn magazine girls that he had peeked with his friends.

His desire for sex grows so strong; it overwhelms him. He wants to try it like the magazine, but he can't find a girl to act out his fantasies. In his room, he masturbates often resulting in lack of energy and focus.

He could not resist the temptation of getting some porn magazines from the boys. He buys them through the boys. And he hides them in his bedroom, and starts spending more and more time with those magazines. He gets behind his school work and loses touches with friends.

The porn addiction eats him alive. Whenever he gets any money, he buys the magazines. He lies to Mom how he needs money for this and that to buy more and more magazines. He couldn't get enough of it.

HIs participation or involvement with the family and friends is significantly reduced. He cites school work as his excuses. He starts to wake up late for school making excuses that he had to study late for exams or had much homework to do.

He loses so much focus in class that teachers are irritated with him. He distances his friends as well. All he thought about is going home and gorging over the naked girls in the magazine and reading the sexual fantasies. He isn't himself but he couldn't help it: The addiction controls his mind and his soul very methodically.

He lies more than ever. He steals porn magazines from stores. His grades drop. He hangs with the wrong crowd saying things he never did. He tries smoking for the first time. He doesn't like it, but he wants to learn.

Mom senses something is wrong with John, but she thinks it's just adolescent thing beside she is just too busy trying to take care of the farm and the family. She prays to God for his well-being: that is about all she could do. She asks him if he's okay, but his excuses are always the same—the school. Dad says just leave him alone that he'll come around. Dad has no idea how time has changed.

One day, trying to find a missing sock, searching through his room, Mom accidently finds the magazines. There are over thirty of them. She is astounded and loses her words. She couldn't believe what she has found. It takes a while for her to accept the reality. She repeats the same thought over and over again—*Not my little John.* She just takes one of them and decides to face John that night.

That night, Mom knocks on John's door and asks him for a private talk. John quickly puts his porn magazine that he was gorging on under the bed. He responds without any defense and welcomes Mom into his room. Mom walks in to his room and seats on the chair. John is smiling and relaxed sitting on his bed.

"Mom, you worried about me…again? Don't worry. I'm just growing up, Mom." John tries to cover up his poor showing in the family and the school with cool attitude.

Mom closes her eyes. She prays for courage to confront her little John. She pulls out the magazine, and says, "Is this yours?"

He gets the biggest sucker punch of his life and loses his smile and composure quickly. He doesn't know where to look. His head moves in irregular ways. He wants to run out the room. When he recovers some thoughts, he hesitantly answers yes with great fear and shame. He feels very guilty, and does not know what will happen to him. It has been a while he had been punished. He had been in trouble before, but he knows this will top everything.

She could not find a word for a while.

He could not keep his head up.

She says calmly but with strong disappointment in her voice and face, "Look at me…, John."

He reluctantly raises his head up and looks into Mom's eyes unwillingly. He is ashamed. He feels the disappointment in her eyes. He could not look into her eyes.

Her eyes are glaring with a slight tear.

He hurts deeply seeing her cry. He knows it was wrong, but his desire to see the beautiful girls exposed and reading the sexual fantasies has chained him very quickly and strongly. How can he explain this?

She continues, "I know you are growing up. You find girls more interesting, especially sexually. Girls will make your heart beat faster. It's natural. I was your age once. But they are God's creation for your friendship first. You'll find one that meets all your desire in time. But you must learned to be friends with them; if not, you will miss out on all other great things especially true love and even having wonderful sex. Sex between a man and a woman is great, but without true love, it's very devastating for both of them. It becomes just an act of cold desire, not an expression of true care and love. Sex becomes more of devise than part of love."

She finishes her eloquent explanation of love and sex. She has no idea where she had gotten those words. She feels good to reprimand and explain the secret of love. She closes her eyes and quietly prays again.

He sees her crying quietly with tears flowing down from her eyes and rolling down on her cheeks. A few fall on the carpet without a sound but make thunderous strikes into his heart.

She stops for a while to breathe slowly, and swallows her tears, and slowly but with a little shake wipes her tears away with her hands, and opens her eyes with a few blinks, and comely and seriously says some more, "This is an easy temptation for boys to fall in to, but you have to win over it because your lust for girls like this can surely ruin you. Your desire for them is natural but learn to be friends with them first. Girls are not like this in this magazine. They are NOT! If you DID find anyone like this, she will definitely RUIN your life."

From the day he had first seen the porn, he knew it was evil, but the hook was just so deep and uncontrollable. He realized his addiction was quick and quite real: He lost interest in all other things and spent more and more time with the porn magazines. He knew he had to quit but he didn't know how. It was like a strong rope that is tied to his whole body that pulled him to those magazines every second that he was awake and asleep. He prayed to God for courage to throw them away but couldn't. He loved the girls in the magazine, and they became the most important part of his life. He was hopeless.

There are tears just keep dripping like a gutter after a heavy rain on Mom's eyes. She closes her remorse with final statement. "John this is between you and me. I don't think Dad would be happy with this. I beg you as Mother to break this chain." She walks over to him, and hugs him, and leaves the room quietly leaving the porn magazine on the desk.

He repents, and takes all the magazines outside, a little further away from the house, where a small fire won't be an alarm to anyone, and he throws the magazine down on the ground, lights the match he brought, and carefully and deliberately burns them all. He feels free, but he knows the hardest tests were ahead.

He kneels there alone and prays. He doesn't know what to say: He only cries and says, "God, I'm sorry. Help me to break this evil chain." He doesn't know how much of time has passed by. He cries and cries. (He cried for Mom and himself.) He never wants to see Mom cry again.

He walks back home. He must have stay out there by himself much longer than he thought. It is very early in the morning. When he walked in and check the clock. It is 5 a.m. He takes a shower and feels as a new person. He does his homework as much as he can. He knows he is so far behind. About 7, he gets ready for the school, and heads for the breakfast Mom prepared.

Since then he stays away from the porn. It is extremely hard for him, but he never wants to hurt Mom again nor see Mom cry again. His love for Mom is greater the temptation of porn.

After a few months of fighting against the temptation and being away from the porn, his smile brightens the room. He is able to talk to girls with much more ease. He enjoys the school more and his energy is back. He doesn't have as much sexual images passing through him when he talked with girls as before.

CH 102: Cidy and John

Then, Cidy sees a teenager growing up to be a man but with some extraordinary courage and faith. She is impressed how Dad overcomes a lot of adversities and varieties of temptation while being financially pressed. She could not believe how much Dad helped people quietly and secretly with the little money he made.

And it feels as if everything suddenly slows down: Dad is in the army. She knows this is when Mom and Dad met. She knows the story very well: she heard it from Mom many times.

He says, "This is when I met Karina."

She sees John going through trainings and camaraderie with fellow soldiers. He is stationed in Asia—a nation called Korea.

Some of his buddies always tempt him to go to the red-light district with them. He knows it's not the right thing to do. But his buddies, that he had witnessed Christ to, keep insisting saying: "let's just take a look.", "there's no harm in taking a look", or "let's just have a drink with them."

But one day he follows his buddies to the red-light district. He thinks he can handle it, and he thinks what harm is there in just taking a look. The red-light district is very close to where they hang around for a bite of authentic American food— McDonalds.

They stroll around seeing girls in shorts or tights, standing or sitting around their "shop." John sees young Korean girls in twenties or thirties alluring the U.S. soldiers. He feels the temptation but also feels very sad that these beautiful girls are selling their body to make money, and the U.S. soldiers are buying them for twenty, thirty minutes of a quick sex. This is somehow all legal by both governments. He couldn't understand it.

A girl approaches him with a bad accent and bad English, "You, Soldier. Want me...good time. Come in." She leans on him as she tries to drag him inside the shop. His heart starts to beat faster. He feels his lust rising. He avoids seeing the girl's eyes. He resists her but not with all of his strength.

The girl touches his chest, makes circles around his chest, and says something he couldn't hear. He loses his concentration.

"Make love to me." She pulls his arm towards the shop again with more strength.

Suddenly, he wants to preach the Gospel to the girls and to the soldiers around. But he can't. He feels ashamed to be part of this, and regrets that he followed them here.

He shakes his arm free with all his strength. The girl falls down as she loses her balance. He runs away from her.

He returns to the post. He knows he committed sin against God. He asks God for forgiveness for falling for such a trap. Since then, he never visits the hookers' region again.

He didn't understand such an evil business that was happening in such openness.

The US army and the Korean government selling and buying sex for money...it just doesn't make sense. Why would the Korean government allow such evil act to their own daughters? For money? And the Army, don't they know they are feeding this evil business? How can this happen?

He attends the army church (they usually called it—chapel.) almost every day, and especially on Sunday, and other special activities ran by the church. If there was any special training off-post that he couldn't attend church for a while, he always has that special time with God off-post—praising and worshiping with other Christian soldiers he met or witnessed to.

In the church, there is a cute high-school girl—Karina. She is Major's daughter. Major's is a great man of faith and his entire family attends the church faithfully.

When John first sees Karina, he feels Karina as just a cute little girl. John plays with her not realizing that he would fall in love with her soon. They play games and do a lot of church activities together. He usually helps a lot of moving and lifting for Karina, and they teach the little ones the Sunday-school songs with a lot of dancing and give Bible lessons with the puppets.

Although there are only a few kids, John and Karina pour their hearts out, and the kids love it; they scream and jump up and down with John and Karina.

They have such laughter. He really enjoys himself being with her; they are like brother and sister.

John has no attraction for her, but he loves her like a little sister.

Karina is in love with John. She knows she is too young for him or for love. She knows John is not interested in her like a girlfriend. But she is more than happy to spend time with him. She wishes that she can grow up soon, so John can see her as more of a woman than a girl. She writes her feelings in her diary.

As their daily routine of army, school, church, friends, and family passes by, a new year comes and goes.

In two years, Karina feels and sees her body changing little by little, and her emotions go up and down more drastically. She does not know what is happening, but she feels a little more excited to see John. She is embarrassed to see her breast and buttocks grow more fully. She sees her figure more of a woman than a girl, and likes what she sees.

He notices her bosom that has grown much bigger and quite attractive, her buttocks that became rounder and firmer, and her face more womanly and attractive.

What time can do to a girl? What happened to Karina? She changed so much. She a woman, now! She's a kid, but she looks like a lady, now. John thinks himself.

She is woman on the outside, but still a kid inside.

He falls in love with her slowly and surely. He couldn't help but to peek at her more and more. He would involuntarily and voluntarily look for her. Seeing her sight excites him and gives him much pleasure. He notices every feature of her body. Every sight of her leaves an imprint on his brain. He just can't help himself keeping a track of her. He starts to dream and constantly think about her.

During exercises or training, he starts to make mistakes and smiles all by himself like a lunatic. His marksmanship is dropped. But his attitude peaks to the highest. He has found his purpose in his life—Karina. He writes poems and draws her here and there, and always has that dimwit smile on him. His mind is out with Karina somewhere in the other side of the universe. His buddies and his sergeant make fun of him for appearing silly and out of his mind.

She notices him looking at her more often.

One day, He is mesmerized by her beauty, and just stares at her unconsciously. He couldn't help it.

She enjoys his attention, but she blushes. She shies away like a little girl by turning her head around as she bashes her eye lids.

He quickly says to cover up his action, "Sorry, I had something on my mind."

She returns, "It's okay." But she knows that it is a lie. She feels wonderful that he's noticing her. She feels like her dream is coming true. She desires for his love even more.

She speaks of him to her best friend. They kid around about her falling in love with John. She enjoys the teasing. She is warned what she is doing is a taboo in the army. She knows if Major, her dad, finds out, John will be in a serious trouble.

Karina knows she is too young to fall in love with John, but she couldn't help it. She has a special feeling that she just can't explain about him. He is tall and handsome and great with kids, and she loves that: He always plays well with her brother, Paul, which is a big plus. But mostly, his lovely voice and his handsome features are quite a turn-on for her. She couldn't ask anything more in a man.

She writes about her love for him in her diary: what she feels about him, what he said and did to her, and how she would like to be married to him. She treasures every moment with him. She visits the church every time she had a chance hoping she might catch him there.

And he does the same. He is entrenched with thought of her. He has no one to share his feeling. He is afraid Major might find out about his love for her. He knows he can get in serious trouble with Major and the Army, probably sent far away. But his love for her is just overwhelms him. He sees her everywhere he turns.

They are only five years apart: she is only 16 and John 21. She is in high school, and he is in the Army. She isn't too young to be dating, but not with a soldier. It was unwritten rule that soldiers knew by heart, and Major's girl is too young and too dangerous for any soldier.

And they meet at the church often as if they made an appointment with each other, and have a lot of little chat. To them it is just a little chat, but each time they meet, a couple of hour just flies by quickly. They know they like each other. They know they are in love—a love that is not permitted.

Before He fell in love with her, he used to give her hugs and taps, but now he is careful not to touch her although he dreams about kissing and making love to her. Every time he makes a contact with her accidently or purposely, he feels a tiny electric shock that goes through his spine. He sees her eyes and they are the window to a world of delicious love.

She feels the same spark when they give each other high five or when their eyes meet. She feels alive and high. She notices herself having more energy than ever. She skips and hops through the post. She feels everything is more colorful and lively. She feels flowers and trees are singing and teasing her love for John. She sometimes sings with them like a scene in a movie.

Major Jackson, Karina's father, is a nice man and Commander, but when it comes to his kids, he does not fool around especially with Karina. He has sent a few soldiers to different posts for just looking at his daughters, especially Karina. He made his message clear to the soldiers about his intention to any soldier coming near his daughters. But he likes John for whatever the reason, and just didn't pay much attention to John or he just trusted John too much because he likes what he heard about John. He sees John and Karina talk and play, but he disregards them because he trusts John. He has heard reports about John not leaving the post for sex.

John has heard that Major adores Karina quite a lot. There are stories about soldiers being sent to other foreign battalions or other regions because Major didn't like the way they looked at Karina. So, he is very careful not to get caught by Major.

One day at the army base, John sees Karina walking alone. He runs up to her from behind, and scares her. She screams and drops everything that she is holding. She realizes it's John. She is very excited to see him.

She starts to chase John around and says, "I'll get you back. You scared me to death. I hate you. I hate you."

They are laughing and giggling. He wants to hug her and kiss her till the morning comes. She gets exhausted. She is panting. He starts to pick up the things for her.

He puts the gathered things together neatly on the grass. He checks on her. She pouts and turns her head away. He sits next to her. He likes his back touching the side of her. He wants to put his arm around her, but holds it in.

She leans her head on his shoulder. She forgets they are in a place where passing soldiers can see them. She just wants to feel the moment.

She says, "John…." She wants to say that she loves him, but she doesn't have the courage.

He loves to hear her voice. He wants to hear more, and says, "Yes."

She feels her heart rushing. She is embarrassed. She feels she has shown too much of her emotion. She quickly picks herself up, gets her stuff, and heads home.

He tries to help but he feels she turned cold. He chases her down, and says, "What's wrong?" John has no idea.

Hearing his voice weakens her will to leave him, so she quickens her pace home. She wants to scream her love out aloud, but she knows she can't.

He goes ahead of her, and stops her, and asks, "What's wrong? I'm sorry. I won't do it again." He has no idea what is going through her mind.

She pulls away again from him and runs home.

He is alone and dumbfounded. He just stares at her back that is getting smaller and smaller. He bows his head with a disappointment. He is lost.

He is afraid that he might lose her. He returns to his quarter.

Major Jackson sees the whole thing accidently, and quickly acknowledges that they can get serious. He notices the growth of his girl as well. He thinks, *Karina has grown a lot. She maybe a high-school girl but she has a body of a woman. My little Karina...all grown. How time flies.*

Major has been thinking about his daughter and John for a week. He has spoken with his wife about it, but she isn't worried at all. But he is more than worried. He likes John too, but Karina is just too young for a relationship with a soldier. He has high hope for Karina. She is smart and very wise for her age, and she has been a trouble-free girl. She never complains about the army life: Moving to different places every few years could be tough for any one, but she doesn't fuss about it. She cries but never complains.

Major doesn't want Karina and John getting too serious. He knows how easy it is to slip. Although he trusts both of them, he couldn't trust their emotion or attraction. He remembers his younger days when he dated Mary: he remembers how he wanted to go all the way with her every time he met her before the wedding. He knows how hard for a man to hold his physical desire a woman, so he worries about John and Karina because they are hot-blood young.

Major fumbles through his memory of Karina and thinks:

> *Karina grew up to be a beautiful girl.*
> *She was so cute when she was little*
> *but she blossomed to a very*
> *attractive young girl. She started to*

*have boys coming around starting
junior high, but I didn't take it
seriously, because they were just
too young. But now she…being a
junior with a full grown woman's
body…I'm worried. Karina is growing
up fast—too fast.*

Major and Mary realize that Karina is a woman in a teenager's mind. But they thought Karina is more mature than most women in their thirties.

After that incident of with Karina, John tries to be careful with Karina.

Karina is afraid of her feelings.

They are awkwardly distant from each other. They are peaking at each other, but they are keeping a definite distance with time, space, and feelings.

Karina feels so naked in front John. She feels that he knows of her crush on him. She wants to see him more than ever, but she wants to hide from him more than ever as well. She loves him, but confused about the way she wants to interact with him.

One day while walking, John sees Karina passing by. He takes courage, and runs to her, and says *hi*. She is surprised and happy. She couldn't hide her joy as she naturally giggles with a shy smile, and she blushes. He too couldn't hide his excitement and babbles a bit.

They both know they like each other. They both laugh and giggle like little kids doing something mischievous and fun on their own. They stare at each other, and know what they have is love.

He feels guilty for loving her, but wants her so badly that he habitually dreams about making love to her. But for now, he is more than happy to have a little chat here and there with her.

She giggles and laughs at seeing John babbling in front of her. She calms him down by putting her hand on his strong shoulder. His strong and wide shoulder attracts her much. She likes the firmness.

He feels very special to feel her hand on his shoulder. He wants to touch her hand. He sees her beautiful hand, and draws her beautiful, peachy hand in his mind—a sensuous thumb and long and slim fingers.

She speaks with her eyes, *I missed you*.

He hears her eyes singing a love song. He calms down and questions her, "You…ah…going home?"

"I just finished homework with Kelly. I'm going home." Karina can't take her eyes off of John's eyes.

He's thinking about kissing her as he sees her beautiful lips move showing that beautiful white teeth flashing as she smiles and talks. He responds a little too late, "Oh…oh….really."

She feels his attention. She wants to be kissed and be held by him. She turns her head toward home, and sees she is about 5 minutes away. She notice him little hesitant and not knowing what to do. She reaches over to his hand taps his hand as if it was an accident.

He feels the touch, and reaches over and slowly grabs her hand while looking around if anyone is watching. She feels the warmth going around her body as he softly grabs her hand. She feels heavenly. She loves him so much.

She fantasizes for a few seconds:

In a beautiful home, just two of
them…with a beautiful music flowing
in the back ground…. They are
holding onto each other, and
dancing to the music, and caressing,
and kissing.

She feels like a princess in a Disney movie.

He walks her home. Just about 50 yards away from her home, she stops and looks into his eyes. She can't believe she has the love of her dream right in front of her. They stare at each other for a while. She wants to kiss him. He wants to grab her and run away a far.

Mary, Karina's mom, sees two of them talking while holding their hands together.

Karina smiles and says, "Thanks John. I'll see you soon." And she lets her hand go and walks toward home.

He didn't know what to say but to let her go.

Mary thinks about her love with Matt. She is worried as much as she is happy for her.

Karina walks in the house not knowing Mom had seen the whole thing.

Mom doesn't say anything.

Mary hopes the same thing she had for Karina—the true love that she and Major had when they were young. She likes John a lot because he reminds her of Major. She is sort of rooting for her daughter's love, and feels vulnerable for her because of heartache she can suffer from breaking up.

Mary doesn't want to stop Karina from experiencing love, because she knows that's the only thing that really people live for—that true love. And she knows she is so happy because she has that true love with Major. She knows Major is not perfect (quite far from it) but she loves him more than anything else in the world. She would give up everything and more for him, and she wants that same true love for her child, Karina.

One night, John arrives first at the church and walks around near the main door, hoping Karina might show up to the church too. It was very late at night.

Karina carefully gets out of the house, walks though the post, and arrives at the church main door, and finds John there. She is surprised to see him although she wanted him to be there. She feels the destiny with him.

They stare at each other hoping the other will say something first. Finally she speaks shyly but with joy she can't hide, breaking the silence out of awkwardness, "John! What are you doing here at this time of the night?"

He already has what he wants to say in his mind, but he murmurs it. "I wanted to see you. I wanted to hold you." It was like a whisper that she couldn't hear.

She senses John is excited to see her. She could see it in his eyes as he fidgets a bit, and she senses that he didn't hear her question. She is too excited, too.

She says a little louder, "I'm here to pray. I have a few things on my mind."

He deeply falls into her eyes. He responds a bit late. "Great. I wanted to pray too. Let's pray together."

He thinks it would be great to be alone with her during the evening hours: He can hold her and kiss her. It is a dream come true.

Major is arriving at the base a little late because of an event that Koreans held for the remembrance of the Korean War. Driving home, he sees John and Karina walking inside the church.

As they get in the church, John locks the door and turns the light on. She hears the locking of the door as the light colors inside of the church. She knows what coming: It is what she dreamed about—holding his hand, leaning against his chest, and kissing his lips. She hopes he would kiss her like lovers do, passionately and softly.

They sit next to each other at the back row. He slowly reaches out for her. As his hands touch her shoulders, she feels the coldness of his hand which makes her body ring with a pleasure. They could see the wooden cross in the middle behind the podium. The church building is simple but quite elegant and beautiful. They are holding each other as if they are hiding even from themselves.

He turns his head to look at Karina's beautiful face. He is so enamored by every detail of her face: a few freckles, a mark of pimple, long eye lashes, soft pinkish lips that are begging for his lips, somewhat voluptuous cheeks, beautiful brown eyes, lovely blond hair, and a graceful chin line.

She shyly observes John's faces well: a strong pillar like nose, rugged facial features, small but sharp looking eyes with hazel pupils, thin small, unattractive lips, and short army-cut dirty-blond hair.

They can't keep their eyes off from each other.

He feels the warmth of her hand reaching out through his whole body. He loves her soft and small white hand. It feels like a toy. He loves her grown breast that catching his eyes constantly. He wants to touch them. He wants to make love to her. He pulls Karina in slowly to his chest and hugs her genteelly.

How many times have I imagined this? He thinks.

She sighs with pleasure. Her whole body feels like a dandelion globe that are breaking apart and flying away.

He feels heavenly to hold her in his arms. Her soft breast bracing his chest is more than magical. She is soft. He caresses her hair gently and touches her shoulder and back. As his hand caresses the bare skin of her arms, shoulders, and her back, he is more than aroused.

She couldn't help it to let out a soft moan of pleasure. She leans on his chest even closer feeling embarrassed. She feels the excitement in her as her body temperature rises. She tries to hide her arousal hoping that he won't notice that she is excited. She pulls away from him and looks into his hazel eyes. She feels like this is all but a dream. She loves him even to her death.

He licks his lips because they became dry. He feels the intensity rising in his body. He gazes into her brown eyes and brushes his finger through her blond hair. They are soft and beautiful. Each strand of her hair sings a song of love. He can smell her perfume that plays his entire body with a pleasure. He slowly guides her head with his right hand as he leans his head half way towards her. Their lips meet, and they kiss softly.

Major is in his the car. He doesn't know what to do. He wants to jump out of the car and rush into the church, but he remembers how he and Mary did the same thing when they were young. He prays for his daughter. He trusts her, but he is too weak when he comes to his own daughters. He wonders about what could happen with her in the church. He is scared. He drives away home feeling helpless.

Major parks his car in front of his home. He quickly gets out and runs for the door as if he is reaching for a quick cover. He opens the door, and gets in, and shuts the door behind him, and he couldn't make a sound.

This isn't John's first kiss, but he thinks it could be Karina's first. He takes things slowly, but the kisses with her feels like his first too. They kiss and kiss. Time is on hold for them. Each kiss feels like an eternity for them. They confirm their love for each other.

Mary sees Matt (Major) near the door, not moving much. She always waits for him to get home. It's something she was taught by her mom. She knows there is something wrong, very wrong, but she acts like she doesn't notice it.

Mary says, "Hey Matt. You're home a little late."

Matt asks Mary to talk outside. He was afraid that he might lose himself and wake the kids up. They leave home and walk towards an area where they can't be heard with a few benches around.

He says, "I saw Karina and John walk into the church together about ten minutes ago. I didn't know what to do. I'm scared."

She speaks quietly not judging, "I love you Matt. You did the right thing."

He feels comforted. (He never realized how weak he was.)

He is trained to fight a war and trains soldiers for all kinds of havoc. But this thing with his daughter, he could not solve a thing. He feels like one stupid incompetent nincompoop.

Mary holds Matt closely. She kisses him softly and touches him. He kisses her back. It has been a while they kissed under the stars. Soon they kiss like a high-school couple. Maybe it is the fear or the comfort he received, he kisses her passionately. She hasn't felt Matt this passionate for a long time. After kissing lasting an hour or more, they walk home. They can't wait to get home.

It really has been a long time for Mary to feel Matt so passionate.

She feels like a newlywed.

Matt never love Mary so much.

He feels like that high school boy when he first fell in love with Mary.

Arriving home, they make passionate love that they hadn't done in years. After a long love making, he falls asleep like a baby as always. She gets herself together and waits for Karina.

Karina wants more of John, and John wants more of Karina. But it is John that couldn't go any further. She would have given all of her if he asked. She has no idea what is happening to her. She knows better, but with him, she feels that true love.

They do not know what time it is.

He separates himself from her and looks into her eyes—such beautiful brown eyes. They look so beautiful. He is in her eyes.

He says, "I love you. I feel this power and weakness when I'm with you. I don't know what to say but I'm in love with you. Your hair and your legs and your eyes...I can't erased them from my mind. I wanna marry you." He proposes to her without thinking about it.

She cries, "I love you too. I don't know what it is about you, but I think about you all day long. I love your laughter and I love your walk. I love your eyes. I love you."

But they know the truth and the reality that they can't get married unless they eloped. And they knew this was not the way God wanted them to be.

They pray together holding hands and confess their love for each other and their will to follow God's will.

(Cidy has heard about Mom's love story many times. But it felt quite different actually seeing and feeling the whole thing from every person's angle. She feels the every emotion of everyone. She is in tears.)

Mary waits, but now decides to leave it to God. She knows her daughter well. Karina has been more than a perfect child. Mary trusts Karina and God for whatever will happen, and turns herself to bed.

John and Karina walk out of the church. They can't be separated. They hug tight. They kiss on and off. They feel hopeless, yet so much joy.

She finally says, "I gotta go. ...take me home, John."

Night is almost over; dawn is about to break.

He, holding her hand, walks her home. He feels they are one. At the front of Karina's home, they embrace each other for a long time again. They have no idea how late it became. Finally she opens the door and reluctantly walks in as their hands make the final release of each other.

He stands at the door for a while dreaming of her and the night. He can't believe what just happened. It all feels like a movie he just watched, not real.

She breathes a sigh of relief. She is afraid maybe Mom or Dad might be awake and hear her coming in. She has been so trustworthy until tonight. She is scared of this love she never experience it before, but she feels the rush of excitement and pleasure of falling in love. She gets into her bed and can't fall asleep. She relives the night with.

The following week, Major decides all by himself, without consulting with Mary, to separate John and Karina for their own good. He secretly dispatches John to another base in another country.

Sergeant Colbert calls John in to his office by sending a private to find him.

John walks in to Sergeant's office and salutes.

Sergeant tells John to take a seat with his hand gesture. John sit strait on a chair across the desk keeping his soldier's face.

"John…you having any problems?" Sergeant knows something is up, but he has no idea. To him, John was out of ordinary but in a good way. He is a model soldier—never causing any trouble, and always taking care of his fellow soldiers.

"No, sir!" John is surprised by the question. He really has no idea what is coming to him.

"You asked to be relocated?" Sergeant with his solid unwavering tenor tone got to the point quickly. He wants to find out if John requested for relocation or reassignment. He likes John.

"No, sir!" John gives his honest answer without hesitation.

"Hmmm…. Well…Son, here's your relocation paper. You will be transported to your new post in three weeks." Sergeant knows something is up, but has no idea it involves Major's daughter.

John feels heartbroken. He looks at the paper and can't believe it.

"I don't want to be relocated, SIR! I DO NOT want to be RELOCATED, SIR!" John screams and tries to reverse the order.

"...have to take it with the Inspector General. But that will take months. You have to relocate first. Will be discharged if you don't follow the order. You know the drill, Son." Sergeant senses John's disturbance. He's curious but he doesn't want to be tangled with a minor problem. "You may leave, Soldier."

John couldn't move for a while. He heard what Sergeant said, but he couldn't believe it. Sergeant doesn't respond, and keeps his mouth shut tightly. John stands up slowly and reluctantly, salutes Sergeant, and leaves the office. He drags his feet. He feels the whole world just crumbling down.

When he walks out of the building, he turns the corner, and leans on the wall for a while and bangs his fists on it till he can't feel his hands anymore. His fists are bleeding. He doesn't care. He bangs his head on the wall hard. He feels a bit nauseated. He gets tired. He groans. He can't find any word. He cries deeply but quietly.

He wants to go find Karina and cry on her shoulder. He loves her so much. He never felt this strong about a girl before. He knows she is too young for him now, but he loves her with his life.

He wonders if someone reported to Major about his relationship with Karina, or if she told her parents. He is lost. He looks around and feels as if everything turned a bit yellowish. Breathing has become somewhat irregular for him. He feels as if the ground is breaking, shaking, and sinking under him.

Just a few minutes ago, he felt so wonderful, he was praising the Lord, and now, he feels like nothing can make him happy. He groans with unimaginable pain in his heart and soul.

He walks to a more secluded spot. He knows in an hour he can see Karina at the church, but he doesn't know what to do now. He is in deep pain. He beats on the grass and the trees. He can't help it to call out Karina's name over and over again in his heart. He lets the time pass away knowing Karina is waiting for him at the church.

She waits for him. She waits inside the church until 2 a.m., and gives up, and returns home.

He sees her walking out of the church and returning home. He stalks her walking home. He makes sure she gets home safely.

She can't sleep. She is baffled and frustrated. She knows he loves her. She hopes something important came up that he couldn't make it.

He doesn't show up at the church at all even on that Sunday. She realizes something serious has happened.

He avoids her by going to random and distant places in the army base and doesn't attend any church event. He knows he'll be moving in two weeks, and doesn't want to hurt her. He feels this is the best way to depart or separate. He hopes she gets the message—the false message—that he is not in love with her any more.

She knows something is very wrong with him. She finally visits him very late at his bunk. She knows he can't avoid her at this late hour at his own barrack. All the soldiers are shocked to see Major's daughter asking for him. He is astounded that she came to see him at his barrack at such a late hour.

He runs out and takes her away from the barrack. He can hear the boys making all kinds of sounds. He takes her to the church. He runs holding her hand. He feels overwhelming with the joy of holding her hand again.

Karina feels wonderful being held my John again.

They arrive at the church.

He looks into her eyes, and they are more beautiful than he remembered. He wants to make love to her, but he knows he has to let her go.

He says angrily (He fakes his anger.), "Hey...what ARE you doing? You can get in trouble. You CAN'T come to soldiers' barrack like that."

"You KNOW why!" She seers through his eyes and wants to know the truth.

He acts as if there's nothing wrong. "What do you mean?"

"You have been AVOIDING me. You CAN'T avoid me like this. You have to tell me what is going on." She is not backing off. She is willing to die for him, and she feels what he is doing to her is more than unbearable. She would rather die, than feel abandoned by him.

He can't say a word for a while, but finally decides to tell the truth. "I've been assigned to another base. I wouldn't be able to see you anymore. I'll be going away in two weeks."

"WHY? DID you apply to be transferred?" She bites hard with her words.

"No...I love you.... You know I love you!" He confesses his feelings for her without knowing.

She responds automatically, "I love you too."

He takes her into the church. They sit at the same spot as usual. They hug and cry. They kiss for a while. They promise to each other that they will stay in touch, and they will get married when Karina graduates from high school. They fall asleep together.

She wakes up and realizes it's very late. She wakes him up, and they quickly leave the church. At the door, she clings on to him as he smells her and caresses her soft hair. He is aroused enough to make love to her, but he knows he has to let her leave.

She suddenly breaks apart and dashes home. John follows her with his eyes, and he walks toward her home making sure she enters home safely.

They meet each other every night till he leaves for his new base.

Night before he leaves for Turkey, they meet at the church as usual. Only a few words are spoken. They kiss and hug through all night till 5 a.m. As 5 a.m. strikes, she runs away from him and runs for home. He tries to catch her but it's already dawn. He fears someone might see them.

Later that day, he leaves the post to catch the flight. He is devastated, but he is grateful to have the love of his life. He gets on the army plane that will be taking him to another foreign land. He prays quietly, "God, thank you for Karina. Please keep our love true."

At school, she looks through the window knowing he is up there somewhere, and prays, "God, protect my John. Please help us keep our love true."

Since he left, she waits for John's call or mail, but she doesn't get any of it. She waits for a week, and two, and three, and she gets none. She slowly loses all the perks and spirits she had. She realizes Dad separate them. She knows Dad did it because Dad loves her.

She doesn't complain like any other thing, but she loses herself.

Mom and Dad see Karina without life in her face. They are devastated as well.

Mom realizes what happened, and doesn't complain to Matt because she knows he did it out of love and fear. (She had to support Matt.)

They decide to move to Germany hoping Karina will return to her old self. They move three months after John left.

John, after being moved to a new base, couldn't reach Karina. He tries calling and sending mail, but nothing gets through. He tries to find where she is in every possible way but no one would tell him. They keep telling him its military secret, classified information, that they can't help him. He loses all the hope.

Almost a year passes since he had last seen Karina. He receives a letter from someone he never heard before. He opens it, and to his shock it was from Karina. She has found him.

Since then they have been writing letters and secretly meeting each other but mostly writing for nine years. After nine years of loving each other through writing, secretly meeting each other for a week here and there, they get married.

But a year after the marriage, a day after Cidy is born, driving to the hospital to see Cidy and Karina, John sees an accident.

A light-blue four-door sedan is quickly cut off by a commercial truck. It looked like the truck didn't see the light-blue Chevrolet 4-door sedan driving close by on the next lane to his right in his blind spot. To avoid an accident, the sedan quickly swerves to the right but too quick and flips and rolls over like a toy. The sedan skids on its roof and slows down on the side of the road. Smoke is coming out of the car. Cars stop, and people are standing around the flipped sedan from a distance to watch what will happen. It is a spectacle in making.

It is like an instinct for John: he stops, and runs over to the flipped car, and helps the trapped people. People are just watching him afar. They know the danger.

He approaches and sees that there are two boys and a mom that is heavily bleeding. He breaks the driver side window with his knee, and tries to pull out the lady. But she refuses and insists that kids be pulled out first.

He has no choice but to get to the kids out first. Smoke gets bigger and thicker, and the foul smell of smoke is nauseating. He breaks the back window with his knee, and pulls out two little boys. He takes them to the safe distance, and goes back.

He hears cops arriving with siren piercing his ear. He knows instinctively that there is only a minute or two left to save the lady. He quickly leans over and tries to pull the lady out. The lady turns her head and says *thank you*. He slowly pulls her, but that instant, the car blows up like a bomb. The lady and John die instantly.

Cidy is overwhelmed to see the actual accident. She is proud her dad for his bravery. She hugs him tight, and says, "Dad, you are my hero."

John says, "You see that handsome little boy. That's…Jake."

"…Jake? …You mean…Jake…my Jake?"

"Yap…. That's him."

"You…saved…the boy that…I'm in love with…."

"He's deeply in love with you, too. God has been planning for you two to meet before you were born."

She hugs her dad and cries some more. He cries with her.

They laugh and have a wonderful date: They go see movies, walk through parks, swim together, fish together, and talk and talk. She spins 40 days and nights with Dad doing the things she had only dreamt about.

As they are walking along the streets of Paris, France, John suddenly hugs Cidy tight and says, "I love you. I'm always with you."

CH 103: The Party

In a flash and not noticing anything had happened to her, Cidy drives back to the party. She feels something weird, but nothing she can pin point to. She feels happier than ever; she feels exhilarated. She is overflowing with love for life and people. It seems as if everything turned a little brighter.

She wants to call everybody but calls her number one fan—Mom, Karina.

She says, "Mom, I love you," before Karina could say anything!

"You told me that this morning."

"Well…I just wanted to say it again."

"You silly. You at the party yet?"

"Yah…almost there."

"I hope Jake asks you out."

"Mom…. What about the God's plan for me? You think Jake is in it with me?"

"Well…. If he asks you out, date him. If his not with the God's plan, dump him."

"What a swell idea…." Cidy chuckles.

Cidy arrives at the hotel a little late than expected. She sees many are here already to get ready for the show and the party. She sees Jake's truck and feels happy to spot it. She winks at Jake's ride and blows a kiss to it. She giggles a little.

She walks into the ball room. It looks perfect. She searches for Jake at the party and quickly locates him near the stage.

Jake checks the tune on his guitar. He stands tall and relaxed but searches for Cidy with his eyes constantly. His eyes meet with Cidy's, but he veers his head aside to act as if he's not interested in her.

Cidy sees a spark in Jake's eyes. She comes around, behind of him, and gives him a big smile and says, "Good to see you, Jake. Ready for the show."

She wants to stop and have a chat, but she is a little too nervous. She gets just enough courage to side step next to him, just enough, to give him a full look of herself. She gives him a little peek of her smile, and quickly paces away.

But, he notices something unusual about her. He calls out for her, "Cidy...ah...ah...CIDY, CAN I see...your NECKLACE?"

She turns around hearing her name. She also hears the word—necklace. She hears her heart pounding. She slowly walks back to Jake with a great anticipation.

"What? Necklace...my necklace?" She reacts because it wasn't something she expected. She smiles, but feels very shy, and stands near him. She can feel her heart pounding louder and faster. She tells herself to calm down.

"Yes.... Can I see your necklace?" He never imagined he would be calling her name out like that. He is surprised by his own action as well, but he had to see her necklace again. He reaches for the necklace almost with unbelief and subconsciously.

As she looks at her own necklace, he quickly touches the necklace, and stares at it for a few seconds, and is stunned.

She feels quite awkward as he touches her chest and the necklace. He is so close to her. She feels nervous and excited. She thinks he is going to make a move to grope her breast.

He questions her in a serious tone, "Where did you get this... this necklace?"

"What...? Whaddyiu mean...?" She reacts.

"This necklace...it is what my mom used wear. I have a picture...her wearing it." He lets the necklace go, and reaches in for his wallet to show his mother's picture.

"Oh...really." She just realizes she is wearing the necklace of the lady—the children's lady Dad saved. She swears she was wearing something else. She usually keeps it home to remember Dad.

He shows the picture of his mother—a beautiful lady with a long, lovely strait brunette hair with the same necklace on her.

She tells him the story about how her dad died saving the children from a car accident. She says, "The necklace belongs to the children's mom."

He quickly pulls her over to a more secluded corner and tells her that the story and the necklace match his family's story.

They compare the date of the fatal accident. The date matches. They can't believe what had just happened.

He suddenly feels enormous courage to ask her out. "Cidy. I had a crush on you for years. Can I take you out for a dinner?

It is a dream-come-true for her. She wants to jump for joy, but clams her mouth for a few seconds.

With a cute smile and bashing her eyes, she says, "No."

He catches on, and gives a smirk.

They talk a little more.

She asks for permission to be excused because she has to make sure the party gets on a roll properly. She goes around checking all the details while greeting all the people.

She meets her favorite uncle and aunt— Peter and Rhonda. They share some words of wonderful fellowship.

The talent show starts. A magic show starts off the show. It is a great success. The next is Cidy and the *009 Girls*. They go on the stage, and make clowns out of themselves, and finish off by dancing to Michael Jackson's Thriller dressed in cute animals.

Jake comes on the stage on second half of the show. The audience goes wild. Girls are shouting his name. He is a little bit embarrassed, but enjoys the attention. He sits down on a high chair and puts the guitar on his lap, and clears his throat a couple of times.

He sees Cidy and gives her a wink. The audience didn't catch it. He wants to say this song is for Cidy, but skips it. He starts to strum the guitar, and slowly get into the rhythm, and sings the songs. He makes another homerun with the song.

Girls are screaming as if Jake's a superstar, and guys go wild for him. He is shy and hides from the crowd quickly.

The talent show is the best they had. The quality of the talent has gotten much better. Everyone is more than entertained: They feel great camaraderie with each other.

The first prize is won by a rock group, *2 Short 2 Long*, singing a few of ABBA's hits. The *009 Girls* win the second prize. The third won by a dance-performing group—Grease It Down.

As the show is about to be over, Mark gets up in the stage, and asks MC for the mike. MC hands him over the mike.

Sandy's eyes get real big seeing Mark upon the stage. She has been avoiding him all night although she couldn't keep her eyes away.

Mark announces loudly, "Ladies and my fellow friends. My heart is pounding with the truth. I must shout this truth to you, to the world, tonight. Tonight, I want to propose to the lady of my life, my dream, for I can't live without her! SANDY! SANDY is my TRUTH and my LIFE! I LOVE YOU, SANDY! Would you dance with me for the rest of my life?"

Sandy is shocked and don't know what to do. She is screaming with joy and shock.

Cidy quickly gets next to her. Sandy is staring at Cidy with her eyes shivering, and she is on her toes jumping.

Mark looks over to Sandy and sees she likes it, so he pulls out a ring and screams out to the world, "I LOVE YOU, SANDY. Would YOU be my WIFE?"

Everyone is shouting, screaming and hooting. They have seen something like this on TV or movies but not in real life. They are all shocked to see what is happening.

Cidy nudges Sandy to go up to the stage.

Sandy cries with her mouth covered by both hands, and runs up to the stage. She stares Mark with tearful eyes. Her mascara is already smudged a little from her tears.

He kneels down in front of her and presents her with the ring, like a knight presenting his sword to his king. He proposes, "Be my wife, Sandy!"

She nods and gives her left hand to him, and screams and cries at the same time, "Oh…yes, YES, YES!"

He slowly puts the ring on her wedding finger, but it won't fit. He smoothly moves on to the next finger; it slides right in her pinkie.

People are laughing and giggling. Finally the crowd goes out of control: Everybody is shouting and screaming with the joy. People are clapping and hooting. They start shouting, "K.I.S.S. K.I.S.S. K.I.S.S."

He reaches over her, pulls her in, dips her, and stares her eyes for a few seconds, and gives a hot and intensive kiss.

The crowd goes wild.

He pulls her back up.

She is breathless.

The *009 Girls* rush up the stage and start to scream and jump with joy. They are all hugging and celebrating.

Mark is sort of pushed aside, but Jake comes over with guys. They give Mark high-fives and shake his hand. Jake hugs him and says, "You are the MAN! You manned up. I gotta hand it to you, Mark. You ARE awesome!"

Finally, Sandy walks over to Mark, and hugs and kisses Mark like lovers do. He makes funny gestures as if he is in heaven. The company employees are screaming and shouting like high school kids. They are loving the night.

In the heat of the celebration, Jake takes Cidy's hand and pulls her out quietly, and takes her out to parking lot. He has never made such a move on a girl like that, but he is desperate to get to know her more.

She knows she has to stay for the party and the girls, but loves what he is doing to her: she follows him like a little puppy.

He takes her to his truck.

Next to his truck, he gets close to her, and looks into her beautiful golden brown eyes. He wants to kiss her like he had been dreaming about for years.

He says firmly, "Let's get some coffee!"

She likes His tone of voice. She smirks. "Latte, Cappuccino?"

He opens the squeaking door for her (He is somewhat embarrassed by the squeak), and responds, "Let's find out?"

She steps in. She can't believe what's happening. Her dream is coming true, but she is still afraid she has to let him go. He closes the squeaking door feeling a bit embarrassed.

He steps in and turns the truck on.

While driving Jake reaches out for her hand, and holds it like he had been holding for it years. He likes the feel of her soft and long fingered hand. There is something magical that he couldn't explain. He feels warmer. But he knows he would have to be separated with her if she won't follow his calling. He is afraid, even more afraid now that she is near him.

She likes his large and thick hand covering her thin and long-fingered hand. Warmth reaches every part of her body. She tightens her grip giving back to him the sign that she likes his touch. She feels like it is all but a dream.

They smile at each other while listening to Christmas songs on the radio. There are just a several days left for Christmas.

She gets a call from Tammy as expected.

"Where are you, Cidy?" Tammy interrogates with a serious and worried tone.

"I'm…with…a boy." Cidy slowly confesses just enough.

"A man…you mean! How could you? We are all searching for you." Tammy lashes at Cidy.

"It wasn't planned. It just happened. I'm sorry. I'll make it up to you girls, soon. I tell you all it about it tomorrow. I promise." She makes a quick apology.

"Good luck." Tammy gives up.

They arrive at Denny's (It opens to late hours.), and get in. They sit next to each other and order two drinks: coffee for him and milk shake for her. They talk for hours looking into each other's eyes.

But they avoid talking about the calling they received. They both fear that they might lose each other if they bring it up.

She takes courage and asks him first, "Jake…. I need to be honest with you. I'm going to quit the company soon…and I'm going to go work…for God." She tries to catch if there is any hesitation in him, but sees a smile, a welcoming smile.

"I wanted to say the same thing, but I was afraid to say it because I might lose you. I'm ashamed. I too…. I received my calling this morning." He confesses and feels relieved, but he feels bad that he wanted to hide it. He repents that he doubted God.

They are in love and amazed that they both received the calling this morning. They confirm they are destined for each other. They are feeling quite high, and they know they are in for an adventure that God has planned for them.

She asks another question she meant to ask for years, "You ever sent me roses on Valentines?"

He smiles and tells the truth, "Every year with initial J."

She giggles. "I knew it. Thank you. I love your poems. But…to test if YOU really sent them, please recite all five of them."

"…Now?"

"Are YOU 'J' or not?"

"Sure, I know all of them by heart. The last year one says," Jake recites the poem:

> Each day as the sun rises,
> I think of your smile.
> I breathe your scent,
> For you are my life.
>
> Each night as the star blinks,
> I dream of your love.
> I hold you in my arms,
> For you are my love.
>
> The sun shines.
> The stars glow.
> But I dream of you,
> I dream…only you,
> For you are my love.

Before he could recite the second one, she gives him a peck of kiss on his cheek. He blushes,

414

and loses his mind, and can't continue. She teases and laughs.

Time dances away quickly, but for them, time stop moving. It is almost 3 am that they realize they need to go home and get ready for work.

They walk out of *Denny's*. He reaches over for her shoulder, and they walk naturally like lovers do.

He opens the door for her, and the door squeaks as usual. He is embarrassed again, but she loves it. He gets around the driver side and gets in the truck and turns the engine on. She scoots over and sits very tight, right next to him, like she had fantasized so many times.

He likes it, but feels uncomfortable. He puts his arm around her. The radio music flows with the Christmas songs. They sing to the song together. They are making music together.

About ten minutes later, they arrive at the hotel. He parks his truck next to her little Metro. He gets off his truck quickly, and runs around his truck to quickly open the door for her.

She scoots over to the edge of the door, and waits, and gives her right hand to him as he opens the door. He takes her right hand with his left. He feels a sensation flowing from her hand to his hand to his whole body as he holds her hand. He couldn't help but to give a smirk. He wants to hug her as she gets out of the truck, but he lets her go thinking there will be other days.

She hopes he gives her a hug, a good tight hug that she can feel like they are bonded as one.

As he lets her go, she feels a little disappointed. She walks over to her car as he follows her with his eyes. As she tries to open her door, he sees her beautiful figure from behind. Every part of her, he dreams of touching, and reaches out for her almost subconsciously.

She feels his hand on her shoulder, and feels the love reaching down to her toes. She shakes a bit as she turns quickly and falls into his chest.

He carries her a little and leans onto his truck as she rushes into him. She wants to run away because of the overwhelming feeling of pleasure from his touch.

He clings on to her like she is his life. Like playing an instrument, his hands cascades through her long brunette hair that shines under a beautiful blushing moon light and twinkling inquisitive stars. He feels every part of her body touching him, and smells her beautiful hair. He is more than aroused. He wants to make love to her, right here, right now.

She almost falls asleep in his arms. She feels more than heavenly. She feels so natural and comfortable.

Soon, she realizes she needs to go home and come right back to work. She turns around and tries to get into her car. But she turns quickly back around and gives him a sudden kiss on his lips.

He is blinded but feels heavenly. He loses all the words and becomes just a big-eyed statue with an opened mouth. He starts to kiss her back passionately.

They kiss for a while.

She separates herself from him reluctantly. He latches on. She giggles at his respond. She is having the time of her life. She quickly gets in to her car (before she changes her mind), turns the engine on, and lowers the window. He reaches out. And their hands meet, and are held together; and their eyes are locked in. They are lost and found. He wants to say so much but can't say a word. She knows how he feels and can't let go. Finally, he lets her go. She slowly drives away while waving her hand, and gives him the look of love as long as she can.

He tracks her driving away; he can't take his eye off of her, and then her car, and the space where she was as she disappeared from his sight. He stands at the parking lot all by himself stunned, and looks up to the sky and notices a few shining stars. The night is closing, and the morning is about to dawn. It all feels like a dream—a dream he never wants to wake up from. He thanks God.

On her way home, she wants to call everybody especially Mom. She is driving on the cloud. She thanks God.

Driving back home, he suddenly remembers a dream he had a few years back (He just didn't think much about it because it felt like a scene from a Disney movie. He disregarded it and had forgotten about it):

> In a wilderness, Jake walks by himself. He feels lonely and scared. There is little life in all things; people are very weary and weak.
>
> He prays and starts to sing songs of Jesus Christ, but there is little change.
>
> Than Cidy comes along and holds his hand. They walk and hop together like kids in love and joy.

He feels as if love surrounds him. He feels powerful. He holds her tight and says, "I love you."

She says, "I love you."

They start to sing together, and the wilderness shows life: flowers and grass grow, animals run around with joy, and the people become healthy and start to dance and sing, praising God.

CH 104: THE MORNING AFTER

Cidy slept maybe an hour or two, but she is wide awake. It's 6 a.m. She calls Mom and tells her everything.

Karina is amazed, shocked, and happy. She wonders, *How can this be? John saved the life of his son-in-law. Is everything planned by God?*

She calls her best friend, Cindy, and tells her what just happened to Cidy, and Cindy is shocked and amazed as well.

Jake is up and calls Dad. He has not spoken with him for a year. He tells Dad what had happened.

Jake's Dad, Karl, can't believe it.

Karl had so much pain in him for so long about his lost wife, but today it feels like the pain is all washed away. He feels the touch of God in every part of his life all over. He gives praise to God.

Jake calls Cidy. They decided to meet soon at work. They miss each other. For some reason, they are not tired at all. They are very refreshed. They meet each other at the parking lot. They hug and hold on to each other for a while. They want to say so much but holding on to each other felt more than natural.

He takes her hand and leads her to the main door. She is a quite embarrassed to walk in with their hands together, but she lets him be. She tries to hold her tear in because of joy and thankfulness she feels from God. She feels so much love from Jake, God, Mom, Dad, and everyone.

They greet Peter.

Peter notices it right away and winks at them.

Cidy and Jake move on to the elevator. They are too early to meet anyone else, but she looks around to see if anyone is watching. They get in the elevator, and he looks at her eye with intense love. She leans her head on his chest.

The elevator stops and opens the doors. They get out. They are staring at each other. They cling onto each other, and the time stops for them.

They are just holding on to each other as if they are going to become a tree there. Some time has passed, but they can't feel it. When the elevator opens again with several of the company's employees in it, they are caught in the action.

They quickly separate and walk in the office as they are stared at.

While following her with his eyes, Jake says, "I see you, soon. I love you." He walks over to his part of the floor.

Embarrassed, she nods. "You'll see me, soon."

Soon the word gets around the company about Cidy and Jake.

The *009 Girls* rush into Cidy's office. All the girls talk at the same time, questioning the validity of the story about Cidy and Jake that they heard from the vine. There is a big commotion.

She laughs and ask them to calm down, so she can answer them. But the girls swarm around her and don't give her a space and time to think or talk. She is just laughing enjoying the moment.

Tammy steps in naturally. She screams, "QUIET! SHUT UP! Hold it!"

The room gets quiet.

Tammy makes a firm statement. "I'll take the question one at a time. Raise your hand if you have a question."

Everyone raises their hand with urgency with hoots and squeaks.

But, Sandy raises her hand speaks before asked, "What is going on? When did this happen? Jake! Jake's not your type! I don't understand it. You were hugging Jake this morning? Is that true? Are you crazy? What are you gonna do now?"

Tammy stops Sandy with her right hand gesturing to stop, and says, "Cidy, you owe us an explanation."

Cidy doesn't know where to start. She is trying to make this simple as possible and says, "First thing first. I want to congratulate Sandy. She is incredible. I love her. Mark and Sandy will have many awesome babies."

The *009 Girls* clap and hoot.

Cidy continues after the girls quiet down, "As for me, I don't know where to start. I liked Jake from the day one, but never knew it would turn out like this. I don't know how he got to me. We never spoke more than 2 minutes before yesterday. I fasted for a husband two years ago, and God spoke one word— Jake. Since then I have been waiting for him to ask me out. But yesterday, when I wore this necklace that Mom gave it to me, we found out we know each other."

Sandy pops in, again, "What? What about the necklace?"

"It is a special necklace. My dad saved a couple of boys from a car accident and…died trying to save their mom. This necklace belongs to that lady."

"Well, what's that got to do with Jake?" As soon as Sandy asked that question, everyone is struck with awe.

"It belongs to Jake's mother!" They say it in harmony and in unison; they know it belonged to Jake's mother. Everyone is astounded. They can't believe it.

Cidy continues, "Jake and I, we have the same dream, too. We are going to work for God."

It is another sucker punch for the *009 Girls.*

Tammy is hit the hardest, and she questions, "Do WHAT? Work for God! What is that mean? You are gonna quit? Is that what you are saying?"

Cidy tries to answer honestly, "I'm not sure when and how, but Jake and I…we are going to be involved in some sort of ministry."

The *009 Girls* are lost and shocked.

They are trying to piece together a love connection and a losing of a dear friend at work as well. They don't know what to say or do. They are looking at each other as if they are lost.

Cidy is looking at each one of them knowing her days with them are very few. She instinctively knows she has maybe two months with them, the most.

Jake works busily when Mark runs over. A lot of work is piled up. Mark punches him on the shoulder and screams at him so that the whole department can hear, "You DOG! You DID Cidy. Didn't you? How far did you go? You sneaky little devil. I'm impressed."

The accounting department is in a shock mode. They stop working, and they all come around to Jake and Mark to hear the details. Jake feels the eyes bearing down on him.

Mark keeps teasing.

Jake is smirking and laughing. He is very happy and shy. He opens his mouth and states calmly as a matter-of-fact tone, "I dated Cidy last night. Nothing happened. I gave her a hug this morning. That's all."

"Hug? That's not a hug. That's making love in public. That's INDECENCY with capital 'I'. Even I don't do that." Mark just blabbers out with great joy. He's having fun.

"Mark! I just hugged her a while. Come on, man? Now people would be saying something very perverted. Stop it, Mark." Jake tries to control the damage hoping there's no weird rumor going around.

"Too late, Son. Should've thought about that before you put on the show." Mark's badgering continues.

"It was you who put on the show. Come on, Mark. So when are you gonna get hitched?" Jake tries desperately to change the subject.

Mark knows he got Jake in the corner. "You pulled off more than a hug in front of a crowd pouring out of the elevator this morning, Dog. You were staging it to show off. SssTuuud! Wooo.... Jake, you pulled a fast one over me, over us. I never thought you had it in you. SssLick."

Jake tries again to change the subject, "Come on Mark. You are the talk of the town with yesterday's stunt. I have never seen anyone pull off such a stunt. That was like a scene from a movie. When you guys getting married?"

Everybody's attention shifts to Mark. He is all smile from head to toe. He jiggles a bit like one happy jello. He jumps, spins like a dancer, and screams out a one loud word—*yes*.

And he continues, "Today, if I have it my way. …I don't know. We have to meet each other's parents and so on. You know the drill. Next year, April, March, February. Sooner the better for me. I can't keep my hands off of her. I got to get this thing done by today. You know what I mean?"

Everybody laughs.

Mark proudly tells of last night, "I couldn't pass the first base even after she agreed to marry me. I kissed her for a while and I tried to touch her…you know. She slapped my hands. I got slapped a lot yesterday. Sandy's driving me crazy!"

With admiration, everybody laughs and soaks in every word Mark speaks.

Jake is thinking about his marriage too. He realizes he has got a lot ahead.

It's Friday, and Mark and Jake can wait to meet the love of their life after the work is done.

ABOUT AUTHOR

My name is Derrick Lee.

I'm reaching 50 in a couple years but I don't feel it especially in my mental level, although my body tells a different story: it takes longer to recover after a sporting event—I didn't think I ran that much but the pain in the morning doesn't lie.

I grew up mostly in Houston, TX, but I lived quite a bit in Seoul, Korea. I'm foremost Christian, and the rest. I'm a bilingual Korean-American.

My greatest pain in my life is the divorce I had several years ago. I think I forgave my ex but I can't talk to her. I still wake up some mornings thinking I'm still married to her. Nine years of marriage do leave indelible marks in all things that I do. It's funny how our brain works.

I have a little girl who is sixteen. She is my prayer: I hope she will face the challenge of being a Christian warrior.

I like to collect things: sports cards, memorabilia, and affordable antiques. My favorites are Hakeem Olajuwon, Payne Stewart, Earl Campbell, Nolan Ryan and Craig Biggio. I collect various little things that retrieve the memories of the past.

I plan to become a missionary in a few years. I'm currently going to Korean Full Gospel Church in Houston. Their motto is—*All Generation,*

425

All Nations, All Languages. It is a church that truly tries to be humble before the Lord and do the work of the Lord. And I work with InterCP (http://www.intercp.net), an organization focused on sending missionaries to unreached tribes and nations. And I support GFA (Gospel for Asia: www.gfa.org).

I hope you enjoy the story.

You can contact me via e-mail (agonyoffaith@yahoo.com), or know more about me at http://www.agonyoffaith.com.

Hope to hear from you.

Die for Christ,

Derrick Lee

SPECIAL THANKS TO MENTORS

I thank God for my mentors. I'm so glad God taught me how I should live with great role models. These are the people who have given me encouragement, strength, love, tears, and laughter.

My parents: With all the difficulties living in a foreign land they never gave up; they live honest and diligent life I can't help but to emulate them.

My Pastor and his wife: He and his wife are much older and retired now, but their teaching and lives they lived are the way that I want to follow.

My current Pastor and his wife: I never seen a couple in ministry sacrifice and risk so much to Christ. They are truly awesome.

My friends: They are awesome. They make me laugh and encourage me. I love being with them.

Thank you God for my mentors.